PRAISE FOR MY DEAD TRUE LOVE

"*My Dead True Love* is a captivating and inspirational story about love, grief and healing that touches your soul in ways you didn't know were possible. Kim Pierce sure knows how to take her readers on a suspenseful journey to a place beyond our physical existence."

— Oliver Tappe, author of *(UN)SICHTBAR* (IN)VISIBLE, and Monroe Institute Outreach Trainer

"You took me on a journey, and I didn't see the end coming. ... I loved it."

— Robin Craver, Reiki Master, Medium

"A sensitive exploration of grief and a compelling exploration into the concept of the afterlife, *My Dead True Love* mixes reality and fantasy into the relationship of several women (and one girl) in the emotional aftermath of a meaningful loss. Absorbing and thought provoking."

— Sophia Dembling, author of "Widow's Walk" *Psychology Today* blog

My Dead True Love

a Novel

Kim Pierce

My Dead True Love

First Edition

Published by Lucobu Books
Dallas, TX

Cover design: Eric Labacz

ISBN 979-8-218-04815-0 Paperback Edition
ISBN 979-8-218-04816-7 Digital Edition

Library of Congress Control Number: 2022914258

Printed in the United States of America

v12

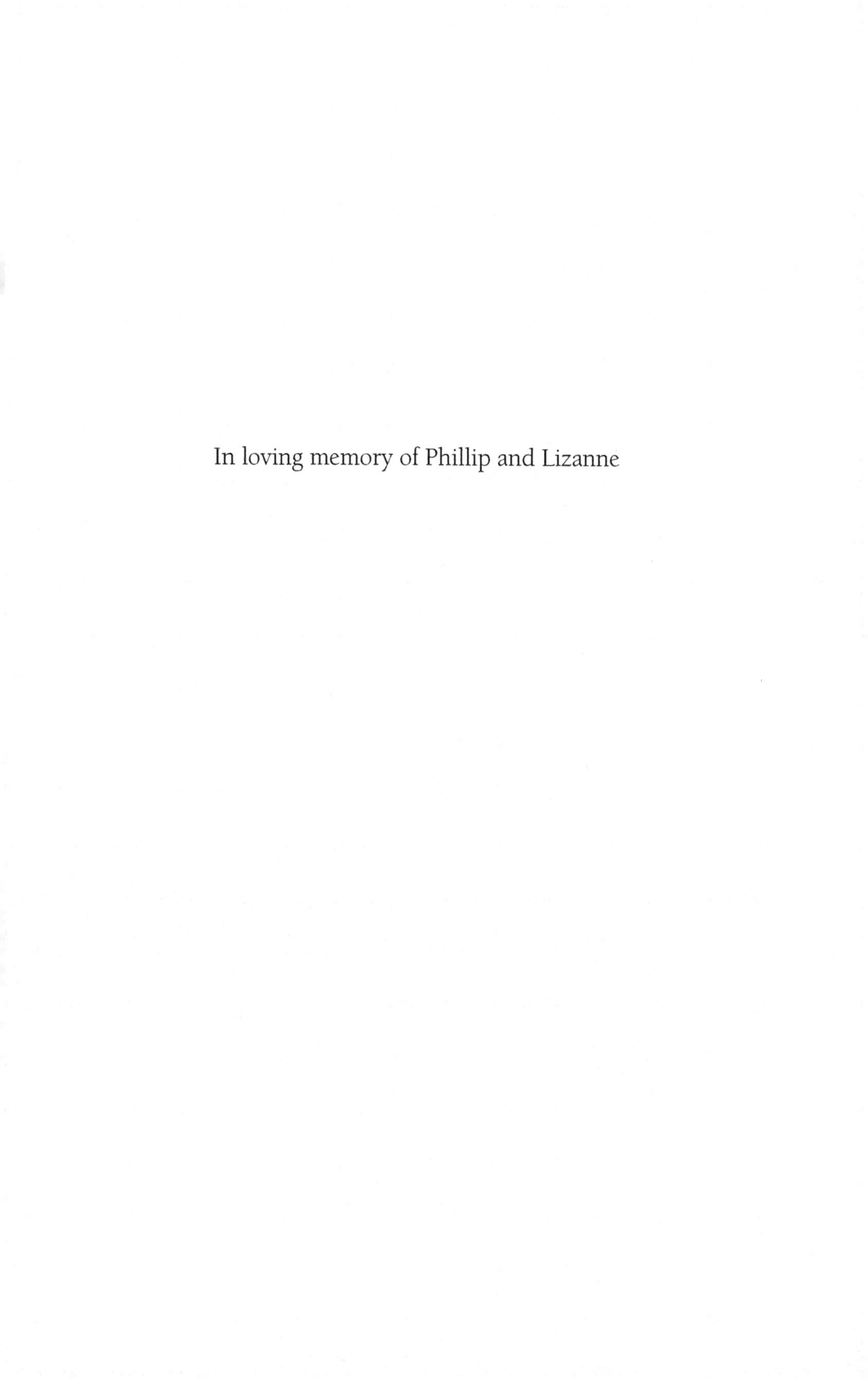

In loving memory of Phillip and Lizanne

CHAPTER ONE

As I watched the lights of Dallas draw closer, from distant twinkling to a shimmering carpet beneath the belly of the plane, my heart leapt at the thought of getting back to Gregory and Olivia. I imagined the two of them, my fiancé and my twelve-year-old daughter, standing at the gate, jumping and waving, eager to hear if my news team had won the award.

I looked down at the beveled edges of the pen-and-quill trophy poking out of my leather carry-on. I couldn't wait to show it to Olivia—the tangible recognition for the long hours of sifting through records and conducting interviews, the writing and rewriting that pulled me away from her. Our investigative series on housing discrimination meant slumlords would now be held accountable. "Here's why Mom does what she does at the newspaper," I'd say to my budding adolescent, "to make a difference in people's lives."

After landing and taxiing to the gate, the plane's doors opened and I zigzagged up the jet bridge through the slow-moving current of passengers, scanning the waiting crowd for the glossy black curls that framed Gregory's angular face. Olivia would be bobbing up and down, trying to get a glimpse between people's shoulders, not quite tall enough to peer over them.

I saw neither.

Was I disappointed? Yes. But this sometimes happened, I reminded myself. Gregory took his work so seriously—as I did mine—that he would get absorbed and lose track of time. He'd look at his watch and quickly arrange for someone else to meet me or pick me up so he could finish what he was doing, usually a deadline sprint for a business presentation or grant proposal. It drove me crazy, but I loved him for it. We understood each other.

I was not entirely surprised to see a different familiar face in the crowd. My best friend, Connie, signaled with a flick of her hand when she saw me.

She was alone. Where was Olivia?

My normally serious friend looked more somber than usual. Connie was a sturdy Midwestern farm girl with short-cropped blonde hair and a muscular build. We lived in the same apartment complex, where Gregory had also rented a unit just a couple of months earlier, bringing him and me one step closer to our plans for a life together. When Connie took the trouble to wear makeup, it added a glow to her moonlike face and emphasized the fullness of her lips. But she rarely bothered. It was as if her plainness were purposeful, to mask the intensity of her smoky gray-blue eyes. They were the kind of eyes that could look right through you. Except they didn't. Out of respect. An old soul, friends said.

"Thanks for coming," I said, breathless. "Where's Gregory? Something come up?"

Connie hesitated, then nudged me forward with her hand.

"We need to sit down," she said.

People hurried past, lugging carry-ons, wrangling toddlers. One kid was absurdly wearing flip-flops, a complete mismatch to the brisk fall weather. A couple of women were arguing about Monica Lewinsky and the soiled "blue dress." As people rushed by, overhead lights threw a harsh glare across their faces, sharpening their features and washing out their skin. A voice droned over the loudspeaker.

"Where's Olivia?" I said, resisting Connie's suggestion. "She was supposed to be here with Gregory."

"She's fine," Connie answered. "She's with her dad."

With her dad? This made no sense. It was Monday, and Monday was my day in our custody rotation. On this Monday, the plan had been for Olivia to walk to our apartment after school, where Gregory was supposed to pick her up so they could meet me here together. Gregory and I had arranged it so she'd only be home alone for a couple of hours, tops.

"Please, we need to sit down," Connie repeated.

I glanced around the gate area. I didn't want to go back there.

"I need to get my bag," I insisted. "Don't want to be here all night."

Before I could completely pivot toward the baggage claim, Connie grabbed my arm and prevented me from taking another step.

"Ann, stop. Gregory had a heart attack."

I gasped.

How could that be? Gregory was the picture of health. All those distinctive curls bouncing on his daily run. Skin glistening in the sun. Taut and muscular. He looked forty—ten years younger than his real age.

"What? Where is he?" I said, shifting mental gears. I assumed this meant we'd have to stop and see him on the way home. "They didn't take him to Parkland, did they?" My mind was leaping ahead to Gregory in the hospital. "Did a story once on a good cardiologist there. Got the card somewhere. Maybe with me..." I started fumbling with my purse. "Maybe I can get him to see Gregory." I looked up. "I need to get my luggage...."

Connie turned me to face her, clamping both my arms in a vicelike hold. Her eyes locked onto mine.

"Ann, he died."

Gut punch.

Then the words rushed around my head like a gust of snow. Everything surrounding us—the rush of people, the ambient sounds, the glare of the lights—fell away as I struggled to absorb her words. Like trying to inhale at high altitude or press through a whiteout. You think news like that is going to shake the ground you're standing on.

But it didn't. There were no feelings. No tears. No pain. Just the odd sensation of snow. Then feathers. Like I'd been hit by a feather pillow that exploded. Or trapped in a snow globe, buffeted by swirling, blinding feathers and snow.

"Ann, he died."

The words seemed to come from someplace far away. No matter how my mind raced and buzzed, grasping at the sounds—*"Ann, he died"*—shock won out, throwing an impenetrable shield between me and the offending news.

Connie guided me to an empty seat in the baggage claim area. I didn't so much sit down as my knees buckled.

"When? What happened?" I said, struggling to find words.

"I'll tell you all I know," she said, "which isn't much, as soon as we get out to the car. For now, let's just get your luggage."

I just stared at her, mute. Unable to protest. Her eyes softened. Now I could see how red and swollen they were. She'd been crying. It also registered that she was wearing tattered sweats. She had come to the airport in haste.

"What about Olivia?" I managed, barely above a whisper. Where was Olivia?

"She's with her dad," Connie said again, fresh sorrow washing across her face. "She knows. This all came up very fast. Earlier today. I called him after the police brought her to me—I'll explain in the car."

I nodded numbly, sinking back. Connie draped her arm lightly around my shoulder and took my other hand.

We sat without talking until the baggage carousel buzzer roused us.

Once we were in the car, Connie filled in some details. It happened Saturday. Two days ago. Gregory had been on the landing outside his front door. A couple of neighbors—students—saw him fall. They called an ambulance. Connie's words pulsed in and out. Some getting through, some muffled and lost.

"Then the police came and got the manager to unlock his door Sunday so they could search his apartment," Connie said.

"Why? What for?"

Something about clues to his next of kin, Connie said. Couldn't find anything. Monday morning—this morning—an officer showed Gregory's photo around the complex.

"When they showed it to me, I was stunned," she said. "I told them he was your boyfriend and took them to your unit. We knocked on the door and rang the bell several times, but there was no answer."

"No one home," I mumbled, struggling to wrap my head around her words while simultaneously pushing them away. It couldn't be true. Not my Gregory.

"I had my key," Connie said, "but they didn't want to go in without you there."

Connie's words were a blur. She told the police I was out of town. They took her contact information. They left.

Connie paused, eyes steady on the road as she pulled onto the highway that would take us from the airport to our apartment complex in town. I closed my eyes and fell into the rhythm of her driving.

"I tried to call your boss at the paper," Connie said, "but it went to voicemail. I wasn't even thinking about Olivia until the cops brought her to my door."

"Oh my God, Olivia."

"She wasn't by herself for long," Connie said. She told me how Olivia had walked home from middle school, just as Gregory and I had planned, and when the police came back, Olivia answered the door.

"That's when they brought her to me, and we called her dad. He came and got her."

"You mean that's how she found out? From the police?" I was horrified. "She's just a kid. What were they thinking?"

"I know, Ann. I don't know. Things were confusing."

A fresh thought darted across my mind.

"What about Stella?" Gregory's mother was in the hospital having surgery, and only a handful of people knew. "Do you know if anyone talked to her?"

"I don't know," Connie said glumly, "but I assume they have by now. Or will soon. Olivia helped the policemen find her address on your Rolodex, and she helped me find your flight information. This part just happened, Ann. Hours ago."

I fumbled for my keys after Connie parked outside my apartment. Once inside, she poured us some wine.

No need to tell her where things were. She knew my apartment as well as her own. As well as Gregory knew it.

As Connie and I sat together on the couch, tiny wisps of feeling began to seep through fissures in my protective cloak. I put down my glass and leaned into Connie, who held me as I cried. Not the deep belly sobs that would come later, but the steady drip-drip-drip of melting snow.

"I don't understand," I said, pulling back. "Gregory was so full of life. He was so looking forward… We were planning a future together…." I looked helplessly at my friend through teary eyes. Not Gregory. Please not Gregory. He was my soulmate, the "one" we all wait a lifetime for. And pray to God we'll find.

She nodded. "I know."

"I can't believe he's just… not here," I said. He was only fifty, barely five years older than I.

I could see him. Smiling. Pulling open the sliding-glass patio door. Me and Olivia in a race to greet him.

Oh how I miss that already.

"He helped me get this couch," I said, running my fingers across the lustrous taupe leather. "He haggled with the salesman to get the price down because there were spots on it.

"He practically stole it," I rambled on, "wearing him down till he called a manager over to finish the sale and get rid of the thing. Or maybe Gregory. Once we got it home, Gregory cleaned it the way his mother showed him, rubbing the spots till they disappeared. So proud of himself."

I wrestled with the torrent of memories, torn between wanting to savor and pushing them away. Everything I touched, looked at, or thought about was radioactive with memories of Gregory.

I barely noticed when Woodward, my ginger tabby, arched his body against my hand, demanding to be stroked. He and Bernstein, his sleek tuxedo companion, had this way of trying to soothe me—or distract me—when I appeared to be in distress.

"Where is he now?" I asked, reaching for a notepad and pen on the coffee table so I could retreat to the safety of reporter mode.

"He's at the medical examiner's. They..." Connie hesitated. "You know they have to do an autopsy when someone dies like that."

"Dies like what?"

"You know, an unexplained death..."

"I didn't even think about that." Too many other thoughts crowding my mind. "So he's just lying in the morgue?"

Connie nodded.

I resisted the truth of it even as I wrote it down: *Dallas County ME.*

Jesus. First he dies. Then some pathologist's scalpel is about to violate his body like it's an animal carcass. I knew too much about the medical examiner's knife, how MEs carve up bodies and weigh the organs and peer into cavities, then sew things up and roll the remains back into an icy drawer. The body I loved. The person I loved.

Reduced to incisions. Probing. And cold. Hard, unyielding cold. I shuddered.

"Yes, I think so," Connie said.

Suddenly my arms and shoulders felt leaden. I slumped back into the couch. The wine was starting to have its effect.

"I'm tired. So tired."

Connie took the notepad and pen from my grasp and put them back on the coffee table.

"There'll be enough time for Brenda Starr," she said, "starting tomorrow. Can I help you up to bed?"

"No. Wait, no." I pushed back weakly. "I've got to call Olivia. Got to be sure she's okay."

I picked up the phone off the end table and dialed her dad's number.

"Hello?" he answered in his familiar drawl.

"It's Ann," I said haltingly. "I… I… just wanted to find out how Olivia's doing and…"

"She's okay. Enough, I guess."

"And you don't mind if she stays with you a few extra days? I know this is awfully sudden, but…"

"She can stay as long as you need. I'm real sorry, Ann."

I managed to thank him and asked him to pass the receiver to our daughter.

"Oh, baby," I said. "I'm so sorry. How are you doing?"

"Kinda numb." Olivia hesitated. "Kinda hasn't sunk in."

"Yeah. Me, too." My mind was blank, still shrouded in shock. "'You okay to stay with Dad for a few days?"

"Yeah." Her voice sounded as flat as I felt.

"I'm so sorry," I repeated. "I'm not much help. I'm so… lost right now, I don't know quite how to be there for you. I want to be. But I'm overwhelmed." Getting the words out was like slogging through soft, wet snow.

"Yeah. I want to see you. But Dad's helping me. It all happened so fast."

"Is there anything I can do?"

"Just be there. I need to know you're there."

"I'll do my best."

"Thanks, Mom. Love you."

"Love you, too."

"I'm taking you upstairs to bed," Connie said after I hung up, "and I'm not leaving you alone tonight."

"No, no. You don't need to."

"Please stop trying to be so darned self-sufficient."

I could hear her exasperation—like she was dealing with a child who refused to put on her pajamas.

"Yes. Okay. I guess."

"And I'll feed the cats," she added, picking up our wine glasses.

I barely noticed Bernstein on the staircase looking at us, switching his black tail. He didn't seem hungry at all. Come to think of it, neither had Woody.

Supporting me around the waist, Connie urged me gently up the stairs to my bedroom. She switched on the lamp on my nightstand, bathing the room in a gauzy glow.

So tired.

I sat on the bed, then lay back on a pillow, not even undressing, moving like an automaton, eyelids heavy as Connie gently slipped off my shoes and drew the coverlet over me.

"I'll be downstairs," she whispered close to my ear, then she turned off the light and left the door cracked.

I wanted to surrender to sleep. Or maybe just close my eyes and rest. I felt wrung out and hypersensitive, as if the top layer of my skin had been scraped away.

Then as shock—sweet, protective shock—wore off, waves of pain flooded every cell. Something nameless had been ripped out of me. Except a physical sensation would have been preferable to this psychic agony, which had no parameters.

Suspended between sleep and wakefulness in some nether twilight of pain, I understood intellectually that Gregory wasn't there. But I couldn't comprehend how all that he was could just cease to be. Death… what was death?

In my drifting state, I saw him standing in the entryway at the bottom of the staircase wearing his favorite cream-colored pullover. And shorts—he wore them in all kinds of weather. So vivid. I smiled. I could feel the exhilaration of seeing him, hurrying with Olivia to greet him. A race to see who could get to him first. I could see his eyes—fierce and yearning—looking at me as he caught Olivia up in his arms. He masked his emotions from others, but I could see behind the mask.

"How can you be here one minute and not the next?" I cried out silently.

It happens. Just happens.

Only nights before, we'd slept together in this bed, entwined like grapevines. Skin to moist skin after making love. With my hand resting on his chest, I'd felt his heart beating. Oh sweet, excruciating memory. My mind flashed on the movie where a grieving Superman rolls back time by flying around the earth so fast he reverses events and Lois Lane comes back to life. I wanted that. Wanted to do that. Desperately. I understood Superman's anguish.

To never see Gregory alive again. Never touch him or be touched by him. Never engage in our repartee. Share our private jokes and knowing glances. Never see him burst through the door. Never smell grill smoke in his hair. Never get called away from tossing a salad to come quick and see a sunset. Never feel our nakedness beneath the covers. "Never" is the mantra of grief: Never. Never. Never. Never. Never.

CHAPTER TWO

I awakened before dawn from a fretful sleep, eyelids dust-storm gritty and still feeling scraped raw, my heart as leaden as it'd been the night before. Coming down the stairs, I was met by the aroma of fresh-brewed coffee. Connie had a cup waiting for me.

"How's it going?" she asked, gently shooing Woodward and Bernstein out of the way so she could fold up the blanket she'd used on the couch.

"Not so great," I said. "No. Really shitty."

We stood for a moment in silence.

"I know," she said, acknowledging the unspoken between us.

What do you say?

I was glad she'd stayed the night.

"If you're okay," she said, "I do need to get home and clean up before my first client comes." Connie was a masseuse whose schedule was typically packed. A lot of people turned to her for relief from pain and, some insisted, even healing. We had known each other since college and became closer after my mother died in a terrible wreck. I'd grieved then, but it was different from this. That's when I came to appreciate Connie's uncanny insight and comforting presence. When Olivia and I moved here, into the apartment complex where Connie already lived, Connie and I became inseparable.

"Yeah, I'm okay enough," I said, sipping the coffee and warming my hands on the cup. "Thanks for staying with me."

"No big deal. I'm here if you need me. Anytime."

I watched as she gathered up her things to leave.

"Call me later," she said.

"I will."

Once Connie was gone, I pushed through the white, sodden heaviness that had overtaken my mind, intent on what I needed to do. The first thing was to get in touch with Gregory's mother. To find out whether anyone had told her. Whether anyone was with her to ease the shock.

We were not close, but with Gregory gone, I felt an obligation—if not to Stella, then to him—to make sure his mother was okay. I felt protective because she really was all alone now. Or maybe it was about more than that. Maybe through her, I could understand Gregory better.

Ever since his father had died, Gregory had taken care of Stella in the Lebanese tradition of sons and mothers. He looked after her yard, her car, her finances. He made little repairs around the house and balanced her checkbook. She wasn't even Lebanese, but he still did all these things, according to his father's culture. To Western sensibilities—to my sensibilities—their relationship seemed overly involved. In the years before the accident cut my own mother's life short, my mom and I talked maybe twice a week, sometimes daily. But she had her life, and I had mine.

Not so Gregory and Stella, who were bound together like two saplings pressed so close they nearly grew as one tree.

"I'm all she has," Gregory would say solemnly when I challenged him about what I judged to be unhealthy closeness. I was even a little jealous of the time he spent with her. Now, in a way, she might be my only connection to Gregory.

I put my coffee cup in the sink and unplugged the coffee maker, determined to go to the hospital where Stella was recovering from surgery. I needed to find out if she'd been told and how she was doing. It was the least I could do.

Moist-eyed and still foggy from the operation, Stella turned her gaze from Bob Barker and *The Price is Right* to look up at me as if she expected something.

"Have you seen my son?" she implored, fingering her rosary. "Where is that tardy boy? I haven't seen him in days!"

I must have looked astonished. They'd told me at the nurse's station that her pastor and the hospital chaplain had come by the previous night to deliver the terrible news—about the same time I heard it. But Stella showed no trace of awareness that this had happened.

Here in her hospital room, Stella's cheerfulness was unsettling.

I just wanted to be sure she understood what had happened—because she needed to know and because she would be asked to make decisions as the next of kin the police were searching for. I wanted to cushion the worst of those questions. Was there a little part of me that hoped we might forge a deeper connection? Yes. Through her, I might hold onto Gregory a little longer.

Don't bet the farm.

"Stella..." I began, turning down the TV and taking a seat on the bed.

She looked at me with a beatific smile. We'd never had much one-on-one time, although Gregory was living in her garage apartment when we met. It's temporary, he said. To get back on his feet, he said. But from the beginning, he'd been determined to keep Stella separate from his world with me. Still, there were times he'd brought me and Stella together in a very controlled way—like Mother's Day brunch or when we stopped in at a family Christmas party. Once in a while, she'd cook dinner for us. Stella usually chatted lightly about her two favorite topics: her dolmas and how proud she was of her son whom, she noted, was the first in the family to earn a college degree.

"And not just one," she'd say, "but two."

"Oh, Ma," Gregory would say, looking pained. "That was a long time ago."

"But it's still wonderful," she insisted, patting his cheek. He cringed.

Stella and I didn't go much deeper than that, although now I wanted her to tell me again the stories she'd shared about Gregory growing up.

"Stella," I repeated as she watched me from her hospital bed. "Don't you remember?"

No change in her expression.

Stella had once been statuesque, so fetching in her youth that she'd modeled hats for Neiman Marcus in the late 1940s. I'd glimpsed some photos—modeling outtakes—that she kept in her home. In them, she gazed out with a coquettish smile from under the brim of a stylish hat, blonde curls hugging the nape of her elegant neck.

Here in the hospital room, hooked up to IVs and monitors, she looked much smaller, but she still was a substantial presence in her mid-seventies. Even now, with graying tendrils matted against the back of her head, I could see how her classic Northern European beauty had softened the more chiseled features Gregory inherited from his Lebanese father.

"Don't you remember?" I repeated. "Didn't Father McCallister and the hospital chaplain come see you?" Stella's eyes dodged sideways as her expression briefly darkened. I placed my hand over hers, something I'd never done before. Her face brightened.

"Did you bring me a present?"

"What? No. I just came as soon as I could. That's all I knew to do."

My words tumbled out stiffly. I had no emotional ballast to respond to such a random question. It felt like talons digging into my skin.

"I need a present."

Stella gazed up expectantly as I fumbled for something more to say. Just then a nurse scurried in.

"Good morning, Mrs. Malouf," she said to Stella, her crisp scrubs matched by her starchy manner. "It's time to check on your incisions."

"Are you family?" the nurse said, nodding at me.

"Yes, kind of," I said.

"I'm so sorry for your loss," she murmured.

"Thank you," I said, averting my eyes as she lifted the covers to inspect the area around Stella's incisions. It had been laparoscopic, but because of her age, they'd allowed more time in the hospital to monitor her recovery.

"This looks good," she said. "Better than good. There's some bruising around the sites, but that's normal. How are you feeling?"

Stella was someplace else.

"Did you know I thought aliens were coming from the TV to abduct me after the anesthesia?" Stella hungrily grabbed for the nurse's arm, her eyes as incandescent as the stars for which she was named—and as empty as the spaces between them. "Were you there when I did that?"

"No," the nurse said. "But I heard all about it from the other nurses," she added, cocking her head to one side.

The nurse looked at me.

"This isn't unusual. People imagine all kinds of things as the anesthesia wears off after surgery."

"Does she remember being told about her son?"

"My son? Did you talk to him?" Stella looked first at me, then the nurse.

"No," the nurse said to Stella. Her smile tightened. "Can I slide you up a bit?"

She grasped the hospital pad under Stella and inched her toward the head of the bed, adjusting the pillows, making sure the drainage line and catheter were where they should be, and repositioning the blanket.

"Use the call button if you need anything," she said, pointing to where it was draped over the bedrail. "Okay, Mrs. Malouf?"

She left us alone. I wished she'd stayed.

"Stella..." I was determined to resume, trying to catch her eyes, looking for something to latch onto in their vacuous depths.

I'd never had to deliver bad news to such a slippery recipient. I was always the one in control, asking the hard questions in the aftermath of some calamitous event. "This is your house? Where were you when the tornado struck?" "Did you know the deceased? Were you close?" I'd stand there, reporter's notebook and pen in hand, and wait for their answers.

I tried a different tack with Stella.

"Has anyone come to see you?" I asked.

"Why, Ann. I didn't notice you there," Stella said without affect. Was this the anesthesia or her growing dottiness that Gregory so often complained about?

"How's that schefflera doing?" she asked.

"Schefflera…?" I repeated, vaguely remembering the frail, spindly potted plant she'd thrust into my hands the last time I'd been to her house. Stella was a collector of plants—castoffs, throwaways—that other people tossed to the curb. Gregory told me how she would cruise through the neighborhood before first light on her way home from early mass and rescue them from certain destruction. Back at her house, her patio was a jungle of derelicts she'd collected over the years, some so tall they strained against the patio awning.

"It's on my patio," I said, "where it can get good light."

"Good." She smiled warmly and patted my hand. "I hope you remember what I told you. Don't fertilize it. Don't water it too much. It'll perk right up."

The schefflera was one in a small parade of gifts Stella had bestowed upon me. Once it had been a ballpoint pen plucked from a pencil holder on her desk—"It will be just like new when you put in a refill," she'd said. I chuckled the time Gregory showed up at my door with an overripe banana. "Guess who wanted you to have this," he said, tossing it onto my kitchen counter. We laughed. But I was mildly curious as to why Stella felt so compelled to give. I wondered if it were a way to prove to herself that she was a good person. A generous person. A pious Catholic.

"The schefflera *has* perked up," I said, as she regarded me carefully. "Thank you for that. Who's taking care of your plants while you're in the hospital?" I ventured, still searching for an entry point to the subject of Gregory's death.

"Wanda, of course. My next-door neighbor."

I'd run into raspy-voiced, chain-smoking Wanda and her sweet white German shepherd every time I'd been to Stella's house.

"Is she your best friend?"

Keep it light.

"Yes, she is."

"Has she been up here to see you?"

"Oh, yes. Of course she has." Stella sparkled. "She brought Princess with her."

I knew this couldn't be true. The hospital didn't allow children, much less animals. But I took the opening.

"Did anyone else come to visit you? Do you remember when Father McCallister and the chaplain came by last night?"

"No! Did they really?"

I had to retreat mentally.

You can do this. You can.

I glanced around the room—a cramped, featureless space in an aging hospital that had never been updated to accommodate modern technology. The paint was fresh and the venetian blinds were open, but the bed was too big and everything else had to be wedged in around it.

"Did I ever tell you about the time I was driving back from the Rio Grande Valley with Gregory and Bubba?" Stella asked out of nowhere. It was one of her favorite stories, repeated often.

"It's a wonderful story," I said. "How does it go again?"

"Oh my goodness," she said, drifting dreamily back to the 1950s.

"When the boys were little—Gregory, you know, was twenty-one months older than Bubba—it would be time for their father and his cronies to go down to the Valley to check on the cotton crop. Did I tell you they were cotton brokers? We'd drive down to spend a few days with them—well, with Johnny, their father—and the boys loved to play in the pool and eat oranges right off the trees. But one time when we got ready to come home, we got a late start. Johnny stayed to do business—oh, the drought was terrible that year—and I had to drive back alone with the boys. I got so tired. So tired…"

Her voice faltered.

"You got so tired…" I picked up the thread, leaning close to her, "… that when it got dark, you could barely see the highway. Bubba was asleep in back, and you made Gregory sit on an orange crate in the front seat and watch the road for you, all the way home."

"Yes, that's right." She brightened again. "I told him he was my eyes, and he sat there just like a little soldier, staring at the road. He took his job so seriously. I told him he was my little man."

Stella paused.

"Have you seen him today?" she said.

"No, I haven't," I said, bringing my hand to my face to muffle a sob. The image of Gregory as an earnest little boy was my undoing.

"Ann, what's wrong? Why are you crying?"

Stella grabbed for my other hand, trying to pat it.

"I can't believe he's gone," I managed, sotto voce.

"What do you mean?" She looked worried.

"Don't you remember?" I struggled once again to find the right words. "Don't you remember Father McCallister and the chaplain coming to visit you last night?"

"Yes," she began, "I remember something like that..." Her voice trailed off as her face grew clouded.

"Did they talk to you about Gregory?"

"I think so."

Looking out the window, she pulled her hand away from mine and brought it absently to her throat.

"Did they tell you Gregory had... a heart attack?"

I hated what I was saying, felt so brittle saying it. Hated hearing the words.

The effect on Stella was immediate.

"He... what? No. No!"

Agitated, Stella began clawing furiously at the covers, trying to tear them off her body and grab the side rail in an attempt to swing around and escape the bed. Only she couldn't. All she succeeded in doing was jostling the twin tethers of her IV and catheter.

"Where is he?" she demanded, flailing and sagging half out of the bed. "I've got to go to him."

"Stella. Stella!"

I pressed the weight of my body against hers as she listed toward one side, and I tried to corral her thrashing limbs, terrified she was going to break something loose. Her strength caught me off guard. Where was that damned call button?

"You can't walk...Surgery...You've got to stay in the bed."

My words got no traction as we struggled against one another.

"No, I do not! You can't stop me! Get away from me! I've got to see him!"

Spittle flying, she flung angry words and flailed her arms, shaking me off and trying to scrabble over the covers.

"Stop, stop, STOP," I repeated, feeling utterly helpless as she squirmed and bawled and tried to push me aside.

We must have been making quite a racket because in seconds, the same nurse and a beefy aide flew into the room and all but pounced on her. I backed against the wall.

"Mrs. Malouf! Calm down!"

The nurse grabbed her firmly by the chin and shoulder and bellowed inches from her face as the aide expertly immobilized her and her IV arm with his strong grasp.

"You're in the hospital" the nurse shouted. "You just had surgery. You're going to tear your stitches if you don't stop."

As abruptly as it began, Stella's fit deflated, like a wave roaring to a crest and falling back upon itself. The caregivers nudged her back into place.

"It's not true, is it?" she said, beseeching the nurse. "He didn't die, did he?"

I felt helpless and ashamed, witnessing the realization of Gregory's death creep anew into her consciousness.

I yearned to go to that place of denial with her—just like the scene in *West Side Story* when Maria doesn't want to face the truth about her beloved Tony and brother Bernardo. "Make it no' be true," she cries when Anita forces her to face the fact that Tony has killed her brother.

Please God, can't we just "make it no' be true" now?

"I'm so sorry, Mrs. Malouf," the nurse said.

Stella turned to me, quivering like a frightened child. Eyes pleading.

"Ann! It's not true. Tell her it's not true."

"I wish I could," I said, aching for us both. *I wish I could.*

As the pain emanating from Stella crashed into my own, it overwhelmed the close confines of the room. Everything inside me broke open again.

"Let me talk to her," came the appeal of another woman, stepping forward so quietly I'd not noticed her slip into the room.

This had to be the chaplain, a gray-haired woman of uncertain contours beneath a loose-fitting sheath. I was more than relieved for her to rescue us from the moment.

Stella and I both seemed to be drowning. She patted Stella's hand and greeted her tenderly.

"Do you remember me, Stella? I'm Pastor Rosemary."

Fear, recognition, and dread collided on Stella's face.

"Look, I brought you a hairpin. Like you wanted last night."

Stella looked at the fancy bobby pin in Pastor Rosemary's hand as if it were a gleaming, precious jewel. The pastor reached over and pushed back a lock of Stella's hair and wove the pin in above her ear.

"There now. Is that what you wanted?"

Never taking her eyes off Pastor Rosemary, Stella felt for the clip with the wizened fingers of her free hand.

"Yes. Yes, thank you."

"Let's close our eyes and pray, shall we?"

She might have been crooning a lullaby to a small, fearful child.

The nurse pulled back and motioned for me to come with her and the aide.

"She'll be OK," the nurse whispered. "We need to leave."

CHAPTER THREE

I waited outside Stella's door for Pastor Rosemary.

"Excuse me," I said tentatively as she came out. "Can I talk to you a minute? I'm Ann. Gregory's… fiancée." I didn't know what other word to use. Boyfriend sounds so silly in your forties.

"Oh, I am sorry," the chaplain said. "What a terrible thing for you."

There was something in the way she said it, so open and welcoming, that I briefly had to shut my eyes and resist the press of urgent tears.

"I want to ask you about something," I said.

We found an alcove down the hall with a couple of chairs. A small table was wedged between them, a box of tissues on top. It was just enough to cloister us from the hospital noises, except the overhead calls for doctors.

"How can I help?"

The chaplain folded her hands in her lap as if she had nothing to do all day but listen to me.

I wasn't quite sure how to start so I just got right to the point.

"I'm fairly certain," I stammered, "that Stella has no immediate family besides Gregory, and I'd like to help her, if she'll let me. The medical examiner has already called me to identify the… body, and…"

The words felt like chalk in my mouth. The body I loved. The body I loved with all my heart and soul and…

"… there'll be questions about what to do next," I said. "Like where his… remains… should go. I want to see if Stella would like me to at least start making some of the… arrangements. You must see a lot of situations like this."

I was groping for what to say, unsure where I was going.

The chaplain seemed to be mulling the situation.

"That's very kind of you," she said, making my pain and effort feel fully *seen*. How did she do this—this nondescript woman who would never draw attention in a crowd. I found myself breathing easier and feeling less tense in her presence.

"If you feel certain she has no one else to turn to, I think it would be entirely appropriate," she said. "I wish more people would do what you're offering."

Her answer was a relief.

"I'm glad to hear you say that. Thank you. Would you be willing to go back in there with me when I talk to her about this?"

"I'd be glad to," she said warmly. "Is there anything else?"

I felt like she was reading my mind. Or was it my body language, like I do with people I interview for the paper? No, it was something more. She radiated a contagious tranquility, almost a sense of knowing. Not unlike Connie. No wonder her presence had calmed Stella.

"Yes," I said, feeling nominally better and sliding back from the edge of the chair. It was so easy to talk to her.

"There's Gregory's apartment," I said, a vision of his Spartan unit playing across my mind. "I'd like to clear it out for her. Even if she wanted to do it, which I don't think she does, it's on the second story, and the stairs would be a problem."

"Isn't that an awfully big task to take on?" the chaplain asked.

"Not really. We live—*lived*—in the same complex, and he was just moving in from the garage apartment at his mother's house. He had his clothes and a few things. Some kitchen stuff. But he'd only been there two months. That's why the police didn't find anything about next of kin."

The chaplain looked down at her neatly folded hands, then looked into my eyes.

"I know you're feeling tremendous grief right now, Ann. Does it seem like you're trying to do too much? Maybe you could just help her find someone to do these things?"

"For some reason that doesn't feel like enough."

In my heart, I wanted to be the only one, or at least the last one, to touch his belongings. If there was something precious in that apartment, I wanted to be there to recognize it, take custody, and cherish it.

Hold on to that thought.

"I'm a journalist," I said. "I've dealt with people who have lost loved ones. I know a little about this—from another side. Doing something for Gregory's mother seems more productive than just sitting and wallowing and..." I lost my track, momentarily riven with pain.

"Doing is a way of putting off the worst of the pain," the chaplain said, holding me steadily in her gaze. "There's nothing wrong with that, but know you'll have to face the grief at some point."

"I know," I said. "I know."

She waited.

"Are you and Stella close?"

"No. The whole time Gregory and I were together—only five years—he held his mother apart from me. He always seemed to flash a little warning light that said, 'Don't go there.' But now that he's... gone... my heart goes out to Stella. I want to do something for her. For him. For her. Maybe for us."

"It would be wonderful if the two of you worked through some of this together."

It was as if her words hit a trip wire. The tears I'd been walling off started spilling over in uncontrollable sobs. Pastor Rosemary reached for a tissue and handed it to me.

"I'm sorry," I sniffed. "I feel so raw. This isn't like me. I don't even know you. And I'm not religious."

"Don't be so hard on yourself," Pastor Rosemary said. "It's true, I'm a chaplain. But what I do has little to do with religion. Faith, maybe. I like to think I walk with souls."

Listen. Listen to her.

What were those unbidden words in my mind that quickly crumbled to dust?

We returned to Stella's room where the chaplain shepherded Stella's wandering thoughts back to the discussion each time she strayed. I took a notepad and pen out of my purse so I could keep track of Stella's wishes.

I started with the least volatile topic, the apartment.

"I don't know what's in his apartment, and I don't really care," Stella said, simultaneously waving it off and growing weepy. "I suppose his clothes. No, just give those away. He was a dresser, just like Johnny. I just wish he'd stayed at my house. This never would've happened."

One question down.

"The next thing is… I'd like your permission to arrange a memorial service," I said tentatively. "I think Gregory's friends would want to pay their respects to him." Then I added, "And to you."

Whatever I was saying seemed to float up out of nowhere. I'd never given a second thought to a memorial service. But now that I considered it—yeah, that sounded like a good idea.

"You mean a funeral?" Stella focused on me, eyes narrowing. "I'd want a funeral. With Father McCallister. I'd want that for my boy."

"Okay," I said, underlining the item on my note pad. Memorial. Funeral. What was the difference? I was impatient to wrap this part up, thinking ahead to the more pressing questions.

The hard questions.

"Gregory is at the medical examiner's office right now, and they've asked me where the family would... ah... like him to go...?" It was as delicately as I could put it. For both of us.

The color drained from Stella's face as she nervously fingered the sparkly bobby pin above her ear.

"He's going to be here soon," she said, eyes tracing wildly around the room. "I just know it."

"Stella," Pastor Rosemary demurred from the foot of the bed, "he's not coming." The words engulfed all of us like swirling snow. But it was gentle, powdery snow. "You've suffered a terrible shock, Stella. You and Ann. I know you both loved Gregory so much but... he isn't coming. And you must try your best to answer these painful questions."

I sat on the bed, set my pad and pen down, and once again clasped Stella's hand as she stared past me, eyes locked on the chaplain.

"He's not?" came the tiny squeak.

Stella's countenance begged the chaplain to recant.

"No, sweetie," the pastor said with great tenderness. "He can't be with us, except in spirit. And we must do what's proper with... the shell that remains."

Oh God, I wanted her to stop. With every syllable, her abiding kindness ripped me further open, the brume of her soothing voice penetrating past muscle to bone. It was all I could do to contain what felt like a waterfall trembling behind the thinnest veneer of calm.

I couldn't hold back forever but reasoned I needed to clamp down—bracket—until I was somewhere safe. Like home. With Connie. I focused on what I needed to write down as soon as my hand was free. I had set a goal for myself—to tell Stella the truth—and I was going to achieve it. Every leak in my resolve was met with a furtive swipe of a tissue. I would face the pain later, I told myself. Later.

"He has to go where all the Maloufs go," Stella said hoarsely.

"Where would that be?" Pastor Rosemary persisted.

Her slow pacing and careful word choices indicated she had had this conversation many times. Weariness in the lines of her face suggested it didn't get easier.

"Moore-Tate," said Stella, resigned. "He has to go to Moore-Tate."

The high-end funeral home served the city's most prominent families.

"What about after that?" I asked meekly.

"What do you mean, 'after that?' You mean heaven?"

"No, no," I said, then sidestepped. "Would you like me to start making… arrangements?" The phrase cut my heart like a piece of jagged metal. "I could at least get things started, until you're able to take over yourself."

Stella said nothing but muttered under her breath. She began fingering her rosary. I adjusted my pad and pen.

"There's just one more thing," I said. "I believe Gregory would want to be... cremated."

The request sounded savage, unattached. But it was important. Even urgent. In the only conversation Gregory and I had had about dying, he'd said he definitely did not want to be buried. "All dressed up and nowhere to go," he'd said, making light of the unthinkable. My mind pushed away the image of a headstone: 1948-1998.

"But what about his soul?" Stella said, practically blubbering. "What would happen to his soul? Isn't that a sin?"

"No, I don't think so," Pastor Rosemary offered, clearly surprised by my question. "I think his soul will be perfectly protected, if that's the course you choose."

Stella looked doubtful.

"Gregory and I talked about this a long time ago," I said, emboldened by the pastor's response. "He told me it was his preference if anything ever happened to him. Truly, I wouldn't ask except to honor that wish."

"How do I know it's what he really wanted?" Stella said, eyeing me suspiciously.

"I wouldn't bring it up if it weren't. This is hard for me, too."

The chaplain's beeper went off, and Pastor Rosemary looked down to see who was paging her.

"Excuse me," she said, "I need to take this." She left the room.

"And Father McCallister says it's okay?" Stella continued.

"We can ask him," I said. "I'll ask him."

Stella seemed to relax, but her fingers never budged from the rosary.

"Only if he says it's okay. He has to say it's not against the church."

Never mind that Gregory wasn't Catholic. His father had insisted Stella take the boys to the local Baptist church, to better fit in with Dallas society. Neither religion took with Gregory. I envied Stella the certainty of her Catholic beliefs.

"What about the rest?" I continued. "What if they ask about... a casket? Or maybe a different container. Something simple? And maybe we could hold the service at Moore-Tate? I think they have a chapel... Or..."

"Oh, that would mean so much to me," Stella chirped.

"What?"

"Taking care of the details. You taking care of this." Stella beamed at me with a cherubic smile.

What a relief. I'd gotten through. Made a connection. I was just about to reach over and hug Stella when she snapped her fingers, taking me aback.

"Just don't spend a lot of money" she added in a sharp tone. "Gregory wouldn't like that. No frills. Keep it cheap. I'm done talking about this."

I stifled a laugh.

One minute she's overcome by the loss of her son. The next she's as dismissive as a monarch. Technically, as the next of kin, Stella had to sign off on everything. But she blinked on and off like a broken neon sign. I chalked it up to the pain meds. Or ebbing anesthesia.

"Okay, Stella. I'll do what I can."

"Thank you, thank you."

Her words followed me out the door.

I asked at the nurse's station if there was a public phone I could use.

"You can use this one if it's just a quick call," the attendant said, lifting it up onto the counter. "Just dial nine to get out."

I made my first "arrangement"—for Gregory to be transported to the funeral home adjacent to the cemetery where so many Maloufs rested in eternal repose. And would I make the formal ID of the body? they asked again. I said I would.

Later that afternoon, I drove to the funeral home, wishing Connie could have been there with me. But she had a full lineup of massage clients that day.

Inside Moore-Tate's imposing façade, a funeral director greeted me at the front desk, which was set up to look like a concierge stand. She asked me to wait while they readied a room for Gregory, as he'd "just arrived." I sank into an overstuffed wingback chair in the waiting area, which was fashioned to simulate a formal library, with imposing oil landscapes hanging from forest-green walls. My gaze fell on an English hunt scene with stately dogs and horses. Then another: a pastoral lake below scudding clouds.

In minutes, a primly dressed young woman who looked as if she'd be more at home drinking margaritas with friends motioned in my direction.

"Please follow me," she said.

As she opened the door to a softly lit room, I could barely make out a figure tucked in a quilt on a gurney so that only the head and arms were visible. I was seized by an impulse to say it wasn't Gregory at all and this was all a big mistake. But no. Even from the doorway, I'd know that profile anywhere. My whole body went limp, confronted with the irrefutable truth that my most precious love was dead.

"Yes, ma'am," I said flatly. "That's him."

I rushed to leave as quickly as I could.

CHAPTER FOUR

"Of course I'll be there," Connie said when I asked about helping with Gregory's apartment. As much as I wanted to do it, I didn't want to face it alone. "You know I will. And I don't have any clients this afternoon."

We crossed the parking lot and wound through the overgrown courtyard that led to Gregory's apartment. I buttoned my cardigan against the late October chill. Connie, who'd grown up in Nebraska, wore a tank top. We were thinking this would be a quick trip. For recon. We'd assess what we needed to clear out and where it should go. I'd make a list with the pen and pad I'd brought. Lists gave me a sense of control.

As we climbed the stairs to the second-story landing where Gregory had stumbled and fallen just short of his front door, I willed my eyes to un-focus, like children do, blurring everything in my field of vision.

But I couldn't resist imagining Gregory hauling himself up the same stairs we were ascending, willing himself to climb each step despite what must have been mounting pain, pushing against whatever tightness constricted his chest, whatever dizziness might have preceded his fall, sure he could make it on will alone. He could operate on pure adrenalin. My eyes fuzzed over again just enough to avoid seeing the probable spot where he collapsed. I looked instead toward the black iron railing around the landing and to the parking area below, where the ambulance probably pulled up. My throat tightened. Too much reality. I shook it off, pushed it down, and concentrated on reaching the door.

With a quick twist of the key, I unlocked it. Once inside, Connie pulled it closed behind us.

There wasn't much to see. The maroon leather chair and ottoman. The floor lamp. His radio. The week's newspapers neatly stacked on the floor. A glance toward the kitchen revealed dishes still in the rack, ready to be put away, and a towel carefully folded next to the sink. The bedroom door was cracked, and just beyond I could see the blow-up mattress he slept on.

"Gregory refused to stay at my place while he saved money for furniture," I said, stopping in the tiny hall just outside his bedroom. "He also refused to buy on credit. He was old-fashioned like that."

"Sounds like he was determined to do this his way," Connie said, standing in the living room, hands on hips, surveying the small space.

Pushing the bedroom door fully open, I resisted looking in the closet, where I knew Gregory's clothes and shoes would be impeccably organized and arrayed. Not yet, I thought. Not yet. Just looking at them would trigger a fresh onslaught of memories. Stella was right: He was a dresser. She told me once how as a child he would carefully lay out his clothes and shoes for school the next day.

But as much as I wished to avoid the closet, something tugged me toward it.

Look. You've got to look.

With Connie at my elbow and tears barely at bay, I scanned the jackets and shirts and slacks, grouped by color and style, and marveled at all his shoes. He definitely had a thing for shoes. Stepping gingerly into the walk-in, I caught a flash, a tiny disruption, from the corner of the closet. What was that? It seemed to come from behind the pair of tan Ferragamo lace-ups, where a box hugged the shadows.

"What's that?" Connie said.

"I don't know."

I moved some shoes out of the way, then bent down to get a closer a look. It was some sort of collectible object, a chest no more than two feet tall, about three wide, maybe eighteen inches deep, its dark wood-and-tooled-leather surface rubbed to a rich patina. The top looked like it would just pop open, and there were flat, shallow drawers down the front. It might have been made for jewelry. Or a draftsman's tools. Perhaps treasure.

"You've never seen it before?" Connie said.

"No. Did you see that flash of light?"

"Flash of light…?"

"Maybe it was a reflection. Or something. From the corner. Maybe I just imagined it."

Suddenly nothing was more important than getting the chest where we could see it. Together we tugged it out of the closet, absurdly careful to replace the shoes we'd moved to gain access.

I knelt to open the top, but it wouldn't budge. As I struggled to dislodge it—the maker had crafted a particularly snug fit—Connie disappeared into another room.

"Maybe this will help," she said, returning from the kitchen with a dinner knife. The unfamiliar chest was a welcome distraction. It gave me a little breathing room, a few moments to push back the dull, persistent pain.

Working between the edges, I used the knife to pry the top loose, careful not to mar the finish. Gregory valued fine things and took meticulous care of them. Not one leaf on the floorboard of his '92 Celica. Not a loose thread on his suits. Shoes shined, always. I could never live up to that standard. Cat box stinky. Desktop in disarray. Laundry to fold, always.

When the lid jerked open abruptly, Connie caught it before it swung into the wall.

"Easy," she said.

Although Connie wasn't saying a lot, I could feel her watching me closely. She'd have been a good mother, striking just the right balance between protection and encouragement. But she'd never had kids.

"I want to see what's in it," I said.

Yes, you do.

"Are you sure you're up for this?"

"Yeah, I can do it," I said.

Connie crouched next to me.

I recognized some of the items in the top compartment: A photo of us at the beach. A crude spoon rest Olivia made from a tile. Red and yellow maple leaves, presumably from Lost Maples in Central Texas, where we had hiked. These were interspersed with old passports, expired driver's licenses and his car title—all held down by a clear, round paperweight with iridescent flecks floating at the center.

Eager to see what else Gregory might have stashed in this private chamber, I lifted out the compartments one at a time and placed them in a semicircle around us. In each lay a careful arrangement of items, most unfamiliar to me. Although their significance might remain forever unknown, I couldn't resist examining them all for any clue to the man I loved.

I picked up the photos of a knockout redhead and a smiling young girl and thumbed through them. No names, nothing on the backs.

"I'm pretty sure this is his ex-wife," I said, "but I have no clue who the kid is."

Connie shrugged.

"You want me to write down what we find? Like an inventory?" she said.

"Yeah, that's a great idea."

Connie took the pen and notepad I'd brought and started writing.

There was a business card from an Oklahoma cemetery.

"Why would Gregory have something like that?" Connie wondered out loud.

"Maybe something to do with a client," I said, searching my brain and coming up empty.

And what was the small paper bag incised on each side with starbursts? As I picked it up, I caught the faintest whiff of smoke. I held the bag to my nose and confirmed it was the source, then handed it to Connie, who also puzzled over the aroma.

"A luminaria?" she said.

"No clue."

She scribbled a note.

I unfolded a piece of pink tissue paper and found it held a lock of soft brown hair tied with a tiny red bow. Someone's baby hair?

"Why would Gregory have a lock of baby hair?" I mused out loud. I brushed it across my lips before passing it to Connie to record.

"And would you look at this," I said, picking up a snapshot of a dark, square-jawed young man hugging the neck of a German shepherd. No writing on this one, either. I noticed one edge was neatly cut, like something had been trimmed from the original.

"Looks like a hunter," Connie said. "I wonder who he is."

"I don't know. Maybe his brother."

"Well you know who this is," Connie said, fingering a handful of formal wedding portraits, clearly a younger Gregory with the ex.

There was his birth certificate. Mother: Stella Jolanta Kaczmarek. Father: John Gregory Malouf. A gold band. A gold Saint Christopher medal.

"That's a surprise," I said, holding up the medallion.

"Maybe he was more religious as a child."

I doubted this.

In the bottom tray we found his diplomas from Vanderbilt and the University of Texas. His old ID from the Department of Agriculture.

And beneath those, at the deepest, seemingly most secret level—or perhaps least important—a series of childish drawings inscribed "To my angel" and "I luv u," made with colored pencils on pages torn out of an artist's sketchbook.

"What do you make of these?" Connie asked.

"No idea," I said, suddenly dizzy.

I'd become completely absorbed and then overwhelmed by the contents of the chest, especially by those drawings. Were they from his childhood? A relative? Thinking about them—and all of this—made my brain hurt. The Gregory I knew lived in the moment and scoffed at sentimentality. But here were private things he'd secretly kept and declined to share. They must have meant something to him. I felt unsettled. Strange. Had to be grief blindsiding me, throwing me off balance.

"What's going on?" my friend asked.

"I don't know. It's like, a rush of feelings. All jumbled up. I can't quite pinpoint…"

My heart was pounding, and I was having difficulty inhaling air. I was sweating. Seeing what was in the chest, even the chest itself, had unleashed uncertainty about who Gregory was and how well I knew him. The feelings were all jumbled—love, doubt, despair, anger. Made no sense. All I wanted was to wake up and roll over into Gregory's arms, as if it were all a bad dream.

"God, I just can't take this all in."

"Easy, friend," Connie said, touching my arm. "You know what the diplomas are. You know where he went to school. You can guess what the gold band is."

"But some of it… I've never seen…. Feel so fragile…"

Turmoil was combusting beneath the surface.

"I don't think I can do anymore right now," I said, my strength utterly depleted. "I've talked to his landlord. We have some time…."

I grasped for words.

"You don't have to do this today," Connie said firmly. "You don't *have* to do it ever."

"I know."

I could feel a return of the snow, whipping around me, insulating me.

"But I want to."

"Let me just slide these back in," Connie said, returning the drawers and trays to their place. "I've got everything written down. And we can always take up where we left off."

Before she closed the lid, she held up the paperweight, whose iridescent specks seemed to fling light around the room like stardust. Connie appeared mesmerized by it. She held it up in the palm of her hand, outstretched toward me, and I took it from her as if it were fragile as an egg, laying it carefully next to the other items in the chest and closing the top.

"Do we want to leave the chest here?" she said.

"No. Yes. I can't deal with it right now."

"Don't you think—"

"I just can't."

We slid the chest next to the wall and closed the bedroom door. Then we left the apartment. About halfway down the stairs, I felt a pang.

Take it.

"Wait a minute," I said.

"What now?"

"I think I do want to take the chest to my apartment."

Connie sighed.

Together we grappled with it, each supporting a side and walking it from his apartment to mine. It wasn't particularly heavy, just awkward to carry. Once we got it in the light, we saw it wasn't actually brown. The lustrous bronze-and-forest-green surface gleamed in the late-afternoon sun, almost as if it were drinking in the light. We set it in the corner of my living room, next to the couch. All I could think of was sleep.

"I need to take a nap."

"I can stay while you do," Connie said.

"No, that's okay. I'll be okay."

"Are you sure?"

"Yeah. I need to withdraw. Like into a fetal ball," I added, weakly attempting humor.

"All right," she said. "I have a few calls to make. But you call me as soon as you wake up."

"I'll do that."

Connie let herself out, and I curled up on the couch, closing my eyes and hoping for sleep to deliver me, however briefly, from my slow-motion hell. Eyes shut tight, I willed myself to slide back across time to an evening right before my trip. A fantasy now. A welcome escape drug.

Olivia and Gregory had been huddled on the couch, and he was helping her with her homework. They were engrossed in science and math. As I listened without listening, I could hear fragments of his explanations and examples—so clear and easy to grasp. Watching them from my desk across the room, I drank in the sweetness of the moment. I loved them both so much.

"Hey, guys," I said. "I need a few things from the drugstore. You at stopping point?"

"Yup. We're wrapped up here," Gregory said, clapping a book shut.

"I've got an idea," Olivia chimed in. "Let's walk." The drugstore was only a block away, and the evening was gorgeous. Why not? We scrambled to see who could get out the front door first—a little spontaneous competition that Olivia won. High clouds, alternately pink and orange in the dying light, streaked across the dusky autumn sky as we marched arm-in-arm down the street, like we were off to see the wizard.

When we got to the drugstore, Olivia and Gregory dashed off. After I'd gotten what I needed, I found them cavorting on the shampoo aisle. Olivia was leaning back, arms glued to her sides, on a red dolly while Gregory wheeled her up and down the aisle. "Don't worry, I've got you," he said, merry as an elf. Olivia giggled.

Seeing Gregory act like a big kid was such a welcome break from his serious nature. I remember thinking they might get chided for breaking the rules by some self-important store manager. But I hadn't the heart to tell them to stop. They were having too much fun.

"That's not setting a very good example," I finally mustered for a half-hearted scold. Gregory's smile grew wider, and he twirled Olivia to a halt.

It felt good to be so happy. Later that night after Gregory had gone home, Olivia confided, "Mom, I think it would be okay if you married Gregory. He's nice."

I wanted this gauzy half-dream to never end.

Should have married you.

"Ummmm."

I couldn't work my mouth to answer.

CHAPTER FIVE

It was already dark when a ringing phone interrupted my reverie.

"Hello?" I said groggily.

"'This Ann?"

"Yes."

"This is Ben. Gregory's cousin," came a clipped male voice with a little too much bravado at the other end of the line.

"Cousin?" I couldn't recall this particular cousin.

"Not a literal cousin. Just a 'cousin.' Family member. You and me met at a Christmas party." Springs squeaked in the background, like someone leaning back in a big chair.

Christmas party? The guy who spilled a drink on me?

"I called to let you know I'm taking over the arrangements now."

"Wait a minute."

I sat up, shocked awake by his words, and dislodged Woody from my feet.

"I don't know who you are," I managed to say, "but I've already put some things in motion that Stella asked me to."

"Stella?" He laughed in a booming voice. "She didn't say anything about that when I went to see her. She just told me you were cleaning up his apartment. It was the funeral home that told me you'd been by."

"We talked," I stammered. "Stella and I. About cremation. Roses. A service at the funeral home…"

"Nothing to worry about now. I got it."

"It's not a matter of worrying about it," I said, alternately frantic and testy. "We set some things up. We agreed. His friends are already gathering remembrances—"

"Yeah, well, thanks for your help. But I'm paying for it, and I got it from here."

"Now wait a darned minute. You can't just dismiss what his friends and I have already started."

"Sorry, but I'm taking over the arrangements," he said. "I'll take it under advisement whether we need a service. I'm meeting with Stella tomorrow morning at the hospital. If you want to come, I'll let you know then what I decide."

I was sputtering, unable to speak.

"And hey," he added, "do you know if he had a will?"

"A will?" You go from upending my plans for a service to asking about a will?

"In his apartment." The squeaking was continuous now, like he was rocking in the big chair.

Fuming, I thought back to the things in the chest. No will.

"No, I don't think so. But listen, you—"

"Figures. Just like his father. Anyway, I got the arrangements handled. That's the bottom line here."

"But I..." Pushing back on Ben felt like trying to slow a dump truck.

"Look, come by Stella's room tomorrow at ten, okay? I gotta go. Bye now."

Click.

And just like that, I was whipsawed out of the picture. Another piece of Gregory ripped from me. And my good intentions with Stella? Tossed aside like flotsam.

"I can't believe it," I said in a rage after dialing up Connie. "Suddenly I'm nobody, and this shady cousin is somebody."

"That's awful," she said. "Just awful."

"I don't know what to do. I can't go back to Stella. Who knows what she'll say. Or agree to do. But I can't call this Ben guy back. I don't even know his last name or phone number."

"You don't need this right now."

"No, I don't," I said, feeling that scraped-skin vulnerability again.

"I think you just have to wait till tomorrow and make your case. In the meantime, let his friends keep doing what they're doing."

"I know, damn it. I know."

The next morning we assembled in Stella's hospital room, where sunlight barely penetrated the narrow blinds. Such a pale, indifferent room, filled with sour, antiseptic odors—except for a moment when something familiar, out of place, something I'd swear was Gregory's scent wafted past my nose. Unmistakable. What the…?

The others didn't seem to notice. Stella propped up in her bed. Ben tapping his foot. The funeral director fumbling with papers. I chalked it up to my overactive imagination—what else could it be?—as we crowded in around the bed to finalize decisions and get Stella to sign off. Even if Ben *was* going to pay for everything, Stella still had to authorize the plans. But it was clear who was in charge.

Ben towered over everyone, his big belly amplifying his presence. But he was not sloppy. His white shirt was tucked in tight, and when he bent over to talk to Stella, his creased black trousers pulled up from his ankles just enough to reveal black silk socks and expensive, tasseled leather loafers. His collar-length black hair was slicked back. He hadn't gotten the Mediterranean curls, but he did get the distinctive family nose.

"Should I cross off the service in the chapel, then?" the funeral director asked Ben, as if Stella and I were not in the room.

"No," I interrupted before he could answer.

"Why do we need a service?" Ben asked, looking annoyed that I was still bird-dogging the arrangements.

"It's expected," I said fiercely. I was fully awake and present now. I wasn't about to let it go. At the very least, I was going to make a case. "Gregory touched so many people. At the chamber of commerce. The university. The business incubator he ran. His childhood friends."

"Well, I don't know about any of that." Ben scowled.

I girded for a fight, ready to defend what I'd just said.

"But, whatever."

His response came as a surprise.

"Yeah, leave it in." He glowered at me. "But you handle it. And keep it cheap."

Stella piped up.

"Are we talking about a party?"

"No, Stella," Ben said.

"And cremation," I persisted. "Gregory would have wanted to be cremated."

"It's in there," Ben said gruffly. "I left the other stuff in there, too. Now can we get on with this?"

I took a step back. He turned to Stella.

"Here." He thrust the contract and pen in front of her. "Just sign this."

She traced her wobbly signature where he pointed.

Then the funeral director pulled a clear plastic bag from her pocket.

"These are the effects that were found with your son when he died," she said, and handed it to Stella.

Seeing its contents was another gut punch. What I saw told me exactly where Gregory had been minutes—just minutes—before his death. Inside the bag was a Perrier-Jouet keychain with a single key on it. The key to my apartment. I'd given it to Gregory when we officially became a couple. I wanted to snatch it from the director's hands.

I resisted, but the keychain made this clear: Gregory had been at my place only minutes before he collapsed and died. I'd wondered why he had fallen on his front landing instead of by his back door—the entrance he used when he drove anywhere. He had been at my apartment, had walked there to feed Woody and Bernie. That's why they weren't hungry when Connie and I got there.

"I believe that's the key to my apartment," I said a little too shrilly.

All faces turned to me. Waiting.

"Could I possibly have it back? Please?"

"It looks like the key to *my* house," Stella said, holding up the plastic bag.

"Now, Stella," Ben broke in. "That's not your key. That's not the key to your house. I know what your key looks like. That's not your key. You need to give that to Ann, if it's hers."

"But it's mine. It's my boy's."

"Well, yes," Ben said, raising his voice. "But really, not." He turned to me. "You got your house key on you?"

"Yes," I said.

"Give it to me."

Fumbling with my purse, I handed Ben my keychain as he wrested the plastic bag from Stella's grip and pulled out the Perrier-Jouet keychain. He let the bag drop on her bed.

"It's mine," Stella protested.

"Look here," he said to her, holding up the two identical keys, one on the Perrier-Jouet chain and one from me.

"See that? Perfect match."

Looking confused and hurt, Stella said nothing.

"That's my key," she said with a pout. "It came out of this bag of my boy's."

"Now Stella, we're not going to make this worse, are we? I'm giving Ann the key."

"That's the key to my house," Stella said, unmoved by Ben's demonstration.

"I'm giving it to Ann," Ben asserted with finality. "Here." He thrust the two keys into my hands.

"I'm sorry, Stella," I said, uneasy with the way Ben had patronized and dismissed her. "Perhaps I can find something else of his to give you from the apartment, something that would mean more." My mind flitted briefly to the gold Saint Christopher in the chest. She would appreciate that. I was torn between wanting to shield Stella from Ben's bullying and getting back the Perrier-Jouet keychain, which suddenly meant so much to me.

"It's mine," peeped a persistent little voice.

"That's enough," Ben blustered. "We're done here."

Stella shut up and glared at him.

When I got home, I buried my face in what had been Gregory's pillow and cried till I was cried out. Over a key. I'd come undone over a key. It was just a key.

CHAPTER SIX

"I could barely drive home," I told Connie when she came to check on me before dinner. "Even if I know it's irrelevant where Gregory was, I can't stop thinking about the fact that he was probably here feeding the cats just before..." Connie watched and listened as I sputtered at the other end of the couch, tucked into the cushions like a nesting squirrel. She grabbed a tissue from the end table and handed it to me.

"Tell me again what made you think this?"

"The keychain. The Perrier-Jouet keychain," I said, pointing to it on the coffee table. "That confirmed where he'd been...." I choked, unable to finish the thought. "It ripped something away again. I'm raw again, just like the first night."

Connie held up the keychain, white flowers embossed on its flat, green-and-gold silhouette of a champagne bottle. The key to my apartment was still attached.

"It makes me want to cry again," I said, looking at the keychain.

"Because it brought you a step closer to his final moments?" Connie said.

"Yeah, I guess. I don't know."

"Come sit closer to me." Connie patted the couch. I slid toward her, leaning into her warm, solid presence. Just touching shoulder-to-shoulder made me calmer.

"I feel like I'm sliding into a pit," I said, less frantic. "Like I'll never get past losing him."

"Understandable," Connie said. "You've been bombarded with so much in what—just a few days? Don't be so hard on yourself. Besides, piecing together all these clues about where and how he died, you're doing what comes naturally. It's in your DNA. As a reporter."

She paused.

Connie often took her time saying what she had to say. It was unclear whether the pauses were for emphasis or for formulating her next thought. Maybe both.

"You found out what happened just before he died. The same thing you do when you write stories. Only, this time, you're in the story. It ratchets up your grief. You can't escape into your work this time."

"Jesus, you ought to be a shrink," I said, comforted by the assurance in her voice and the logic of her words.

"I've just known you a long time," she said. "You know you do it, too. Retreat into work."

"When I'm writing a story, I feel like I'm in control," I sniffed, shifting to sit more upright. I stared at the pale carpet as dust motes cavorted in shafts of light above it. I made a mental note that it needed cleaning.

"You can't do it that way this time," Connie said. "This is harder. You just don't have that buffer between you and the event. It's also not like any loss you've ever faced before. Losing your parents doesn't count. I mean, it *counts*, but this is a different magnitude."

It was true. While I had mourned the loss of each of my parents—especially my mother after that damned T-bone wreck—this was different. I know my dad meant well, but he didn't help things after she died. He avoided talking about it, as if that protected me. Maybe him, too. Gave away all her stuff. Remarried fairly quickly. When he finally died, he was old and frail. We never talked about what happens after death. Besides, he had lived a long life.

"The only thing worse than this would be losing a child," I said. As the thought suffused my consciousness, my gut went all grippy. Good God, Olivia. She was all I had now. I was glad we were checking in daily.

Connie nodded, seeming to gather her thoughts.

"I'd like to suggest something that might make what you're going through a little easier."

Connie sat forward, clasping her hands together.

"I know it might sound counterintuitive," she said, "but I'd like you to consider spending some time alone with his body."

"I already did that."

"No—really be with him."

Connie let the words settle.

My knee-jerk reaction: No, no, and no. The closest I'd been to dead bodies was the doll-like figures in funeral coffins. I'd never done homicides at work, although I'd seen the grisly unpublished photos. But behind her words was something tantalizing I couldn't put my finger on. There were things Connie had a sixth sense about, and this might be one of them. If it would diminish the pain… yes, I would consider it. Already my mind was skipping ahead: It was Wednesday, and we would have to make special arrangements with the funeral home, since Gregory was going to be cremated, probably Friday. My mind leapt to random thoughts. If I saw him, he would be "as is." There would be no embalming. No tarting up for viewing.

"Tell me again why I would do this?" I said. "You're talking about someone I loved. It sounds pretty ghoulish."

"It only seems ghoulish because we've completely lost touch with how to handle death in this country," Connie said with the barest trace of exasperation—not directed at me, I was pretty sure. "How to engage, to mourn, understand…" She stopped and drew an unhurried breath. "In a lot of religions, there's been a revival of customs to prepare the body for burial—and by extension, the soul, for its journey."

Connie was shifting the way she explained things. If I'd been taking notes, I'd have underlined this.

"With Jews, it's usually some ritual form of bathing, dressing, and watching over the body before its final journey. Usually by a small group of people close to the person who's passed. It's part of grieving. Very intimate and cathartic. I'm not talking about exactly this, but the thought keeps recurring that you might be comforted if you spent just a little time alone with him. Maybe even touched him."

"Touch what? His lifeless body?"

Yes, touch.

I wasn't sure I wanted my last memory of Gregory to be in death. Even though I'd already identified him at the funeral home, I still clung to the image of him driving away from the airport that final morning, waving goodbye. Full of life. Juicy.

As I struggled with the dichotomy, an old memory surfaced.

"Have I ever mentioned Tiger?"

"I don't think so," Connie said.

As if on cue, Woody reached out and stretched toward Bernie in their nook above the TV.

"Tiger was a cat I had once," I said. "When I was ten."

"How's that?"

"A cat. You know how much I love my cats."

Connie nodded.

"Tiger was one in a million, a beautiful brown tabby with soulful green eyes." I could see him in my mind's eye, feel him as if he were there, lifting his chin for me to scratch, collapsing against me and closing his eyes in feline bliss.

"I loved Tiger. I could dress him in doll clothes. Hold him in my lap and play with making his claws go in and out. Carry him like a baby. Push him around in my baby buggy. Tiger just purred. At night he slept in the crook of my arm, and in the morning I'd find his little head next to mine on the pillow. I loved him so much."

The memory of that sweet intimacy was immediate.

"Then one day after school, my mother told me he'd been hit by a car."

"I'm so sorry, Ann."

I paused as the ache for Tiger melted into my outsized anguish over Gregory, like tears swallowed up by rain.

"I begged my mother to let me see him. But she said 'no,' even as she assured me he looked like he was sleeping. I knew I *needed* to see him. But she was firm. 'No, you don't.' I remember how those words cut. The more I insisted, the more she hardened. 'It's better you don't,' she said. 'I'm your mother, and I know what's best.' And her eyes went cold.

"That was that." I brushed my hands together in a finished-up gesture. "She was done and never spoke of him again. I got the message that I shouldn't, either."

"What a sad story. And this reminds you of Gregory now?"

"I've always believed that seeing Tiger, even stroking his lifeless body, would have given me some sense of closure—though I hate that word." Things were never "closed"—nor would they ever be the same. "I haven't thought about Tiger's death in years, and now it seems suddenly fresh. Like it happened yesterday."

"I'm not thinking 'closure' in the present situation," Connie said, stretching to get up off the couch and walk to the window, pulling aside the sheers and staring at the cars parked in front of my unit.

"Closure is overrated," she said. "I'm thinking more about processing."

I was startled by the sound of someone peeling rubber outside, probably a student. The complex was full of them. Professors, too. How many of them had lost someone? How many had gone through what I was going through?

"So my proposition doesn't sound completely unreasonable?" Connie said.

"I don't know. There's a big difference between a cat and a person."

Yet I intuitively trusted Connie. Even if I couldn't fully wrap my head around what she was saying. We were talking about the body I'd made love to less than a week ago. A week ago! How quickly things can change.

Like walking through a door.

What a strange thought.

"If I say yes… will you go with me?"

She let the sheers drop and looked back at me.

"I won't go in the room with you, if that's what you're asking. But I'll go and wait outside."

The next day, all my uncertainty, my doubts and fear of revulsion fell away as soon as I was standing alone next to Gregory's body in a small, formal viewing room at the funeral home. As before, Gregory was on a gurney with a quilted gray blanket wrapped tightly around his body from the armpits down—the way a woman might wrap a towel around her body after a shower. The blanket covered everything except his shoulders, upper chest, arms, neck, and head.

Seeing him up close like this, I forgot my hesitation and wanted to drink in every detail. Sear them into my mind so I'd never forget.

At first, I just observed. Inspected, really. Here were the face and lips I'd kissed a thousand times, the eyes through which I'd plumbed the depths—or at least wandered the shallows—of another soul. The ears into which I'd whispered "I love you" countless times. I whispered it again.

Something rustled in the distance.

"Is that you, my love?" I said, straining toward the sound.

Shhh. No time for words.

His color was drained, in its place an opaque waxiness. Hesitantly, I touched his face. It was cold, like the inside of the refrigerator where he'd so recently lain. All his features were slightly flattened and the crook of his nose, sharpened. Some well-meaning mortician had combed his hair back, accentuating his receding hairline. Gregory would have hated that. Gingerly, I pushed it into a more natural arrangement.

Standing at his head and feeling more daring, I leaned down to smell his forehead, intent on drinking in his scent one more time. But I was met with disappointment: There was no scent here like the powerful jolt I'd experienced in

Stella's hospital room. In its place was only an unfamiliar plastic odor—not unpleasant, just not him. Death had stolen his scent. Slowly, I traced the outline of his ears with my fingers and followed the crest of his brow and the line of his strong chin, still rough with stubble. I was struck by the weight of his head as I rolled it between my hands. It had never seemed so heavy when the life of his muscles lifted it.

I ran my hands down his neck, over his strong shoulders, down his arms to his hands. You can love someone for years and be hazy on the fine details of their features. It was as if now I had to look at him with my hands as well as my eyes and burn the memory into both senses—every line and crevice; the faint mole on his upper lip; the bend of his long, elegant fingers. He was perfect and unscathed, save for the thick black thread where the autopsy incisions were sewn closed on the back of his head and his chest, extending just above the blanket line. It all felt natural, like a meditation.

I wanted to touch his feet, to see again those uniquely slender toes, but they were beyond my reach, tightly bound beneath the blanket. I loved those toes that he wiggled in the grass on our first date. Such lovely toes. One time when we were at an Assyrian art exhibit, I looked up at a massive wall relief of soldiers in battle thousands of years ago to see dozens of toes exactly like Gregory's. Here, truly, were his forebears. We marveled and had a good laugh.

Standing next to him in this alien setting, I realized how much I loved this body—its shape, its smell, the form of it—and how difficult it had been up until that moment to separate the body from the life that was once within. I loved the way Gregory's spirit moved and animated this body—with confidence, but not swagger. He seemed so comfortable in his skin, even with the long, jagged scar that disfigured his torso.

As I stood beside him one last time, I was struck by the thought: The man I love is gone.

After brushing his forehead lightly with my lips, I backed away slowly toward the door, stretching my farewell and taking in the whole of him one last time. Then I withdrew and closed the door firmly behind me. I felt strangely peaceful. Connie got up from her chair and met me in the hallway.

"You were right," I said. "I'm still sad, but he's not there. The man I loved isn't there."

"No," she said.

"Without his energy, the body is simply a shell," I said, feeling grief pool in my belly. "'Makes me wish my mother had listened when I said I wanted to see Tiger."

"Maybe you needed that experience to fully appreciate this," Connie whispered.

CHAPTER SEVEN

In the hours after my interlude with Gregory's body, my grief wasn't diminished so much as changed, like pain that travels around your body. I still longed for his touch—his fingers pressed to my skin, the security of his arms enfolding me. I missed it all like a drug. But my resignation was more settled, less ragged. Death was more clearly a line of demarcation. Seeing his body gave rise to a troubling question I'd never considered in any depth before: What happened to the essence of who he was? What happens to the essence of any of us after we die? It was inconceivable that all his Gregory-ness had simply ceased to exist. I was not a religious person so I did not expect to turn there for answers. I had always relied on the security of my mind and rational thought to understand the nature of reality. I guess I bought into my father's denial: I just never much thought about what might come after physical death. If anything.

Now the question churned in the back of my mind like a low hum as I set about my next terrible task. I had volunteered to select the clothes Gregory would wear to the crematory—Olivia called it the creamery—on Friday and had to get them to the funeral home by mid-morning. It was another irrational act of guarding jealously what I felt to be mine. I simply couldn't permit anyone else—Ben for instance—to go pawing through his closet and picking the first thing they saw and tossing it in a bag.

I was determined Gregory would be well-dressed in death, just as he'd been in life. Even if all of it was destined to go up in flames. Aren't we all ashes to ashes and dust to dust at some point? But as I stood in his closet surveying the suits; the slacks and jackets; the neatly hung, precision-ironed shirts; and the ties, it felt so surreal. It's just not something you ever think about having to do. I was picking out clothes to be incinerated with his body. That body, again. Only I didn't cry this time. Instead, an odd hollowing spread across my chest as I selected first the dark gabardine slacks, then a collarless silk dress shirt requiring no tie, his nearly new Cole Haan lace-ups, and a belt. I hung the slacks and shirt carefully in a garment bag and tucked the shoes, belt, and a pair of socks in a small tote.

I wondered briefly if I should bring a pair of Jockeys.

Free-balling in the crematorium.

Then thought better of it with a sardonic chuckle.

Thankfully, the rest of Friday I was engrossed in helping plan the service that Ben had ceded to me. But I didn't have to do a lot. Some of Gregory's friends—a bunch of type As—along with Connie and a handful of my colleagues from work swarmed over all but the most personal decisions. They'd gotten the word out, set up the service, sorted through tributes, and coordinated dozens of mundane details. I secured the chapel at the funeral home and called Stella's priest, who agreed to officiate even though there would be no mass. It would be a celebration of Gregory's life, with friends and hopefully family reading their remembrances. Father McCallister would read for people who were shaky or shy about delivering their own. I wasn't sure I'd be able to read mine. I hoped Ben and other family members would be there, if for no other reason than to see how much Gregory meant to the people around him.

Before Connie came to pick me up on Saturday—she insisted on ferrying me to and from the service—I lingered in front of the full-length mirror in my bedroom. Had it been only a week since Gregory had taken me to the airport to attend the convention? How insignificant the award seemed now.

Numbly going through the motions, I put on just enough makeup to subdue my freckles and mask the hollows under my eyes. I tried to pencil some shape into my wispy brows but hesitated when I got to my eyes.

Those Natalie Wood eyes.

Gregory told me how he loved my big, brown eyes, though mine were neither as dark nor as intense as his.

I outlined what he teasingly called my skinny "white-bread lips," then filled in the color and brushed my wavy, chestnut-brown hair the way Gregory liked it, with soft finger curls trailing down the nape of my neck.

It was as if I were dressing to go out on a date, one last date, with Gregory. He even gave me the dress I was wearing—a long-sleeved, black jersey A-line with a turtleneck. He surprised me with it one day out of nowhere.

I sat on the edge of the bed for a moment, closing my eyes and imagining he was there. I tried to remember the things he'd said so I could feel his love all over again. "I loved you from the first moment I laid eyes on you," he used to say. I remembered the night we met at a patio party and talked the whole time. Later, as we fell in love, he'd trace my lips with his fingers before kissing them. I could almost feel him doing it again. "I love your freckles," he'd say. "Love kissing them. Love kissing all of you." And it would start… like steam heat rising…

"Hello! Hello up there!"

My escape fantasy vanished at the sound of Connie's voice.

"I'm up here," I said, slipping on my black suede pumps and a necklace of green-and-gold beads my father brought back from Italy. Gregory always liked the way the dress set them off.

"I let myself in when you didn't answer," Connie said.

"I'll be down in a minute."

I started to finish my makeup with mascara, then thought better of it. Mascara runs. I tucked a tissue inside my sleeve and went down the stairs.

"How are you doing?" Connie asked on the way to the service.

"Okay, I guess."

"Sorry I couldn't spend much time with you yesterday."

"That's okay. You're doing a lot."

"What you got there?" Connie said, eyeing a brown paper wrapped parcel on my lap.

"It's a portrait of Gregory."

"To put up front?"

"Yes. He had it taken earlier this year for a brochure. The photographer insisted on framing it for me when he heard about Gregory. He brought it by a little while ago. Wouldn't let me pay for it."

Connie dropped me off at the chapel door and went to find a place to park. The chapel itself was a big, boxy, beige room that provided a neutral backdrop for whatever ceremony a client might desire. I unwrapped the portrait and placed it next to a black-and-white of Gregory's sixth-grade Little League team already nestled between a couple of floral sprays. I'd not seen the photograph before and wondered who brought it. Most of the boys kneeling or standing with him in the frame would be taking their places in the pews. The organ warbled through Pachelbel as people filed in.

I turned from setting up his portrait on the altar just in time to see Connie come inside. Behind her, Olivia came through the door with her dad—the first time I'd seen her in a week. I rushed to greet her, and we held and hugged each other a long time.

"How have you been, sweetie?" I said, pushing a few stray strands of hair off her face.

"Okay. I've missed you."

Her eyes were red.

"I've missed you, too."

It felt so good to hold her. Tears or not, she was so radiant and fresh-faced, with long lazy curls and unaffected grace. She looked mature beyond her twelve years—poised in the pretty black velvet dress I'd bought her to wear to an art show opening with Gregory and me. She liked it so much she carried it back and forth between her two houses, mine and her father's. The reminder made my heart ache—for both of us.

"Oh, sweetheart." I hugged her again. "This is so hard for all of us. But starting Monday, we'll get back to our regular schedule."

"Good. There are some things I really just want to talk about with you."

"I know this is hard," I said to her. "But we'll get through it. Together."

Then I looked over at her dad.

"It means a lot that you're here. And that Olivia's been able to draw strength from you."

"I'm sorry, Ann," he said. "I'm glad I could be here for her."

"Would you like to come sit with me and Connie?" I asked Olivia.

"If you want me to," Olivia said, shifting her feet and looking down. I could tell she wanted to stay with her dad.

"You don't have to," I said gently.

"Then I think I'll sit with Dad this time." Our daughter wedged into the pew next to him, but not before squeezing my hand. "I love you, Mom."

"Love you, too," I mouthed.

As the pews filled, I looked around for Stella and still didn't see her. Perhaps she hadn't felt well enough to attend after all. Connie, I could see, was already finding a place in the third row, next to one of Gregory's friends from elementary school. When it was nearly time for the service to begin, Father McCallister cleared his throat, then made an informal request for folks to please find their seats. I took my place, tucked safely between Gregory's friend and Connie. All those boys, now grown up, had stayed in touch and made me feel welcome in their circle.

"Hope you like the team photo I found," the friend next to me whispered in my ear.

As I started to answer, something fluttered in the corner of my vision, and I turned to see Stella working her way down the center aisle to the family pew, grasping her neighbor's arm. She walked stiffly, steadied by a cane, shoulders back with obvious dignity, draped in a dated but elegant navy frock with a white lace collar that set off her silver-white hair. The only person she allowed at her side was her next-door-neighbor Wanda, a slight, bent woman with hard dark eyes in a face lined like a shar-pei's. Wanda had an affinity for polyester, in contrast to Stella's yesteryear high fashion. Gregory told me they were an odd couple whose friendship grew out of being neighbors. Both widows, they leaned on each other.

Abruptly, Stella stopped and turned to a young man seated at the end of a pew.

"Did you know he was *my* son?" she asked a little too loudly. The young man looked up, blinking. Whispers rustled through the crowd.

"No, ma'am," he said softly. "I'm sorry, I didn't."

Stella smiled. After a few more halting steps, she paused and pressed the question again, this time to an older woman on the other side of the aisle.

"Did you know he was my son?"

I watched as people shifted in their seats, looked down, tried not to stare. Someone dropped a program. Someone coughed.

"Stella, stop," Wanda stage-whispered out the side of her mouth where a cigarette would normally have dangled. "You're making people uncomfortable." Wanda's spindly arms and legs were overwhelmed by her too-large black pantsuit as she shuffled next to Stella.

"Did you know he was my son?" Stella continued her drill as through she hadn't heard.

"Of course, Mrs. Malouf," said a middle-aged man. "I'm Duke. Remember me? From Little League."

"Oh my goodness," Stella exclaimed. "You're all grown up. I didn't recognize you."

"I could never forget you, Mrs. Malouf. You bought the whole team Popsicles."

Stella beamed.

"Can I help you get to your pew?" he asked.

"No." Stella was firm. "I can do it."

Again and again, she shambled forward, stopped, and asked the question.

"Did you know he was *my* son?"

"Yes," said a woman close to the front. "From Ann. She had so many good things to say about Gregory—a reflection on you, I'm sure."

"Why thank you."

In silence Wanda steered Stella the rest of the way forward. The two of them sat alone in the first pew near the pulpit. No other family had shown up. Not even Ben.

Father McCallister waited for the two women to settle in before he began the service with a greeting and a prayer.

Yes, let us SPRAY.

I almost giggled at the quirky, unbidden thought that sounded just like something Gregory would say in one of his irreverent moments. Father McCallister intoned about the fact that Gregory was taken from us suddenly and asked God to forgive him his sins and Jesus to accept him with waiting arms. We recited the Lord's Prayer together. Then it was time for the remembrances. One after the other, the anecdotes tumbled out—from friends, coworkers, some people I didn't know. I loved listening to all the stories about Gregory and the way they came together in a mosaic of his character: his eagerness to help young entrepreneurs, the time he rescued a tiny owl, his recipe for great steaks.

One of the entrepreneurs Gregory had counseled, a Boomer with a neatly trimmed goatee, spoke admiringly of Gregory's steady hand through a rough patch: "Gregory had a knack for finding a path to order through chaos." He had a lot of practice, I thought.

A sob caught in my throat, and I felt for the tissue in my sleeve when one of the men from his grammar-school pack said, voice breaking, "I figure for Gregory right now it's eternal summer between the fifth and sixth grades on the Field of Dreams. *Nos vemos, compadre.*"

Father McCallister had barely gotten the name of Gregory's ex-wife out before the energy in the room shifted, sucked up by this figure striding toward the pulpit, her long black taffeta skirt swooshing in rhythm with her movements, flaming red tresses trailing behind her as wild and free as a mustang's mane. Our eyes met briefly.

So this was Elizabeth, the overweight shrew Gregory had railed about? She was striking. A head-turner. Not at all what I expected. Once rooted behind the lectern, she started by saying she had known Gregory since college. He had never mentioned that. As I thought about it, he'd never really told me anything about how or when they met, or how long they'd known each other, or why their marriage hadn't worked out. He simply hadn't talked about it, except to diss her. This woman was so unlike what I'd envisioned. I couldn't take my eyes off her.

"The sun was his healer," she said. "He cut out cartoons in the *New Yorker* with pinking shears so he could send them to friends.... He loved quietly and deeply.... A little girl once told him that he was her angel, an angel sent by God. And it was true."

I glanced sideways at Connie to see if she'd caught that last bit. An angel sent by God? Did this have some connection to the angel reference in the drawings we'd found in the chest in Gregory's apartment? If so, maybe Elizabeth could unravel the riddle. Or riddles.

But my friend was concentrating on something in the vicinity of the altar. Brow knitted, neck strained, eyes narrowed, she seemed to be looking just beyond it. Her rigid body telegraphed, "Do not disturb."

I turned my attention back to Elizabeth, feeling a little jealous at the intimacy of her words. I recognized the Gregory she described. She obviously had been in love with him and maybe still was.

Finally it was my turn. Although many of the remembrances up to that moment left me teary, I felt shimmering inside. Throughout the readings, it was as though I were being showered with love. I got to drink in Gregory for just a little while longer, through the eyes of others. I felt subdued and fragile, but also radiant and alive. I slid down the pew to the center aisle and made my way to the pulpit, there to see for the first time how full the chapel was—overflowing really—with maybe three hundred people there for him and me. Rows and rows of upturned faces. Olivia. Her dad. Our friends. So many newsroom colleagues. Suits I didn't know, probably from his business incubator or the chamber of commerce. I was surprised to see that Stella seemed to have nodded off, her head drooping against Wanda's shoulder.

I unfolded a piece of paper and began.

"I remember meeting Gregory..."

I told about our first date at the restaurant with literal garden seating and how he'd slipped off his shoes and wiggled those long Assyrian toes in the grass. I told them how we had five wonderful years—years made sweet by simple pleasures, like cooking together and reading the paper on Sundays. People chuckled when I mentioned washing our cars. Anyone who knew Gregory knew he loved his Celica. As I spoke of the car, something like a caress washed over me, and my flesh tingled against the silkiness of the camisole beneath my dress. It was as if he were right there listening to me say how much I'd appreciated him and how we'd never taken each other for granted. I said I only regretted not telling him more often how much I adored him. My thoughts skittered briefly again to the deliciousness of his fingers lightly dancing inside my thighs. In that moment, a blast of love rushed into my heart, so strong—and yes, *erotic*—my whole body vibrated. I was careful not to betray this subtext as I walked slowly back to my seat, cheeks flushed with what people surely assumed was sadness.

Father McCallister was set to start the final blessing when he was interrupted by a smartly dressed young Black man sprinting up to the pulpit from the back of the chapel.

"Wait. Please wait. I have one more tribute to offer."

A murmur fluttered through the pews.

"That's one of the guys from the business incubator," I whispered to Connie, who failed for the second time to acknowledge me, still fixated on… something.

We all waited and watched, curious. I expected the young man to pull some notes from behind the handkerchief tucked neatly in his suit breast pocket. But no. Instead of launching into a speech, a sonorous baritone rose up out of that slender body and expanded to fill the entire chapel with a soaring a cappella rendition of "Amazing Grace." It took my breath away and so lightened and illuminated the gathering that we all stood—first one, then another, and another—and spontaneously joined our voices with his.

"I thought that was wonderful," I said to Connie on the way home after the service.

"Sorry. I missed a lot of it," Connie said.

She seemed unusually tense and distracted, just as she had throughout the service. My friend who up until then had been so calm, reassuring, and supportive. Now she appeared to struggle with her composure as she drove the short distance home.

"Is anything wrong?" I asked, not really wanting to cloud the moment but also concerned for her well-being. Her chest heaved as she glanced in the rearview mirror.

"I don't know," she said, wheeling into the complex and stopping in front of my unit, where a few slender trees were dropping gold and amber leaves onto a small flowerbed.

"Can you give me a clue what's going on?"

"Ann," she said slowly, "I think I saw him."

The words came out thick as wax.

"Who?" I put my hand on her arm. "Who did you see?"

She was trembling.

"It's hazy," Connie continued, then shook her head. "No, it isn't hazy at all. I saw Gregory. I feel like he was watching the whole thing."

"Gregory?" My pulse quickened even as I scoffed. "What do you mean Gregory?"

"Over the altar."

"What the…? What are you talking about? What did you see?"

My mind failed to register what she was saying.

"Him. Gregory. Your guy. I could easily make out his face—he was smiling—and, absurdly, I could see he was wearing a sports coat and tie."

I was dumbstruck. I simply couldn't grasp it.

"I… I… don't know what to say."

"I know it sounds crazy," Connie said. "But it was so clearly him. You tease me about being a magic Christian, but this… I couldn't take my eyes off… his radiance." Tears gathered at the corners of her eyes. Her face was suffused with softness. Then it shifted. "But I couldn't flow into the feeling. Memories of my father's fury kept rearing up."

"Your father. What's your father got to do with this?" I was aware of the abuse she had suffered at his hand growing up, but I wanted her to say more about what she saw.

"Visions. He would say visions are the devil's work. I grew up with so much shame and fear. And this vision really activated my fear because I couldn't control it. Couldn't look away."

She pressed her fingers to her forehead. I could see she was shaking.

"Undeserved shame," I said, almost in a whisper.

"It was definitely Gregory," Connie declared, forcing herself to return to the vision. "As clear as if he were standing next to me. Smiling."

"If you saw him"—and I still wasn't believing—"did he see you? Did he see me?"

It made no sense, but I had to know more.

"I don't know. I tried to un-see him. I really did," she said, turning to me, something akin to terror twisting her face. "This 'seeing' is a part of me that triggers so much shame—and reactivates the trauma. Like shell shock." Red mottling crept up Connie's neck and onto her cheeks.

She saw him. The words slid off my brain as if she were speaking in tongues. What did that mean?

"Could it have been your imagination?" I offered wanly, not wanting that to be the case.

"Yes, I suppose it could."

Neither of us believed it.

I waited.

"What would it mean for you to 'see' him?" I pressed.

Tell me. Even if it makes no sense.

"That there's something wrong with me," came her acrid reply. "Deeply, terribly wrong. At least that's what my father would say. And a lot of other people who make judgments about what I can do." She slammed the car into park a little too aggressively.

"There's nothing wrong with you," I said, getting out of the car.

Connie shut down.

"I need to go home for a while," she said.

Tell. Me. More.

CHAPTER EIGHT

Sitting at my desk the Monday after the service, I struggled without much success to write thank-you notes for the flowers, the cards, the reminiscences, and enough casseroles for a month of meals. The spark of Connie's revelation burned like a stubborn ember—refusing to die and yet not strong enough to catch fire—nearly overwhelmed by the immediacy of Things That Must Get Done. But focus eluded me. I tried to imagine life without Gregory, and each time, I descended into brooding about what my daughter and I faced. Our new normal took me back to when it was just Olivia and me in cozy mother-daughter solitude. Not terrible, but like returning to black-and-white after being awash in Kodachrome. We were good together, she and I. But Gregory added so much to our lives.

I was grateful when the phone at my elbow jangled, interrupting my bleak thoughts.

"Ann Stewart?"

I couldn't place the throaty, sandpaper voice at the other end of the line.

"Hello?" the voice persisted. "Is this Ann?"

"Yes, this is Ann," I said finally. "Who's this?"

Was that whimpering, perhaps an animal, in the background?

"This is Wanda. Wanda White. Stella's neighbor."

Wanda. I knew I'd heard that voice before. I still could see her walking Stella to the front of the chapel at the service.

"Yes, Wanda. How are you? How's Stella?"

I felt a little guilty for not reaching out to Gregory's mother sooner. She'd seemed so lost and forlorn at the service, even with Wanda stuck fiercely to her side. I spoke to them only briefly afterwards, when I handed Stella the framed portrait of Gregory from the altar.

"You take this, Stella," I said. "I know Gregory would want you to have it."

Don't be so sure.

What was this? My hectoring alter ego?

"Why thank you, dear."

Stella seemed grateful to receive it but never fully engaged, eyes wandering and darting about the crowd. Perhaps because she was still on the pain meds—and struggling with Gregory's death, as I was.

"Stella's not good."

Wanda's clipped words brought me back to the phone. It was impossible to tell if she was angry or always talked that way.

"What's going on?"

I braced for her answer.

"You've got to come over. Right now. Stella's beside herself."

"Okay, I can do that," I said, relieved she wasn't asking me to do more. "Can you tell me what's going on?"

"It's Gregory," Wanda said.

Of course it's Gregory.

"What about Gregory?"

What, specifically, I wanted to ask.

"She can't stand looking at him. On her mantel."

"You mean the ashes?"

Oh. I put my pen down. The box from the funeral home.

"Yes, you've got to come over. She wants to talk to you."

"Okay, okay. I can be there in a few minutes."

"Good," Wanda said. "Bye."

Dial tone.

Wanda answered after I rang the bell at Stella's front door, Princess at her side. The bristle-coated white shepherd looked up, hopeful, tail switching back and forth. Gregory told me all the dogs Wanda had ever owned were white because of her name: Wanda White. He said Wanda rarely went anywhere without her loyal, tail-wagging companion.

Wanda had been smoking; I could smell it in the air between us.

"Come in," Wanda said, leading me to the den at the back of the house. On my few previous visits, the den had been where Stella held court. On those occasions, she'd been sitting in the recliner which was across from the TV and fireplace. A nearby TV tray still held the remote and the *TV Guide*.

But this time Stella wasn't sitting in the recliner. Wanda sat there instead.

Stella was slumped on the oversized contemporary gold sofa wearing a lumpy turquoise patio dress machine-trimmed with Mexican embroidery. Her eyes were puffy against her splotchy, sagging skin, and her hair was untidy, pressed against the back of her head as if she hadn't bothered to comb it after she got up. Several wadded-up tissues littered the gold shag carpet at her slippered feet. She held one in her hand.

"Oh, Ann," she said, sitting up as I came into the room. I carefully skirted the black lacquered end-table that jutted out into the doorway, avoiding the shade of the Jetsons-style lamp. Gregory told me that when the family had been forced to downsize, Stella couldn't part with these symbols of their onetime affluence. Just as she hadn't been able to part with her *I Love Lucy* frocks. Or Johnny's suits.

Her worried eyes followed me as I sat down beside her.

"I can't do this," she said.

"What's wrong?"

I turned to Wanda, who was perched on the edge of the recliner, Princess pacing at her feet.

"What's the problem, Stella?" I asked, looking back and forth between the women.

"She can't stand the fact that her son is in a box on the mantel," Wanda finally said, arms fixed across her chest.

I scanned the mantel above the fireplace, searching among the candlesticks, a Bible, and several faded children's photographs. There it was, the maroon plastic container about a foot square and a few inches deep, standing upright. Nothing distinguished it in any other way, not even a label.

All our love, reduced to this.

"I can't do this," Stella wailed, looking at me.

I still wasn't sure what she wanted.

It was strange to engage Stella in this intimate way. It went against Gregory's efforts to keep the two of us at a distance from one another. I found his attitude curious, as she just seemed like a harmless old woman. Maybe a little dotty. And despite his outsized devotion to her, he seemed to have so many issues around her, starting with her "superstitious" Catholicism, as he called it. Her contempt for the women in his life. The obstacles she threw up when he wanted to sell the liquor store they co-owned. Her faked heart attack during a robbery. All his complaints and characterizations gave way to one truth now that he was gone: She was a connection to him. I clung to the belief that we could help each other in the aftermath of this shared tragedy. I yearned to hear her stories about Gregory.

"What is it you can't do?" I said, taking Stella's hand, the one that wasn't clutching the tissue.

"I'm sorry now that I approved this," she said, gesturing toward the box.

I wasn't sure how to respond. In my heart I knew this was what Gregory would have wanted, but the final decision had ultimately been Stella's, as next of kin. It was her decision and hers alone. Had I pushed too hard? Did she feel pressured against her will? Or was this a kind of buyer's remorse? One thing for sure: We couldn't go back.

"Do you remember we talked about this?" I said gingerly. "I was going to take his ashes to places he liked, so he'll be free of that little box and out in the world he loved. I could even take the box with me now, if you like."

"No."

She shook her head and pulled her hand back.

"No, I can't stand that."

I'd fought ardently to honor Gregory's wishes—it was all I had of him now—but I didn't want to make Stella's pain worse. I thought we'd come to an understanding, Stella and me. I looked helplessly across the room at Wanda.

"Tell her what you want," Wanda said, nodding to Stella and pulling a cigarette out and lighting it.

"I want him in the family plot," Stella sputtered, "with the family. With Bubba and Johnny… and me when I die."

Bubba, Gregory's only sibling, had been killed in a hunting accident—the details were murky—and of course Johnny was the boys' father.

"I can't bear him being someplace else. Or just blowing around like dust. Dust! That's worse." She wrung her hands. "So much worse."

With pleading, pained eyes she looked like a hostage, as though someone were holding a knife to her throat. She seemed sure I could rescue her.

With no help from Wanda, I struggled to find the right words. Was it my grief or Wanda's smoke that was making it hard to breathe?

"Stella," I said steadily, "you are his next of kin. You get the final say on what happens. I am so grateful you agreed to let him be cremated. But if you want him to be buried in the family plot, then that's what's going to happen. It's up to you. Not me."

Instantly her face was transformed, like a crying child distracted by a toy.

"Really?" she said, pawing at my sleeve. "You'd do that for me?"

"It's not up to me. This is your decision."

"Thank you."

Stella straightened up at once, as if remembering herself.

"I know it's the right thing to do. I'm sure it's what Gregory would want. Father McCallister said it would be better, too."

I doubted her priest had said burying the ashes in the family plot would be better than scattering them, but I wasn't about to challenge her. As much as I liked a good debate, this wasn't one I'd be wading into. I had gotten him cremated and, in that, fulfilled his wishes.

The truth was, Gregory wouldn't care where his ashes ended up—or even, ultimately, whether he was cremated or not. When I meditated on his body at the funeral home, I thoroughly grasped that whoever or whatever he was had gone. Departed. Vanished, at least, from the flesh. It was time to give Stella whatever it took to ease the pain so naked in her eyes. There comes a point after a death when you have to put the needs of the living first.

Wanda stubbed out her cigarette and shifted in the recliner, as if to signal that it was time for me to leave. I welcomed the opening and surrendered to her mute invitation.

"Is there anything else you need me to do?" I said, turning to Stella before I stood to go.

"There's really not," said Wanda, jumping in. "She can call Ben herself."

Wanda wasn't being rude, just direct. I could see that she recognized when Stella had reached her limit. Maybe she noticed that I had, too.

Before finishing our goodbyes, Stella rose abruptly and shuffled out of the room. Suspended in awkwardness with Wanda, I wanted to break and run for the front door but moved instead with measured steps. I even stopped to give sweet Princess, who was nosing my legs, a good head rub.

"Wait!" Stella called out as I reached the front door. "Wait, I have something for you."

Oh, no. I remembered all the other times Stella had implored me to wait, then thrust some unwanted object, like the schefflera, into my hands. Gregory said I wasn't alone. She did this gift-giving ritual with everyone who came to visit.

"I want you to have these," she said, looking at me through rheumy eyes. "These were Gregory's."

She placed two little bronzed baby shoes into my hands.

"Oh my God, Stella. I can't take these."

So much for meaningless gifts. It was as if she'd handed me a couple of gold ingots.

"Yes, you can. I want you to have them." She patted my hands. "I have Bubba's."

I could feel Stella watching for my reaction.

"Why… thank you," I said. "Thank you very much. I will take good care of them."

"Those were Gregory's," Stella said. "His first shoes. He was such a darling baby. He was my little man, you know."

CHAPTER NINE

Once home, I stroked the bronzed baby shoes, running my fingers over the shiny copper-colored surface, trying to imagine them on a diminutive Gregory. They were maybe four-and-a-half inches long, the left one ever-so-slightly wider than the right. The smooshed toes suggested his little feet had made lots of baby tracks in them. It was as if I could feel the energy of the little person who pattered around in those shoes, full of toddler purpose and determination. My face felt hot. Tears were scudding close to the surface. Holding the little shoes made me so sad for the life cut short. For a future that would never be. For the open wound in my heart. Twisted up in this raw sorrow was the sense of needing to be there for Stella. If I could somehow make up for the hole in her life, maybe it would help fill the one in mine.

But I'd have to bracket this for the time being. It was Monday, and I had agreed with Olivia's father that I would pick her up after school from her friend's house.

Her father and I shared custody, meticulously splitting each week so Olivia had school time and fun time with each parent. This was the first time other than vacations we'd broken that pattern, and she'd stayed with her dad the whole week. I missed her but had to admit I'd been overwhelmed most of that time. I knew I hadn't had the emotional reserve to meet my own needs, let alone hers.

Resuming our regular parenting pattern would be a concrete step toward normalcy, even if I couldn't fathom how my daughter and I would go forward. It was as if a chasm had opened up, and I had no idea how to bridge or fill it. Olivia was only twelve, but she had bonded with Gregory over the past five years. His energy was different from—complementary to—her father's. Both were quiet, stoic men. But where her dad was intuitive and worked with his hands, making museum display cases for a living, Gregory was a brainiac who used his intellect to overcome the limitations of his family.

Without thinking, I reached for the key to Gregory's Celica, which I had moved from his parking place to one right outside my back patio to better keep an eye on it.

Good idea to drive it.

Yeah? But maybe not now. Not the first time I pick my daughter up after what's happened. I put the key back on the hook, grabbed my purse, and headed for my own car, a sturdy, reliable Volvo parked next to the Celica. But when I went to start it, the engine sputtered. What the heck? I cranked the key over again. Click-click-click.

Shit-shit-shit. I could hear Gregory telling me it was time for a new battery. And now, dammit, my car wouldn't start. Looks like I was being more or less forced to take the Celica.

Told you so.

I grabbed the key again and slipped into the driver's seat of the sleek, midnight-blue two-door. Having always ridden as a passenger, the driver's seat felt unfamiliar. In the way that some men love cars, Gregory loved the Celica, a cream puff set of wheels with sporty, elegant exterior lines reminiscent of a Jaguar XKE. And despite Gregory's outwardly reserved manner, I detected a surge of excitement in him each time he drove the car—for which he was proud to have paid cash. His eyes shone with satisfaction and even joy.

I ran my hand over the dashboard. Angled to face the driver, all the elements of the instrument panel were within easy sight and reach. Gregory repeatedly praised the car's ergonomics. Now I understood. I turned the key, and the engine roared to life like an eager stallion. Easing the gearshift into reverse, I backed toward the alley. It'd been a while since I'd driven a stick shift, but the sense of it came back easily. Like riding a bicycle. Only better.

It felt so good to drive the Celica, even the short distance to Shannon's house, where Olivia was waiting on the porch with her friend. As she approached the car, I rushed around to greet her. Could she have gotten more mature since the memorial service? She seemed to grow and change before my eyes. I hugged her, and she hugged me back.

"I've missed you," I said.

"Missed you, too."

Pulling back from the embrace, she turned to look at the car, then back at me.

"What are you doing in this?" she said.

"The Volvo wouldn't start. I hope you're not upset."

"No," she said. "Just surprised."

I opened the door for her, and she hoisted her backpack into the back. She turned to wave to her friend, then slid into the passenger's seat.

"I needed to drive it," I said a little too nonchalantly after getting in. "Cars shouldn't sit indefinitely. They need a workout every so often, just like us."

She gave me an "uh-huh-sure" glance.

"Look, it's not hurting anything," I said. "And I do need to drive it at least once a week."

"I'm not blaming you," my daughter said, inspecting the ebony interior. "It's such a cool car."

Yes, it was. I had a growing attachment to it as one of the few places where I experienced a tangible sense of Gregory. Not like what Connie said she saw at the service or even that unexplained scent in Stella's hospital room, but a sense of his presence in life. The Celica's interior still gleamed from the last time he detailed it and, aside from a little dust, the car was as immaculate as ever. Driving it felt deliciously wonderful and forbidden.

"Is it ours now?" Olivia asked as she burrowed into the creaminess of the leather and drummed her fingers on the console between us, opening it up to see what was inside. Still neatly stored there: Gregory's CDs along with breath mints and a hair pick. Not a comb or brush. A pick. To subdue his curls.

"It's Stella's, honey."

"Stella's? But she can't drive it. Why wouldn't she give it to you?"

"She might need the money."

"You mean she'd sell it?"

"Yeah, probably."

Damn it, Gregory. No will, which I presume is the case, and everything you owned goes to your mother. Not trying to be selfish. But yeah, I really would have liked the car.

We drove in silence except for the engine's low thrum. First gear. Second gear. Third to fourth.

"Do you think of Puke when you drive it?" Olivia wanted to know. Puke was the nickname Olivia had given Gregory when they were roughhousing one time. He wouldn't let her up quickly enough, and she got so mad she cried out, "Stop it, Puke!" The name stuck.

"Yes, I do. I think about him so much anyway, but it's different in the car. Like being a little closer to him. What about you?"

Talk to me.

"I don't know. Yeah, it reminds me of him."

She looked out the window.

When I pulled into the parking space behind our apartment, Olivia jumped out and unlocked the back gate to the patio, swinging it closed behind her—a habit, so that Woodward and Bernstein wouldn't escape. She seemed in an unusual hurry. Me, I lingered, drinking in the car's sumptuous lines. The only imperfection was a slight discoloration on the front left bumper, from the time Stella had grazed it with her car. Gregory was livid when he told me about it. Stella had stood there, he said, looking from the bumper to him and back and saying, "Your insurance will pay for it."

"Like hell it will," he told his mother. "You're the one who hit *me*." He went inside her house and called her insurance company to report the damage.

"Olivia, dinner," I called from the bottom of the staircase. For the briefest second I thought I heard a key turn in the front door behind me, as if Gregory were arriving to join us, as he often did for the evening meal. Here to tell us his death had all been a big mistake. Over and over, those wishful flashes invaded my thinking. Would they ever stop? Did I want them to? I reached to check the doorknob. It wasn't locked. That made no sense. I locked it tight.

Olivia looked weary as she made her way down the stairs. The fullness of her silky brown locks couldn't mask the way her shoulders rounded forward. She let her feet clomp heavily on each carpeted step. It was hard to miss the loss of innocence in her face, the downcast expression, the somber knowing in her eyes.

"What'd you do in school today?" I asked, attempting to jump-start a normal conversation as we sat down to a beef stew from our casserole stash.

"Nothing, really."

This was so awkward. Olivia and I rarely had difficulty talking to one another. I couldn't tell whether it was Gregory's death or just normal adolescent hormones starting their inevitable march. Maybe the collision of the two. I wanted to know what she'd been feeling and how she'd been processing the situation. But I resisted prying. Push a teenager—which she wasn't quite yet—and they pull back inside themselves like a poked snail. Gregory's absence hung over us like a gray haze.

"I miss him, too," Olivia said, picking up her knife and fork.

"How'd you know I was thinking about that?"

"You look so sad," she said, shrugging and cutting her beef and vegetables into smaller pieces. Was I that transparent?

"I feel kind of guilty," I said. "I've been so wrapped up in my own feelings that I've left you on your own. Or feel like I have."

"Not really," she said. "I have some questions. But not yet. I talked to Dad. Some of my friends. And I have my horses at Papaw's. I rode a lot, and that helped." Olivia had a special connection with horses, and her grandparents kept three for her in their pasture south of

Dallas. A natural rider, she often preferred to grab their mane, knees pressed in bareback, and take off galloping.

"It's not the same without him, is it?" I ventured.

"No." Olivia put her knife down. "You can't talk to everyone about death. I mean, really talk about it. They get all twitchy."

I nodded, amused by her choice of words.

"Yeah, the topic makes people uncomfortable," I said. "Sometimes, you just need someone to listen, yes?"

"A bunch of kids at school just avoid me," Olivia said. "They look the other way when they see me coming."

My heart broke for her.

"I hope not everyone does that."

I hated that she was having to navigate such difficult terrain at her tender age. It seemed so unfair. She should be looking forward to becoming a teenager and worrying about whether she'll get to go to the Friday night football game. Not death. Not suddenly losing someone.

"No," she said. "David and Lara have been really nice."

We continued our dinner without talking. The silence between us felt warmer and less fraught.

"You remember the day you came home from the airport?" Olivia said.

The worst day of our lives?

"Sure," I said.

How could we forget?

"The worst thing was when the policemen came to the door," Olivia volunteered. "I was eating nachos.

Waiting for Puke. I was looking forward to going to the airport."

"Yeah?"

I wanted to hear more. I wanted to prompt. I waited.

"I saw this police car drive up and park in a space near our door. I went over to the window and peeked through the curtains to see what it was doing. The policemen got out, but I couldn't hear anything. Then I went over and crouched by the door and opened the mail slot to see if I could hear any better. I hoped they weren't coming to our door."

"I'll bet," I said under my breath.

"But they did. They knocked on the door, and I opened it, and one of them asked me if I knew Gregory."

She slowed here, looking down. I could barely conceal my fury at these insensitive cops.

"They told me Gregory had had a heart attack and died." The color drained from her cheeks. "The first thing I thought was, 'This must be a joke,'" she said. "And then I remembered: Policemen don't joke."

She looked at me with doleful eyes.

"My heart dropped like an elevator," she said, barely above a whisper. "I couldn't stand up anymore and sat down on the stairs."

I wanted to rush around the table and scoop her up in my arms, the way I had when she was little after she'd scraped a knee or felt the sting of an unkind remark. But there was no invitation—verbal or non—for me to do this. So I kept still and waited.

"After that, they took me to Connie's." She pursed her lips. "I helped them."

I was dumbfounded at what had happened to her. I didn't care whether she helped them. This was too much, way too much, too soon for someone her age.

"Oh, baby." This time I did walk around the table and bend down to wrap my arms around her shoulders. She put her hand on mine. "I wish there was something I could say that would make this all easier. But if there is, I don't know what it is. At the risk of sounding too mom-ish, this is grown-up stuff you shouldn't have to deal with. Not yet."

"Yeah, I know," she said and pulled her hand away. "No kiss and a Band-Aid."

I hated that the police had sprung the news on her the way they did. She was only twelve! Later they apologized. They said they hadn't realized she was so young, that she seemed older. And they were desperate for any lead on Gregory's next of kin. Which, darn it, she provided. Still...

When we were done, I started clearing away the dishes. Olivia gathered up what was left from the table. Going through the motions of rinsing the plates and silverware for the dishwasher and putting the placemats and napkins away was comforting. This was routine. This was predictable.

"I think Gregory liked kids, even though he never had any of his own," I said as I poured the dishwasher gel into its compartment and snapped it shut. Olivia closed the door and turned the appliance on. "And I think you were special to him. Did you feel that?"

"Yeah. I knew he liked me, even when I called him Puke."

Gregory could be curt with people, but when it came to Olivia, he tolerated her the way a cat tolerates the mauling inflicted by its young. I'd catch him just gazing at her from some deep, interior place—and not in any odd or lascivious way. She seemed to touch something in him. Other men might have considered her baggage. He seemed to genuinely love her.

"Did you and your dad do anything special for Halloween this year?" I asked, leaning against the sink, trying to lighten things.

Olivia shook her head.

"I hung out with friends at Matt's house," she said. "I wasn't in the mood to do much else."

"I understand," I said.

"Gotta finish my homework now."

She turned and headed back upstairs to her room.

After watching the ten o'clock news, I went upstairs, too, and peeked in on Olivia, whose room was across the tiny hall from mine. She had fallen asleep, still fully dressed, an open book splayed across her chest. Woody was curled up in an orange ball next to her. I laid the book gently aside, slipped her shoes off, and covered her, trying not to disturb the two of them. I wondered if sleep was as elusive for her as it had become for me.

In my own room, I pulled my clothes off and slipped into a tee, then brushed my teeth, flipped off the light, and pulled up the covers. In the darkness, I thought about what Connie said she saw, then put it aside. I conjured Gregory's face in my mind, his smile, the sweetness of his breath, his searching kisses, his solemn eyes that seemed to conceal so much, belie so much. When we slept, he held on like he never wanted to let go. I imagined his caress, the way his hands moved so effortlessly to my intimate places, and I hungered for the warmth of his body next to mine. My fingers found their way between my thighs, where I was moist with anticipation. I couldn't resist a half-sleeping orgasm, even if it was a pale facsimile.

As I hovered at the edge of sleep, the name "Ira" percolated up through my consciousness. Ira who? It was like someone whispering in my ear.

Ira. Don't forget Ira.

The name swam around and around as I slipped from the precipice of consciousness.

Sometime later, Olivia let out a sharp cry.

Instantly awake, I rushed to her room.

"Olivia! Are you okay?"

She blinked and looked up at me, questioning.

"You cried out," I said.

She rose to her elbows under the blanket I'd tucked over her and shook her head as if trying to throw something off. Woody was on his feet, head-butting her arm and mewling softly.

"I dreamed we were in the back room," she mumbled sleepily, "and I heard someone unlock the gate, and the hinges squeaked. I looked up, and it was Puke in a white sweater and shorts. Sliding the glass door to let himself in. Sweater… glowing. I threw my arms around his neck and said, 'Puke! You're not dead after all!' And he said, 'No, I'm not dead. Of course I'm not dead.' Then I woke up and you were sitting on my bed."

"You cried out," I repeated.

"I dreamed he wasn't dead, Mom, and… just for a moment, in my dream, he wasn't."

I reached down and pulled her close to me.

"Oh, baby. I'm so sorry."

Her sobs were contagious as I cradled her in my arms and we held each other, rocking gently.

CHAPTER TEN

"You sure you're okay?" I said to Olivia the next morning as we got in the Celica to drive to school.

"Yeah, Mom. It was just a dream," she said, closing the door and fastening her seatbelt.

"A powerful dream."

"Yeah."

"Not trying to pry," I said. Of course I was prying. "I just need to check in. Hear that you're good."

"It's weird," Olivia said. "It's like it was wonderful when I believed he was alive. And then it was awful."

"And…?"

We pulled up outside the middle school.

"And nothing." She shrugged. "I'll go to school and find my friends. We'll get through this."

My heart caught in my throat.

"Gotta go. Love you." She was out of the car.

The way she said it—"We'll get through this"—was like a dagger. Between that and Gregory's baby shoes and her dream, I was sinking. Drowning.

I called Connie as soon as I got home.

"Hello?"

"I'm in a state," I croaked. "Again."

"What is it?"

"Olivia said something that touched me, made me sad, and she had a vivid dream about Gregory last night, and Stella gave me Gregory's bronzed baby shoes, and… and… I feel ripped open again… scab off… and…" I blubbered. "I'm desperate to know more about what you saw at the service. I can't get it out of my mind. I keep wondering: Could it really have been Gregory? Is he out there somewhere? I feel like I'll go mad until I know. But then I know I can't know. My mind says it isn't possible. And *that* makes me crazier. Around and around and around this goes in my head, and you're probably the only person in the world I could say that to."

"Oh, Ann." Connie's own voice faltered. "Can you come down to my place so we can talk about this in person? There's something I've been hesitant to share with you. But something tells me this is the time."

I had no idea what she might be talking about. But I'd take it.

"I'll be down in a second," I sniffed, dabbing at my eyes with a tissue before hurrying to her apartment.

When she opened the door, I was surprised to see she had drawn her heavy drapes and the room was aglow with candles, maybe a dozen, on the coffee table, the counter between her living room and kitchen, on the bookcases and other open real estate. The effect was stunning, like being inside a tiny, cloistered chapel.

"Whoa," I said. "What's with all this?" I gestured, palm outstretched, at the luminous room. "Looks like you're some New Age-y diva." It was the same gently taunting voice I used when I called her a magic Christian.

"This isn't anything woo-woo," she said. "I do it to put my massage clients at ease. When they're real uptight, the candles and some tea calm them down. You were so distraught on the phone just now, I figured it might work for you, too. But looking at it from your perspective, yeah, I guess it can seem a little woo-woo."

"I do feel less frantic," I said, "whether it's the candles or just being with you."

"Come here," she said, taking my hand. "You sit here."

She directed me toward her maroon velvet sofa. Then she poured a cup of steaming tea from a clear glass pot on the low table in front of us and placed it in my hands. The fragrance of jasmine wafted up from the warm liquid. Tiny white buds floated on the surface. Connie sat facing me—cross-legged, Indian style—with her own cup. The scent of sandalwood from unseen incense suffused the air.

With mesmerizing deliberation, Connie took a sip of tea, drew a slow, deep breath, and looked at me.

"I have hesitated to bring this up with you until now." She paused. "But there is a whole side to my life I've never shared with you."

"I don't understand," I said. "I thought we talked about everything."

We were old, close friends. As far as I knew, we had pretty much shared everything since we were college freshmen. She'd saved my life when my mother died, providing a rudder then, when I'd felt lost and alone.

"I haven't talked a lot about religion and what that really meant growing up in my house. Or the paranormal side."

"Paranormal side? I kinda know about that. It's why I tease you about being a magic Christian." I was pretty sure Connie knew I didn't believe any of it.

"There's much more you don't know. Things I've told almost no one."

"Oh."

"Like I've never told you about this 'seeing' thing in any depth. But after what happened at the service... I feel like I need to."

Connie's words were slow and measured, as if she were in a confessional. She looked down at her tea before continuing.

"Your... circumstances... keep pushing me. I see you suffering, and I feel like there's something I need to say, and it's related to the stuff I've never mentioned before."

"I don't guess I've made it easy, always kind of kidding you."

Still, I sat forward, as if to press into her words. I would listen.

"It started when I was a little kid. The first time I 'saw' someone was my grandma, shortly after she passed.

She was smiling and waving at me. I told my dad about it and thought he'd be thrilled to hear she was okay."

Connie pursed her lips and slumped.

"And...?"

"That was the first time he held my head in the toilet and flushed it."

"Oh, Jesus." She had never shared the specifics of her abuse with me before.

"It got worse. Making me kneel on broken glass. Holding my hands over an open flame. You've seen those scars. His repeated attempts to 'cleanse' my soul left me with a visceral fear I can't control except to shut it out. Wall it off."

Connie's round face glowed in the forest of undulating lights, and individual flames reflected in her eyes. They failed to dim the harshness of her revelation.

"The toilet flushing ended when my hair got caught in the trap and I nearly drowned. My mother shoved my father out of the way, grabbed some scissors, and cut my hair as I was gagging and choking. I thought I was going to die. She wrapped me in a towel with one hand, raised the scissors over my father's head with the other, then charged past him, carrying me, screaming he'd never do that again. I remember her shouting, 'You take your effing demons and go straight to hell. You don't touch a hair on this child's head.'

"'But her soul, Martha,' my dad whimpered.

"'NEVER again,' she screamed. And it never happened again."

I was stunned.

"That's horrible. I can't believe a parent could do that."

Except after working at the paper, I knew they could.

"I was so confused because he kept saying how much he loved me," Connie continued. "But his fire-and-brimstone never let up. It didn't work, either. He couldn't make it stop. I just kept 'seeing.' And doing other stuff. Learned to keep it secret. But the deep sense of shame never left me. I still have nightmares. Get terrible shakes. I feel like if people knew this about me, they'd think something was wrong with me, like he did. So I try to control it and wall off the shame."

"I just can't believe it," I said, shaking my head.

Connie fixed my gaze.

"That's one side." Her tone shifted, "I also have this tug, this urging, that pulls me to embrace the psychic side. Like seeing Gregory at the service. The seeing has always come unbidden."

She closed her eyes and pressed her fingers briefly to her temples.

"What happened at the service brought this up again for me because it was more intense than anything I've ever felt before," she said. "It felt out of control. Like bleeding through. Like some sort of spiritual incontinence."

I could hear fear in her quavering voice.

"That's… that's just ridiculous," I said. "No matter what this is that happens to you, there's nothing wrong with you. I see you. I see your heart."

"I thought you might think I was crazy," she said, visibly relieved.

"No, you're not crazy. But it is a unique… skill. Or whatever you would call it."

"Sometimes when it happens, I feel like something or someone is lifting a veil," Connie said, looking less anxious. "Other times I wonder whether I'm being suckered by something evil. Temptation? Enlightenment? I don't know. I just don't know."

She sighed, not waiting for an answer.

"But I keep coming back to this," she said. "I feel an urgency to share with you. Pressed to tell you. God forgive me if I'm wrong."

She paused to sip her tea. I did the same. I knew what she was doing, and I was grateful: She was slowing things down, as much for me to digest what she was saying as to pace herself in the telling.

For the first time I saw how deeply this internal conflict affected her. I was sorry I'd teased her about being a magic Christian.

"What do you want to tell me?" I coaxed softly.

"First a little more about what I saw at the service."

Serenity had returned to her voice.

"Did Gregory have a message? Did he say something?"

"No. No." Connie smiled and shook her head. "I don't 'hear' things like that," she said. "He just appeared to me. He looked solid, like you and I look to each other. He was wearing a sports coat and slacks. And a tie. He was just floating there, above the altar, and his face was radiant. Lit up. Dare I say with joy?"

I brought a hand to my chest, hoping to quiet my quickening heart. What she described contradicted my deepest convictions but also stirred me.

"Before we go any further with this, I need to say a prayer," Connie said.

"Okay."

We put our cups down on the table and took each other's hands and closed our eyes.

"Lord," she began, "please guide my words and thoughts as I share with Ann what you have revealed to me. Give us the wisdom to discern that which comes from you and how this information may be used in your service. Please protect us, now and always. Amen."

"Amen."

Her words barely registered. I couldn't get the image out of my mind of Gregory somehow hovering behind the altar.

We opened our eyes, and I felt calmer. I wasn't one to believe in prayer—which had always seemed too much like asking for things—but my anxiety had subsided, and warmth spread over my chest. I waited, eager to hear what was so important to tell me.

"Have you ever heard of John Edward?" Connie said.

What? It was like Connie just completely shifted tracks. I hoped my disappointment didn't show.

"What? No."

"Joel Martin? Patricia Romanowski?"

"No. And no."

"Bruce Moen?"

"Sorry, no."

"Stay with me. I'm bringing them up because I know how you are, how you need data."

Confused and in overload, I just sat, waiting.

"They are psychic mediums."

I slumped. No wonder I hadn't heard of them.

"I don't know much about mediums," I blurted out. "But a friend of mine had an experience that makes me really skeptical."

Connie sat quietly.

"She contacted one of those people in Clarksville, where everybody's supposed to be a psychic, and the 'medium' kept asking questions and told my friend she couldn't 'read' if my friend didn't answer them. By the end of the session, my friend was in tears."

"I know what you're talking about," Connie said. "I have issues with those kinds of 'mediums,' too. But the ones I'm talking about are different. They don't feed off body language or vocal clues. They've actually been subjected to legitimate research."

"Legitimate by whose measure?" I said, flipping into reporter mode.

"They're part of a handful—and I do mean handful—who've been scrutinized under the glare of hard science. No one knows exactly what they do or how they do it, but they appear not to be playing parlor games."

Mediums. This wasn't what I expected—or wanted—to hear.

"But what about what happened to you at the service? Are you telling that's the same thing?"

"Not really. They're connected. But different."

Connie pressed on, but I remained skeptical. Yet if there were even a shadow of truth in what she was saying, it would point toward something of us surviving physical death. Not heaven or hell. But something. Perhaps I was wrong to dismiss this whole side of my friend's character.

"I've come to believe there are legitimate mediums," Connie said. "It's like they really can tune in to souls who have passed."

"Is that what you were doing at the service when you saw Gregory?"

"No. It's not the same, although I stumbled onto the medium thing when I started trying to understand what happens to me."

"The fact that this whatever-it-is happens to you—someone I know and trust—makes me take it more seriously. But I'm still really skeptical. You're going up against a lifetime of rational thinking, drummed into me by my dad."

"I know. Just hoping you'll trust in our friendship enough to hear me out about these 'real' psychics. Here's how Sumi Koslow explains it. You heard of him? The guy at the university supposedly studying paranormal stuff?"

"I don't think so."

"I guess they keep it pretty quiet. Anyway, he thinks people who have died—their spirits or souls—exist at a different vibration, like waves on a light continuum. Almost literally." Connie lapsed into something like a teaching cadence. "What these mediums seem to do is modify their own vibration—speed it up—so they can receive information. They don't wait for you to feed them clues. They tell you what they're receiving, like a radio tower."

Connie lost me. She might as well have been talking about dancing on the rings of Saturn. Was it the fog of grief, or was she talking about something way over my head? We're all like radio towers?

Connie poured us each more tea.

"I'm having an awfully hard time understanding this."

"We can come back to the explanation when you're not so frazzled," she said. "The thing is, and I'll just keep it to this, I want to tell you about Sasha."

I leaned closer.

"I met her through some of my therapist friends. She's one of the 'legitimate' types I was talking about. I have to admit that even after Dr. Koslow tried to explain it to me, I was still skeptical—until I met her. She was passing through Dallas last summer, and I sat in on some of her readings as an observer. The person being 'read' always sat behind a black screen or in another room so Sasha couldn't see them. The room was darkened before and after, so she couldn't get visual clues.

"It was impressive. She actually 'read' something spontaneously about me that no one could have known. I mean, I didn't even know it."

"Sounds interesting. What happened?"

"At one point, she called out, 'There's someone here who's coming through for Bonnie or Ronnie, who's a grandmother. She's showing me a ring, a gold ring. She says it's yours. It's meant for you. She's showing me what look like colored tubes. Or pieces of chalk. *It's there*, she's telling me.'"

"And what did you read into that?"

"Bonnie. Ronnie. Connie. They're so close. Do you know I'd been looking for my grandmother's ring since I saw her after she died when I was a little girl?" Connie said. "It connected us; it was set with a garnet, the birthstone we shared. I even dreamed about it. But got nothing to help locate it."

I started getting chills just listening.

"I went to my parents' house and climbed up into the attic to look again where a bunch of my grandmother's things were still stored. Then I saw her sewing kit, and it hit me: Maybe 'colored tubes' could be spools of thread. So I opened it, started fishing around, and was drawn to a tiny velvet pouch. I opened it, and there was the ring."

"Wow. Just... wow."

Here was my most trusted friend talking about something I would never have given any credence to. And yet weren't these "facts," too? Facts about her experience?

"That convinced me it wasn't an act or dumb luck. And she wasn't picking up something in my mind telepathically. Later I asked her if she'd do a reading for a friend's niece, after a classmate died in a car wreck. I saw the girl's anguish transformed to peace after the reading and what supposedly 'came through' Sasha from her deceased friend."

"So when you saw Gregory, was he also trying to tell you something?"

"No, that was something completely different," Connie said again patiently. "I see things and I feel things that randomly come to me. And I know how to… that's all."

Connie shifted in her seat as she said this.

"I could feel his mood, his satisfaction. But that's not like what Sasha does. She gets pictures and impressions. Even words and phrases."

I was doing my best to square what Connie was saying with my belief in rock-solid reality, the kind you can touch and verify using hard science. I'd grown up a Methodist, but eventually came to believe that Biblical teachings were just too limited to explain the cosmos.

"Anyway, after Sasha left for the West Coast, my therapist friends and I spent long hours discussing what we'd witnessed. I told them about finding the ring. They were blown away.

"But here's the kicker, Ann. Sasha can 'read' long distance. She does this whole bilocation thing. At least that's what my friends say. You can be nothing but a voice on the phone, and she can still pick up the vibrations of those on the other side who are connected to you."

"So what does this mean to me? What, exactly, are you suggesting?"

"I'm saying she might be able to do a reading for you. About Gregory. *With* Gregory."

"A reading with Gregory? You mean actually contact him?"

My brain felt like a big fuzz box. Could what she was saying possibly be true? I dared not hope. This contradicted everything I knew and stood for. Still I clung to that tenuous reed: Connie said she saw him. She seemed to have an understanding, even acceptance, of so many things I'd previously dismissed. Maybe this was possible, too.

"I think it's worth a try," she said.

Our tea had gone cold. I held my hand over my cup as Connie started to pour more.

"But what about the other guys you just mentioned? Why not go to one of them?"

"You may not have heard of them, but lots of other people have. They've written books, they're in demand, and the wait for a reading is long. Like months. Even years. Plus, you usually have to go wherever they are. I read their books at Dr. Koslow's suggestion, and it occurred to me that Sasha does the same thing. She's just way below the radar."

I wrapped my arms around my knees and rocked quietly.

"Dr. Koslow says they're all connected, these things that happen," Connie said. "Not the fakes. But what

I saw at the service, and the readings like Sasha's, and other stuff—they're real. I don't understand it; I'm just going by what he told me. And what I've witnessed and experienced."

I wanted it to be true, even as my instincts railed against it.

"I took some time to pray about Sasha," Connie said, "given my mixed feelings, and I asked whether I was doing the right thing, telling you about this. What I keep coming back to is it's important for you to hear this from me. No, what I'm getting is even stronger: I feel like I'm being compelled to share with you.

"'Course, I can't make you do anything with it," she quickly added, providing an escape hatch.

"Thanks," I said. "This is a lot to digest."

While I mulled over all Connie had told me, she got up and turned on the overheads. With a twist of a dimmer switch, the room and the mood lightened. Then she started blowing out the candles. I joined her until we had extinguished every one. As we swatted at the resulting haze to create little swirls in the air, I noticed a couple of books under the coffee table.

"Are these the books you were talking about?" I said, reaching down to pick up the John Edward title and one coauthored by Martin and Romanowski.

"That's two of them," she said. "Two of the best."

"Would you mind if I borrowed them?"

"Not at all. I put them there hoping you'd notice."

"But this thing you did, or do, where you saw him? It means you're psychic, too, doesn't it? For real?"

"I wish it were that simple."

CHAPTER ELEVEN

I stacked the books in my living room next to Gregory's mystery chest when I got home. Connie's revelations had given me a lot to think about. But as much as I wanted to dig into the books and see what they had to say, any talk of mediums and their "legitimacy" would have to wait because Gregory's ex was coming over any minute, and my thoughts swiveled to that.

I had reached out to Elizabeth while we were milling around after the service. Other people brushed away their tears or treated me like I'd shatter, but she hugged me as if I were an old friend.

"I found a small chest in Gregory's closet that I've never seen before," I'd told her. "I wonder if you know anything about it?"

"His 'secret' chest? Ha. Yeah. I know something about that."

I took an all-or-nothing stab at enlisting her help.

"Would you be able to help identify what's in it?"

"Sure. Just tell me when and where."

We agreed to meet while Olivia was at school. My days were still fairly open, although that would change soon, when I returned to work. Then Elizabeth turned to hug another acquaintance.

I opened the front door to a flamboyant woman. This time I looked more closely at the half smile and hooded eyes. It was impossible to discern what might lie behind them. But there was no escaping their oddly seductive, inviting appeal. A large brooch clasped her sweeping brocade shawl, and her fall of copper curls seemed positively electric against the elaborate fabric. She offered her hand in greeting.

"Hello, Ann," she said, as her eyes met mine. "Again, I'm so sorry."

"Thanks. It's a loss for all of us."

I squeezed her hand and swung the door wide to welcome her in.

I struggled to reconcile the woman stepping into my living room with the one Gregory had so often described. His ex-wife was angry. Fat. Got under his skin. Let him down. Pissed away money. Couldn't handle business. The only time I'd ever seen her, aside from the memorial service, was once as Gregory and I were leaving the mall.

"You see that flashy redhead?" he'd said when we got to the car. I nodded, vaguely aware of the woman we'd passed. But yes, you couldn't miss that hair.

"That was my ex-wife," he said with a strange mixture of pride and sadness. For the briefest moment, he expressed something other than hostility toward her. I turned to look at her again, but she was already gone.

"Oh this is nice," Elizabeth said as she paused to take in the apartment's living room and peek through the doorway at the rooms beyond. "I've always wondered what these looked like on the inside." Olivia and I lived on so-called "townhouse row" at the northern edge of the apartment complex.

"Thank you," I said. "It's really just glorified student housing."

"And what a great location," she said, ignoring my remark.

She seemed unaffected and genuine. I saw no evidence of the shrew Gregory had railed against.

"Is this your daughter?" she said, walking over to my desk and picking up a framed portrait of Olivia.

"Yes," I said. "She's at school now."

Elizabeth was silent. Time seemed suspended as she regarded my daughter.

"She's quite lovely. She looks like you, with those big brown eyes. And such a serious expression."

Natalie Wood eyes. Like yours.

"Oh, she got plenty of impishness from her dad," I said. "And those big, pouty lips."

"Were she and Gregory close?"

"Yes. It's like she lost her third parent."

Elizabeth put the photo back down.

We stood a moment without speaking—sizing each other up, I suppose—before I invited her to have a seat on the couch. I sat down next to her.

"Look, I know this situation is awkward," I began. "Me the fiancée, you the ex-wife…"

"Yeah, I can only imagine what he's said about me. Medusa unbound."

"Oh no, that's not what I meant…."

I tripped over my words.

"But it's very likely what *he* meant." She let out a belly laugh.

Bunching up her considerable green velvet skirt, she stretched out her legs, revealing black cowboy boots.

"Ours was not a friendly parting."

"I gathered," I said. "I also know you were married for, like, ten years—double the time I knew him. And I know I ought to feel jealous…"

Elizabeth stared at me, waiting.

"But I don't."

"No?"

"No. You were close to him. He was close to you." I paused. It was difficult, even counterintuitive, what I was trying to say. "I could hear this in the intimate way you talked about him at the service."

I clasped my hands as my words spilled out haltingly.

"I don't even know how to say this," I continued, "but I understood. It's not like you're a rival. You're more like a sister. Or something like that. Someone I have a common bond with. He's gone, and the hurt of that…"

I looked away. Tears were percolating up, boiling over again. Would this fountain of grief never cease?

I rushed to add, "The hurt of that doesn't leave room for trivial bullshit like jealousy." There, I'd said it. My heart was pounding.

"We… shared… him. Like no one else can understand."

Someone understands.

"You don't know how that hits home for me," Elizabeth said calmly, pressing her hand to her chest. "When I found out he'd died, I started grieving all over again.

"It was ridiculous," she said. "We've been divorced for nearly eight years. We were never getting back together. But…"

She seemed to push something down as she spoke.

"I was so glad he'd found someone like you," she said, gazing at me, "who could help him heal in ways I couldn't. He and I… we… were both so hurt. As much by circumstances as each other."

Now Elizabeth was groping for words.

"His heart and spirit were broken," she said, casting her eyes down. "I probably contributed to that. But from what people said who'd seen him since we broke up…" Her gaze rose to meet mine again. "It sounded like he found something in you that made him whole. Your daughter, I think, was part of that. So thank you. Thank you for your honesty."

Elizabeth reached over to squeeze my arm. Then she turned to scan the room, as if searching for something.

Her eyes alighted on the chest nestled between the couch and Gregory's big leather chair, which Woodward and Bernstein had taken over.

"Gregory loved that piece," Elizabeth said. "From the first moment he saw it at auction, he had to have it. Let's take a look at what's inside, shall we? That's why I'm here, right?"

"Right."

"Do you mind if we sit on the floor?"

Elizabeth surprised me with the suggestion.

"No problem."

She plopped down, and we scooted the chest out from its corner.

"Gregory said you were in the antique business," I said, as I sat down on the floor with her, leaning against the ottoman. "Is that still the case?"

"Yes. It's what I do. Antiques and collectibles. Gregory and I used to shop the auctions together. It's not nearly as much fun without him."

I heard the same wistfulness I'd heard in her heartfelt words at the memorial service.

"The chest was a private cubby for him," she said, rubbing her hand lightly over the tooled emerald-green leather and wood. "He never let me see what he kept in there, and it's one of the places where I didn't snoop. At least, not a lot."

"What do you mean?"

"Gregory was fond of secret places. Maybe I should just say secrets. He didn't always tell me everything that was going on. So I'd have to do a little sleuthing on my own to get the full story."

"That makes two of us, although it looks like he told me a lot less than he told you. I didn't even know this existed."

"Mind if I open it?" Elizabeth looked to me for permission.

"Please do."

For the moment, I felt less like a bereaved fiancée and more like my old reporter self, drawing out a new source. I desperately wanted Elizabeth to tell me everything she knew about what was inside the chest. But I didn't want to spook her. I was actually relieved when she took the lead in opening it.

"Yeah, well, Gregory could be unpredictable, so I'm pretty much prepared for anything," she said with a harrumph.

I waited for her to elaborate. Instead, she turned her attention to the chest.

She pulled at the top, slowly and patiently coaxing it open.

"Would you like to use this?" I said, holding out a table knife I'd gotten from the kitchen.

"That'd be great. I'll hold the chest steady, and you work the blade around between the lid and the body."

Gently twisting the knife blade into the thin crevice between the top and body, I was careful not to mar the wood. Elizabeth and I were so close I could smell her perfume, a scent I recognized but couldn't place. What with her strong grasp and my twisting and lifting, we finally managed to pop the lid.

"There!" she said. "If you take an old candle and rub it on those two surfaces," she added authoritatively, "it will open much more easily."

Elizabeth inspected the items in the top tray, including the photographs of what I now surmised was her with the young girl, and a handful of prints from her wedding. As she studied these, her face took on a different quality, loosening around the brow and mouth. She touched each image as if caressing an amulet, and her eyes grew moist as her lips formed almost a pout.

"Oh, yes," she said more to herself than me. "Those were sweet days."

She picked up the Oklahoma cemetery business card and huffed, pitching it back in the tray.

"He looks so young in these photos," she said as she examined the old passports. "And you know what this is, right? His Utah Ag ID?"

"Yes, he told me how much he liked that job."

Elizabeth let out a sigh.

"If only he hadn't had to come home," she said.

Barely out of school and established in his promising job, Gregory was called home from Utah by his mother after his father suffered a massive heart attack.

"Yeah," I said. "He told me how he left his job and never went back. What a shame."

Elizabeth got a faraway look.

"He told me about looking out the window by his desk after that call as it started to snow," she said, "then snowed harder, and how he lost himself gazing at the snow."

Refuge in the swirling snow. He'd never told me about that, but I understood.

Elizabeth held up the glass paperweight and turned it in her hand.

"I don't remember this," she said. "The way those center points reflect light is so unusual."

It threw iridescent teal and emerald beams across the wall and front-window sheers. She put it down.

"And I've never seen this Saint Christopher," she said, briefly examining the shimmering medallion. "Looks like real gold."

One by one she put the items back, set the tray to one side, and looked deeper into the chest's layered chambers, eventually reaching all the way to the bottom. When her eyes fell on the childish drawings, she let out a gasp.

"I had no idea he kept these," she said in a subdued voice, slowly unfolding the sheets of manila paper and running her fingers over the pastel lines of one, tracing the letters "To my angel."

"What are they?" I could see that they meant something to her. "What can you tell me?"

So much for holding back.

"They were from a little girl who loved him very much," Elizabeth said in an oddly distant voice. Her armor seemed to fall away as she pored over the drawings.

The confident woman who'd marched through my front door had softened to the point that she might melt into a puddle at any moment.

As she reached for the pink tissue paper enfolding the lock of hair, Elizabeth began rocking back and forth and broke into what can only be described as lowing, like someone keening over the dead. Her shoulders quaked as she tried to contain her emotions. It was as if she'd fallen into a trance and forgotten I was there.

"Oh my God, I'm sorry," I said, not knowing what to do. "I didn't mean for this to upset you. I had no idea..."

"No, no."

Surfacing from her altered state, she waved me off.

"It's not you. It's Gregory." She spat out his name, and her face reddened. "Damn him. I thought I was... I wasn't prepared for this."

She looked back again at the scribbled drawings while she absently brushed the ginger-brown tuft tied with a thin red ribbon against her cheek and lips. Rivulets of tears drained from the corners of her eyes.

"Damn him."

I grabbed a box of tissues off a nearby table and offered them to her. Elizabeth took one and dabbed at her eyes, smearing her mascara.

"No, it's me who should be apologizing," she said, pushing the chest away and standing abruptly.

"I'm very sorry," she continued, picking up her purse, "but I can't stay. I was wrong. This is so... I... just... can't do this now."

She gave me an imploring glance and turned toward the front door, shawl drooping half off her shoulders, skirt swirling around her ankles.

"But what are these?" I beseeched her, desperate to know what had set her off and why.

The opportunity to identify what was in the chest was slipping away, slipping toward the front door.

"Elizabeth…" I pleaded.

"I just… can't… right now," she said, rushing down the front steps as if fleeing a fire.

"Can I call you later?" I called helplessly behind her.

"Yes," she said, slamming her car door shut.

Staring straight ahead, she started the engine. She threw the car into reverse and peeled away like a teenager.

With a knot in my stomach, I gathered up the drawings, re-cradled the lock of hair in its tissue, and laid the other items from the chest in a neat circle on the floor. Before replacing them in their respective trays, I got an old candle and rubbed the surfaces where the chest's lid and body met, as Elizabeth had suggested—a "doing" I could accomplish. When I had gotten all the way around the edge, I closed the lid. Then I opened it again. Absently, I opened and closed it a few more times, still wondering what set Elizabeth off.

The drawings? No. It was the lock of hair. Soft, ginger-colored hair. Not hers. Not his. Did Gregory have a love child he'd kept secret?

CHAPTER TWELVE

The next morning after dropping Olivia off for school, I drove to the paper for my first day back at work. It had been almost two weeks since I had concerned myself with city council meetings and apartment fires. As I stepped off the elevator, the thrum of the newsroom tugged at me like the call of tribal drums. After my fog of grief, it was time to get back. Past the reception area, phones were ringing. The bank of TVs over the metro desk buzzed with local news and CNN, their droning interrupted only by the occasional squawk of a police scanner and muffled conversations. Deeper in the news-gathering hub, more TVs overhung the foreign desk, their screens flanked by clocks set to time zones around the world: London, Moscow, Beijing, Baghdad, Tokyo.

Walking toward the far side of the maze of desks and cubicles, I could see my work station from a distance piled high with press releases, story files, random notes, and other news-gathering detritus—plus everything that had been there prior to Gregory's death. It wasn't as bad as the TV critic's cubicle, a virtual landfill of promotional videocassettes and releases, but it was bad enough. Before rolling up my sleeves to tackle the imposing stack, I poked my head in my boss's office. Bill leapt around his desk to greet me with a bear hug.

"Ann, welcome back," he said, releasing me but still holding one of my hands between his beefy palms. "We've missed you. I'm sorry you're having to go through this."

He dropped my hand and leaned back against his desk.

"Thanks," I said. "I appreciate everything you and the paper have done. I'm blown away that so many people have been willing to help out. I know we all pitch in when someone goes on vacation, but this was—"

"It was the least we could do," Bill said, straightening his bow tie and running a hand through thinning brown hair. He was about ten years my senior, and this was as personal an exchange as we'd ever had. We were close, yes, but in a writer-editor kind of way.

"We wanted you to have all the time you needed."

"Thank you," I said. "But before I dig in to work in earnest, I'd like a few hours' grace to clean off my desk."

I pointed to the mess.

He laughed and clapped me on the shoulder.

"Do what you need to do."

I took off my jacket, stashed my purse under my desk, and sat down, rolling my chair around to see if anyone had changed the adjustments. They hadn't. My eyes alighted briefly on the photo of Gregory, Olivia, and me at an outdoor festival, still stuck to my cubicle wall with a pushpin. I turned it over so it wouldn't be a persistent reminder of all I'd lost, all that had changed.

Seeing the commotion around my cubicle—nothing goes unnoticed in a newsroom—coworkers began dropping by and expressing their sympathy. Many were the same people who had brought me covered dishes or attended the memorial. I was grateful for this sensitive reentry.

"I'm so sorry, Ann. Glad to see you back."

"Sorry about your loss."

"It's good to see you. This can't be easy."

"Let us know if there's anything else we can do."

Each time someone spoke during those first awkward hours, I experienced my emotional frailty anew. Constantly on the verge of tears. Unable to do much besides mutter a heartfelt "thank you." But at least they weren't turning away or avoiding me, as some of Olivia's classmates had with her. In all my years of covering accidents and homicides and stories about sick kids on my metro beat—even after my parents' deaths—I never realized how much it means for someone to acknowledge loss. I'd been an avoider. One of those people who would shy away from contact, from saying much of anything lest it "upset" the grieving person. Presuming that was best. Was I ever wrong.

Between coworkers' brief visits, I concentrated on clearing my desk and work area, slowly and methodically poring over every document, press release, scribbled note, newspaper clipping, printout, and file folder—sorting, culling, organizing. Things that needed immediate attention, here. Phone messages I needed to return, here. Files for ongoing projects, here. Stuff I needed to get to, another pile. Everything else went into a trash bin. Here, at last, was something I could control. It distracted me from thinking about the phone call from Gregory that would never come. Stopped me from dialing his number again just to hear his voice on the answering machine. Kept me from staring at the dates so recently circled on my calendar. Dinner on the Thursday after his death. Lunch the following week at our favorite Italian restaurant. I ripped off the pages. Never. Never. Never. Never. Never.

As I was tossing the last of the extraneous matter into the bin, a whirlwind topped by pink, spiky hair blew by my desk and leveled impish eyes at mine.

"Look who's back and dressed to the nines," she threw out breezily, "and in your best flirty heels." Never breaking her stride, Raiza plopped down in the cubicle next door and tapped out one of her sarcasm-tinged emails: "Lookin all sexy 4 ur dead true love?" She was the only person who dared joke about what had happened. And, in a strange way, it was just the right tonic.

"no frumpdum 4 me" I tapped back.

Raiza had been one of the first people to show up on my doorstep after Gregory died. She'd had a tub of chicken salad tucked in the crook of her arm. Connie had answered the door—at that point, Connie was running interference at my apartment—and after handing the salad off to her, Raiza rushed to embrace me. Sobs tumbled between us. No words were needed.

When she stepped back, there were spots where my tears had fallen on her purple satin blouse.

"I can't stay," she said, pulling away like a cat that's reached its limit for contact. "But I knew you might not be eating right."

"I haven't thought much about food," I said, although the memory of her chicken salad made my stomach rumble.

"I'll see that she eats it," Connie called from the kitchen.

"Gotta go now," Raiza said, reaching for the door. But not before turning back toward me, both of us still watery-eyed. "Hang in there, sweetie."

And with that she was off down the front steps as quickly as she'd come.

Back at the office, after the initial email blast, Raiza went silent, then surprised me by pushing the trash bin out of the way and rolling her chair all the way around to my side of the divider.

"You know what?" she said. "I think I know what Gregory's purpose was in your life." With eyes wide, she was uncharacteristically serious, leaning so far toward me she looked like she might fall out of her chair.

"What?" I said, with no clue where this was going.

"He came here to make you be a good dresser!" she exclaimed before letting out a stream of cackling peals that cut the tension like high-frequency waves shattering crystal.

Her outburst complete, she turned serious.

"How's it going, really?"

"It's okay. Okay enough."

"Sorry, baby. I wanna hear more, but right now I got a story to finish by four."

A quirky character renowned for her jarring laughter, Raiza zigzagged through life in a way some people found annoying. But her eccentricity got her into places other reporters couldn't go. Besides, she was the only Rhodes Scholar on the floor, which generated its share of respect and jealousy. I was one of the few people in the newsroom who could sit next to her without being distracted by her outbursts.

I'd learned long ago to look beyond the attention-grabbing affectations and random guffaws to the substance well hidden beneath. We didn't spend a lot of time outside work together—our circles and interests were too different—but we did share a mutual love of good food, which led us to check out new restaurants together, especially offbeat ones. On those rare occasions when she came over to the house—usually to replicate an intriguing dish or meal—Olivia flitted around her like a hummingbird.

With a front-row seat, Raiza had witnessed the progress of my relationship with Gregory from its beginning, insisting on baking a Lebanese pine-nut tart for the first time I invited him to spend the night. Her email notes in taunting patois became routine in the months and years that followed. If my phone rang and she wasn't absorbed in a deadline, her pointy spikes would pop up behind the divider. As soon as she recognized what she called the "dreamy look," she'd roll her eyes and drop back down.

Soon enough, an email would land in my in-box along the lines of "coo coo. giggle tee-hee... lemme guess. the boyfriendz on the line."

I'd chuckle and shoot something back like, "ur so jelous ur hair blushes."

And so it would go.

After lunch I found myself in a conference room with coworkers, discussing how to cover an upcoming bond-proposal package.

Welcome back, baby.

While they debated the pros and cons and how to approach each proposal, I drifted, losing myself in the brilliant blue fall sky and the crisp backdrop it created for the gleaming downtown high-rises. As I admired its beauty, I was saddened to think Gregory would never see such a view again. Damn grief, with its intrusive little reminders of the harsh divide between before and the new normal.

"Ann, have you got this?"

The sound of my name wrenched me back from the postcard-perfect skyline.

"Ann?"

"Yes? Sorry. No. Didn't hear all that."

I fumbled with my notes.

"It's okay," said Gillian, the lead editor on the package. She put her hand on my arm. "Most of what we talked about is on the assignment sheet. Just look over the parts with your name on them and tell me if there's anything you need to know."

God, people were being nice. At no other time would I have gotten a pass for zoning out during a meeting. I'd have to learn to gently banish thoughts of Gregory when they intruded like this.

As if you could.

After the meeting broke up I was back at my cubicle organizing my notes on the project when our society editor, Ruby Nell, came sashaying toward my desk. I knew she was coming my way because she was looking straight at me. This was not a woman who normally had two words for me on any day of the week. I was not of her social strata; no one at the paper really was. Except maybe the publisher.

"Ann? How ya doin', hon?" she said, dripping with the Texas charm she used on all the big shots at the galas she covered.

I wondered what she really wanted.

Before I could get a word out, big-mouthed, brassy Ruby Nell—even her honey-blonde hair was big and brassy—leaned down and regarded me in a chummy sort of way.

"I have something to tell you, and I hope you won't be offended by it."

She was so close, I was at eye level with her horsey teeth flashing behind candy-apple red Mick Jagger lips. I thought I might gag on her magnolia blossom perfume. Please, deliver me.

"Go ahead," I said. "Shoot."

Just listen.

"I don't know quite how to say this," she said, "so I guess I'll just say it."

"Best way," I agreed, nodding my head, mustering a fake smile.

"I was at a party on Halloween, and…" suddenly she dropped into sotto voce, "we were doing a séance." She said it like it was something deliciously forbidden, like going to see a porno flick. "You know. Around a table. Touching hands."

She waited. I nodded.

"Yes, I know what séance is."

"Not that we were serious, of course, about ghosts or anything." Now she was backpedaling. It was curious, her awkwardness. Not like our Ruby Nell at all.

"That's okay," I said. "I won't judge you."

She seemed relieved and returned to her story.

"We were all kind of giddy and drinking," she said. "And, you know, no one thought anything real was going to happen."

She punctuated the telling with a flip of her wrist that made her bangle bracelets jingle. Then she leaned down on elbows in a half crouch next to my desk, thought better of it, and pulled up my spare chair. I was trapped in her magnolia haze.

"Anyway, all night, the medium supposedly made contact. A guy's dog even came through, and we listened and laughed. Nothing really serious, but then…"

Ruby Nell lowered her voice still more and glanced outside my cubicle, like she wanted to be sure no one was in earshot.

"… she says, the séance lady says, 'Is there anyone who hasn't gotten a message from the beyond?' Well, I spoke right up. 'No one for me,' I said. Everyone laughed. She told us to settle down and she'd try again. So we did, and this medium went back to her trance and said, I swear she said this: 'Do you know someone named Ann on the other side?' I said no, I did not, and she said, 'Is she on this side?'

"I nearly wet my pants when she said that. I said, 'Yes, I know an Ann.' You, Ann. You're the only Ann I know. Well, darned if that medium doesn't go back under her spell or trance or whatever, and she says, 'Tell her that Gregory—*Gregory*—says he loves her and was called away suddenly on urgent business.'"

The hair on the back of my neck stiffened.

"But that's not all," Ruby Nell said in a voice so soft I don't think even Raiza, straining from the next cubicle, could hear it.

"After the séance, the lady pulls me aside. She wanted to be sure I took the message seriously and that I'd really tell you. She said to me… she explained she was clair… *sentient*, someone who just 'knows' things, like a sixth sense. But she said this was all mucked up by this this Gregory spirit. She said, 'This is the first time I've ever been *shouted at* from the beyond.' Seriously, that's what she said. Like she *heard* someone shouting at her for the first time from the spirit world."

I had no words.

"I hope I haven't upset you, hon," Ruby Nell said, buttery as your mama's best biscuits.

"No, no." My mind was reeling. "I just don't know what to say."

"I'm sure it's just some crazy coincidence," she said, flapping that arm again, setting off the bangles. "But just in case it's not…"

That's just what Gregory would say: "called away on business."

"Thank you for sharing," I managed as the magnolia mist dispersed. "Sounds kinda weird, but I appreciate your telling me."

"Glad you're not pissed," she said more loudly, flashing another toothy smile, and with a wink, she rose and turned to leave, skirt swishing jauntily. Bye, Ruby Nell.

The second she was gone, Raiza popped up above the divider.

"Let's go get some coffee," she said.

This was code for meeting in the lunchroom, away from prying eyes and ears in the newsroom. Everyone did it.

"I just finished filing," she added. "I've got about a half hour before we have to edit." That meant about a half hour before sitting down with the originating desk editor to go over her story.

"Okay."

The newspaper's lunchroom was about the size of a middle-school cafeteria. The dining area had recently been repainted industrial gray and outfitted with something that looked like Steelcase chic. We could hear the lunch crew cleaning up, with pots clanging and water sloshing. Out on the line, they'd left a supply of snacks and beverages.

We grabbed a couple of coffees, took a table by a window, and I filled Raiza in on the parts she missed about the séance. I even told her a little about what Connie had mentioned, the whole medium thing. Then I pressed her.

"What do you think when you hear stuff like this?"

"You mean do I believe it's possible that someone can be someplace after they die where they can reach out? At a party séance? Really?"

Raiza cackled loudly and her pink topknot shook.

"Honestly," she said, calming down, "I don't know. I'm skeptical—aren't all journalists?—but I try to keep an open mind. Homicide or woo-woo—just gimme the facts." She took a sip of her coffee. "I suppose if you believed in this stuff, you could surmise the medium at the séance was an entry point for him. An easy vector."

"Yeah? I never thought about it that way. But do you think it's even possible there's a someplace where dead people or spirits or whatever you call them 'talk' from?"

"Dunno."

Raiza dropped her kooky façade and spoke without affectation.

"There's been some paranormal research—even some at the university—but I've never followed up on it. I might be a lot more interested if I'd just lost someone."

She could be thoughtful under that pink pixie do.

"I can understand wanting to check it out," she added.

"Thanks," I said. "Sometimes I think I sound crazy."

"Crazy? Of course it's crazy," she said, letting out a guffaw. "But no. You have to explore every possibility. To do less wouldn't be you."

Then she slapped her hands on the table.

"Wouldn't you know he'd shout?"

I just smiled. This was Raiza's way of telling me she'd gone as deep as she could for the moment. We dropped our mugs in a bus tray and headed upstairs.

We'd been back in the newsroom only a few minutes before my phone rang. I clicked into work mode.

"This is Ann Stewart. Can..."

"This is Ben." The voice at the other end of the line chopped off my sentence without so much as a "hello."

"Ben?"

"Ben. Gregory's cousin."

That Ben. The cousin who appropriated the memorial arrangements, but also managed to get my key back from Stella.

"Oh. Hi."

"Did you know that Gregory had an IRA with Fidelity?" he asked.

I imagined Ben sitting behind a massive oak desk in some dark paneled office, a bottle of Dalmore 12-year stashed in a side drawer.

"No, I didn't."

"Well, guess what. He named you the beneficiary. Had about ten thousand dollars in it, too."

"Oh, my gosh," I stammered.

"Come by my office and we'll get you started on the paperwork," he said, reeling off the address and location with staccato precision.

I scrawled them on the back of a press release.

"Thanks," I said, once again caught off guard by his domineering demeanor. "I'll try to come by tomorrow."

"Good. See you then."

Fidelity IRA? A little alarm went off in my head. Was that what I thought I'd heard in a dream? The name Ira? Could all these seemingly random events somehow be connected? There was Connie's deal with Gregory over the altar. The odd scent. The Sasha thing. Olivia's dream. The weird Ruby Nell encounter. The Ira dream.

I knew, standing back and evaluating my own mental state, that I was vulnerable to suggestion. I wanted to believe that something of Gregory's essence survived. But my dogged, data-driven side persisted. I wanted to believe it only if it really was true. Was all this "evidence"? Or an overactive imagination?

Figure it out.

I took out a fresh yellow pad and made some notes before returning to the world of municipal bond proposals. Or trying to, anyway. Ira = IRA? Words in the dream = "Remember Ira. Don't forget Ira." Then I jotted down everything I could remember about Ruby Nell's story: He was called away on business. He "shouted" at the medium. And what was the word Ruby had used? Clairsentient? "Look up meaning," I wrote. "Follow up on research Raiza mentioned." I underlined "research."

These were things I could do. Why did all this make my heart beat faster?

Connie had been staying with me off and on throughout the first weeks and made a point of dropping in when Olivia got home from school if I wasn't going to be there. Neither of us wanted her to be alone in the apartment yet, even for a few hours.

"So, Connie," I greeted my friend, who was there on the couch when I got home from work the first day, "what is clairsentience?"

"Why do you ask?" she said, looking up from her book.

"Don't answer a question with a question."

"Ha. Why not?"

"No, seriously. A funny thing happened at work today," I said as I kicked off my shoes and put down my purse and jacket. "No, two funny things happened. Three." I gave her a rundown of the séance story, the call from Ben, and the "Ira" incident.

"So the medium at the séance said she was clairsentient," Connie repeated slowly, as if mulling over the information. "That means she feels things. Intuits. Not like Sasha, who is clairvoyant and clairaudient.... More like me...."

"Whoa. Stop. Back up."

Connie waited for me to sit down. I took out the yellow pad I'd started at work.

"Now. Go slowly."

"'Clair' is the root word," she said. "It's French for 'clear.'"

"Got it. And you said clairsentient is..."

"... feeling," Connie finished the sentence. "Like getting impressions. She is a medium. All mediums are psychics, but not all psychics are mediums."

I took notes as she talked. This would help me understand.

"Yes. So when that medium said she was shouted at, she was experiencing clairaudience—hearing information. Sasha does that. She's also clair*voyant*, meaning clear seeing, because images come to her."

"So what do you make of the séance thing?"

Connie shrugged.

"Who knows? It could be a coincidence—although that's a pretty impressive coincidence—or there could be something to it."

"That's pretty much what Raiza said. I want to believe it. But I also want it to be true because it *is* true, not just because I want it to be."

"Okay. You said Raiza mentioned research. Do you know if she was talking about something specific?"

"Not really."

"Why don't you ask her about that? She might be talking about Dr. Koslow—Sumi Koslow—the friend I mentioned who's studying some paranormal stuff right here at the university."

"What does he study?"

Connie hesitated to answer.

"Connie, what?"

"He studies out-of-body experiences."

"Geez, Connie," I said. "What the hell does that mean? Is this more stuff you haven't told me about?"

"Y'know, I don't *have* to tell you anything," Connie fired back, then adding less harshly, "There's a lot I haven't told you. You know I'm private about some things. And it never came up."

Connie lapsed into cloak mode—it made me think of *Star Trek's* cloaking device that rendered Romulan vessels invisible. At those times, her gray eyes were like one-way mirrors that took in much, offered back little.

"That's no answer," I snapped, immediately sorry to have done so.

Lighten up.

Just then familiar footsteps padded down the staircase.

"Hi Mom."

"Hey there," I said to Olivia. "How're you doing?"

I wanted to run and throw my arms around her but thought better of it. So many things like that were feelings out of my need, not hers. The body language—head down, shoulders hunched, kind of dropping step to step—wasn't inviting. Stopping just above the last step, she leaned over the banister, fingering and chewing the ends of her hair.

"Fine," Olivia said. "How're *you* doing, back at work?"

"Weird. Tired. Awkward."

"Sounds like school."

"Which part?" I said, searching her face to see if she would add anything more.

"All of it." Olivia shrugged. In went the snail. "I've got homework to do."

She spun around and trotted back up the stairs.

CHAPTER THIRTEEN

"Are you going to be home in the next half hour or so?" It was Elizabeth on the phone. The way she'd fled the last time, I wasn't sure I'd ever hear from her again. It had already been nearly a week.

"I will be here, yes."

"Is your daughter going to be there?"

"Not for a couple of hours. I have to go pick her up at four thirty."

"Good. Because I want to share something with you that might be too much for her to handle."

Would this be something about Gregory that I didn't know? Would my guess be right? Something about a love child?

I could barely suppress my anticipation.

"I'm here," I said. "Come on over. Please."

I wasn't a hundred percent sure I was prepared to hear what Elizabeth had to say, but she might never volunteer the information again. I'd just have to wing it if things got dicey.

"Okay. See you in a few minutes."

I put out a fresh hand towel in the downstairs bath and had just begun straightening the living room—stacking newspapers, fluffing pillows—when the doorbell rang.

"Wow. That was fast," I said as I opened the door.

"Yeah, well, I have to do this before I lose my nerve." She flashed a lopsided grin and stepped inside. "I can only do this once."

I was again disarmed by her warmth and forthrightness. This time she wore a smart black velvet jacket over an ankle-length, print skirt in ochre and brown stippled with black. The hem brushed another pair of cowboy boots—black on brown. She'd pulled her flaming red hair back into a tight, becoming chignon with random curls framing her face. I surmised this was how she dressed for work.

"May I sit here?" She motioned to a spot on the floor in front of the ottoman.

"Yes, of course. Sit anywhere you want."

She sat down on the floor and placed a small black velvet satchel next to her.

"Is this about what's in the chest?" I asked.

"It is."

"Should I move it closer?"

"If you wouldn't mind."

All business. Getting right to the point.

I dropped to my knees and, as I stretched out, my cropped sweater hiked up to reveal a turquoise-and-silver belt buckle at the front of my jeans. Elizabeth gasped and did a double take.

"That belt you're wearing… It's not…?"

"Gregory's?" I said. "Yes, it is."

We both looked down at the buckle as I pulled the chest closer to her.

"I… It feels good to wear it. Like I still can touch a small part of him. I've worn it every day since…"

Elizabeth stared at the belt.

"You should know it's quite old and valuable," she said before finally looking away. "We got it on a trip to Santa Fe."

This seemed like a natural place to ask a question.

"How did you meet Gregory?"

Elizabeth sighed and let her shoulders fall.

"I met him in college at a New Year's Eve party," she said, "where he shocked me by kissing me full on the mouth at midnight. He took my name and number, but I never heard from him until *years* later, right after his dad died, asking very politely if he could rent a room from me. He was hoping I was single and still lived in Dallas!

"What the hell," she said, as if verbally slapping her knee. "I needed the money, and we were all young and stupid back then. The 'room' lasted two nights. On the third night, he slipped into my bedroom. Before we knew it, we were making love. Oh my God, he was such a good lover."

Momentarily losing herself in the memory, she looked up and said, "I'm sorry."

"No, no," I said. "I… I know what you mean. Weird to say. But I do."

I flashed to our first encounter—Gregory's slow hand, the aching for each other, our explosive union—yes, the man knew how to make love. What an oddity that Elizabeth and I could share this intimacy we both experienced with him.

"If it just hadn't been for that damned store," Elizabeth said, "and the way it chained him to his mother."

"You mean the liquor store?"

"And that selfish bastard father of his."

After a career as a cotton broker, Johnny had opened a liquor store in his retirement years. Not a smart move. When Gregory got home from Utah after his father died, the store was on the brink of bankruptcy, and Johnny's foolish investment had wiped out the Maloufs' savings.

"Johnny left Stella with nothing except a measly widow's Social Security," sniffed Elizabeth, crimson rising on her freckled neck. "So there was Gregory, bound up in that damned mother-first tradition. Take care of her or risk the scorn of the tribe. No ridicule for Johnny—he was dead. No, the sins of the father landed squarely on the son. He tried to resist. I think that's why he moved in with me and not her."

"Geez."

I knew part of the story. Gregory told me he felt duty bound to shore up the store's accounts and provide for his mother, even if it meant giving up that job he loved at the Department of Agriculture in Utah. The store was his inheritance, whether he liked it or not. In Texas, if you die without a will—as Johnny did—your wife and surviving children evenly divide the estate.

Gregory took on the store as a challenge. Resurrecting the business meant hands-on organizing of inventory and staff. And he created two sets of books: one for the IRS and one for skimming, to increase under-the-table cash flow. I was shocked when Gregory told me this as casually as he might describe choosing a new color scheme for a house. He acted like it was nothing. He did what he had to do, he said. He and his mother inherited the store fifty-fifty, so they were like oxen burdened with a single, unyielding yoke.

"I swear if I still smoked, I'd light a cigarette right now," Elizabeth said.

"Can I offer you a glass of water instead?"

"Yeah. Thanks."

I left her fuming.

Returning to the living room, I held out a tumbler, then sat back down on the floor by the couch with my own glass. She took a long draft and seemed less agitated.

"Okay," she said, "let's take another look at what's in that chest." As she eased it open, her face flickered with satisfaction. "You waxed the surfaces, didn't you?"

"Yes I did. Just like you said. It was good advice."

Elizabeth lifted out the two top trays and set them aside, going straight for the drawings and the lock of hair in the bottom one. She peeled off the tissue like delicate petals off a flower and brushed the curl against her lips. I worried she was getting ready to bolt again.

Her next words came slowly and thickly.

"Did Gregory ever mention… that he had a stepdaughter?"

She cocked her head and watched for my reaction.

"No," I gasped.

A stepdaughter? My hand went to my throat.

"No, I guess he didn't."

I could hear the disappointment in Elizabeth's voice.

A stepdaughter?

Before continuing she withdrew a handful of snapshots from the black velvet satchel and handed them to me. There was Gregory with a laughing, smiling little girl. Tawny curls. Lanky arms and legs, not unlike Olivia's. Faces caught in unguarded moments of love and laughter. They were snapshots from a picnic on a sloping lawn spread with an old-fashioned checkered tablecloth in the shade of a cottonwood tree with its characteristic heart-shaped leaves. A wicker basket lay open nearby. But my attention was riveted on Gregory and the girl. They looked so happy.

"This… is… Megan," Elizabeth said, doling out each word as if stringing pearls on a necklace. "She is—or was—Gregory's stepdaughter."

The information hit me like a physical blow. But she wasn't his child.

"Wait a minute," I said, truth dawning slowly. "This is *your* daughter?"

Elizabeth nodded.

"Oh my God, she's beautiful. Where is she? What happened?"

I couldn't fathom why Gregory hadn't mentioned her. He told me about Elizabeth. About his marriage. The robbery at the liquor store when he'd been shot. But it was like each story, each aspect of his life, was a separate compartment. His mother, with all her complicated needs, in one compartment. His dad's Lebanese family, with all its demands, in another. Work was a compartment. His marriage was a compartment. My view of his world was only the compartments he wanted me to see.

But a stepdaughter. Why wouldn't he have told me about a stepdaughter?

"I think I know why he never mentioned her," Elizabeth said, anticipating my thoughts.

She took out another photo from the small bag. It was the same little girl, this time barely recognizable: Ashen. Wizened. Eyes closed. Curled up in a hospital bed. A shadow hooked up to IVs and nasal oxygen.

"It broke his heart when she finally died of the cancer," Elizabeth said steadily.

"Broke *his* heart," I said, watching Elizabeth closely. Cancer. My resolve to maintain a professional façade wobbled. "What about *your* heart? I... I can't imagine losing a child...."

I flashed on Olivia and swung from astonishment to gut spasms.

"You don't want to," Elizabeth said, looking at me squarely. "Just like people don't want to imagine what you're going through. No one should ever have to go there."

I couldn't help myself. I wept silently as she talked, struggling to regain control. I didn't want her to stop.

"The pain never goes away," she said, softening, "but time dulls it. After a while, you don't wake up every day feeling like your heart's been ripped out. This was years ago."

I managed to recover my composure.

"I don't know what to say except I'm so, so sorry."

"I know," Elizabeth said. "I know."

She turned back to the chest.

"I had no idea he kept some of her drawings," she murmured. "Or the lock of her hair."

She brushed the lock against her lips again and closed her eyes.

His stepdaughter's hair. I felt like the wind had been knocked out of me. We sat in silence as I struggled to make sense of this revelation, and to fathom Elizabeth's loss.

Elizabeth leaned back against the ottoman. I unconsciously touched the turquoise on the belt buckle. Something else made more sense now: a reference Elizabeth made during the memorial service.

"What did that mean, what you said at the service," I asked, "that Gregory was her angel?"

"Megan was my only child, and her biological father was out of the picture," she began. "She died just before her thirteenth birthday. She and Gregory were crazy about each other."

"Tell me more."

"She developed a very rare cancer, an adrenal carcinoma," Elizabeth said, letting out a deep sigh.

"And that is...?"

"A tumor on her kidney. She probably contracted it from asbestos at her school. It was an old building. She played the alto sax, which Gregory loved. Despite being so young, she loved jazz and was crazy for Coltrane. John Coltrane! Can you imagine? Practiced constantly. At home. At school. That probably accelerated her illness, but you couldn't prove anything. The doctors said she was probably inhaling asbestos every time she filled her lungs. By the time it was diagnosed, she was stage four and inoperable. We were devastated."

Eyes cast downward, Elizabeth's focus turned inward, as if I weren't there. She spoke as if in a trance.

"All through her illness, Gregory took care of her. When Megan was well enough to get out of bed, he took her anyplace she wanted to go—restaurants, antique malls, the park. And when she wasn't well enough, he brought things to her. Gregory would buy her dresses, knowing she would never be well enough to wear them. He would bring them home and lay them on her bed and tell her where he was going to take her when she put them on—like to see *The Lion King* on Broadway. Only she was too sick and never got to go. He bought stuffed animals, CDs, trinkets—anything to make her smile. He even hooked up a speaker system from her bedroom to ours so he could listen as she slept. And when she would cry out in the middle of the night from the pain, he insisted on going to her. He learned how to give shots so he could give her the pain injections. Then he would lie down next to her until she fell asleep."

If it was possible, I loved Gregory more in that moment than I ever had.

"Please. Go. On." Please don't stop now.

Elizabeth paused, as if summoning courage to continue.

"Until the robbery, everything in our lives had come to revolve around Megan," she said. "Everything conformed to her needs as we tacitly acknowledged the unspoken. We were losing a little more of her every day. I was with her at Baylor when she died."

I shook my head. With each revelation, a new wave of sadness crashed against my wobbly defenses.

"Oh, Elizabeth, my heart breaks for you."

As it should.

"She looked so peaceful once it was over. I swear I saw her soul leave her body. It was like she was just sleeping. Except… she wasn't. At the same time, Gregory was at Parkland fighting for his life. He wanted so desperately to say goodbye to Megan."

That was a jolt.

"What do you mean 'fighting for his life'? Don't tell me this was the same time as when he was shot."

"You got it," Elizabeth said, gathering her skirt around her legs and holding on to her knees. "It all happened simultaneously."

"Are you friggin' kidding me?"

"You know about the robbery, right?"

"I don't know what I know anymore."

Good God, could this get any worse?

"That's when he got that awful scar."

The scar. Yes. The jagged scar that skirted the bottom of his rib cage.

He explained it to me early in our relationship as easily as if he were describing a summer rain. Stella and their employee were behind the counter dealing with an electrical problem when a guy walked in waving a gun around. It happened so fast. The three of them looked up, and there he was. When Gregory lunged for the gun, it went off, and the bullet pierced his liver.

"The ambulance hustled him off to Parkland," Elizabeth said.

My ability to absorb this new, more complicated version verged on collapse.

"When the surgeons couldn't repair the wound from the front, they flipped him over onto his stomach to get at it from the back, which is why the scar ended up being so long. No time for niceties."

Gregory had tossed it off as no big deal. Elizabeth's roller-coaster narrative continued.

"Then the bleeding wouldn't stop. He took sixty-eight pints of blood. The body only holds ten, for Chrissakes. It was like pouring blood down a sieve. I got there as soon as I could. But at that very moment, Megan was in crisis at Baylor."

The color was rising in Elizabeth's face.

She cradled the baby-fine lock in her palm.

"I'm driving back and forth between them each day, knowing one of the two people I loved most in the world was dying, and the other might be. Four days after Gregory's crisis passed, Megan asked me if Gregory was going to be okay. When I said yes, she said, 'Good. I'm so tired.' She died the next morning. Fifteen minutes after Megan passed, I was on my way to Parkland to tell Gregory. He never got to tell her goodbye. It was the first time I'd ever seen him cry."

New waves of anguish swept over me. For Elizabeth. For the loss of her daughter and her fear of losing Gregory. For his loss—all this sealed up inside of him.

"It hurt to see him so inconsolable," Elizabeth said.

The air was heavy between us.

"He couldn't stand it. Couldn't stand the pain of losing her like that. He buried it so deeply in his heart that it lodged there as surely as the bullet that pierced his liver."

With this revelation, I started shaking uncontrollably and gasping for air.

Elizabeth scooted closer and put her arms around me. With her touch, my dammed-up torrent broke. As she rocked me, I heaved with long cathartic sobs—the deep belly sobs I always knew would come. I felt her sobbing, too.

We clung to each other like shipwreck survivors and wept for a long time. Eventually the waves of pain and tears subsided, transmuted into something simply open and vulnerable resonating between us. Being with Elizabeth was like drinking from a deep, clear well when you're so thirsty your mouth is swollen and your lips are cracked.

"I am so sorry," I said finally. "So, so sorry. For you. And for Gregory."

"Thank you."

Tenderly, she returned Megan's drawings and lock of hair to their place in the chest. She examined the business card for the Oklahoma cemetery again, then placed it on top.

"After Megan died, things were never the same between us. Things happened. He went on emotional lockdown."

Just then, Olivia traipsed through the front door, surprising both of us. We had just finished repositioning the chest next to the sofa.

"Mom," she said, then looked to Elizabeth. "Hi. Janie's mom offered to drop me off early, so I said yes. Have you guys been crying?"

"Yes," I said. "But it's okay. It's a good kind of crying."

Elizabeth stood, picked up her purse and satchel, where she'd replaced her photos, and moved toward the door, her gaze lingering on Olivia.

"It's good to see you again, Olivia. I'll bet you and Gregory had some good times together," she said warmly, wiping her eyes with a tissue.

"Yes, we did. I liked him a lot."

Olivia scooted her backpack out of Elizabeth's way.

"Thank you for everything," I said. "I know this wasn't easy for you."

"I'm just glad he found you," she said. "He chose good women."

"Yes, he did."

Our eyes connected one final time. Then she left.

"What was that all about?" Olivia said, slipping her arm around my waist.

"She told me some things about Gregory that help me understand him better."

"She seems really nice. Are we going to see her again?"

"I hope so. I really do."

CHAPTER FOURTEEN

With so much weighing on my heart and mind, I wanted to put off reading Connie's books a little longer. But no. Curiosity overruled reason, and I felt compelled to pick them up. Were the weird, woo-woo-ish events since Gregory's death real? Connected? Something a "medium" could shed light on?

My rational side dug in: Wasn't this just so much naked desperation, grabbing at anything?

But what about what Connie saw? Or says she saw.

She wouldn't lie.

Why would Ruby Nell come to me with such an outlandish story if there weren't some kernel of truth to it? She was many things—flamboyant, self-important, narcissistic. But cruel? Not her style.

And what about the dreams and the effing IRA, for heaven's sake?

For heaven's sake? I laughed out loud.

Don't drive yourself crazy.

At this point, the books were like a welcome escape. So I picked them up.

Thumbing through the John Edward title, I found myself drawn to the passage where he asked, "How does one tell a real psychic from a fake?"

Okay. How?

It was the perfect morsel to tempt me to read more.

This sentence caught my eye: "Do they come through with accurate, detailed validation, or is it all vague generalities?"

I thought of Clarksville. Then Sasha.

In another section, I was impressed with his explanation of the confusion that can arise from literal versus figurative images in the "reading" process. I thought about Sasha's spontaneous reading for Connie and how Sasha's "colored chalk" turned out to be spools of thread. While not quite accurate, there was no question the image led Connie to something prized she might otherwise have never found. Hard to write off something that specific as coincidence.

Edward also freely admitted there were mysteries about how he received information. And I was comforted to learn that he didn't buy into the medium thing altogether at first.

"One day I'd stop," he wrote. "Once I got a Real Job."

I had to admit this was completely at odds with the chicanery my friend had encountered in Clarksville. I flashed back to what she told me, how the reader kept asking sneaky questions—"You're over forty, aren't you?"

We learn in the news business never to do this, that it's unethical to lead with questions like that except in very unusual circumstances. There didn't seem to be any mystery to how the Clarksville medium was "getting" her information.

Interesting that Edward referred to the work of Martin and Romanowski, who cowrote the other book Connie gave me. I'd taken it upstairs to my bedroom for nighttime reading. Before long, I was devouring both books. I was particularly moved by an account of a "contact" experience between Janis Joplin and her sister. It felt personal for me because I'd met Laura Joplin once when Janis was alive. A chance encounter through the paper. In her book *Love, Janis,* Laura wrote that the ascendant blues-rock singer who overdosed at the age of twenty-seven had reached across the physical-nonphysical divide to her.

Both books were peppered with examples that encouraged the reader to decide whether the contact was real. They sounded real as written. But skepticism was my business. Anecdotes are not data. Wanting to believe doesn't make it so, and I was fully aware of how badly I wanted to believe. The possibility of contact was like offering morphine to someone in pain.

You want it so much.

As I read the second book, I was struck again by the fact that none of these authors were engaged in a hard sell or slick presentation. They just wanted you to consider and add up the anecdotal accounts in which something seems to have happened. They weren't peddling an agenda, other than to suggest we should all be more open-minded about the possibility of communication between the living and the dead. Draw your own conclusions.

Both books—and the possibilities they opened up—were drilling little holes in my resistance, feeding a hope I dared not acknowledge. Before Gregory died, I casually considered there might be *something* after death. But the physics were complicated, and who had time to dwell on it? I was busy living. In the same vein, I never considered "psychic stuff" as anything more serious than playing with a Ouija board, where I was certain a very flesh-and-blood someone was moving the planchette. The thing I wanted most, the thing I hungered for, was certainty that something of Gregory survived physical death. Gregory's death had changed everything. I had to know if some aspect of him was still out there. No, it was more than that. I wanted that connection. Once more. If such a thing were possible. Like the title of Edward's book: *One Last Time.*

At one point, I had been reading well into the night. I closed my eyes, nodding toward sleep, only to be startled as the book slid off my chest and hit the floor with a thud. When I reached down to pick it up and put it on the nightstand, a piece of paper floated out of its pages: "Sasha Butler 503-555-0189." Printed in Connie's handwriting. I smiled. Why did this not surprise me?

The next morning I made up my mind to call Connie's medium. Olivia was at her dad's, and Sunday was probably as good a day as any to find Sasha at home. I wasn't getting my hopes up. Or was I? No, I told myself. I was doing this because this is how I investigated things. This is what I know: Follow the thread, see where it leads. Here, too, was something new to "do," a distraction from my chronic aching for Gregory.

After a good cup of coffee and the Sunday paper—Gregory and I used to always read it together in bed—I got dressed, sat down at my desk, fished out a fresh yellow notepad, and wrote "Sasha" firmly across the top, with the phone number.

"You guys think I'm doing the right thing?" I queried Woodward and Bernstein, who were lolling together on Gregory's maroon leather chair. They looked up briefly.

Taking a deep breath, I dialed.

"Hello?" The voice on the other end was male and gravelly.

Not Sasha, I was pretty sure.

"Hello," I said, putting on my best professional demeanor. "My name is Ann Stewart. I'm looking for Sasha Butler, and a friend of mine said this might be her number."

"Yeah, when she was staying here she used it," came the husky reply. "That was a few months ago. But she's not here now."

"Do you know how to contact her?"

"Hmmm. Lemme see. Can you wait a minute?"

I could hear rustling in the background.

While I waited, I tried imagining what Sasha might look like, envisioning her on the plump side, with long wavy hair, wearing hippie tie-dye and fake baubles. She probably didn't shave her legs or armpits. I could see her driving around in an old, battered camper, broken down as often as not.

I drummed my fingers on the desk and looked again toward the living room, where I could just see the corner of the wooden chest, aglow in sunlight spilling through the sheers. I was used to waiting on calls, but this guy seemed really slow. Maybe he couldn't find her real number. Maybe this would be a dead end. My heart sank.

"I don't think she has a phone," the voice said back on the line, "but I do have the number of a friend that keeps up with her pretty well."

I pictured the owner of this voice with wild hair and a scruffy beard.

"You want that?"

"Yes, I'd like that very much," I said.

I wrote the number down under the first one. "Thanks for your help."

I repeated this routine through a daisy-chain of four more calls. Tedious calls. Nerve-wracking calls.

After the fourth I sat for a moment, collecting myself. I hadn't anticipated making more than one call to reach Sasha. I suddenly felt fatigued. Each time I was forced to deviate from the predictable, it was like another layer of muck to slog through.

Fed up, I dialed Connie.

"Hello?"

"Who the hell is this Sasha woman?" My frustration erupted. "That wasn't her number you gave me. I'm calling people, and they're all over the map about where she is and how to get ahold of her. And if she even has a phone. Is she some fly-by-night?"

"Whoa. Wait a minute," Connie backpedaled. "I thought that was her number. That's why I put it in the book. Maybe it's changed."

"That's an understatement. I keep calling and getting *another* number and *another* number…"

"Take a breath." Connie bristled. Woody smacked Bernie with his paw. "The fact that the number's wrong doesn't change what she does."

"I know. I want to call her but I'm… It's too hard." I sounded like a petulant child. I tugged Woody gently away from my tuxedo baby.

"I know you're upset. I'm sorry. I thought I was helping."

"Sorry, too. I don't mean to attack you. It's just so… frustrating."

Weepy one minute, out of control the next. Was this ever going to end?

"Look, call me if you don't reach her. Maybe I can help you track her down."

"Yeah, I can do that. Thanks. Sorry."

"Let me know if you can't reach her."

"Okay. Gotta keep trying. Thanks. Bye."

Logic versus desire. Push-pull. Gregory, Gregory, Gregory. Every thought corkscrewed back to Gregory. I slammed down the phone and went over to the chest. I ran my hands over its smooth surface, so finely crafted. So Gregory. Out of nowhere, I felt my heart catch, and I broke into sobs. It was as if the initial shock and pain came crashing down on me again. Oh, Gregory. Where are you? I curled up next the chest and wrapped my arms around it, like some permutation of a Harlow monkey. I laid my head on it and sobbed.

Then, like a spigot, the tears shut off. I'd cried enough. There weren't any more. Not for the moment. The cats just watched as I dried my eyes and returned to my desk, determined to tear up the page with the phone numbers on it and be done with this notion of contacting a medium. It was silly and stupid. It was too hard. Too painful.

I reached down, grabbed the page, tore it off the yellow pad, and mashed it into a little ball. Just as I was about to drop it in the wastebasket, the yearning came creeping back and paralyzed my arm.

What if it works?

I couldn't let it go. "What if" this was the one way I might find out if Gregory was still out there? "What if" this led to a real opportunity? To do what?

To feel our hearts connect.

Oh my God, this was what I really wanted. The desire was buried so deep I nearly missed it. I teased the page back out into a flat but wrinkled sheet. I wrote Sasha's name and the numbers on a fresh page of the notepad.

After two more calls, the person assured me I had *the* number. The supposedly real number that would link me to Sasha. Darting thought: These calls and their long-distance charges were costing me a small fortune.

So what?

The possibility of contacting Gregory one last time was more important. I dialed the number.

One ring. Two rings. Three rings.

Oh great, she's not there. Oh shit, she's not there.

A woman answered on the fourth ring.

"Hello?"

"Hello. Is this Sasha Butler?"

"Yes? Who's this?"

Finally, I was talking to her. Relief flooded my body.

"I'm a friend of a friend," I said, careful not to reveal who I was or where I was calling from.

"Okay." No affect. Flat.

"I wanted to inquire about a reading," I said. "Do you do them? Can you do them long distance?"

"Yes, I do them," she said without equivocation. "And, yes, I can do them long distance. I just have to be at a number I can use."

"You don't have a phone?"

"Nope. Never in one place long enough to sign up for one."

"Well... would you do a reading for me?" I groped for words. "I'm not sure how to do this. What's the protocol?"

"I charge fifty dollars," Sasha began, as though she'd made this speech many times before, "and I need you to send me something personal from the person you want me to contact. It can be a hair clip, a piece of jewelry, a scarf—just something that they handled a lot that meant a lot to them when they were alive."

"Okay." I thought about what I might send. Something neutral. Nothing that would give away his identity or help her guess who he was. "What about a small beanbag toy?" Gregory kept a whimsical little stuffed spider on his desk that I'd rescued when his childhood buddy and I cleaned out his office.

"Yes, that would be fine."

"How long have you been doing this?" I asked.

"How long? Since I was a kid. Not something I went looking for." I could almost hear her shrug. "It's a way to pick up a few bucks. When would you like to do this?"

When? I hadn't even thought about that. I looked at the calendar on the wall behind my desk.

"Would Wednesday night work?" I asked. Olivia would be at her dad's then.

"Yeah, works for me. You do understand this call has to be on your dime?"

"I do. Should I call this number?"

"Yeah, that should be fine. Just be sure to put cash or a money order in the mail so I get it before then."

She was worried about the money.

"Can I get the beanbag toy back?" I asked.

"If you send me a self-addressed, stamped envelope." Her voice was edgy.

"But I don't want you to know who I am." It sounded so petty to my ears.

"Great. Like what, I'm going to look you up? Where would I go? How would I do that?"

"I just don't want anyone to have any room to criticize what you come up with," I stammered. "I don't want them saying you somehow got the information by other means. I have friends who would do that."

"Look." She paused as if she were exhaling smoke from a cigarette. "You'll have my address. Send the self-addressed stamped envelope after we're done."

"Okay."

We set the appointment for six p.m. my time the following Wednesday. She gave me her mailing address, I repeated it back to her, and we said our goodbyes.

Once we hung up, I tucked the writing pad away in a safe place. All that dialing and redialing and the uncertainty about whether I would actually reach her had wrung me completely out. As if to console me, Bernie jumped into my lap, curled up, and purred.

The following Monday, I was at the post office as soon as it opened.

CHAPTER FIFTEEN

In the days leading up to the reading, I found myself misplacing things. Having trouble concentrating. Eating sporadically. Lots of drift, except for reading and rereading the books from Connie. I studied them so intently I could've aced a pop quiz. That, plus the unexplained psychic weirdness around me, left me giddy with excitement as the reading inched closer. I allowed myself to consider that contact with Gregory might be possible.

Oh baby, please.

This allowed me to push down my doubts. So many anecdotes in the books seemed real and lined up with what had happened to people I knew. Like Connie. Ruby Nell—that one still floored me. In a way, the books were prepping me for what was about to happen. Telling me how to give feedback without leading or being led. How to interpret what might come up. How to listen. They were the perfect backgrounders for what was coming, just like research before an interview. No one but Connie knew what I was doing.

Wednesday after work, the countdown to six p.m. was on. I set up my desk like I was working, with a blank page on my computer screen and my phone-cassette-tape-recording system next to the monitor. A little suction cup attached to the back of the handset would pick up the conversation from the phone. I'd be typing in notes as the reading progressed, backup in case anything went wrong with the cassette. A glass of water was the final act of preparation in my ritual. I looked at my computer clock: Thirty minutes to go. The only thing missing was the yellow notepad with Sasha's number on it, and the others I'd dialed through to find her.

"Now where did I put that?" I wondered out loud.

I riffled through the stack of papers to the left of my computer where I expected it to be, where I kept documents still active for current projects. I pulled out a notepad, but it was the wrong one. I thumbed through again, more slowly. Nope. Not there. I scoured my "done" pile on the right, where I put notes and items once a project was complete. Not there either. Maybe I slid it next to the bookends or between the reference books I kept on my desk. I pulled each one toward me to check.

Not there.

I pushed my chair back to survey the desk and contemplate where the notepad might be hiding. I remembered putting it in a safe place, but where was that? I jerked open the drawers on the left side of my desk and went through those. Not there. I did the same with the right. Not there, either. I turned and closely scanned the bookcase behind me. No reason to think I'd put it there, but still I had to look.

I took a shallow breath. Where could it be?

There was simply no way I'd misplace something that important. No way. I looked at my computer screen: Twenty-five minutes. Panic rose like water starting to slowly boil in the bottom of a pan. First one little bubble. Then another little bubble. Then another. And another. Where the hell is the yellow pad with Sasha's number on it?

Reason dictated it must be on the desk. It had to be. I was so sure of it that I again flipped through the well-ordered stacks on either side of my computer. The yellow notepad was nowhere to be found. I went through the standing books again. It just wasn't there.

I ran up the stairs, taking them two at a time, to my bedroom, picked up the books and magazines in the basket next to my bed and flipped through those, knowing I hadn't put it there, but checking all the same. Maybe I'd moved it someplace, not thinking. I'd been misplacing things, hadn't I? But I would never misplace something this important. I knew I wouldn't. I just wouldn't.

So where was it? The clock beside my bed caught my eye. Twenty minutes. Oh God, where was it? What did I do with it? What am I going to do?

I ran back downstairs and thumbed through my Rolodex. I was certain I hadn't added Sasha's number to the file but still I checked. How stupid could I be? Why hadn't I written it there?

Then I thought about the books Connie gave me and dashed over by the couch where I'd stacked them. I held each one up by the front and back covers and shook it. I could always go back to that initial number that started the chain of calls, I reasoned wildly, and re-establish the link to Sasha. It was a crazy long shot. But I'd have to have that original wrong number from Connie that eventually led to the medium.

Finally, I fished the crumpled paper with the first number on it out of my trash can. I grabbed it and picked up the phone.

Here goes nothing. Oh God, this has to work.

I dialed the first number with shaking fingers, and the man with the gravelly voice answered.

"Hello?"

"Hello," I said, throat constricting as I fought to maintain composure. "I'm the person who called about Sasha Butler's number. Could you possibly give me that number again? I seem to have misplaced the one you gave me...."

"Yeah, I think I can find that again. It was her friend's number I gave you, right?"

"Yes," I said. Come on, come on.

"All-righty now. Here you go." He rattled off the number.

"Thank you!" One down. My ears throbbed.

I dialed the second number. I felt as if I couldn't draw a deep breath. Everything was shallow. Tight. My shoulders felt like armor plates.

The phone rang. And rang. Oh God, please let her be there. And continued to ring. No answer. No message machine. I replaced the handset in its cradle.

I wanted to melt into a puddle but steeled myself.

Don't give in to panic.

Will not. Puddle. Panic.

The phone rang, and I jumped like I'd heard gunfire.

I grabbed for the handset greedily.

"Hello?"

"Ann?" It was Connie. "I felt like I needed to call you."

"Oh my God," I said, then blurted out, "I can't find Sasha's number. I've got the reading in like five minutes, and I can't find the number. I tried to backtrack from the first one you gave me, but one of the people wasn't there, and I'm having a nervous breakdown and I've looked everywhere—"

"Stop," Connie said the way a parent would firmly shush their child. "I have the number."

"What?"

"I have the number. Out of the blue, I remembered where I put it. The real number. Not the one I wrote down and put in the book."

"Oh my god."

Take a breath.

I tried to calm myself, but my body and mind were in full-bore fight-or-flight.

"Then I got this unmistakable impression I needed to call and give it to you. Like kicked in the butt to call you."

"Oh my God."

Slow down.

I unclenched my jaw and pushed back the sensation of needing to throw up.

"It's okay now," Connie soothed. "It's really okay. Let me give you the number."

"Yes, please do," I gulped. Starting with 503, Connie read off the digits, and I copied them onto a notepad. I kept trying to calm myself down. I had the number now. The real number.

"Thank you," I said. "Thank you so much."

"Seems like we both just got a nudge," Connie said with a wink in her voice. "Now make that call. We'll talk about it later."

With one minute to go, I dialed Sasha's number.

"Hello?"

"Yes, hello."

My body went limp. Briefly I explained what had happened and turned on the tape recorder.

"I'm so sorry," she said. "Do you need to reschedule?"

"No," I said firmly, cradling the phone on my shoulder. "I'm ready." I wasn't about to risk losing her again.

"Okay. Let me tell you a little bit about how I read."

CHAPTER SIXTEEN

When Sasha was finished with the reading, I thanked her, and we said our good-byes. I rewound the cassette tape, checking to be sure it had done its job. Yes, Sasha's voice was clear and strong. I also filed the backup notes I'd made on the computer. Then I lay my forehead on the back of my hands on my desk and cried so hard my ribs ached.

When I looked up, an hour had passed. Did I fall asleep or lose consciousness? The mix of exhaustion and exhilaration left me feeling like a baby bird that's just expended all its energy cracking open its shell. Relieved. Awed. Taking in the new world. I sat up and wiped my eyes and pushed back the strands of hair that were stuck to my face. My neck ached from holding the receiver up to my ear with my shoulder. My hands dangled limply. But my heart was light.

I grabbed a tissue and blew my nose. Connie had gotten me into this, and now I needed her to help decipher the content. Reflexively I had the phone to my ear again and was dialing her number.

"Hello?"

"Connie. It's me."

"Well, hello me."

"I just finished the reading with Sasha," I said, feeling calmer. "I wondered, if you're not doing anything..."

"Let me guess: You want me to help you make heads or tails of it."

"Yes, exactly. I'm spent—but in a good way this time. It's... I feel this sense of relief and hopefulness and... I need you."

In the mirror behind my desk, I regarded a caricature of myself: red patches overlay my fair skin, puffy lips where mine were normally stiletto thin. Swollen eyes, as if someone had bopped me. Lank brown curls. Who was this woman?

"Of course, my friend," Connie said. "Would you like to come here, or would you like me to come there?"

"Whatever's easiest for you," I said. It seemed like we were practically living together since all this had happened.

"Tell you what: I'll pick up some food and come there. 'Cause I bet you haven't eaten."

"I like it," I said, sounding more like my old self. And she was right. I couldn't remember the last time I had eaten. "That'll give me time to pull myself together and make printouts of my notes. I got pretty good notes because she went slow."

"Okay. Be there in a few."

"Thanks," I said, my gratitude surfacing from a liquid place of love the reading seemed to have accessed.

I washed my face. Catching a whiff of my armpits, I gave them a quick scrub, too. I changed into a fresh sweatshirt over my jeans.

After Connie arrived—she didn't bother to knock anymore —she absently unpacked a couple of Caesars and slices of quiche, putting them on plates and adding forks. She wasn't looking at what she was doing but almost askance, absorbed in her own thoughts. I poured us some chardonnay, jittery and careful not to spill, and grabbed the pepper mill and cloth napkins. Gregory's cloth napkins. Gregory was funny about that. He always insisted on cloth napkins. Now I had a drawer full.

"Let's just eat first," Connie said. "Then get into the reading. It isn't going anywhere."

"You're right."

"This is the first time I've seen any spark in your eyes since this happened," Connie said.

"I gotta tell you, the reading reached something in me," I said, savoring a bite of quiche Lorraine. It was the first time in a long time I could remember food tasting like something other than cardboard.

"Can you say more?"

"Sure. There were moments—you'll see—when it seemed impossible that what was coming through was coincidence. Like your colored chalk. I mean, I'm trying to keep my journalistic skepticism, but a few moments were so clear-cut."

I felt tingly inside just talking about it.

"Would you do it again?"

"Yeah, I would."

It was good to get some food in my belly. Grounding in its way, just like Connie's presence.

Once the table was cleared, I gathered up the printouts and tape recorder.

"Let's do this on the couch," I said.

We settled in facing each other, and I put the tape player between us. Just a couple of regular gals listening to a conversation between a psychic and a spirit on a Wednesday night.

"So here's what I have," I said, handing Connie a printout.

"Whoa, you can read this?" she said, chuckling and turning it sideways.

"Yeah. My typing's kinda sloppy. But yes, I can read it."

"It looks like code. I had no idea reporters had their own secret language."

Now it was my turn to smile.

I flipped on the tape recorder, and Sasha began with her explanation.

Visual images rush by very quickly. I have to grab onto what I can, which is often incomplete. Sometimes messages are spoken, as though I have you on the phone in one ear and someone—Spirit—is whispering to me in the other. I will get an image or message, then I'll attempt to translate it and repeat that translation to you.

Names may come across as sound-alikes. Jim might come out as Tim or Kim. Or simply the letter 'J' or James. Spirits will use images that are meaningful to you, or they might use ones that are meaningful to me.

As I'm bringing messages to you, I need input back. Not additional information. I just need to know if an image or word makes sense to you. Then I can compare your feedback with what I sense Spirit to be saying. If I feel Spirit is saying something different, I will tell you.

I stopped the recorder to get Connie's reaction.

"That's essentially the same thing she says at the beginning of every reading," Connie said, flipping the lamp on behind her to get more light. "Play some more."

I think you're going to need a lot of work on your physical body—your neck, your shoulders, your lower back. It seems like you need a lot of body work. It would be of benefit to get that work on a continuing basis.

"My heart sank when she started in with that," I said, reaching to turn on the lamp behind me. "I thought the reading was going to be a bust—my money, my time, my hopes down the toilet. But wait till you hear this."

I started the tape again.

Somebody's brother crossed over and is here. He was young when he crossed over. He wanted to come in and say "Hi." There's one that's coming in who's committed suicide. There's more than one coming in. There's a brother here with this person that committed suicide. He's saying, "No accident."

He repeats it. He wanted to come in and say no one could help him but everybody tried. He has a dog with him that belonged to him or you. I think he's also trying to show me a necklace. Like a disc on a chain.

"What…?" Connie said. I stopped the recorder. "I've heard of more than one spirit coming through, but it's rare."

"Really? You know something about that?"

Connie sighed.

"Yeah."

This makes some sense to me, I heard myself say on the tape. *But not all of it.*

"How did that make sense to you?" Connie wanted to know.

"Gregory's brother was killed in a hunting accident when he was twenty-one. Gregory told me he had been with the hunting party, but never said a lot about it. Just, 'that was then, this is now.' He did say it was horrible when the police came to tell Stella."

"How awful," Connie said. "And what an unusual turn for a reading. Not something you were expecting."

"That's for sure."

I switched the tape on again.

I'm getting chance. No, chants. The kind you sing or say. Does this mean anything to you?"

No, I said on the tape.

"Wait, stop," Connie said, looking incredulous. "That doesn't mean anything to you? You've got to be kidding. How many kinds of chants do we know? From music history? *Medieval* chants?"

I stared back at her, blank and questioning.

"GREGORIAN chants, Ann." Connie practically shrieked, throwing her arms up and in the process nearly sending the tape recorder to the floor. Then she reached out to clasp my hands, which had started trembling.

"Oh my God. I completely missed that."

In the glow of the lamps, Connie's face looked positively golden.

"That's the kind of thing that blows people away," she said. "It's specific to you. It's not even 'Greg,' like rhymes with 'leg' or 'peg.' It's *Gregorian.* Gregory. It goes so far beyond coincidence."

"I… I don't know."

I was stunned that this had gone right over my head. I wanted to believe so much. But I still had doubts. I was being dutifully skeptical.

"Couldn't this still be a lucky guess on Sasha's part?" I asked.

"The whole thing could be a series of lucky guesses," Connie said. "There will always be that possibility. You have to weigh the odds, given the specifics."

"Sometimes I wish I weren't my father's daughter." Through the front window, I watched the streetlights come on in the darkened night.

Connie's brow crimped.

"What has that got to do with this?"

"The nuclear engineer. Everything for him was rational."

I turned the recorder back on.

I hear somebody saying, "I was quite the reader, quite the intellectual...." He says, "I didn't expect it, and I know you didn't want me to go, but I had to." He says it in a funny way: "My bank account was up," meaning his life was up. He had used it all. He talks about being a good mathematician. He worked with a lot of money, a lot of math, a lot of figures.

"The thing is," I stopped the tape, "that generally fits, but it's something you *could* play the odds with and say for a good show, if you were faking it."

"Is that how it struck you?"

"No. But I still can't quite wrap my head around this. Even with that specific part about the brother being there, where it's like Sasha was receiving from two entities. Spirits, whatever. And the Gregorian chants."

Why, then, did my heart feel so at peace?

Connie stood up and put her hands on the ottoman and bent over, stretching from the hips, flexing first one knee, then the other.

"Let's keep going," she said, plopping back down on the couch.

There's a mother in the physical side. Somebody's mother. They're talking about a mother and wanting to send her lots of healing.

"She definitely says 'they' in that part," Connie said. "Is that picture from Gregory's chest—the one with the young hunter and the dog—is that his brother?"

"I think so. But I'm not sure. The thing with his brother happened before I came along, and he never showed me any pictures. I could ask Elizabeth about it."

"Good idea."

There's also something about a heart problem or the stoppage of a heart, losing his grip and slipping. It's like something he didn't expect. He was very surprised. He's showing me a Coke bottle. It reminds him of a Coke bottle? He's pointing to the lettering. He says something about he was technically gone when they found him. "It was my time to go," he says. He just says again, "How did I get here?"

"This is one those passages that really touched me," I said, "even though I know it sounds fake. I mean, that's what happens when you die. Your heart stops. But I don't get the Coke bottle. He didn't drink soft drinks at all."

"Yeah, I always thought of him as kind of a health nut," Connie said. "Like he'd be the one who'd order a salad when everyone else was eating enchiladas."

"He might drink too much wine, but I don't think I ever saw him with a Coke."

"Maybe that's another question for Elizabeth."

Somebody says they loved to be tanned. He says he doesn't have to worry about that now.

"That's another zinger. It gave me chills when she said it. Gregory loved the sun, loved lying in the sun and being tan. Remember what Elizabeth said at the memorial? 'The sun was his healer.'"

There's something about throwing in the towel. Did he get shot in the head? He keeps thinking about getting shot. I'm seeing his heart stop.

I stopped the tape again.

Connie spoke first.

"Didn't you tell me Gregory nearly died after he got shot during a robbery?"

"Yes, but he was shot in the side. Hit in the liver. His *brother* was shot in the head. In the hunting accident."

"Two sons shot. God, Stella's been through a lot," Connie said quietly.

My friend stared at me, then reached out to press my hand. Her touch was warm. Tears pooled in my eyes. In Connie's, too.

"She's lost her husband and both her sons," I said. It was easy to fathom how someone forced to absorb so much loss could lose a part of their sanity. "Maybe I should be more patient with her."

"Maybe you can. Let's go back to the tape," Connie gently urged.

He said he liked to drive fast. He liked driving. He keeps talking about the car. He wants you to drive it. He keeps saying, "Drive it." He says, "She's not supposed to have the car. You are. You could sell it if you wanted to, but it's your car. It's a good car."

"Ah, the car," Connie said as I paused the tape. "He talks about the car."

"Now that part is weird," I said. "Almost an… instruction. When I went to do the paperwork for the IRA at Ben's office, he said it was probably enough for the car if I wanted it, and did I want it."

"Do you?"

"Of course I do. But there are so many other things I could do with that money…."

Now it was my turn to get up and move around. I clasped my hands behind my back to stretch my chest.

"Really?" Connie interrupted.

I shook my arms out and sank back into the cushions.

"I told Ben yes—yes, I would like to own it. I felt a little ashamed. It seemed so selfish to want the car."

"There's nothing wrong with wanting it," Connie said sternly. "Nothing at all. So stop feeling guilty."

I hit the play button.

He says, "I was a classic man, a stylish man." He liked the very best of everything—wine, cars, the good style of life. He says, "I also liked good restaurants. Don't forget that."

"Another specific reference," I said. "He was a Neiman's-Ferragamo kind of guy. That thing about restaurants feels like it was aimed right at me. Going out to eat and watching people was one of our favorite pastimes."

I thought back to our favorite patio table at an Italian place. It overlooked the valet stand. We loved watching the swells come and go.

Somebody likes to ride horses. He's talking about riding horses. She's either wanting a relationship or marriage? A relationship? How old is she? She's too young for a relationship. He says tell her not to worry about me.

"Is he talking about Olivia? And her horses?" Connie looked baffled. "But the part about a relationship makes no sense."

"Actually, it does," I said. "I hear this as like a split-second interpretation on Sasha's part. Things coming at her, and her talking almost stream of consciousness. This is something no one would've caught except me or Olivia. It goes back to when she and Gregory first met, when Olivia was seven. Olivia had a crush on him and wanted to marry him when she grew up. She changed her mind after he played too rough once and pissed her off. The 'Puke' incident."

"Good grief," Connie said. "That's subtle. And I don't think anyone could make that up."

We reached the point in the tape where Sasha invited me to ask a question of the spirit, if I wanted to.

I said, *What do I do about Stella?*

The answer was swift: *Spirit says she's telling a lot of people you're trying to get things away from her. She's seeing herself as a victim against you. I feel like this woman is not all right in her head. He's pointing to her head. He just says, "Be kind but be careful."*

He says time and again he whispers in your ear that he loves you and he has always loved you from the moment you have been together. He says, "I was madly in love with you."

With that, we'd come to the end of the tape, and I switched off the recorder. We both sat back on the couch, contemplating what we had just heard.

"What do you think?" I asked.

Connie considered this, then shook her head.

"No," she said. "The question is what do you think?"

"I'm curious. Confused. I want to believe, but… I think I'm really tired right now," I said, suddenly gripped by weariness.

"It's been a long, emotional day, hasn't it?"

"Yeah."

"I think you have a little bit of a tendency to lapse into reporter mode, even in a moment like this. You want to hear my response. But yours is the one that matters."

"Yeah, I know. I'm just not sure yet what I make of this."

"Are you okay with all that's happened?"

"Not with Gregory dying. But what we've been doing here, yeah. Although there was that rough patch earlier. I'm sorry I yelled at you—and glad you came to my rescue."

"I was nudged to do that. Don't forget."

"Yeah." I smiled at my friend. "I think I need to get some rest."

Connie got up and began to gather her things, gently pushing aside Woody, who was draped over her purse.

"You've done a lot today," she said.

"Thank you so much for everything—for listening with me, for dinner…"

She smiled and pulled me up off the couch into a warm hug.

"I'll call you in the morning," she said as she left.

I felt drained. Cleansed. Elated. Subdued. Without thinking much about it, I went to the pantry looking for a candle. I found a fat olive-colored one and brought it back out to the living room along with a red Fiestaware plate and a book of matches. I put the candle on the plate and steadied it on the ottoman. Then I swiped a match, lit the wick, and turned off the lights, leaving only the flame in the moonlight coming through the sheers.

As the flame danced and bobbed, I watched from the big leather chair I'd rescued from Gregory's apartment and allowed myself to sink into my feelings. The rawness of grief had not subsided, but it was entwined with a new sense that something had broken open. Something had changed. I wanted to believe that our souls had touched, however briefly.

CHAPTER SEVENTEEN

"Oh, isn't this fun?" Stella tittered, holding up her hands and drumming her fingers together. "It's like we're having a party."

Having just come from confession, she wore high-waisted, navy bell-bottoms with a sailor look that harkened back to the 1940s. Wherever her current mind resided, her fashion sense lived in the past. Wanda, looking more mantis-like than I remembered, sat across from us in the TV lounger. Princess made barky-whining sounds, as if she didn't want to be there.

"Hush now," Wanda said, bending down to hold the dog's muzzle in her hand and stare into her eyes. Princess hushed.

Ben had pressed me about whether I wanted to buy the Celica, and after the reading, I was sure it was the right thing to do. That's how we came to be gathered—Ben, Stella, Wanda, Olivia, and I—in Stella's overstuffed den, beneath a pall of smoke from Wanda's cigarette habit. Judging from the pervasiveness of the stale odor, I guessed the two neighbors had been seeing a lot of each other. I was wedged next to Olivia, who had asked if she could come along, at one end of the oversized sofa. Stella sank into the other end. With the flamboyance of a ringmaster, Ben held court from in front of the fireplace.

"Let's get on with this," he said, taking up half the space in the room not because he was so large, but because of the way he loomed. I scanned the mantel behind him for the box containing Gregory's ashes. It was no longer there among the photographs and memorabilia. Stella must have somehow gotten them buried in the family plot, probably with more of Ben's intervention—the same way he had taken over the funeral arrangements and was here to orchestrate the selling of the beloved Celica. I sensed in him the same fealty I'd seen in Gregory to the cultural imperative about taking care of women. Especially mothers. As Stella's closest living male relative, he was bound by this code.

His assertive nature, which had annoyed me during the memorial arrangements, gave me cover with this dubious gathering. You could say he brought a measure of control to unruly elements. Kept wandering minds focused. Badgered parties toward a goal. His goal. To sell the car. Which in this case coincided with my desire to buy the car. Despite misgivings about the parties gathered for this exchange, I was certain I was doing the right thing. So certain after the reading with Sasha that I drove Olivia and myself to the proceedings in the coveted automobile. It was parked out on Stella's driveway next to Ben's black

Mercedes, and it would belong to us when we drove it home.

"Now you're here because...?" Ben began, scrutinizing Wanda and pushing back a straight, slick lock that had fallen over his eye.

"I'm Wanda, Stella's next-door neighbor," she said, stroking Princess's head. "I'm her friend."

"I still don't get why you're here."

It was like he could bellow softly. Even at a perfectly civilized volume, his voice resonated and bounced around the room.

"Stella asked me to come," Wanda said, drawing up into the lounger and casting a glance across at Stella on the couch.

"Yes. Yes, I did," Stella said, looking for a moment like a startled chipmunk. "She's my friend."

"Okay. Whatever," Ben boomed.

Before Ben took complete control of the proceedings, Wanda puffed herself up to ask, "Will you please explain to me how Ann ended up with that money?" Wanda was talking about the funds from Gregory's IRA, the same funds that were making it possible for me to purchase the Celica.

"Gregory named her the beneficiary," Ben said, then turned to me. "It was a surprise to me, too."

When Wanda noticed Olivia's bewildered expression, her tone eased. "It's nothing against your mother," she said, stroking her gentle dog. "We just figured any *estate* would go to Stella."

My daughter said nothing. I was beginning to regret bringing her.

"I understand," I interjected. "I had no idea he even had an IRA."

I tried to envision Gregory filling out the document and signing it when he opened the account. He wasn't expecting to die. I imagined him thinking about us and smiling. Then deciding to write my name there, an affirmation of our future together.

"I don't think it's right," Wanda muttered, crossing her arms.

"But that's how it is," Ben said. "And if I understand correctly, Ann and Stella have agreed on a price for the car, and we have a sale here. Am I right?"

I sighed. Ben was used to being right.

"We talked a few days ago," I said, as much to Wanda as to Ben. "I told Stella I probably couldn't pay the blue book value, but if she could see her way clear to lowering the price to what I could afford, I'd take good care of the car. Like Gregory did. The money from the IRA made it possible for me to do this."

"Now isn't that sweet?" Stella said to no one in particular. She seemed positively sunny.

"But, Stella, that's not what you told me," Wanda snapped. "You told me she was trying to Jew you down and steal it from you."

Wanda's voice had an edge, no matter how hard she tried to curtail it.

Olivia's eyes grew wide at the word "Jew" used as a verb and looked up at me. Something else to explain later.

Wanda took out a cigarette and started to light it. "Anybody mind if I smoke?" she said without waiting for an answer.

Olivia made a squeaking sound, and I squeezed her hand.

"Fine, fine. You smoke," Ben said, oblivious to Olivia's truncated objection. Truth is, I wasn't crazy about her smoking in the small, stuffy room, either. I just wanted to get on with it.

"May I have a glass of water?" Olivia piped up, stifling a cough.

"Why, of course you can," Stella said in a motherly tone suggesting how she might have spoken to her boys when they were young.

She rose from her end of the couch, marched into the kitchen, and brought back water in a jelly jar.

"Thank you," Olivia said, downing the water and sinking deeper into the couch.

"Can we get back to the business at hand?" said Ben, who had seated himself on the hearth in front of the fireplace.

He leaned forward, elbows on knees, car title in one hand and pen in the other. Now we were getting somewhere. I had the feeling that in other settings, he'd be holding a cigar and a glass of scotch.

"So what's the price you agreed on?"

"Seven thousand dollars," I said.

That left about three thousand to pay the taxes and have a tiny nest egg.

"And it's worth what?" Ben asked, raising his eyebrows.

"It's worth about eleven thousand," Wanda sniffed.

"Yes, it is," Stella chimed in. "It's a very nice car."

Eyes alert, she sat forward with her hands folded in her lap like I imagined she once did as a child behind her desk in school.

"But you agreed to sell it to Ann here for seven thousand." Ben grilled Stella. "Is that right, Aunt Stella?"

He didn't try to conceal his impatience. Crescents of sweat ringed his white shirt under the armpits.

"When did I agree to do that?" Stella said.

Princess let out a sharp yip. Olivia was so startled she dropped the empty jelly jar on the carpet.

I reached down instinctively, perhaps too quickly, and righted the jar, searching my brain for some way to extricate Olivia from something far more awkward than I'd anticipated. But my daughter was ahead of me.

"Can I pet her?" she asked, looking at Wanda.

"Sure," Wanda said.

My daughter crouched down next to Princess, whose tail started thumping on the matted shag carpet.

"She likes you, honey," Wanda said, warming to Olivia.

"She's nice," Olivia offered back.

Ben cleared his throat.

"Can we get on with this?"

"We talked on the phone a few days ago, Stella," I said in a jittery rush of words. Geez, did I need to record my conversations with her? Was she this prone to forgetting?

I couldn't put my finger on it, but it seemed like the mood in the room had shifted.

"We did?" Stella eyed me with suspicion. "I don't remember talking to you," she said, shaking her head slowly from side to side.

Silence. Ben tapped his foot. Why was everyone looking at me?

Olivia opened her mouth to speak, but I jumped in first.

"We talked a couple of times," I asserted, "and one of those calls was about the car. Remember? I told you how much it would mean to me."

My voice sounded sharp.

Stella reflected for a moment.

"We never talked about the car," she declared, slapping her knees. "I'm sure of it. And what's more, I might not want to sell it at all."

Her narrowing eyes bored right through me. What the hell was this?

"You see what I mean?" Wanda said in her best "I'm right" voice. "Stella doesn't remember any such conversation."

Wanda started coughing. Hacking, really.

All I could think about was everyone looking at me and no way to escape. I was furious at being cast as the bad guy. Furious and distressed. I fantasized about joining

Olivia and Princess on the floor. Maybe there was a way to disappear into the voluminous shag.

"Now wait a minute, Aunt Stella." Ben's voice rose, annoyed. "*You* said she was ready to buy it. *You* said you'd agreed on a price. That's what you told me."

"She told *me* they never talked," Wanda said, huff-puffing on her cigarette, her righteous certainty renewed. The lounger creaked as she changed positions.

"We *never* talked," Stella parroted. "And I'm sure she stole some things from me." Her head swiveled in my direction. "Do you still have a key to my house, Ann?"

"I do not," I said, fighting rising frustration and the urgent need to escape. "And I've never stolen anything from you. I would never do that."

I reached absently for Olivia's hand, but it wasn't there. Olivia was moored to Princess, her safe harbor.

I couldn't believe my predicament. If I stood my ground, I made Stella out to be a liar. If I didn't, it looked like I was trying to game her out of the car. Damn it, Gregory, this is crazy.

"Mom?" Olivia returned to the couch. I could feel my chest going hollow, like I might disappear. I wanted to disappear.

"I think we better go," I said, picking up my purse. I couldn't get a decent breath without gulping.

"How can we go?" Olivia wanted to know. "We drove over in Puke's car."

I burst into a coughing fit so the others wouldn't hear the nickname.

"Is somebody going to be sick?" Stella asked.

"No, no. I'm sorry. I don't know what came over me. I'm very sorry," I said. "Look, I can't stay here and listen to this." I directed my comments to Ben. "I just can't."

Then I turned to Olivia.

"We have to go."

"Now wait. WAIT," Ben roared in his best silverback voice. But it was too late. The closeness of the room, the suffocating smoke, the sting of unfair accusations, and my brittle state—not to mention disappointment... I felt I would shatter if I didn't get out of there.

"Mom, what are we doing?"

"Just come on," I said as calmly as I could. "Imverysorrywehavetogo."

"But Mom." Olivia tried to get my attention. "I heard you guys on the phone."

"Never mind. Just come on."

In little more time than it took me to string the words together, I was slamming the front door and we were heading toward Hillcrest, the street at the end of the block. It would be a long walk home.

"What'd you do that for, Mom?"

"I couldn't stand them calling me a liar," I said, wiping away tears. "I couldn't stand the disappointment of losing the car." And I was disappointed. Bitterly. Damn you, Gregory. "I felt overwhelmed. I'm sorry. I'm sorry I dragged you into it."

"What do we do now?"

"We're walking," I said. "Can't you see?"

CHAPTER EIGHTEEN

It was a long three miles to our apartment as cars whooshed past on the busy thoroughfare. Rushing home from church to catch the Cowboys game, no doubt. I pulled my jacket tighter around me. A blue norther had whipped up while we'd been at Stella's, and the cold wind stung our backs and necks as we continued walking to stay warm. With only a pullover sweater, Olivia wasn't dressed for a blustery fall stroll.

At least we had a sidewalk—not always the case in this city of cars. Cars! It's just a damned car, I tried to tell myself. But I was raging with disappointment. At some irrational level, I was certain whatever I had left of Gregory—his energy—was tied up in that car. It meant so much to him. I remembered when he bought it, how proud he was. He'd been driving an old beater when he picked me up on our first date. I barely remembered that car. What stood out was the way Gregory opened the door for me.

"What a fool I've been to think I could take Stella at her word." I bristled, forgetting Olivia was right there. "Oh, sorry, baby."

"It's okay, Mom. It was getting really weird in there. But we should have taken the car. I'm cold."

She was shivering. She was right. I could have driven the car away. This walking drama was irrational.

"Stella claimed we never talked or settled on a price!" I railed. God, was I exasperated.

"But I was there when you talked to her on the phone," Olivia said. "That's what I wanted to say. She talked so loud, I overheard. Why would she lie now?"

"I don't think she means to lie," I said carefully. "I think she gets confused. And she just lost her son."

"We lost him, too," Olivia said.

Yes, you did.

"But we're not seventy-something years old."

I wondered if there were any way to reach beyond Stella's ditziness and really connect with her.

"Are you still thirsty?" I said to Olivia as we approached a corner convenience store.

"Yeah. Kinda. I don't know."

"Well I know we're both cold. Let's get something to warm us up before we go the rest of the way." We ducked into the store and picked up a couple of hot drinks: coffee for me, hot chocolate for Olivia. The cups warmed our hands.

Once back outside, we crossed Northwest Highway and found a sun-warmed bench by the playground at a small park. Trees shielded us from the worst of the biting wind. The air was still chilly, but the sun felt good. The kids cavorting on the swings and merry-go-round didn't seem to notice the cold at all.

We'd been sitting on the bench about fifteen minutes when we were jolted by the baying of a car horn.

"Hey," blared a voice in the distance as a swarthy man waved from the driver's side of a large, predatory black sedan. Ben. We got up and walked toward him, tossing the remains of our drinks in the trash.

"I've been driving all around looking for you," he said, clearly exasperated. "How the hell did you disappear so fast?"

"Sorry," I said, standing by the car and wishing he hadn't just cursed in front of my daughter.

"We're on our way home."

I bent to look in the passenger's side window he'd opened as the wind slapped at us again.

"Want to give us a ride the rest of the way?"

"Just get in," he said.

I climbed in front, and Olivia got in back. The car was cozy, and the luxurious leather seats were warm, like someone had just been sitting in them. Ben threw the leviathan into reverse and headed back the way he'd come.

"Wait. What are we doing?" I said. "This is the wrong way."

"I'm taking you back to Aunt Stella's."

"No, you're not," I insisted. "Either take us home or stop the car. We're not going back there."

"Mom…"

Ben acted as if he hadn't heard me. Then he pulled into a church parking lot and stopped. He angled his body to face me.

"You're gonna buy a car, remember?"

"I remember being called a liar," I said, crossing my arms and unable to stifle my petulance. Ben looked huge in the driver's seat, hunched over the steering wheel.

"Aunt Stella's not a hundred percent there, if you know what I mean," Ben said, tapping an index finger to his head. "Plus, she forgets things. She means well, but she forgets."

"Wanda didn't seem to think she was forgetting."

Oh, stop it.

"She's almost as batty as Stella," barked Ben.

"I heard them on the phone," Olivia piped up.

Ben ignored her.

"Look. You want the car, right?"

"Do I ever."

"Then leave it to me. Let's get in there and get it done." He popped the car out of park and into gear.

"Just don't get up and walk out again. No matter what she says. Agreed?"

"Okay." How could I say no to my new ally?

When we got back, the den reeked of smoke. Wanda hadn't missed the opportunity to light up again.

"Mom, could I just wait outside?" pleaded Olivia, coughing and suddenly less concerned about the blustery cold.

"Yeah, sure, she can go," Ben said. "She can take the dog, too."

Wanda was indignant.

"Wait a minute...."

"They'll be okay," Ben said with a dismissive wave as he removed his overcoat. "We got business to conduct. The fewer distractions, the better."

My daughter, the distraction.

"Do you have the check?" Ben said, looking at me like he was conducting a marriage ceremony, getting all the parts and players aligned.

"Yes. It's right here," I said, retrieving an envelope containing the cashier's check from my purse.

"Stella," I said, looking toward her at the other end of the couch, "if you don't think the price is fair, say so now. I don't want you doing anything you don't want to do."

Stella looked at me as if I had just spoken to her in Chinese. Her eyes were as wide and blank as Orphan Annie's. She cocked her head to one side. "I'm doing a good thing," she said, and as she did, the outer corners of her eyes pinched up. "He was *my* son, not yours."

I glimpsed the fierce protectiveness she must have brought to the household when Gregory and his brother were growing up.

"Yes, Aunt Stella, we know he was your son."

Ben took the envelope from me, ripped it open, and examined the check before turning his attention to the title, which he pulled out of his jacket pocket.

"Here's what I'm going to do," he said. "I'm going to sign this title with Gregory's signature, and we're going to send it through that way."

I was horrified at his suggestion that we skirt the law, although I'd seen this same law-bending practicality in Gregory. Ben waved his arm in a flourish before signing the title.

"So we can avoid the red tape of putting it in Stella's name, then in your name."

"You shouldn't do it that way," said Wanda, taking a long draw and coughing without covering her mouth.

"No, but we are going to do it this way so we can get this over with," huffed Ben, turning his attention to me. "Did you get the mileage for me?"

"Yes," I said, unfolding a small piece of paper I'd kept in my pocket. "Fifty-five thousand eight hundred, give or take."

He scribbled that onto the form. Then he signed it and handed it to me.

"You mail it in like this and don't worry about it," he ordered. "It's easier this way, and no one's going to find out." He looked hard at Wanda. "Or care."

After a quick glance at his watch, he turned to Stella.

"Aunt Stella? I need you to sign this." He brandished the cashier's check and gave her the pen. "I'll put it in your account."

Obediently Stella signed and gave it back to him. Was this automatic obeisance, this bowing to bullying, an echo of her marriage to Gregory's dad? As soon as she was done signing, Ben tucked the check in his front pocket and patted it.

"Well, all right."

Ben stood up.

"Are we done here?"

We all stood, as if on silent command.

"Thank you," I said to Ben.

I was grateful he had taken charge, although I shuddered at the illegality of the signature. Then I thanked Stella as Wanda glowered at us and stubbed out one more cigarette.

Stella just stared at me. Or through me. And said nothing.

Wanda headed toward the front door, which I heard her open.

"I really like your dog," I heard Olivia say. She was stroking Princess's head and neck when I got there. Princess panted and wagged her tail.

"Thanks, honey."

"Wait," said Stella, as if a light were going on in a randomly lit marquee. "Don't you have time for some hummus and baba ghanoush?" she said to no one in particular, standing in the middle of the den. "I made some tabbouleh."

"No, no, Aunt Stella."

Ben put his hands up and reached for his overcoat by the door. "I'm watching the game with the boys, and it starts in a few minutes. Gotta go."

He gave her a peck on the cheek and strode out the front door. Poof. He was done.

"We need to go, too," I said, standing at the door with Wanda. "But thank you for the offer."

Wanda folded her arms across her chest and ignored me. All I could think about was getting out of there.

"Well, you can at least take some for dinner," Stella insisted, scurrying into the kitchen and, before I could protest, returning and pressing a greasy paper bag into Olivia's hands.

"There you go. Some of my best hummus, tabbouleh and dolmas," she said, then turned to me. "You need to come back so I can teach you how to make dolmas. They were Gregory's favorite, you know."

"Thank you. Yes, I'd like that," I said to be polite.

I doubted I'd take her up on it, but the way she was reaching out was touching and sweet.

As we walked down the stone path toward the car, Stella and Wanda waved. Princess sniffed at some leaves on the lawn. Wanda seemed resigned. I was just relieved to finally be getting away.

Once Olivia and I were in the car, we shut the doors on one world and entered another.

Now I could breathe. The Celica was ours. It was a long way from having Gregory back, but at least we had this memento, this steel-and-leather object he cared so much about.

Sasha had been right about the car, after all. Gregory had come through. And in a way I never imagined. I started the engine and slid the shifter into reverse. What a beautiful, sweet hum the engine made compared to my old sedan. It felt so good not just to drive it, but to know it was mine, even if I felt more like a custodian than an owner.

"Wow," said Olivia, opening the glove box and snapping it closed. "It's really ours."

"Yes, it is," I said triumphantly, giving it a little gas and accelerating out of the driveway and into the street.

CHAPTER NINETEEN

It took me a few days to work up to calling Elizabeth.

"I've got something I'd like to show you," I said.

"Really? What?"

"I'd rather show you in person. I think it'd be easier," I said.

"Really? Can you hint at what it is?"

"I just think it'd be easier in person."

"Fine. When?" She wasn't frosty so much as matter-of-fact.

"How about Friday?" I could take part of the afternoon off because I'd been working long nights on a story.

"Yeah, that works. But why won't you tell me what this is about?"

"It's complicated. Just... trust me." Such a weak comeback. "By the way," I said, shifting topics, "I bought Gregory's car from Stella with some IRA money he left me. I thought you'd appreciate that."

"The Celica? No shit. Good for you. She sure as hell couldn't use it. I'll bet Gregory's glad you got it."

You got that right.

"Ben helped with the transaction. Did you know Ben?"

"Oh yeah. Piece of work, that guy."

"So would you like to come over, say, on Friday, then stay for dinner with Connie and Olivia and me?"

"Yes, I'd like that."

"How does three o'clock sound?"

"Fine. See you then. This better be worth it," she added with a little laugh. I couldn't tell if she was teasing or not.

"God, I hope so."

For me, as much as for Elizabeth. I ached to believe Gregory had actually contacted me. Connie was so certain. And even my logical mind couldn't dispute that so much of what Sasha said rang true, beyond coincidence or good guesswork. But still I couldn't shake the tiny toehold of doubt. I looked forward to what Elizabeth would say after I shared the contents of the reading with her.

When Friday rolled around, I took Elizabeth to a special place on campus where we could talk uninterrupted while Connie and Olivia prepared dinner.

"This was one of our favorite spots," I said, as we settled onto a shaded, concrete-and-wooden bench at the edge of the commons. Oak trees encircling the commons had grown into stout regal giants from saplings planted when the school was still new, their stands interspersed with clusters of lacy pond cypress.

"Easy to see why," she said, looking around.

"Gregory and I used to come here and people watch," I said, gazing across the grassy patch at the center of the university where students played spontaneous pick-up games and held animated discussions.

We'd make up stories about the people we saw. Some in a hurry—head down, death grip on books. We'd imagine what class or lab they were late for. The dawdlers, they were dreamers, and we tried to guess their dreams. And it always cracked us up when we spotted some fuzzy-cheeked kid smoking a pipe, trying to look grown up. Gregory was good at making up their stories.

"We used to people watch, too," Elizabeth said, her loose auburn tresses catching the autumn sun.

Why did that not surprise me?

I'd brought a printout of the reading—which I'd cleaned up so someone else could decipher it—for now safely ensconced in a satchel.

Go slow. Give her time.

"I've driven by this a million times, thinking how inviting it looks," Elizabeth said.

"I like walking here from the apartment. Now, without Gregory, I come over by myself."

"Isn't that hard?"

"No. It's not like I just associate it with him," I said. "I still love the feeling of a campus, remembering what it was like going to college."

"Hmm," Elizabeth said, nodding. "So many possibilities. So many ways to stretch. But once you get away… life overtakes you."

"Yeah," I said. "I still can't get over all you've endured. Your beautiful daughter and—"

"I've had time to process it," Elizabeth said, putting her hand lightly on my arm to stop me. "You never get over losing a child." I could hear sadness in her voice without the rawness I felt about losing Gregory. "But time lessens the intensity of the pain. As it will for you."

I wanted to believe her.

"I don't think Gregory ever had the head space for that," she said. "To process the sadness and guilt over losing Megan, I mean. He just bottled it up."

"Things get complicated," I said, adjusting my headband to keep the fine hairs from tickling my face in the breeze.

A Frisbee came our way, and Elizabeth plucked it out of the air like an ace first baseman and flung it back. The student who'd thrown it cheered.

"So, you had something you wanted to show me?"

"I do."

I reached for the printout and took a deep breath.

"I feel like this requires some explanation," I said. "First, are you familiar with psychic readings?" I just managed to get the words out, with no clue how she'd take them.

"What, like fortune telling?" Elizabeth looked askance.

"No, no. This is different. It's where a medium—a person—supposedly tunes in to someone who's died and brings back a message."

Elizabeth continued staring at me. Nothing easy about this.

"I've heard of such things," she said at last. "Always figured it was bullshit. You aren't telling me you went to a psychic, are you?"

I stiffened against the skepticism in her voice. Maybe I was making a mistake.

"I talked to a medium. A kind of psychic, yes." There, I got it out.

"Aw, Jesus." Surprise, shock and confusion telegraphed across Elizabeth's face. Her brow clouded under copper wisps, which she absently shoved aside.

"You don't strike me as someone who'd fall for that—"

"Wait a minute." I cut her off. "Wait. I need you to hear me out. If you can't do that… we may as well stop right now."

"No, no. Sorry to jump down your throat. It's just so—" She threw up her hands.

"Delusional. I know it sounds delusional. But it's not the only woo-woo thing that's happened."

"What in the world are you talking about?"

"Connie is certain she *saw* Gregory at the service. Above the altar."

"And you believe her?"

"Yes, I do," I said firmly. "Because it's Connie. I used to tease her about her psychic streak—called her the magic Christian and stuff like that. But she's got something like a sixth sense. Seeing him rattled her. The way she described it rattled me."

"That's some crazy shit. But I suppose I have to listen now."

"Look, the only way to really do this is to suspend disbelief, just for the moment," I said, exasperation in my voice. "That's what I've been having to do. And it isn't easy. There've also been some unusual dreams and... I really want to show you this reading."

Elizabeth pursed her lips. Not convinced in the slightest, I was certain. But at least she had acquiesced.

"I went to a medium—well, I didn't actually 'go to' a medium. She did a reading long-distance. Over the phone."

"What? That sounds like a first."

"I have a selfish goal in this," I continued, ignoring her sarcasm. "I want to find out if anything she said means anything to you." I handed her the printout.

"Is this like that John Edward guy?" she said after giving it a once-over.

"Yes," I said. "Have you read his book?"

"Hardly. Just heard about it someplace. On *Oprah* or something. Sounded pretty far-fetched."

"I thought so, too. Before this."

Breathe.

"But there are moments in the reading... and now I'm not so sure. Connie got me to do it. She witnessed this medium in person and definitely believes she's legit."

"Connie again. You must really put a lot of faith in her."

"I do."

"I think I need to know this Connie better."

"Anyway, after our last meeting—yours and mine—I felt like, you know, you and I made a strong connection. And I thought maybe there's information that would resonate with you." Which would help confirm that it was Gregory coming through.

"Can I take it with me?"

"Yes… but with the understanding that it's only for you. Not to share."

She gave a little snort—like "Really?"—and studied the printout more intently.

As prickly as Elizabeth could be, it felt good to be with her. Or more precisely, I hurt less in her presence. As much as I could bare my soul to Connie, here was a woman who understood loving Gregory at a visceral level. When I looked in her eyes, I believed I could see a reflection of the love I felt for him. The love I felt for Olivia reflected in her love for Megan, although I still could not completely wrap my heart around her loss.

A gust of wind rustled the pages in her hands.

"My God," Elizabeth said, letting out a gasp.

"What is it?"

"This part about the brother is just plain spooky." She looked away, brow creased, as if less certain of her doubts. She put the reading down. "Did you know about Bubba?"

"Just what Gregory told me. That he had a brother he wasn't close to who was killed in a hunting accident."

"That's always been his story," Elizabeth said. "His and Ben's. But that's not what this says. It's more like the whispered story. How strange to specify suicide. That's creepy."

"Are you saying it *was* a suicide?" I asked.

"Not one-hundred-percent sure either way," she said, "but the party line—that it was an accident—was pretty cut-and-dried. People shut down—more like clammed up—anytime I wanted to know more. Eventually I stopped asking. But maybe it wasn't BS."

"Did Stella know?" I asked.

"Good question. Everyone sure as hell tried to keep it from her."

"You know, this would explain some of Stella's possessiveness toward Gregory," I said. "And I'd think losing him would magnify both losses. You lost your daughter, which is horrible. Stella lost both her sons. Even if just for a moment, doesn't that make you sad for her?"

"No, I never thought of her that way," Elizabeth said. "She's still Stella."

"Do you think this is related to the photo in the chest?" I asked. "The one we think is Bubba and his dog?"

"I wouldn't be surprised. It's so odd how it was trimmed on one side, like someone cut something off."

"I noticed that, too."

"The two of them were so different," Elizabeth said, "if Gregory's to be believed. Bubba was a social wannabe. Gregory was studious and athletic. He resigned himself to being an outsider in their richy-rich, whitey-white neighborhood. But Bubba wanted in. Did Gregory tell you about the time the police found Bubba dancing down the middle of Preston Road? When he was in high school? High as a kite?"

"No. Never."

"Figures. I can only imagine there was a knockdown, drag-out in the Malouf household that night. Each parent blamed the other for Bubba's 'problems.' Gregory told me that much."

"And kept a picture of him. Bubba, I mean."

"Yeah, Mister No-Photos-Please. He didn't like to be in them, and he didn't like to keep them. At least he said he didn't."

"I actually hate that. I have so few to remember him by."

"To be honest, my impression was that by the time we got together, he just didn't give Bubba or his death much thought. And as you must have figured out by now, this isn't exactly a forthcoming family. They disliked outsiders, and Stella and I both qualified. We would never crack their tribal circle."

I got a queasy feeling.

"Plus, Stella took up so much space in his life. When we were married, it was like I was married to Stella, too. And that damned liquor store. For whatever reason, he couldn't break free. Couldn't live with her and couldn't live without her."

"Why did you put up with it?" I asked.

She cast a stern look my way.

"Why did *you* put up with it?"

"He convinced me that she wasn't part of our future plans," I stammered. "He was always talking about what we were going to do together. Our future together."

"Ha. She'd have found a way to weasel in." Our conversation was reprising Elizabeth's bitterness.

"But he did move away from her," I said. "Two months before he died."

"You loved him that much, didn't you?" Elizabeth said. "And you just hoped he'd somehow slip free of her."

"Oh, what, and you didn't?"

"Point taken."

"There's so much of this I didn't know," I retorted in mild protest. "And I didn't interact much with Stella—like he tried to keep us apart."

"Lucky you. Well he didn't shield me. He brought it home. Every night."

Elizabeth face flushed with fierce warrior anger.

"You know the business card from the Oklahoma cemetery that's in the chest? That's where I buried Megan while Gregory was still at Parkland with the gunshot wound. It's where a lot of my family is buried. Much, much later, he begged his mother to let Megan be moved to the Malouf family plot here in Dallas. That's how much he loved my daughter. And me. Do you know what Stella's answer was?"

"What?"

"'NO.'" Elizabeth spat out the word. "'She's no kin of mine.' Snapped her fingers in his face. When he got home, he was devastated. Again. 'I don't know what I'm going to do,' he told me. 'I hate her so much.' He was furious. And heartbroken. It was the second time I'd seen him cry."

We sat in silence.

"Let's get back to the reading," Elizabeth said and returned to flipping through the printout, this time more carefully. "I've never had anyone to talk to about this with," she said, "and it's like pulling a scab off an old wound."

"Is there anything else in the reading that stands out to you?" I hungered to hear the words that would align in my heart like the right key in a tumbler.

"Oh, yeah." She smiled, less agitated. "I love the part about the sun and wanting to be tanned. Some things never change. And he was a classic man. Yeah. He was that."

I nodded in recognition.

"Do those seem like coincidences to you?" I asked.

"I don't know. I just don't know. . . ."

She wasn't as openly hostile as she had been at first, as she seemed to drift further into her own feelings.

"There was a heart in him," she began, her brassiness muted, "that never seemed like it could fully open. Like he was always in defensive mode. And from such a young age. No thanks to that family of his. . . . I wish I still smoked."

Elizabeth looked at me and mustered a sad grin.

"Did he tell you about the earring incident? When he was a little kid?"

"I don't think so."

"Johnny came home one afternoon raging and bellowing, he says, and Bubba ran and hid under his bed. But when Johnny started grabbing at Stella's ears, grabbing to tear the diamond earrings out of them because he was wanted to pawn them, Gregory—like seven years old—wedged himself between the two adults and demanded his father stop. 'That's no way to treat a lady,' he said." Elizabeth paused, wiping away a tear. "Then Johnny smacked him, and Stella smacked Johnny."

"Oh my God, that's horrible. What a horrible way to grow up."

"Gregory could be harsh like them," she said, referring to the Lebanese clan, "but there was a sweetness about him I never saw in the rest. I remember one time at a Christmas party at another 'cousin's' house after we got married. Stella and all the extended family were there. We went in separate cars because Gregory had come from the store with several cases of booze, and I had just dropped Megan off to spend the night at a friend's. I get there, and it's everything Gregory hates: the big gaudy house, schmoozing, lots of drinking, a cigar haze, all with a Middle Eastern oud throbbing in the background. He unloaded the liquor in the kitchen, shot me a quick glance, and slipped out the back door.

"I stayed a little longer, perplexed he'd left so quickly. But he did things like that. I learned not to question. Pretty soon, no one at the party was talking to me—you know, the outsider he married—and I figured I could slip out without being noticed.

"When I pulled up in the drive behind his car, everything at home was dark except the front walk leading up to the house. He'd lined the entire length with luminarias, each paper bag illuminated by a single candle. It took my breath away. Gregory had decided this was more important than the Christmas party. When I got to the front porch, he was sitting on the porch swing, waiting for me."

She paused, lost in the memory.

"You know that faded paper bag in his secret chest?" Elizabeth swallowed hard. "That was one of the luminarias."

I was touched anew at his tenderness—his exquisite, hidden, protected tenderness.

"Maybe this would be a good place to stop for now," I murmured.

As the sun began to dip from view, we made our way back to the apartment. Just before crossing the street between the campus and my complex, we paused to admire the evening sky, streaked with giant clouds the color of pink champagne.

"Wait," Elizabeth said, taking hold of my arm just before we started crossing the street and pulling me to sit on a bench.

"What is it?"

"The Coke bottle." She locked eyes onto mine, refusing to let me evade her gaze. "Did he ever tell you about the cocaine incident?"

"What? No." I said. Cocaine? She couldn't mean Gregory.

"I wouldn't think so. It happened before Megan got sick, when we were making a lot of money skimming at the liquor store and managing Stella at arm's length. Dallas was such a Rolex and Mercedes town, and coke was freely available if you knew the right people. Cheap, too. Did we indulge? You bet."

"So you think that's what the Coke bottle's about?" I asked.

"I do. It so fits. But I bet he never told you about the coke incident. Scared the pants off him. Me, too. That part about losing his grip and slipping right here." She pointed to a page and started reading: "*There's also something about a heart problem or the stoppage of a heart, losing his grip and slipping. It's like something he didn't expect. He was very surprised. He's showing me a Coke bottle. It reminds him of a Coke bottle? He's pointing to the lettering.*"

"What did you think that meant?" Elizabeth asked.

"That he probably lost his grip on the staircase and slipped and stumbled onto the landing in front of his door before he died. I couldn't really figure out the Coke bottle."

"That's what makes this so-called psychic stuff so slippery," Elizabeth said. "You made an assumption. But I am almost certain, if this thing's real, this refers to an incident when we had some friends over and were hanging out in the front yard. We'd done some lines, and the other couples had moved to the lawn. He and I were popping beers, and he stumbles backward and catches himself on the fender of the Mercedes. Drops his beer and grabs his chest and crumples to his knees. I freaked and said, 'What the heck was that?' And he says, 'It felt like my heart stopped.' There was terror in his voice. In his eyes. I'd never seen him shaken like that. After I helped him get up, one of the guys came over, made a sarcastic remark about dropping his beer, and handed him another. Gregory and I locked eyes briefly, but he'd already flipped back into charm mode. That was it. Nothing was ever said again."

I was at turns exasperated and incredulous at all the things Elizabeth was telling me. Things that Gregory had conveniently left out of his story. It was like we each knew different versions of the same man.

"Frankly, I doubt it crossed his mind to tell you," she said. "To him, it was a closed chapter. Over. Done. He probably saw no reason to open it again. With you or anyone."

"It didn't bother you that he might have had a heart attack?" I said.

"Hell yes, it bothered me. But we had enough issues, what with Stella and the liquor store."

Stella. Stella. Stella.

"Thank you for being so candid," I said, touched by her frankness. "I can see why he loved you. You went through some unspeakably hard times together."

"I'm just glad he found something like redemption with you before he died," she said.

"What do you mean, redemption?"

"He always thought he failed Megan. Not being there with her when she died. Not able to bring her down from Oklahoma. But he found another little girl to love, your daughter, and it seems like he was really trying to clean up his life. He lived way closer to the edge with me. And you got him to leave Stella. That was big."

My first urge was to deflect her words. I couldn't escape the feeling—knowing what I knew now—that I pushed him too hard, expected too much. Yet another person expecting too much. Maybe I set too high a bar for integrity and respect. I flashed on the time I told him I couldn't keep my heart open if he yelled at me. He never raised his voice again. Had he broken the pattern from father to son? Or had he simply buried that part of himself, leaving it to lie unattended and festering? I couldn't see past my own guilt. And what of Stella? For all her faults, she seemed more than ever like a wounded bird, alone in the world.

"I think I know what I need to do now," I said.

"What do you mean?"

"Stella asked me over to make dolmas," I said, watching the light fade. "Maybe I could connect with her then. I could bring the reading and the Saint Christopher, maybe bring them up if there's an opportune moment. Best-case scenario, I could share a little bit about the reading. I mean, don't Catholics already believe in mysticism? Wouldn't that be a good thing? To bring her a message from both her sons? So she'd feel less tortured and alone?"

"I'd rather walk through a pit of rattlesnakes. Barefoot."

"You don't think it'd help her? I think it would."

"I think it's a bad idea."

We crossed the street to the apartment complex just as the street lights were coming on. Connie and Olivia greeted us at the front door with sparkling wine and canapes: smoked salmon and cream cheese on crostini and skewers of baby tomatoes, basil, and mozzarella. The air was scented with marinara sauce simmering on the stove. Connie had started dinner, and Olivia had been helping her since getting home from school. I could also smell garlic toast crisping under the broiler.

"Hi," Olivia said, proffering the appetizer tray.

"Your timing is perfect," Connie said, handing each of us a glass.

"I don't think you two have met," I said, looking from Elizabeth to Connie.

"Elizabeth, this is my good friend, Connie," I said. "Connie, Elizabeth."

The two women exchanged greetings as we all sat down in the living room.

"These are so good," I said, taking a crostini. "You guys make a great team."

"Did you have a nice walk?" Connie asked.

"We did," I said.

"Did you go to the bench on the commons?" Olivia wanted to know.

"Yes, we did," Elizabeth said, wiping crumbs from her lips with a napkin. "Do you like that bench?"

"Not so much," Olivia said. "I'd rather run on the grass. With a kite."

"Is that something you and Gregory used to do?" Elizabeth said, patting a spot on the couch next to her.

"Oh yeah. But what I really like..."

Connie and I exchanged a quick glance and slipped out of the room to finish preparing dinner.

The evening turned out wonderful at every level. Salad, spaghetti, garlic toast, and Chianti for the grown-ups. Relaxed conversation—a break from the intensity. Without having planned it that way, I had pulled Elizabeth together with the two most important "women" in my life: Connie and Olivia. It felt like a circle was complete.

After we said our goodbyes, Olivia retreated to her room for homework while I picked up the phone and dialed Stella's number. She answered right away.

"Hello?"

"Stella, this is Ann. How are you doing?"

"Why I'm fine," Stella replied warmly.

"Listen," I began, "you know how you invited me to make dolmas with you?"

"Yes?"

"I think I'd like to take you up on that."

"Oh, Ann, that would be wonderful!"

At last, I was making progress.

CHAPTER TWENTY

Stuffed grape leaves, a traditional Middle Eastern appetizer, were Gregory's favorite food, especially the ones his mother made. Filled with lamb and rice and dashed with a squeeze of lemon juice, Stella's dolmas were savory and satisfying. Perhaps something lasting would come of our dolma-making if all went well. Perhaps the beginning of a new tradition—a connection that would benefit both of us.

I announced myself with a rap on the side door, which led to her kitchen.

"Yes," Stella called from inside. "Just let yourself in."

"Hi," I said, slipping off my coat and laying it over one of the chrome dinette chairs in the breakfast nook. A printout of the reading plus the Saint Christopher medal were tucked safely in my purse, which I set down next to my coat.

One by one, Stella was sizing up the ingredients already laid out on the counter: the grape leaves, the onions, the garlic, fresh mint, and lemons. The pine nuts. The currants. She slipped her crooked thumb through the seal on one of the brown paper packages, folding it back and smiling approvingly at the glistening ground lamb. She did the same with the second package, filled with wafer-thin lamb chops.

"Oh yes," Stella pronounced. "These will do nicely."

Stella seemed to blossom in her kitchen and had chosen an especially festive outfit for our cooking lesson—a jaunty red June Cleaver frock from the '50s with fade marks down the shoulders from long confinement to a clothes hanger. It had a V-neck and flared skirt. She protected it with a dainty white cocktail apron from the same era.

She might have been an artist or sculptor lining up her paints or tools, so intent was her focus on the task at hand. A rush of appreciation flooded me. Unlike the ditzy woman bordering on dementia I kept encountering since the surgery, this one seemed present and assured. Maybe this was where the real Stella would emerge.

"This is one of Gregory's favorite dishes," she said with authority.

"Yes," I said. "The ones he shared with me were always delicious, and I'm glad I'll get to see how you make them."

I didn't mention the ones she'd given to Olivia after the near disaster of the car purchase. No need to revisit that day.

"You can even take notes if you want," she added cheerfully, "you being a writer and all. It wasn't like that when Johnny made me learn from the shrews in his family. Put that apron on."

"What was different?" I asked, reaching for the granny smock on a peg by the door. I slipped it over my head and tied it at the waist.

"Those Lebanese, they stick together. Like thieves." Stella cackled and pushed the hair off her jowling face with the back of her hand. "Wouldn't let me in."

"So where do we start?" I asked.

"You can start by chopping the onions," Stella instructed, handing me a cutting board and knife.

I started chopping and almost immediately my eyes stung. The knife was as dull as a letter opener and mashed the onions as much as cut them, releasing a surge of fumes. Gamely I pressed ahead, stopping occasionally to dab at my eyes.

"What a pack of hyenas they were," Stella continued, back on family.

"What was so bad about them?" I asked. "Seems like learning to cook from your new family would be a wonderful way to get acquainted."

She took a battered soup pot out of a lower cabinet and, after balancing it unsteadily on the vintage Tappan range, poured a thin stream of olive oil into it. She moved about the kitchen with surprising agility considering she'd just had surgery, displaying only a slight awkwardness when she bent down to fetch things.

"Get acquainted? Oh, no. They didn't accept me. I wasn't *Lebanese*. They were determined to make it as difficult as possible for me," she said. "They wouldn't tell me how much of anything they were using or even what they were doing," she said, waggling a finger in my face.

"I'm so sorry."

As I mash-chopped the onions, Stella methodically prepared the other ingredients, explaining each step and browning the ground lamb last. Wonderful aromas wafted up from the pot, and I forgot about my stinging eyes.

"They rushed around and pushed me aside like a child. And when I took out a tablet and pencil, they all said, 'Oh, no, no, no. *Secret.*'"

"What was so secret?"

"Nothing!" She threw her hands up. "They just wanted me to know that I was an outsider. Not how I'm treating you. Made my life miserable any way they could. Deliberately made it hard for me to learn the recipes. But I showed them. Yes I did. Now my dolmas are better than theirs," she added triumphantly.

"Or they would be." She shook her head. "Most of those old hens are dead."

Stella was more animated than I'd ever seen her, almost dancing around the kitchen, completely absorbed by the dolma-making, and happily so. She was seasoning the meat with oregano, mint, garlic, and something I couldn't identify.

"Is that lemon I smell?" I asked.

"No. No lemon yet. You must mean the sumac. A Lebanese spice. It was so difficult to get when Johnny and I first got married. And I hated asking his mother for it."

"Why'd you have to do that?"

"Because she got it from back east and would lord it over me. She was worse than all the cousins put together. Made me beg for it. Doled it out like it was saffron. But I showed her, too. I did a little research—I'm very good at research, you know—and figured out how to get it myself and never ask her for it again."

Chatty Stella. Gossipy Stella. This was new, and I didn't know quite what to make of it. Now that we were out from under the immediate aftermath of Gregory's death, maybe she was more herself. Maybe we were finally getting somewhere with this bonding thing. Once I'd finished chopping the onions, she took the cutting board and scraped them off into the pot. Mindful not to touch my eyes, I waited for my next instruction.

"There were times I second-guessed myself for marrying Johnny," Stella sighed, leaning against the counter. "But he was so dashing when we met. And he took me to the nicest places. He swept me off my feet."

I knew so little of Stella's story except the thin gruel Gregory doled out, and I was beginning to suspect it might have been just as distorted as his depiction of Elizabeth. He told me Stella came from Philadelphia after the war. Gregory was particularly proud of the fact that she had worked at Neiman Marcus, first in retail and then as a model, making enough money to buy her own house—unheard of for a woman in that era.

As Stella continued sharing the details of Johnny's courtship, I was reminded of how charming Gregory had been with me, the acorn surely not unlike the oak.

"I'll never forget the time Johnny threw his coat down over a mud puddle for me to walk over," Stella said. "Can you imagine? Just like in the movies! It cost a fortune to clean."

She continued stirring the fragrant, sizzling concoction in the pot.

"You and I share something in common," I said. "We both fell for Malouf men."

"When we were first married, we had the babies one after the other," she said, dreamlike. "Gregory was first, Andrew was second." It was the first time I'd ever heard his brother's given name. "We all called Andrew 'Bubba' because that's how Gregory said 'brother.'" Visions of toddler Gregory in those little shoes struggling with the big word flickered across my mind.

"They must have been so cute together."

"Oh, they were." Stella seemed to warm to the thought. "My little men."

Once the meat and onions were done, Stella scraped the mixture into a bowl next to the other ingredients, all prepped and ready except the lemons. Then she turned to browning the chops in the same pot, adding more of the aromatic seasonings.

"This is one of the things that makes mine so good, the way I use the lamb chops," Stella said, as searing meat perfumed the air. "Now it's time to get the lemons ready. Can you juice those?"

Dutifully, I complied.

"What was Gregory like as a boy?"

"Oh, he was darling. So intense. Polishing those little shoes before school. Nose stuck in a book—or shooting baskets with his pal Bobby. Telling me to pack bologna sandwiches instead of dolmas for his lunch. He just wanted to fit in."

Once the chops were done, Stella turned off the heat and removed all but six of them to a platter on the counter, tendrils of steam curling off them under the cabinets.

"When we finish rolling the grape leaves, we'll put those other chops on top and the juices will drip down," she said.

Her attention returned to the pot, where she worked the remaining lamb chops into a single layer.

Was making dolmas pleasant, I wondered, because it reminded her of Gregory and happier times? Or was her mood brighter because we were on her turf, where she felt more at ease and in charge than anyplace else? She seemed patient, even generous, as we worked together to make the grape leaves, as she called them.

We set up an assembly line, starting with Stella pulling individual grape leaves from their jar and smoothing them out flat. I spooned a bit of ground meat, rice, pine nuts and currants onto them. Stella rolled each one expertly, laying them in neat rows on top of the lamb chops in the pot.

"Now here," she said, stepping back from the counter. "You try it."

We traded places.

I flattened out the grape leaf just as I'd watch her do, and she added the filling ingredients. She observed me closely as I slid the filling toward the bottom of the leaf and tucked the sides in, rolling it up to keep the grape leaf tight.

The leaf split.

"No, no," she said. "Roll it snug, but not so tight that it breaks."

She elbowed me out of the way, took a fresh leaf and laid the split one on top of it. I marveled as her fingers moved expertly to wind the new leaf over the old just tight enough.

"You'll learn in time." Into the pot it went. "See? Now you try it again." She stepped back, crossed her arms and waited.

This time, I managed a lopsided dolma. Stella started scooping the filling onto the other leaves I laid out, and I rolled my lumpy, imperfect dolmas, adding them to hers in the pot. When we finished the last one, she took a fork and began laying the remaining lamb chops on top to cover all the dolmas. Then she poured the juice from the platter over them, followed by lemon juice. The aroma was intoxicating.

"Now here's another important trick," she said, as if I were a co-conspirator.

She took out a dinner plate, turned it over, and pressed down lightly on the lamb chops.

"You leave the plate on top while they cook. That way, all the juices get absorbed in the grape leaves. They come out so good. So perfect for my baby."

She covered the pot, lowered the heat, and set the timer.

"Let's go sit in the den, shall we?" she said as she wiped her hands on her apron. "I'll bring some water."

Traces of stale smoke still clung to the den furniture. We sat on the couch, which seemed much more comfortable this time. Glancing up at the mantel, I noticed an unfamiliar photo of Gregory and Bubba.

"Is that new, Stella, that picture of Gregory and Bubba?" I said, sipping my water. "I don't remember seeing it before."

"Well, the photo's not new. But yes, I did just put it up there."

"Is it a particular favorite of yours?"

Her face brightened. "Yes," she said, looking at it across the room. "They were all dressed up for Easter, and I've always loved their little faces in that picture. I found it the other day in a drawer."

Everything felt so cozy, I decided it was now or never if I were going to share the reading with her, though a tiny voice inside urged caution. I shushed it.

"Stella," I began tentatively, "do you ever wonder where Gregory is? If he's at peace?"

"Why, he's in heaven," she said firmly. "He was a good boy. That's where he would go."

"I wish I had your certainty," I said, "about what happens after we pass."

Stella's face twisted into a fleeting frown.

"Aren't you a Christian?" Stella said.

"I'm... not as certain a Christian as you are." My parents had made me go to Sunday school and I'd been baptized. But after my mother died, my dad turned completely away from religion. Retreated into his intellect. And his new wife.

"I suppose I do wonder a little bit if he's okay," Stella offered, as if my uncertainty gave her room to open up.

"I feel like I might have found some answers," I said, "but not in the way you might expect. Do you remember I told you I had something I wanted to share with you?"

"Oh, I hope it's a present," Stella enthused. "I love presents."

"It's like a gift from Gregory."

"From Gregory? What kind of gift would that be?" she said, toying with the edge of her cocktail apron and regarding me suspiciously.

Could she see my heart drumming against my ribcage? The sheen of sweat on my forehead? It felt as if I were about to walk across a suspension bridge that was already swaying in the wind. A little voice whispered, "Don't do it," but I snuffed it out like one of Wanda's cigarettes. Everything had fallen into place for this moment like kismet. It had to be right.

"I talked to a woman in Oregon," I began tentatively. "She says she can talk to souls that have passed from this life."

"She can do what? That doesn't make any sense," Stella sniffed, shaking her head.

Right words, right words.

"She has... psychic abilities," I said, feeling the suspension bridge tremble beneath my feet.

"Psychic? Yes? Well, what is that?" Stella looked at me blankly.

"A very dear friend suggested I contact her," I continued, as if I could not stop the stream of words once it was flowing. "Her words were so comforting to me. I thought you might find comfort in them, too.

"I was very skeptical at first. But afterwards I was convinced that she actually made contact with Gregory. And not only him, but his brother, too."

Stella's eyes widened.

"What are you saying?" She folded her arms. "That's not possible."

"Wait," I said. "Hear me out. Let me read some of the passages to you so you can see for yourself. I have a printout of what she said. Let me get it."

I hurried into the kitchen.

"I'm not sure about this," Stella called after me. "It doesn't sound right."

"It's okay. It really is. I'll be right back."

I didn't expect her to instantly believe it was Gregory and Bubba. But I was hopeful she would recognize Gregory in the reading and take solace in that.

I got the printout from my purse and pocketed the Saint Christopher in my apron, just in case that came up, then returned to sit back down with her.

"It is something called a reading," I said, ignoring the darkening storm in her eyes. "I talked to the medium in Oregon," I said, then corrected myself. "I wasn't *in* Oregon. We did this by phone. I wouldn't have ever tried it, much less believed it, except my friend had watched her work and was convinced she was the real deal."

"Real deal what?" Stella asked with clipped words.

"Real psychic. Real medium," I said in a hushed tone. "I know it must sound terribly odd. But I thought there would be no harm in trying."

I rattled on, ignoring Stella's reaction, then turned to a specific page of the printout.

"See? Look at this part about his fast car."

I showed her while holding out the printout.

"Or about how stylish he was. How he liked to be tanned. Loved the sun. Doesn't that sound like the Gregory we knew? And then there's the part about the two brothers. A brother came through and spoke, too. I wasn't expecting that, you know?"

Stella sat stone-faced.

She glanced at the place on the mantel where Gregory's ashes had been but were now replaced by the photo of the boys. Then, without warning, she grabbed the printout from my hands.

"Let me see that," she snapped.

She put her glasses on and twisted away from me.

"How can you think this has anything to do with my boy?" she snarled. "And why did you circle that?"

Shit. She was looking at the part about Bubba. I had to get the printout back. But she deliberately held it away from me. The bridge shook beneath my feet.

"There's one that's committed suicide," Stella read out loud. "There's a brother here with this person that committed suicide...."

"Suicide!" Stella slammed the reading down—but held it fast—as her indignation flared.

"What suicide? There was no suicide," she said, voice dripping with scorn. "*No one committed suicide.* Your psychic doesn't know what she's talking about. Bubba was killed in a hunting accident. You hear? It was an accident!"

No, no, no.

"I'm sorry, Stella," I said, scrambling to recover the printout. But she continued, gripping it tight. It was too late. She couldn't unsee the words.

"You're making a lot out of nothing," Stella said. "NOTHING."

Before either of us could say another word, the timer went off in the kitchen, jangling my nerves like a minor explosion.

"Time to check on those dolmas." Stella broke off abruptly, tossing the printout aside and scurrying to the kitchen. It felt like the sides of the suspension bridge were coming loose from their moorings, and I was about to plunge into the abyss. Stella seemed to have gained renewed vigor. Not because she believed the reading but because opposition fueled her. Was this how she found the strength to face off with her abusive husband?

Shit, shit, shit.

The smoke alarm started trilling, and I rushed into the kitchen. Something was burning. I could smell that the lamb chops under the dolmas were scorching.

I lunged past Stella and turned off the flame, swiftly grabbing a couple of pot holders and shifting the pot to a back burner. In her haste to reduce the heat, Stella had turned it up instead of down.

"Don't push me," Stella said, rooted where she stood. I was close enough to smell her sweat mingled with perfume.

"I'm sorry," I said, not feeling very sorry, "but the dolmas were starting to burn. The lamb chops."

"It was your fault," Stella said, sneering. "You made me do it."

I rushed to open the back door and fan the air with it so the alarm would stop. When I did, Ben swept through the doorway.

"Whoa," he said. "What the hell's going on here?"

"Ann made me burn the dolmas," Stella shrieked. "She said Bubba committed suicide."

"What the hell, Ann?"

Before I could speak, Stella pushed past both of us, stormed into the den, and returned waving the printout.

"With this." Stella waved the reading in Ben's face.

"What's this?" He snatched the reading from Stella and looked at me.

"It's a reading," I tried to explain. "From a psychic. From Gregory. It made sense. So many answers. Not coincidence..."

You're babbling.

"This is a crock of shit." Ben looked accusingly. "You come in here and you upset Aunt Stella with this hocus-pocus bullshit?"

"It's not bullshit." What the hell was I doing? Melting down, that's what. I had nothing left inside for a confrontation. No energy to mount a defense. Nothing.

"You wanna know what kind of bullshit this is?" Ben was livid, using the printout to emphasize his points. "I've read studies on this shit. Academic studies. Tons of them. These *people*—these *so-called psychics*—are very good at saying just what you want to hear. They make it their *business* to say just the right thing. They know how to do deep research and reel you in like a fish. I'm surprised at you, Ann. You should know better."

"But you haven't even looked at it...."

"I don't have to," Ben snarled. "It's bogus."

"Yes, it's bogus," Stella chimed in. There was that same haughty, know-it-all tone. Just like when she told me how much Gregory liked her damned dolmas.

Their blistering assault withered me, shaming and attacking all at once. My God, what was I thinking?

"My Gregory would never be any part of what you're talking about," Stella hissed. "He was a good Christian boy, and what you're talking about is Satanic."

"It is not," I sputtered. "There's nothing Satanic about this message." I seized the reading, then stuffed it in my purse.

"Only the devil would conjure up something like this. This is pure evil, Ann." Stella was on a roll, growing more furious by the second, sputtering and muttering about Satan.

"You need to leave, Ann. You've upset Aunt Stella." Ben held the door open.

Was that a smile blooming at the corner of Stella's lips? I untied my apron and scooped the Saint Christopher out of the apron pocket. It flickered a moment in the light. I couldn't gather up my coat and purse fast enough.

"Wait a minute." Stella snatched the Saint Christopher out of my hand and held it up, swinging it by the chain.

"What's this? What's this you have?"

Something new shone in her eyes. A wildness. A fury.

"Where did you get this?" she demanded, sweating and breathing heavily, her hair clinging in wilted curls to her face.

"The Saint Christopher? It was Gregory's," I said, noticing that Ben was also eyeing the medallion.

"No, it wasn't Gregory's," Stella screeched. "This was Bubba's! I gave it to him the day he died. What are you doing with it? What have you done to my boys? Did you make a pact with the devil? You made a pact with the devil!"

"Dammit, I did not. I'm trying to tell you Gregory's okay. That he really came through… That… That…" I was gasping for air.

"You need to leave right now," Ben insisted, refocused on dismissing me. But he looked more worried than angry. Why the mood change?

It didn't matter. There was nothing I could do but scuttle down the steps, defeated.

As Ben slammed the door shut behind me, Stella called out in a completely different voice.

"Wait, Ann!" The cheeriness had returned. "You forgot your dolmas."

"Leave it, Aunt Stella."

I stopped at the bottom of the steps, dumbfounded.

"My *dolmas?*"

"Yes" Stella said, jerking the door back open.

"Wait there."

I watched numbly as Stella swiftly scooped several from the pot and wrapped them in aluminum foil before placing them in a paper sack. Ben just scowled.

"Here," she said.

Stella handed the bag to me and smiled—a warm, open smile—as if the past several minutes had never happened.

"I hope you had fun learning to make my dolmas," she said sweetly. "I think you did a wonderful job. Of course you've got to take some with you. Just be sure to squeeze a little lemon juice on them the way Gregory likes them."

I grabbed the bag, hurried to the car, and burned rubber backing out her long driveway. I tried to think about the reading, determined to take comfort in its words, in its message from Gregory, as I had with Connie and Elizabeth. But it was like trying to recapture a dream that fades more quickly the harder you try. Something had changed. Everything had changed.

CHAPTER TWENTY-ONE

I flung my coat and purse on floor and slammed the stupid dolmas down on the counter. Angry tears and self-recrimination flooded me. Why had I gone over there? What was I thinking? How could I be so mind-numbingly bad at reading her? Denial. Wishful thinking. And hadn't Gregory warned me in the reading about approaching her?

The reading. Ben had effectively undermined my confidence with his tirade. And Stella, with her horrible accusations. What was I to make of those? I kept telling myself she wasn't always right in the head. But my normally sharp judgment was as dull as her crappy knife. I'd worked so hard over my life to develop a strong inner compass. How could I have let Ben and Stella completely blindside me? I grabbed the phone, dialing madly. Connie answered.

"What are you doing?" I asked.

"I'm reading before going to bed." I could hear wariness in her voice. "Why?"

"I hate to do this again," I said. "I hate to. But I need to see you. I just got back from Stella's, and I told her about the reading and... and..." I started losing it. Blast it. I couldn't stop sobbing long enough to finish the sentence.

"... and it turned out badly?"

"Yes," I managed. "I feel so bad asking you this, but I don't know who else to call. All I can think is maybe Elizabeth. But she'll just tell me she was right, and I never should have gone over there. And..."

"Where's Olivia tonight?" Connie interrupted.

"With her dad."

"Then why don't you come here?"

Connie did nothing to conceal a heavy sigh. I knew my friend was tired of my leaning on her so much. But I couldn't help it. She was my anchor, my rock.

I was surviving on the thinnest sliver of hope she had given me that Gregory's essence might live on. The possibility drove me. Consumed me. I was strung out on the need to know. Like a drug. It was simply inconceivable that all he was had vanished with his extinguished neurons. Yet if that *was* the truth, I wanted to know *that*, too. And I was going to exhaust every possibility to get to the final answer.

"Ann?"

"Yes," I said, jolted back to the conversation. "I'm really messed up, Connie. I'll be there in a minute. Thank you. I know I'm a pain in the ass. I owe you."

As I strode to Connie's, the brisk November air was like a bracing slap in the face that I needed. I looked up at the stars—it was a brilliantly clear night, as sharply defined as an Ansel Adams photograph. It reminded me how minuscule we are, which launched my haphazardly tethered mind into its newly familiar frenzy. Stardust? Or road kill? Eternal or ephemeral?

I gave a quick rap on Connie's door to let her know it was me, then let myself in. She had put on her robe and fluffy slippers. I felt ashamed for asking so much of her.

We hugged.

"Dolmas?" she asked, pointing to the bag in my hand.

"Yes, ugh." I threw down my coat and put the bag in the fridge. "Stella and I made dolmas, then she accused me of conspiring with Satan, and Ben interrupted us and just ripped the reading and…"

"Wait. What?"

"I've never seen Stella like that. Enraged. Possessed. And so energized by it all. There was no reasoning with her. And then Ben walks in on us and starts dissing everything and I hate that I keep running away from difficult situations, but I… I… just don't have the strength right now to face this shit down."

I felt the thin, fragile veneer I'd been holding up fracture into a million pieces.

It's okay. You're safe.

Exhausted and drained, I wondered if I'd ever feel strong again. I collapsed onto the velvet sofa.

"Just a minute." Connie shuffled to the kitchen and returned with snifters of brandy. "Here," she said, bundling her robe around her. "Sip on this while we talk."

I began spilling the details of my horrible dolma lesson, my tongue and tears loosened by the warmth of the alcohol.

"But here's the thing," I wailed, wiping my eyes with a tissue Connie held out to me. "Something in the way Ben said it—how so-called psychics find out details, how that's what they do, like I'd be stupid to believe them—just withered me. I *know* you would never collude with someone, but he planted just enough doubt that I'm doubting the reading and questioning whether it could have been faked. My brain *knows* you would never do something like that, but he tainted it."

"I'd never deceive you," Connie said, "and neither would my friends, even if we somehow had information to share. I don't suppose it does any good to point out that there was stuff in the reading none of us could have known—not even you."

"But everything Sasha said could have been a lucky guess," I said. "And she was all concerned about the money order reaching her before we talked. I hate this. I feel like I'm back to square one."

With that, I simply ran out of steam and stopped talking. Connie sipped her Cognac.

"I've been asking myself more lately whether my sixth sense is a blessing or a curse—for both of us."

"Why?"

"Because there's something more I want to tell you. And I'm torn. Like, I'm thinking I've already done enough damage. Like, you'll judge me. I still worry that people will think I'm crazy. And I've still got so much… charge… around the awful things my father did to me when he found out I could 'see.' Maybe I should just keep my mouth shut."

"Well you know I'm always going to say trust your gut. And I'm not going to judge you. So I'm not a good person to ask. But whatever it is, what the hell, let's hear it."

In a crazy way, I felt like a mama bear encircling her cub this time. I wanted to protect Connie as much as she wanted to protect me. Even if what she had to say could hurt.

"In a way, I'm a lot like Gregory," Connie said, her face framed in soft light. "I have these little compartments to separate the facets of my life. Like, my family's in one compartment so it won't clash with the psychic stuff that seems to 'surpass all understanding' in another."

"Your dad was pretty rigid about religion, wasn't he?"

"Completely. Refused to accept what I do. Said it wasn't natural. I could never convince him that it just happens. Just like I didn't go looking to see Gregory at the memorial service. But that frightened me because I couldn't control it. Couldn't control what I was seeing. It kicked up old feelings, terrible fears, that something might really be wrong with me.

"I could have kept the vision of Gregory to myself. But I saw your suffering. It felt right to tell you. In all the time I've known you, I've never seen anything hurt you this much. Not even losing your mother."

There was that comparison again. She was right. Over the decades, I'd forgotten how much that hurt—the pain subsumed by the struggle to grow up and define who I was, with female guidance coming only from friends like Connie. Especially Connie.

"I almost hesitate to tell you that there's another way to go at this," Connie said slowly, "to discover what might happen after we die."

"Another way?" I couldn't imagine what she meant. Neither did I have the energy to speculate. I was worn all the way down. "What would that be?"

"I had hoped a reading would comfort you. I had great faith in Sasha—still do—but like she said, a medium can only do so much. And you are a tough case."

This was probably true.

"As hungry as I am for what Sasha said to be the truth," I said, "I can't seem to fully let go of my skepticism. It's in my DNA."

"You might need stronger medicine," Connie said.

"What? Please don't speak in riddles. I'm too damned tired."

Connie looked as worn as I felt. Fine lines spider-webbed the corners of her eyes, and her skin was so pale as to appear translucent. Her hands were cracked and dry, her normally well-groomed nails, chewed.

"Have you ever heard of an out-of-body-experience?" she said.

What now? I thought.

"Maybe," I said. "You said something about it when you mentioned the professor. Isn't it like a near-death experience?"

"Something like that," Connie said, refreshing our brandy.

"Don't tell me you've had one."

"Yeah," she said, then paused. "And not just one."

Her words seemed to overwhelm the small room.

"What does that mean?" I managed to say.

"I've... loosened my consciousness from my body and... moved outside it." She spoke as if she were confessing to adultery, or worse.

"How is that even possible?"

"Oh, it's possible. And very real. In the beginning, I did ordinary things, like look at myself from the ceiling of a room. I've also done what can only be described as cosmic things, like touching the consciousness of others. That includes people who have died."

"What the eff?" I said, incredulous. "And why didn't you tell me this when you told me about Sasha?"

"Why didn't I tell you...? Because this is like all that 'stuff' I do. I can't seem to get past some visceral dread, like people will think I'm weird or psycho."

I took her hands in mine.

"Do you feel that way with me?"

"No. It's more like a knee-jerk fear of bringing it up, reactivating the shame I felt as a child. I don't think I've ever gotten over that."

I wanted her to tell me more about this going out of body. But I also wanted to calm her fears and reassure her that I wasn't going to judge her, no matter what.

"What do you want to tell me about it?" I said, releasing her hands.

"I think it might be important to the answers you're searching for," she said, sounding relieved, "and I feel pulled—urged—to tell you about it."

"What's it like to go outside your body?" I still couldn't grasp the possibility, but I knew how to ask questions.

"It's hard to describe. And I don't want to get you into something you might regret. Or I might regret. Like I feel happened with the reading."

"I don't regret that exactly," I said, stirred by something behind her words, "and it's no one's fault. It did lead me to some good things with Elizabeth and Olivia. Just not the certainty I crave."

"Going out of body… is serious stuff," Connie said. "It can even be dangerous. I've thought it over, and the only way I'd ever agree to show you what it's like is under controlled conditions with someone more experienced."

I wasn't sure what she was talking about. I waited to hear more.

"My friend, Dr. Koslow, is doing research," she said, gazing down, as if she didn't want to look directly at me. "It's a very hush-hush project at the university—yes, the one by our complex. He's trying to figure out whether OBEs are real, from a scientific standpoint. He's not alone in this. There are other labs engaged in the research, too.

He might be willing to lead you through an experience, if I asked him. It would be very far under the radar. In official terms, he'd be testing to see if you're a potential subject for his research."

I didn't fully comprehend what she was saying, but intuitively, it sounded like going out of body probably crossed some line. Like those characters in *Flatliners*.

"There is risk," Connie reiterated, as if reading my mind. "Sometimes when people find what they are looking for, find their loved ones, they don't want to leave," she said.

"Don't want to leave where?"

"The place where consciousness lives after the body dies. They decide not to come back because the desire to stay is so strong."

The last two words were spoken so quietly, it was as though Connie were trying to conceal the fear and uncertainty in her voice.

I wasn't sure what to say. She was talking about certainty at a whole different level in this life-death debate, a certainty she obviously had experienced. That was mind-blowing. I resisted the full impact of her words. My circuits were overloaded. Yet I had to know more.

"What happens to the ones that want to stay?" I asked. I wished for a notepad to record her answers.

"Their bodies hang on for a while, usually in hospitals, hooked up to life support. But eventually the physical shell withers and dies. They never come back. They're classified as idiopathic deaths. No clear cause or reason. At least not one you can record on an official document."

I'd never seen Connie so serious.

"I've held this back from you because we don't know enough about how this happens, and I'm concerned that you might get into an OBE—and not be able to get out of it."

My mind spun with the possibilities. Maybe it was just the brandy and lateness of the hour making me light-headed. She wasn't talking about just contacting Gregory through a medium, which is like being on a very poor quality phone line.

"You're talking about contacting Gregory in person, so to speak, aren't you? Going where he is." Wherever the hell that might be.

"Yes."

I put my hand to my head, which was beginning to pound, and took several slow, deep breaths. There was something both tantalizing and terrifying in what Connie was telling me.

"I think I'd be willing to try that," I said slowly. "But it also sounds scary."

"I know, Ann, and that's what concerns me. I don't want to be the catalyst for something with potentially terrible consequences. You have a daughter. A life. So many people here who need you. Like me. I need you."

Connie knew even before she told me that I would risk anything to get the answer to my question. I'd never felt such urgency until Gregory died—all-consuming and unstoppable. As though his death opened a door that couldn't be shut. I would never rest, never relax, never completely let go of my grief nor participate fully in life again until I knew what had happened to Gregory's spirit. His spirit. Even my vocabulary had changed. I pushed the dangers to the back of my mind. Nothing would go wrong, I told myself.

"I'm going to ask Dr. Koslow if you would be an appropriate subject," Connie said. "You have a more acute agenda than most of the people he works with."

"Like you?"

"Like me. I've been a subject for years and have helped him discreetly find other potential subjects. He always has to tell them about the idiopathic deaths and have them sign a consent-release form. But he doesn't like having to do that."

"Isn't that just part of doing business? Even with research?"

"Yes, and he's never 'lost' a subject. He just hates to plant the suggestion. I'm going to ask him to meet with you, tell you more about it, but don't bring up what I've just told you."

"About the deaths?"

"Yeah, he'll just tell you not to do it if you have any doubts."

"I think this might be as far as I can go with this tonight," I said. "Are you hungry? Do you want some dolmas?"

Connie laughed out loud at my abrupt change of course. Like we had suddenly walked into a shaft of sunlight in a giant dark forest. It was respite we both needed.

"Sure. Why not?"

We stayed up talking about OBEs and what to expect till almost three a.m. before I went home. The next morning, the phone rang, and I rolled over to answer it.

"Ann?"

Oh, shit.

"Yes," I said, shaking the sleep quickly from my head.

"This is Stella. I wanted to call and apologize for yesterday. I didn't mean for you to go away mad."

You accused me of being in collusion with the devil. Why would that make anyone mad?

"Things did get kind of out of hand," I said.

"I went to confession this morning."

"Okay." Why are you telling me this?

"And Father McCallister said what I did was wrong, and I had to apologize to you." She sounded like a little girl. I could picture her at about eight years old, bow in bobbed hair, kneeling before the screen in the confessional, reciting her childish sins.

"I'm sorry," she said. It wasn't like she quite meant it. It was more like she was sorry she got caught.

"Well, thank you, Stella. I appreciate that. I know that's hard for you to say."

"Oh no it's not," she sniffed.

"Well thank you anyway." Now please go away.

"You're welcome," she said in her sweet voice again. "We'll have to get together soon so you can give me back the key to my house. The one you took from me at the hospital."

"Yes," I said, mindful that I had no such key, "we can do that."

CHAPTER TWENTY-TWO

"Raiza?" I called over the cubicle divider at work the next day, where my coworker was furiously tappy-tap-tapping at her keyboard.

"What-i-what?" she answered without missing a stroke.

"I need a favor," I said, looking at the photograph I'd been carrying around from the mystery chest. The one Elizabeth and I assumed was Gregory's brother in his camo gear.

Raiza's keyboard went silent.

"Anything, sweetie. Just name it."

I pulled up a chair in her cubicle and showed her the photo.

"This is Gregory's brother, Andrew," I said.

"I didn't know lover boy was into hunting," Raiza said with her usual flippancy.

"He wasn't. Or at least, he said he wasn't. God knows at this point; I don't know what to believe. I'm pretty sure his brother died on a hunting trip. But there seems to be some question about how he died."

I hadn't gotten much sleep after the dolma-making disaster and late night with Connie. My eyelids felt gritty and my whole body brittle. But I had a renewed sense of resolve about the reading, despite the doubts Ben stirred up. And Connie awakened in me a desire to at least consider the out-of-body thing. Still, I wanted to pause and regroup. Research and verify was my credo, my foundation. So I'd start with the reading. I was determined to independently verify whether any of the things Sasha said were true—and the suicide question seemed a good place to start.

I wasn't accustomed to chasing down information like this, but Raiza was. I would frame what I knew in a neutral way, even holding some information back, to see what my friend could uncover on her own. I was eager to nail down Bubba's cause of death.

"I did find an obit dated Oct. 17, 1971," I told her. "It doesn't say much. Just birthdate, school, next of kin. The usual stuff." Ben was mentioned as the family spokesman.

I showed Raiza a copy of the obit. I also handed her the trimmed photo.

"Hmm, and what's this got to do with your favor?"

"I want to find out how he died."

"Oh?"

As she read the obit, Raiza chewed absently on a purple pen that matched her sparkly purple nail polish.

"It says here it was a hunting accident."

"I know. But I'd like verification. I suspect there's a medical examiner's report floating around, except I'm not sure where. Could be Dallas County. Or some other Texas county. Even a nearby state. I'd like to know what it says."

If—and it was a big if—Sasha and the spirits she was bringing through correctly identified Bubba's cause of death, I could take other parts of the reading more seriously again. The suicide assertion directly contradicted the obit, as well as what Elizabeth told me about the "official" family story. Of course, she got that from Gregory. Not the most reliable source.

"This is sounding like quite a mystery."

Raiza had a glint in her eye. She loved digging into mysteries. And she had the tenacity of a rat terrier. Both qualities contributed to her reputation as a wicked-good investigative reporter. Once she exposed an embezzlement scheme that cost the county nearly half a million dollars before it was discovered. Another time, even the sports staff admitted to grudging respect when she laid bare a racehorse-doping scandal missed on their watch.

"I'm told the brother was once arrested in the Park Cities when he was high—like maybe in his junior or senior year," I said. "The paper might've reported on that, but I haven't looked through the archives to see."

"Why would that have anything to do with his death?"

"Not saying it would."

"What's with the close trim on the photo?"

"Nothing gets past you. Another mystery. I think someone was deliberately cut out of the picture. Bonus points if you uncover who and why."

"How odd. Can I keep this?" she said, running her finger along the cut edge.

I hesitated for a nanosecond.

"Not the original. I'll make you a Xerox."

"Sounds good. What's my timeline?"

"Yesterday." I gave her my best smart-ass smirk. "No, just whatever you can dig up as soon as possible. Dying to know how the brother died. Ugh. No pun intended. Oh, and I wouldn't take this up with Stella."

"Unreliable?"

"Ha. That's one word for it."

The professor Connie had mentioned agreed to meet with me. But Dr. Koslow's tight schedule and high lab traffic meant we would need to rendezvous someplace off campus. We agreed on a popular shopping mall. It was a safe public space where the cover of ambient noise would allow us to talk without being overheard. Connie wanted him to explain in his own words what he did, rather than her trying to explain it for him. She had already told him about my situation.

We nursed our lattes in a small dining area that jutted out like a Parisian sidewalk café into the tony shopping-center walkway. Shoppers' footsteps echoed on polished concrete as voices caromed off the elegant glass storefronts and vaulted ceiling. A tot jumped and shrieked as a yellow balloon bobbed overhead, tethered to his wrist. Knots of teenagers slumped from one window display to the next, absorbed in their adolescent dramas. Everywhere we cast our gaze, there were mall walkers—older men and women in telltale sweats and sneakers, weaving in and out along invisible tracks carved through the more sluggish throngs.

Before long, Connie caught the eye of a tall, bony, bronzed man who gave a wave and signaled that he would pick up a beverage before joining us. Clad in white athletic pants and a blue tennis jacket, Dr. Koslow looked like he'd just come from a round of doubles. As he sat down with his spiced chai, I studied the angular features that set off his black, agate-like eyes. For the briefest moment, his tousled, curly hair reminded me of Gregory's. It was clear both men shared a Mediterranean heritage.

"Hello." Speaking with a faint accent, the college professor greeted Connie with the warm familiarity of an old friend, then turned to me. "And you must be Ann." He extended his hand.

"Yes, I am," I said, giving a firm squeeze. "Pleased to meet you."

After some small talk, Connie said, "I think I explained on the phone why I invited you here."

"Yes," Dr. Koslow said in a hushed voice. "I understand Ann would like to visit our lab."

He didn't come out and use the term out-of-body experience, but we all knew what he meant when he said "visit our lab"—our pre-agreed-upon code for participating in an OBE under his guidance. My situation was slightly different from those of the people who normally were chosen as study subjects. In my case, Dr. Koslow wanted to conduct what amounted to a test run before accepting me into his research because no one had ever participated so soon after the loss of a loved one. Connie, who was a longtime participant, coaxed him into considering me. In effect, she was calling in a favor.

"This is somewhat irregular," he said, shifting in his chair, "but not entirely unprecedented. Connie has been a gifted subject, penetrating levels of consciousness few reach. I trust her judgment. And I believe we can make an exception to strict protocol in this case."

This meant I was skipping the psych eval as well as the six-month waiting period for those who had lost loved ones. "If all goes well, we will also have you return as a test subject," he said, speaking with the steady demeanor of a pilot and a candor that helped put me at ease.

"Thank you for even considering this," I said. "I'm indebted to both of you."

I caught them exchanging a quick glance.

"Can you tell me what I might expect and how you do it?"

Almost as one body, we all leaned closer.

"Sound is the key," Dr. Koslow began, "at least in my research. I use it to bring your brain waves into synchrony. After years of trial and error, we have arrived at a pattern that has the effect of preparing you to release. In the headphones you'll wear throughout the experience, it may sound to you like a Gregorian chant."

Gregorian chant. Got that?

"Can anyone do this?" I asked.

"Yes and no," he said. "Theoretically it's possible. But some people have strong inhibitors that prevent them from letting go."

"How will we know if I'm one of those?"

"We won't until you try it," he said.

"Dr. Koslow was a pioneer in developing the technique," Connie injected. "He started by studying people who went out of their bodies spontaneously. These were everyday people who suddenly and inexplicably found themselves above their bodies—looking at themselves—after lying down, or sometimes during surgery. He wanted to learn as much as he could about how—"

"Well, will you look who's *here*."

It was as if a lightning bolt had struck the center of the table, throwing us all backward. An interloper leaned too close over the faux fence next to our table.

"Hello, Ann," came the saccharine greeting.

"Come back here," growled a familiar husky voice as the faintest scent of old cigarette smoke brushed past my nostrils. Connie and I looked at each other in disbelief.

"Stella," Connie managed. "How are you?"

"She's fine, rebuilding her strength," said Wanda, grabbing her friend's arm to pull her away, but not before adding under her breath, "Now that her boy's in the ground."

Stella jerked her arm out of Wanda's hand. Wanda seemed to burn holes through me with her eyes. I squirmed.

"Hello, Mrs. White," Dr. Koslow said, prompting Wanda to turn and look at him. She loosened her grip on Stella as Dr. Koslow thrust out his hand stiffly to shake hers.

"Oh, Dr. Koslow." Wanda's face relaxed. "I didn't realize it was you. Stella, this is Dr. Koslow. From the university. We work in Lyndon Hall together. I sometimes do his scheduling."

"How do you do?" he said.

"This is Stella Malouf, my neighbor," Wanda said.

I looked at Connie, and she looked at me. We didn't know what to say.

"Very good to meet you, Mrs. Malouf," Dr. Koslow said, nodding formally.

"Are you Lebanese?" Stella queried, fixating on the professor.

"Stella. Stop it," Wanda said. "That's rude."

"It's quite all right, Mrs. White," Dr. Koslow replied, turning to Stella. "Lebanon is a lovely country, ma'am, but I grew up in Spain."

"So you are Catholic...." Stella seemed to want to add something.

"That's enough, Stella," Wanda persisted. "We need to leave these people alone and get back to our walking. We still have five laps to go."

"Yes, well… Oh Ann. Nice to see you."

"You, too."

I could manage only a grimace that I hoped resembled a smile.

Polite goodbyes were offered all around, and Stella and Wanda continued on their way. But not before Stella turned back again and stared at Dr. Koslow. How odd she seemed in this public setting. So unpredictable. The old Stella.

"I'm sorry," Dr. Koslow said, sitting back down. "Where were we?"

"We were talking about the out-of-body… ," I said, catching myself too late. "I mean, 'the visit.'"

Stella was still looking back as Wanda towed her along like a three-year-old.

"Who was that, exactly, with Mrs. White?" Dr. Koslow asked.

"That was Gregory's mother," I said.

"She seems a little… off kilter, if I may be so forward."

"An accurate perception," I said. "She's had a hard time dealing with her son's death. But she would not be open to what we're discussing."

"Let's get back to why we're here," Connie, said, sipping her latte. "We don't want to intrude too much on your time, Professor."

"I appreciate that. Where were we?"

"I was starting to ask you what it felt like," I said, keeping my voice low.

Dr. Koslow spoke slowly, choosing his words carefully.

"It's hard to describe," he said, "and I don't want to set up an expectation. Let's just say people get there differently. But there's a point in the process where you are able to let go."

"One minute you're in the flow of the chant," Connie added. "The next minute, you're outside your physical self."

"That's a very good way to put it, thank you."

"Are there any risks?" I asked, eager to get his perspective on this and unable to resist my reportorial instincts.

Connie kicked me under the table.

"Risks? Ah… well… There is the risk you might not be able to let go. And I assume Connie has made you familiar with… the idiopathic issue sometimes attributed to these activities in the literature. But in my experience, I have seen none of those results."

Crimson crept into Connie's alabaster cheeks.

"I did tell her about those," she said. "But I emphasized that they were uncommon."

She seemed to be backpedaling from the concerns she had shared with me.

"If you have any doubts, you should not do it," Dr. Koslow said with finality.

"No, no," I said. "It's not that. I want to do it, but I want to know what I'm getting into."

"Please forgive Ann," Connie said. "She's a very direct person."

Oh geez, Connie was apologizing for me. And fidgeting in her chair.

"Yes, I can see that," Dr. Koslow said, sitting back. "No offense taken."

He glanced down at his watch.

"Oh dear. I must change and get back to the lab. We are set then? For Thursday? Like you and I discussed, Connie?"

Was that Stella's head bobbing around the corner of a nearby display window?

"Yes, we will be there."

"I deeply appreciate your doing this," I added.

"It's my pleasure," Dr. Koslow said, offering a cordial smile and resuming his professorial demeanor as he rose to leave.

And with that he blended back into the mall crowd.

I slumped in my seat.

"Did I just eff that up?"

"You came close."

Connie's eyes had turned steely and cool. I felt weepiness inching to the surface.

"Oh, damn it. I'm sorry."

Push down the tears. Push.

"No. Just listen," she said. "This is like dance, getting him to do this with you. It's not something he normally does. He's uneasy about skipping the psych test and bending protocol, even though he trusts me. He doesn't need you bringing up doubts—or the concerns I shared with you. I have imposed on our relationship to get him to do this. So please, please, don't bring this up again."

It felt like Connie was lecturing me. Like I'd been a bad child.

"Look," she continued, a little less harshly. "The deaths do concern me. They are rare, but because Gregory's death is so recent and you're so obsessed, you might be more susceptible. I don't know. But I do want you to promise me you'll have your legal affairs in order, just in case."

Ah. Code for making sure I had a will.

"If you want to do this, you're going to have to accept the risk," she said.

CHAPTER TWENTY-THREE

Later in the week, after dinner, Olivia and I sat down on the living room floor to look through Gregory's chest together.

"I'd like to see what he kept in there," she had announced.

At first, I vacillated, unsure I was ready to talk about the contents. Plus, I didn't want to add to the burden of his passing. But Olivia was mature and, since Gregory's death, maturing faster every day. If looking at the objects and learning about Megan would deepen Olivia's understanding of Gregory, perhaps it would also help with her own healing. It was probably time that Olivia learned about the other little girl in Gregory's life.

"These are things that Gregory kept that were special to him," I told Olivia. "Special and private. I didn't know this chest existed."

The phone rang, and I got up to answer it. Raiza was on the other end. I turned my back to Olivia so she wouldn't hear.

"What'd you find out?" I asked.

"That there's not a definitive answer." She sounded miffed.

"Can you say more?" I looked over at Olivia, who was carefully taking the items out of each tray.

"I'll be there in just a minute, sweetie," I called over my shoulder.

"I found the medical examiner's report," Raiza said, "and you were right. It was from another county. Comanche County, to be exact."

"What'd it say?"

"Cause of death: gunshot wound. Manner: undetermined."

"What does that mean?"

"In ME lingo it means they couldn't tell conclusively from the autopsy whether it was self-inflicted or inflicted by another. Whether he shot himself or someone else shot him."

Confronting the reality of the shooting was like another emotional sucker punch.

"That's totally weird," I said. "Makes this more of a mystery, not less."

"I thought so, too. So I didn't stop there."

No, of course not. This was Raiza.

"I did a little more snooping and managed to find an old cop who remembered the case. Said it was a real tragedy, what with the brothers."

I got a sick feeling in the pit of my stomach.

"Brothers plural?"

"Brothers plural. Said there were three of them out on a lease hunting."

"Three?"

"Not three brothers. Turns out it was the two brothers and a cousin who was a little older, but not much. He said the surviving brother, ID'd as Gregory, kept saying at the lease, 'I tried to stop him. I really did. I tried.' Said he was carrying on. The cousin, that Ben guy in the obit, told him to shut up. Said they took statements from both young men at headquarters. But that was after they all drove in from the lease. Cops in their cars; Gregory and Ben in theirs. By then both boys had clammed up."

"Did you see the statements?"

"Nah. Destroyed. The guy said he only remembered the case 'cuz it bugged him that they were never able to pin down whether it was a suicide or a homicide."

"Jesus Christ."

"Yeah, that's what I said."

"If it were a homicide, would it have been manslaughter or murder?" Reporter mode, kicking in.

"No way of knowing so long after the fact. But it sounds like neither Gregory nor Ben was willing to expound on what happened."

"So we'll never know." Unless I can pry an answer out of Ben. I tried to conceal my disappointment. "Thanks for checking this out."

"No problem," Raiza said. "I just wish I could have gotten a better answer."

"Mom!" Olivia shrieked, dropping something on the carpet. I'd completely forgotten I was supposed to be in the living room with her.

"Gotta go," I said to Raiza in a rush. "We'll talk more later."

"Okay. See ya."

I turned to find Olivia shaking her right hand as if something were wrong with it. The iridescent paperweight lay in front of her.

"What happened? What're you doing?"

"It gave me a shock," she said, more startled than distressed. She rubbed her right palm with her left thumb.

"You must've rubbed your hand on the carpet or something."

"No. I picked it up and held it to the light, and it zapped me."

I reached down to touch the glass object. It felt like a paperweight, nothing more, with a pleasantly curved shape that conformed to the palm of my hand. But no zaps for me. Nothing.

"I don't know," I said. "It seems like just a paperweight. Could the cat have brushed up against you before you touched it and made a spark?"

Woody was sitting behind Olivia, licking his paw a little obsessively.

"I don't know. Maybe. I didn't make it up."

"No, no. I'm not saying you did. I'm just thinking there must be a simple explanation." Let's be logical.

Or not.

As we continued examining the items from the chest, I couldn't stop thinking about what Raiza had said. I knew I had to talk to Ben.

"What's this yellow bag?" Olivia wanted to know.

"Put it up to your nose," I said.

"It smells like smoke." She made a face.

I retold the luminaria story as well as I could while Olivia listened, rapt. "He must have loved Elizabeth a lot," she finally said.

"Yes, I think he did."

When we got to Megan's drawings, Olivia was visibly moved.

"Who drew these, and who is the angel?" she said.

I explained who Megan was, what had happened to her, and that Gregory was her angel. Olivia's face grew pensive, her eyes rimmed with red. But she resisted shedding so much as a single tear. The pushback of budding adolescence.

"Can something like that happen to anyone?" she asked.

"Yes, but… ," I said with as much reassurance as I could muster, "this cancer was extremely rare."

"This makes me sad, Mom."

"Me, too," I said, touched by Gregory's capacity for love and disappointed anew that he hadn't told me about Megan. "It's like discovering this secret place in his heart where he held a lot of hurt." As much hurt as losing his brother? I wondered. Perhaps those losses were entwined someplace in his compartments, too.

"Why wouldn't he tell us?"

"I don't know."

"Did he think we wouldn't understand?"

"No, I don't think that's it. I think maybe it hurt him so deeply that he just wanted to forget it ever happened. That's Elizabeth's theory. And then you were there for him to love."

Olivia fidgeted.

Note to self: Don't get too mushy. And don't put her on the spot.

"What I mean is, he locked away the pain. But the experience with Elizabeth's daughter also made him appreciate you more."

"That's not very smart, Mom, hiding pain."

"Yeah. It's not what you or I would do. We've learned to talk about our feelings. And to listen." At least, I hoped her dad and I were seeding these healthier habits. "But he grew up very differently."

"What do you mean?"

"His family wasn't open about feelings, not the way we are. And the adults didn't handle their anger well. I'm pretty sure his mom and dad fought in front of him and his brother when they were growing up."

"That's awful. You and Dad never fought in front of me."

"No, we didn't."

I looked at the clock. It was past time for Olivia to start her homework.

"Can we wrap this up for now? For tonight?" I said gently. "You need to do your homework."

"Yeah. This is a lot."

"And yes. We can look at stuff and talk about it more another time."

"Okay." I gave Olivia a hug, and for a moment we kind of melted into each other.

"I love you, Mom."

"Love you, too."

She replaced the drawings and the rest of the chest's contents, being extra careful with the paperweight. This time, nothing happened when she picked it up and laid it in the top tray.

CHAPTER TWENTY-FOUR

The next morning, I called to make an appointment with Ben on the pretext of having a question about Gregory's estate.

"Sure," he said, "let's meet today." It was like the encounter with Stella had never happened.

When I got there, Ben's secretary buzzed him, then opened the door for me to enter his office. No greeting. No handshake. Ben was on the phone and motioned for me to sit down in the overstuffed chair in front of his behemoth of a desk. I still had only a vague notion of what Ben did for a living. I knew he ran a business of some sort but had no idea whether it was real estate or something more sinister. Not knowing contributed to an underlying sense of apprehension each time I saw him. Today was no different.

"Yeah, I'll get back to you on that," he said, ending the call.

"So, Ann. What do you want now?" He was short with me.

I said I was there to talk about what Gregory had left.

"There wasn't much, as you know," Ben said, leaning back in his big, creaky chair on the other side of the desk.

"Did you find the stocks?" I asked.

"Yeah. Wasn't much value to 'em. But every bit went to Stella."

I couldn't read the titles on the bookshelves behind Ben. Could have been books-by-the-foot, for all I knew. The office smelled rank, like stale cigar smoke. Heavy curtains shrouded tall, filmy windows through which sunlight struggled to penetrate.

I steeled myself.

"I'm here to ask you about something else, too." I kept my voice steady.

"Why does that not surprise me?" he said, annoyed. "What do you want now?"

Go for broke.

"What can you tell me about this picture?" I said, pulling the photo of Bubba and his dog out of my purse and handing it to Ben.

It seemed to catch him momentarily off guard. He put his glasses on, leaned forward, and studied it hastily.

"It's Gregory's brother, of course." He pitched it back across his desk like he was dealing cards. "Where'd you get it?"

"I found it among Gregory's effects," I said, picking it up gingerly. "Does it mean anything to you?"

"Nope."

Ben folded his arms across his belly.

"Are you sure? I also found the obit for Bubba, and it mentions you."

Ben shifted uneasily in his grandiose chair, then sat forward and leaned in to face me across the vast expanse of the mahogany desk.

"Look, I was the family spokesman. It says that, too, doesn't it?"

"Yes."

"So end of story." Ben was not budging.

"Not so fast." Very deep breath. "I saw how you reacted at Stella's to the part of the reading that referenced a suicide. A friend of mine found the autopsy report and located one of the police officers from the case."

"So what?" Ben affected nonchalance, deflecting the words. But he was interested.

"You were there the day of the accident."

"You can't prove that."

"Yeah, I can. The officer remembered you. Told us all about the statements they took from you. How you told Gregory to shut up." Ben winced and looked suddenly miserable. "I think you know more about what happened that day than you've told me. Or anyone. Including the investigating officers."

"Where do you get off?" he barked, flinging his hand in the air. "Where the hell do you get off making accusations about that day?" His voice rose, and his eyes narrowed. A lock of hair fell across his forehead, and he hastily slicked it back.

"I think something happened that day that changed Gregory," I said, trembling but unmoved by his mounting intimidation. "And I intend to find out what it was."

Ben sputtered. His ears turned crimson and drops of sweat tracked down his face. He jerked a handkerchief out of his pocket and mopped his forehead.

"You're outspoken, little girl," he snarled.

"I'm not a little girl," I said, audacious as Cool Hand Luke. I'm prepared for this, I kept telling myself. I wasn't going to stop until he physically threw me out or tried to hit me, in which case I'd already decided I would press charges. "And I'm going to get to the bottom of this. Now, what happened that day?"

"None of your damned business."

"Of course it's my damned business," I shot back. "I have a right to know what happened to Gregory that day. You know what happened that day, don't you? Did you have a hand in Bubba's death?"

"Get out of my office!" he shouted, standing up and banging his fist on his desk. "Right now!"

"I will not."

I stood and matched him pose for stubborn pose.

"I want to know what happened that day and how it affected Gregory. The way he 'took care' of his mother was not normal. My next stop is to talk to Stella."

"Why you little bitch. . . ."

"Why am I a bitch?" I wasn't about to let him intimidate me. "Because I call your bluff? Because I won't leave till you tell me what happened? Not used to women standing up to you?"

At that moment, it was as if someone stuck a pin in an overinflated Macy's parade balloon. Ben's shoulders sagged, he appeared to visibly shrink, and simply melted back into his chair, brow moist, white dress shirt stuck to his damp body.

"Dammit, Ann," he said more evenly, "can't you just let the dead be?"

I sat stone-like, unmoved.

"You're right," he said, still clearly pissed. "I've never told anyone what happened. Not the cops. No one. I was all about shielding Gregory that day. Keeping him out of trouble. Any hint of trouble. Which I did."

"And what does that mean?" I said, easing back down in my chair without breaking eye contact.

We were like wrestlers circling in a ring.

"I'll tell you, but you gotta give me your word you won't go to Stella. God knows Gregory and I protected *her* from the truth all those years, too, and I'm not about to let you fuck that up."

"You have my word," I said, hoping I wouldn't regret it.

Ben's tone became more direct and less confrontational, like when he rounded up Olivia and me the day I bought the Celica.

"It was Bubba's big day," Ben said. "He was going to show Gregory about hunting. Or maybe not. I guess we'll never know." He scowled at me.

"What do you mean we'll never know? If you were there, you know what happened."

"Not really." He shook his head. "But I'll tell you what I saw. And by the way, I didn't tell the police this. So don't go dredging it up with them."

I would keep my word. I doubted they'd be interested in revisiting the case, anyway.

"I was barely older than Gregory. His older cousin by a few years. And Stella made me promise to look after him and Bubba that day. No big deal, I thought. Brought my camera along. Wanted them to have something to remember the day by." He shook his head. "I'm taking shots through the brush, and all of a sudden I see Andrew. He's got the muzzle of his rifle under his chin, and I panic. I'm too far away to do anything but yell. That's when I catch Gregory out of the corner of my eye, lunging for the rifle like he's grabbing a line drive. Just as he touches the stock, it goes off."

I was too shocked to speak.

Ben put his head in his hands and started sobbing. Unburdening after all the years he'd held this in. Then he looked up and pulled out his handkerchief again.

Suddenly I felt sorry for him. But before I could utter a word, he grew silent, wiped away the tears, and looked across at me like I'd just cut him.

"If Gregory and I hadn't stuck to our story—of seeing Bubba pull the trigger but too far away to stop him—they might have tested the rifle for fingerprints, and they would have found Gregory's on it. That would have raised all kinds of questions. We felt terrible about the lie, but I convinced him that Stella couldn't stand losing both her sons. We had to give them a 'clean' consistent story. Gregory carried that around the rest of his life. Never knew whether he caused the rifle to go off or not."

"What in the world was Bubba thinking? Did you know he was suicidal?"

"We didn't know. Didn't know if he went out there on purpose to do that—and to fuck with us somehow by making us watch. Or maybe he thought he was alone. Bubba was an odd duck and loved guns, but he never talked about doing himself in. Whatever was going on in that head of his, Gregory couldn't stand the thought that he might have triggered the fatal shot. He spent the rest of his life trying to make it up to Stella. There. You have it."

He crossed his arms over his chest and sat back.

"Ben, I'm so sorry you had to witness that."

"Yeah. Go to hell."

Wordlessly, he pulled open the middle drawer of his desk and began rooting around under some papers.

"I suppose you'll be wanting this," he said and slapped down a photo of Gregory, smiling in his hunting gear. I slid the snapshot of Bubba up next to it. The edges were a perfect fit. Two brothers. Together—and both gone.

"But why did you cut the photo?"

"After I got them developed and showed them to Gregory, we burned all but this one. Negatives and all. We wanted to forget that day, didn't want anything to raise questions about what happened. But Gregory insisted on keeping the picture of Bubba. I would only give it to him if I cut him out. I don't know why I kept the other half. I don't know why I did that. I put it in the drawer and forgot about it. Until you decided to get nosy."

I put both pieces in my purse and thanked Ben before getting up to leave.

As soon as I got home, I called Elizabeth.

"You're not gonna believe what I'm about to tell you," I said as soon as she picked up the line.

"What? What's up?" she said.

"It's about the day Bubba died. Do you have a moment?"

"Yeah, sure."

"Are you ready to hear what really happened on the hunting trip?"

I recounted the whole story, from Raiza's discoveries to Ben's breakdown. I could hear Elizabeth crying softly.

"That is… so far beyond anything I could have imagined," she said. "And to think he never told me—or anyone else. What a burden on his heart. On his shoulders. God, why wouldn't he talk to anyone?"

"It reminds me of a poem," I said, "about the heart being a strong muscle but a tender vessel…. What must he have felt, with so much guilt and uncertainty and obligation and pressure...?"

"And to keep it bottled up," Elizabeth interrupted. "It was like he worked some of it through by helping Megan. But then to lose her, too..."

"What a strange, sad way to grieve," I said. "Suppressing the pain and trying to ignore it."

We both fell to sobbing. How oddly satisfying to be close to Elizabeth at this moment of shared revelation.

"More than ever I'm convinced he died of a broken heart," I said.

"You're right. I think you're right."

The initial grief of losing Gregory rebounded, but it was softened by my strange connection to this woman he had loved.

"I really appreciate all you've done," she said, "unraveling so much. Answering so many questions. As awful as the answers are."

"Yes, sorry. Yes."

"I think I need to go now."

After we hung up, I made two more calls, to Connie, then Raiza.

Even Raiza cried.

"What a sad story," she said, her professional guard undone. "I guess this verifies your reading," she sniffed.

"Yeah. Just not the way I expected."

CHAPTER TWENTY-FIVE

Lyndon Hall was tucked away in a quiet corner of the campus. The only sound Connie and I heard once we'd entered the Georgian edifice was a smart *clack-ka-clack-ka-clack* of high heels on bare tile somewhere ahead of us. With its ornate stonework and floors polished to a patina by decades of determined footsteps, the building telegraphed its standing as a serious place where scholars and academics like Dr. Koslow toiled at their life's work.

"I'm so nervous," I said, unable to stop the shakes as we turned down the hall that led to the lab.

"You'll be in good hands," Connie said, pushing open a heavy, windowless door with a red light above it. "Here we go."

A small sign next to the door put visitors on notice: "When light is flashing: Do not enter. Session in progress."

The seating area reminded me of nothing so much as a shrink's waiting room: neat, with inviting contemporary chairs in a warm, informal setting illuminated by soft light. The room was bookended with doors: the one leading in and another that presumably opened to the interior lab area. Before Connie could press the buzzer by the interior door, an ebullient young man with shaggy auburn hair and fashionably clipped, two-day stubble opened it.

"Connie. It's great to see you again," he said, shaking her hand. "And this is Ann?"

"Yes, hello."

"I'm Adrian. I work with Dr. Koslow." Adrian's easy, confident demeanor and open smile helped calm me, although I remained as jittery as if I'd just downed a couple of espresso shots. He led us to a small, open area dominated by a freestanding chamber next to something that looked like a cross between a control panel and a piano keyboard. The lab outside the chamber was ringed in blond paneling polished to a satin sheen. All around the perimeter were file drawers and cubbies, a warren of neatly stacked papers and expanding files. The control board itself was on risers adjacent to the chamber, which was like a room within a room.

"Follow me," Adrian said as he stepped up and opened the door to the inner chamber. It had that deadened, thuddy sound of something that is heavily soundproofed. At the center of the chamber were two overstuffed, recliner-type chairs with wires and panels on each side and overhead. Headphones hung between them on a double hook, and what looked like microphones were suspended on wires from the ceiling. Suddenly, what I was about to do seemed more real. More exciting. More terrifying.

"Are the chairs close enough for us to hold hands?" I asked, nerves dancing.

Adrian chuckled. "Yes, they are. But you probably won't need to. Once you achieve the out-of-body state, you lose the desire for physical contact. You connect differently."

This momentarily chilled me. Like I'll never need physical contact again? Is he saying that?

"Have you done this?" I asked, gesturing toward the recliners.

"Yes." Adrian was reassuring. "Many times."

With Connie out of earshot, I pulled him quietly aside.

"Do you think this is risky?" I asked, still not satisfied with the answers I'd gotten from either Connie or Dr. Koslow. I wanted to ask him if anyone had ever failed to return. At some level, I was still spooked by the possibility, although I'd been unable to find any record of such a mishap at this facility. In fact, I could not find solid documentation of idiopathic deaths associated with OBEs anywhere.

"I think the risks are exaggerated," Adrian said offhandedly. "And we've never come close here."

I wanted to probe deeper but left it alone.

We ducked back out of the chamber and joined Connie just in time to see Dr. Koslow walking toward us from a short interior hall. He'd traded his tennis togs for a forest-green pullover with an open-collar shirt. Black slacks, crisp and pressed. I had a flash of neatnik Gregory. Until I looked down. Goofy sneakers. Oh dear. Not like Gregory at all. Would there ever be a day when he wasn't my first thought?

"Hello, and welcome to our lab," Dr. Koslow said, radiating confidence and pride.

"Let me walk you through what will happen. You and I will go into the chamber and get comfortably seated in the two chairs. Adrian will hook us up to the monitors and, as we go through the synchronized-sound sequence, he'll use the monitors to track everything that's happening to our physical bodies. Physiologically, it will resemble sleep. But it's not. Also, I can assure you that you will be in good hands. He and I have both done this many times."

I wanted to believe him, and again I had the impression of a calm, steady pilot. But no matter what he said I still had that chattering sensation in my teeth and felt as if tremors were going off in my body.

I worried: Could I overcome my fears and do this? Or would I completely wash out? Would I get "out," only to be unable to get back in? Connie had spent hours preparing me for this, showing me how to focus on my breathing and quiet my monkey mind, but… I still felt so utterly unprepared. And my questions persisted: How would I know Gregory? What would he look like? Would he see me? Could we touch? What if I didn't want to leave?

Connie moved close to me and slid her arm through mine.

"I know you're still scared," she said. "Just trust the process and do the best you can."

"Yes," Dr. Koslow chimed in. "And if at any point you want to terminate the process, Adrian will be able to read that, too, on the monitors. If that happens, we will stop immediately. You are always in control."

He paused.

"Would you like a drink of water or to use the restroom before we get started?"

Everything was moving too fast and not fast enough. The prospect of seeing Gregory flipped me into giddy excitement. Shaking with fear? No, this new shaking tapped an anticipation I'd dared not let myself feel, as if I were holding back another wall of tears, a dam that would burst when I laid eyes on him—or whatever you do without a body. I still had so many questions that Connie had not answered. At least not to my satisfaction. She was careful not to reveal too much or create an unreal expectation, emphasizing that everyone's experience was different.

"Yes," I said, reeling myself back to the moment. "Water and a pit stop would be nice."

"We'll be right here," Adrian said. "Ready when you are. The restroom's down the hall by Dr. Koslow's office."

He pulled a bottle of water out of a small refrigerator for me, placed it on the counter next to the console, and motioned toward the hall.

When I got back, Dr. Koslow was already inside the chamber, easing into one of the chairs. I took one last look at Connie for courage. She smiled and winked. I entered the chamber and sat down. There was no turning back now. As Adrian hooked me up to the sensors, I practiced the slow, rhythmic breathing Connie had taught me. But I could not prevent my heart from pounding as if I were leading a drum circle.

"Try not to be afraid," said Dr. Koslow, reaching for my hand. Because of the connectors on our temples, he couldn't turn and face me.

"I've done this many times," he said, catching my hand in his. "When I first started, it was difficult to overcome my fears. But I just kept at it, kept my logical side engaged—that's very important—and trusted my guides."

"Guides?" I said, surprised at the use of the term. "I thought this was pure research."

"It is, and yes, spiritual guides. That's how they have identified themselves to us. We can't explain them yet, so we just work with them as an experimental variable.

"We never know exactly what will happen when we go out of body, but my hope is to travel to a place called the park, a common gathering point for those in transition. That's where I think we have the best chance of finding Gregory. The information you gave me about him will be helpful for locating him.

"I'll hold your hand for now if you like, but I think you will be able to concentrate better if I don't. It's up to you."

His voice was as cosseting as the feathery snow that had swirled around me those many weeks before, when

I first learned of Gregory's death. Only this was different. This time I didn't feel blocked off or buffered from the full impact of my experience. It was more like falling into a deep, airy feather bed, where every inch of you is supported in softness and warmth, and you feel relaxed and peaceful. My jitters were gone.

"I'll do what you suggest," I said, releasing his hand as Adrian adjusted my headphones. My hands seemed to nest naturally into the arms of the chair, and I opened my eyes just long enough to see Adrian pull the door closed behind him. Dr. Koslow and I were alone in the chamber.

Slowly, the lights dimmed until we were in total darkness.

"Testing, testing. Can you hear me, Ann?" Adrian had become a faraway voice in my head.

"Yes, I can hear you."

"Okay. I'm going to test for the sound level. When you hear a tone, hold up your hand on the side where you hear it."

I raised my right hand as the first point of sound grew louder.

"How can you see what I'm doing?" I asked.

"I can see you because we use thermal imaging monitors," Adrian said.

The sequence reminded me of a hearing test.

"Now, can you hear this?"

A low tone vibrated in my left ear. I put my left hand up.

"Okay, good."

We went through this routine several more times, until it seemed Adrian was satisfied with what I could hear.

"I think we're about ready," he said.

I wondered if this was what astronauts felt like as the final seconds before launch counted down in their helmets.

"This is just a reminder, Ann: You and Dr. Koslow won't be able to hear each other initially. But I will be able to hear both of you at all times, so if you need something, speak up."

Lift-off, I thought to myself, tingling.

As we reclined in the darkness, my flight out of body began with a series of tones, reminiscent of Gregorian chant, reverberating in my ears. It felt as if they filled my entire head. Then my body. The sounds washed over me like physical sensations, but then I felt as if I were floating on top of them, pulsing on a magic carpet of sound. It was so enveloping that I completely forgot where I was. It seemed like we were rising higher and sinking lower simultaneously. Falling, floating. The tones gradually gave way to drumming. Long, low drumming. I began vibrating in every corner of my being.

The vibrating alarmed me until Adrian's faraway, silky voice broke through: "Relax, Ann. This is normal. Just go with it."

I inhaled into the tremors, like Connie had taught me. No, I'm not breaking apart. I exhaled slowly, as the shaking ratcheted up again.

Before I knew what had happened, something popped, and I found myself hovering a few inches above my chair. I was out of my body! If only by a fragment of space and time, barely inches removed.

But then I wavered, lost concentration or something, and couldn't hold it. I slammed back down into the chair.

"It's okay," Adrian said. "You did great. It's not unusual to require a couple of attempts at first. Let's try that again."

We repeated the same sequence, starting with the low vibration of the chant, the feeling of floating and sinking… trembling and shaking… and another pop. Again, I was a few inches above my body. I concentrated on holding myself steady.

As I "looked" around and perceived nothing but darkness inside the chamber, I started to panic and almost lost it again. That's when something that felt like a hand brushed my arm.

"Hold on there," a voice seemed to say in my head, which was no longer a head.

"I think I'm okay," I somehow intoned with thought.

I'm out of my body. I'm actually out of my body.

"We are in the astral phase, the beginning. Let's explore the immediate surroundings of the lab and building so you can get used to 'seeing' with your noncorporeal self."

"Oh my God," was all I could emit as I looked around us, first at the lab, where I clearly discerned the tops of Adrian and Connie's heads as what I can only describe as energy patterns. Then, as we seemed to float higher, like kites in the wind, beyond the roof, we found ourselves in a cooler energy matrix surrounded by the darkness of the night. The sensation was breathtaking, but I had no breath to take. Moving from place to place felt dreamlike and surreal. Only I was not dreaming.

"I want you to see how familiar objects such as the building look from this vantage point," Dr. Koslow said after we had ascended higher. He wasn't holding my hand exactly. It was more like we had an energetic connection. He seemed to be the one securing it, as though he were holding me in place lest I drift too far too quickly.

I was "viewing" things from a dimension as different as three dimensions are from two. I wanted to run my hands along the exterior brick, but as I tried, the part of me that I thought was my hand slipped right through the masonry as though it weren't there. No resistance whatsoever. I couldn't see anything clearly. It was like we were in a fog.

"It's a little like seeing in darkness," Dr. Koslow resonated. "You will become accustomed to it."

I could see what I surmised were people—moving shapes—on the ground below me. One seemed very familiar.

Is this what Gregory would look like?

"No," I felt Dr. Koslow vibrate. "He won't show up like human energy, which is what you are seeing. We still have to 'go' to where I hope he will be."

The park. The place called the park. My concentration had wandered. I was captivated by an entity moving below us. Fuzzy and unclear, it was like a blurred photo image.

"That one is out of focus," came Dr. Koslow's thought. He saw it, too.

"But why?"

"Either it is near death or otherwise out of sync with life. Not anything for us to approach or be distracted by."

I couldn't help myself. I kept staring, unable to look away, simultaneously drawn to and repelled by the strange entity. As the blur lumbered toward what looked like one of the building's doors, I saw a glint of something shiny.

"What was that?" For no reason I could deduce, I found this image alarming.

"'Could be a soda can. Or a belt buckle."

"Then why can't I look away?"

"Do not let it pull you too much," Dr. Koslow soothed. "I notice the familiarity, too, but it's probably just a student. We still have a distance to go."

I felt the shudder of vibration again.

"You need to focus on me, Ann," I heard the professor say. I sensed some urgency emanating from him.

"You cannot hide anything here," he said with a cosmic chuckle. "It's easy to get sidetracked."

With one last glance at the unfocused figure lurching toward the building door, I rolled my full attention into Dr. Koslow. The bucking stopped.

"Okay now. Concentrate on me and my energy signature. We're going to pull a jump."

I closed my "eyes" and melted into Dr. Koslow's spiraling shape. The building fell away, and everything went black. We entered what I can best describe as a vortex, only that isn't what it was. Two-dimensional words can't describe the spinning, whirling sensation we were experiencing. Were we in the place like a vortex for two seconds or two thousand years? No way to gauge.

I turned my attention to Dr. Koslow and was blinded by a blueish-white light.

"What's happening?" I emitted with unease.

"Nothing bad," he said. "You're just 'seeing' me as I exist fully outside my corporeal body."

"Is that what I look like?" Where were my arms? My legs? I felt them. Why couldn't I see them?

"Yes, more or less. Everyone's signature is different. You are more pink."

Pink. Great.

"Where are we?"

I looked down at myself and my shimmering pinkness.

"We are at the edge of the park, just where I hoped we'd be."

And yes, there it was, a glowing green space of lush, vibrating vegetation that extended as far as I could "see." It was possible to make out trees and bushes and shadows, and here and there what resembled earthly park benches along random paths. I could smell dirt and flowers and hear water gurgling somewhere nearby.

"So I'm really out of my body?" I emitted. "This isn't just some sort of shared illusion?"

"Does it feel like an illusion?"

"No."

"Does it feel real?"

"Oh God, yes."

"It IS real, as real as the room we just left."

"What's happening with our bodies?" I felt a stab of doubt, fearing for my physical self. As I did, something tugged lightly at my midsection.

"They're fine. Like we're asleep. Only the brain waves are different. That pulling sensation is what people call the silver cord that connects 'you' and your body. Please concentrate on your love for Gregory now. I need your help if we are to find him."

I immersed myself unfettered into my feelings of love, still so entwined with the ache of loss. I let myself visualize Gregory as if he were standing before me, let myself feel as wrapped in his love as when our physical bodies had comingled, let myself exalt in the outpouring of my love. His love. But the alternating waves of love and despair—I could not control the oscillation—were almost too much to bear.

"Stay with it," Dr. Koslow encouraged in a whisper. "Stay with the feelings."

A force slammed into my gut, and it was not love. Got to get back, was all I could think. It made no sense, but—

"Hurry!" came Dr. Koslow's command. "We have to leave. Now."

Like being sucked backwards through a kaleidoscope, I felt myself rushing, twisting, turning, tumbling through rotating colors with increased urgency to get back to the astral. Hovering briefly above the lab, I sensed something was terribly wrong.

Adrian lay motionless on the floor like a rag doll, and Connie was thrashing furiously against something emitting waves of red and orange. Glints of light. Alarms went off in my head. I struggled to lock onto the slashing entity as Dr. Koslow and I surged inbound.

I landed with a cosmic thud in the chair next to Dr. Koslow, who was already tearing off the wires and connectors. I threw down my headphones and did the same. Our nearly palpable panic was eerie in the black, dead silence of the chamber. Dr. Koslow raced to unlatch the door from our side, and as soon as he did, Connie's screams dissipated any afterglow.

"Adrian!" Dr. Koslow rushed to his limp assistant's side, pressing his hand against a heavily bleeding gash on one leg. Blood was pulsing out of it, pooling under him.

No time to think.

I rushed up behind the slashing figure just as she—she?—was bringing the metal thing—metal?—down in an arc toward Connie, who was shielding herself with her arms in the small work area, already bleeding from defensive wounds. Was it an ax? A machete?

"*NO… YOU… DON'T!*"

The words spewed from my mouth—yes, my real mouth—as I grabbed for her arm. Before I could stop her—who is "her"?—she swung to face me in one motion.

"You!" She glowered and took a swipe at me. "You she-devil!"

Stella!

I barely felt the knife slice into the flesh of my arm, leaving a bright, garnet line.

"I will stop you," she shrieked. "You can't get my boy's soul. You and your Spanish Satan. I'll kill you both."

Her eyes bulged out, the whites streaked red and yellow, on fire. She had tapped some unseen reservoir of strength, menacing me with a huge knife, its tip inches from my face. Would she really slash my face?

"Wanda told me you'd be here!" she said, feral with rage.

"Call the cops!" I shouted as Connie scrambled toward a phone on the console.

Stella raised her arms over her head, preparing to slash. As she did, a foul, animal stink radiated off her in swells. Her gray-blonde hair was stringy and matted with sweat, and the flaps and folds of her crepe-y arms swung and glistened as she came at me again in the close, cramped space.

"This is going to stop," she bellowed, gasping and jabbing toward me with what I now saw clearly was a carbon-steel butcher's knife. "They're my boys. You can't have them." I didn't even feel the blood sluicing down my arm.

I body slammed her, but it was like hitting a tank. She had at least a fifty-pound advantage on me. As the knife swooped my way again, I dodged the blade and grabbed her wrist, this time wrapping myself next to her vile-smelling awfulness.

"You're insane," I growled, struggling to get my body up next to her and away from the knife-wielding hand as she screeched on about the devil.

Friends close, enemies closer.

She tried to pull me away with her free hand, grabbing me around the neck. Without thinking, I stomped on her foot.

She spat on me. "Goddamn you, you she-devil bitch!"

In the nanosecond as she caught her breath, I grabbed the pinkie of her clawing hand and bent it back, hard.

The knife clattered to the floor, and Stella howled, cursing me but immobilized by the pain. The room was nearly silent except for her sputtering and our animal panting. I swooped down to grab the knife and flung it down the hall, where it landed with a hollow rattle.

It was only then that I heard the distant wail of sirens.

Moving Dr. Koslow aside, the EMTs worked quickly to stanch Adrian's bleeding and stabilize him before placing him in an ambulance and speeding away. Dr. Koslow collapsed in the chair next to the console and held his hands to his head like *The Scream,* a man undone.

"What will I do?" he moaned. "What will we do? Adrian hurt. The lab destroyed. Years of work. Years and years of work. Gone. What now? What now?"

The police easily overpowered Stella who was bleating about her wrenched finger.

"Don't you touch me! I'm hurt. She attacked me," she bawled, wild-eyed and pointing at me.

"Just take it easy," one of the officers said, keeping a firm grip on her arm.

"She's the slasher," Dr. Koslow said, surfacing from his despair. His bloodied sweater and slacks clung to his limbs.

"Am not. She did it," screeched Stella, struggling against the officer's grasp. "You weren't even here."

"No, but I was," said Connie, sitting nearby, another EMT dabbing something on her arms and starting to wrap them with gauze. She looked over the EMT's shoulder directly at Stella. "And you were definitely the one with the knife."

"Liar! Devil bitch. I saw it at the mall. Devils dancing around you. Devils!"

Stella spewed the words, her face contorted with pain as another officer stepped up and, with the help of the first, led her away.

I looked at Connie and started shaking violently.

"It's okay," she said. "You did exactly right. You drew her off so I could call the police. That's why they got here so fast."

"But how did she...?"

"Adrian and I were so focused on you and Dr. Koslow that we didn't even hear her till she was on top of us. And the workspace was so small..." Her voice trailed off.

A blur of blue uniforms and black leather swarmed the lab, now a crime scene cordoned off with yellow tape.

A police officer took Dr. Koslow's arm and led him toward a quiet corner, presumably where they could talk.

Only then did I stop to look around the room and survey the carnage.

The console lay in ruins. Shards of glass and plastic littered the floor. Blood was everywhere—on the console, the floor tiles, splattered up the walls. The overhead lights still worked, but the console was dark.

"Look at this," I said. "Look at this mess." I picked up a tangle of wires.

"Don't touch that, miss," said one of the officers, and I let it drop.

"She slashed at everything," Connie said with a sigh. "The wires. The keyboard. The door." Only then did I see the gashes in the chamber's outer door. "Thousands of dollars' worth of equipment. Destroyed."

I could hear the dread in Connie's voice.

Like everyone else standing around the lab, I was relieved that we had somehow averted a worse disaster. Why, then, did I feel so sad?

CHAPTER TWENTY-SIX

Long hours after the incident, after the police had finished interviewing each of us, Connie and I walked home. To all outward appearances, the world seemed normal in the moonlight—the sleepy campus, the stars, the scant people we encountered crossing the quad.

But from my perspective, everything had changed. Everything looked vibrant and alive, buzzing with a truth new to me: the revelation of a nonphysical scaffolding to the universe. As real as my pumping heart and the rustle of wind through the trees. But also as real as the violence that had just taken place, rattling and unsettling all involved. The EMTs assured us Adrian would be okay, thanks to Dr. Koslow's quick actions. And Dr. Koslow—what about him? Surely the university officials would take into consideration that he'd saved Adrian's life. But through the mopping-up and interrogations, Connie had cast a look at me across the room as if to say we had more to talk about than the aftermath of the crime.

"I know we've just been through a lot," I said as we arrived at her door, "but I've got to tell you what we—Dr. Koslow and I—did before we got pulled back."

"Yeah," Connie said. "I want to hear this. And I need to hear it now, even though I'm wrecked. Where'd you go? Did you find him?"

"No, we got pulled back before we found him. But oh my God, the rest of it..."

Connie turned the key in her lock. "Come inside."

"Is there something I can get for you?" I said, taking Connie's coat as she struggled to slip it off. Underneath, her long-sleeve shirt was stained brown. "A cup of tea? Something to eat?"

For all the blood and gauze—Connie's arms resembled a mummy's by the time the EMT was through—Connie's wounds were superficial. Not so, Adrian's. He would be in the hospital for at least several days because Stella's chaotic stabbing nicked an artery in his leg. Dr. Koslow emerged from the chamber just in time to save him from bleeding to death. Stella must have been losing momentum and strength when she visited her fury on Connie, because Connie's wounds were long, shallow incisions—the kind of scoring you'd make on top of bread dough before slipping it into the oven. Around the patchwork of butterfly bandages and gauze, her skin had already started bruising.

Connie smiled wanly. "A glass of water would be nice. But please, I've got to know just a little more..."

I got a pitcher of cold water from her fridge and poured her a glass. She had taken to the couch and pulled an afghan over her lap, looking so vulnerable, as if the energy had been leached out of her.

But her fierce, smoky eyes shone.

"So you didn't see him."

"No," I said, my excitement at what we had accomplished muted by this disappointment, "but we were so close. I got outside my body—I, oh my God—I was out there. Up in the corner of the room. And then… And then… my 'hand' through the bricks. And… You know what it's like to fly in a dream? It was like that, only it wasn't a dream, and I went so far beyond that. Nothing will ever be the same again."

Connie beamed, if weakly. "It does change your perspective."

"We went somewhere with hyperdrive or a hyperlink or something…."

"A jump," Connie corrected. "We call that a jump. Helps you skip across space like a stone across water."

"I mean, that should have been enough," I said. "But we landed near what must have been the park. Or the edge of the park."

"Um hmm."

"And then it all vanished after I was punched in the gut."

"Yes. Your frantic cue to return. Adrian trying to warn you. Stella took us by surprise."

"And here we are now."

"And here we are now," Connie repeated.

I thought about all she had been through, all she had done up to that moment.

"I have to thank you," I said. "Profusely. For setting this up, for taking the risk, for being there, for..." I fumbled for words. I wanted her to know how much I appreciated everything she had done even if... "I'm sorry it all went so wrong."

"No, stop. No one could have predicted Stella would turn to violence."

"How could Stella even have known we'd be there?" I wondered.

Wanda.

"Ah, Wanda," I answered my own question. "She must have seen Dr. Koslow's schedule with my name on it and gotten suspicious. Put two and two together."

Connie seemed oddly sanguine.

"It's just what it is," she said, all-knowing and Yoda-like. "I want to hear more about where you went. But right now, I'm fading. I need to sleep...."

"But what about your clothes? And a shower?"

"I'm just too tired tonight."

"I'll let myself out, then," I said. I sat next to her and clasped her hands in mine. "I'll call you first thing in the morning."

Our foreheads met and lightly touched.

"Thanks," she said with such sweetness I almost cried.

Back at my own place, I looked in the mirror. What a mess. My hair looked like I'd combed it with an egg beater, as my mother would have said—brown clumps and curls jutted out every which way. Dried blood smeared across my cheeks and nose, on my ears, and I had a gash over my right eye closed with some butterfly strips. Stella had come close to blinding me. I was so relieved Olivia was at her dad's.

None of it mattered. I couldn't stop marveling: I'd gone out of my body—actually gone out of body. I kept replaying what we did over and over. The hyperjump pushed me beyond all bounds of reason, unmoored and euphoric. Unexpected. Unlike anything I'd ever experienced. My entire perspective on consciousness and what it meant to be alive shifted in that moment. Forever. In the short time we were out there—wherever "there" was—my doubts about surviving death, whether Gregory survived death, evaporated. Talk about research and verify. But there was more: For the first time, at least consciously, I experienced an almost mystical connection to something greater than myself.

Unlike Connie, I couldn't wait to shower. Both cats sat and watched, heads tilted, as the bathroom filled with steam. Once I was done, I slipped into sweats and curled up on the couch with some hot chocolate. No way could I sleep. Bernie leapt up beside me and nosed my hand. I stroked him absently. Woody sniffed and licked at my fingers, seemingly determined to obliterate whatever clung there.

Then I lay back with both cats ensconced, closed my eyes and dove again into what it felt like to be in that place, out there. Everything going so well till the pull at my gut....

I was grateful no one had died. But my relief was tempered. I couldn't overcome a gnawing sense of disappointment.

We'd come so close.

My innate skepticism stiffened against this new reality and struggled to surface from somewhere deep in my bones. It was no match for the thrill of being out of body and all its inherent possibilities. I hungered to go back. Taste again. Drink at the river. Touch Gregory. Touch all that lies beyond physical existence. Already this was torquing my earthbound perception. I could feel my focus tugged away from the life I was living here on earth to craving, needing more of something that was logically unattainable until you throw off the shell of your body.

Until you die.

The yearning it aroused was what I imagined heroin addicts must feel, just not as extreme. Completely tuned out to their physical surroundings—eyes closed, mouth agape, lost to the world on some greasy, cast-off sofa in a boarded-up house—transported by the drug to someplace deeply pleasurable inside their own brains. And as soon as they came around to the so-called real world again, all their energy would be consumed in the effort to get back to that place heroin delivered. In a figurative and sometimes literal sense, their compulsion sucked the life out of them. Was I headed down a similar path?

We came so close.

The thought gnawed at me. Right or wrong didn't matter. Supposed to or not didn't matter. All I could think about was traveling through those cosmic mountains and up over a rise that revealed the valley below, surely the edge of the park—only to be jerked up and away, off-course, like pulling the cord on a parachute and getting caught in the upward rush of air.

I couldn't shake my desire to do it again. We had been so close to Gregory. I sensed it. I had to do it again.

But this seemed out of the question. The lab was a shambles. Who knew how long it would take to repair? If it could even be put back together again. And if it could, what then? Dr. Koslow and perhaps a good chunk of his research were completely undone by the destruction. What kind of ruinous inquiries would follow to decide whether this was a legitimate pursuit for a university? Dr. Koslow might well lose his job, his career, over this. What trials and penalties would authorities exact? And what about the rest of us, who had been willing co-conspirators? At best, the powers that be would clamp down on the sort of test ride we had attempted, calling for greater oversight and closer screening of potential subjects. Worst case, if there were enough public outcry, the whole operation might be shuttered.

None of it mattered. I had to try it again.

I would have to tap Connie, my magic Christian. That's all there was to it. She was my only connection. I'd have to press her. Again. On how I might return to that place.

I lay back and closed my eyes, head pounding, thoughts whirling.

Where had we gone? What was space-time? Was that "jump" like warp speed on *Star Trek?* How close did we get to Gregory?

Did he see *me?*

The next thing I knew, the first mote-speckled streaks of dawn were winking through the darkness and a small black-and-white face was staring into mine. Bernie mewled softly for me to wake up.

I called in sick to work, explaining that I'd been in an accident. Not hurt, just a little shaken up. It was mostly true.

Minutes after I'd put the phone down, it rang again.

"Hey."

Raiza.

"Hey, what's up?"

"You mean, 'What the eff's up?' Don't you?"

"Not getting what you mean... ," I said.

"Last night. I got the assignment to write a metro short on the lab mishap. My reward for coming in to work so early."

Lab mishap? My life-changing experience had been reduced to a lab mishap? The wonderful world of journalism.

"I know this isn't the most professional way to start, but what the hell happened?"

Raiza. My very best friend at work. What was I going to tell her?

"What do you mean? What do you know?"

"Saw the police blotter. Injuries. Property damage. Stella. And a note from the night editor that you were there. They tried to reach you but..."

My phone. I hadn't even checked for messages before falling asleep on the couch. It just didn't seem as important as it might have the day before.

I weighed my words. I was on the record, now.

"I was being tested as a possible subject for one of Dr. Koslow's studies," I said truthfully.

"Yeah, that's a nice official line," Raiza said. I could hear her teeth on the end of her pen.

"Yeah," I said with a deep sigh. "If I ever tell anyone in the press what happened, you'll be first in line. But right now, that's all I can say."

"All you can say! I'm your best goddamned friend—and that's all you can say? This has something to do with Gregory, doesn't it?"

"Officially, no. Off the record, yes."

"But you're not going to tell me squat."

"No. Not now. Not for a metro brief. On the record, I'm glad no one was hurt worse than they were. I know that's a sorry quote. You can say I was not there on a story. I was just interested in volunteering for Dr. Koslow's research."

"What's going to happen to that now?"

"I don't know. That's up to the university."

"Did you go out of body, like the buzz on his research suggests?"

"No comment."

"You did, didn't you?"

"No comment."

"You're really starting to piss me off."

"I'm sorry," I said.

It wasn't easy being on the receiving end of a reporter's grilling.

"Can you just take what I've given you and run with it? At some point, I'll tell you more. But right now that's all I have for you."

"That's really sucky, cube-mate." I couldn't tell if she was actually mad.

"I know."

As soon as I could get Raiza off the phone, I called Connie.

Even at hello, my friend sounded rested, even mildly chipper.

"How y'doing this morning?" I asked.

"Sore, but feeling more human. My arms must be bruised as well as cut, the way they hurt." She hesitated. "I really want to take a shower, but I need some help. You up for coming over?"

"Of course," I said, "for whatever you need. And we don't need to take off the bandages or anything. I devised a dandy trash-bag-duct-tape system to keep them dry and in place. Be there in a few minutes."

Connie laughed. "That sounds good," she said. Her laugh sounded good, too.

"Do you want some coffee?"

"That sounds even better."

"Okay, see you in a few."

After feeding the cats, I put on a bra under my sweatshirt, brushed my teeth and pushed my hair back with a headband. Then I jumped into the purring Celica and drove through Coffee Cabana for a couple of skinny lattes.

Skinny lattes? Really?

"Wait," I said. "Make those regular, full-on milk lattes."

I was at Connie's door in less than twenty minutes.

"Hi," she said.

"Hi, yourself."

I held out one of the lattes for her and gave her a gentle near-hug, careful not to touch her arms.

"This tastes good after last night," she said, sipping the hot liquid.

"And since we're going to live forever, we're doing full fat. All the way." I slurped noisily, to cool the hot drink.

We sat at the little drop-leaf table in her kitchen. Her eyes were still swollen from sleep, and she was in her rumpled tartan plaid robe. She looked awful. But she was smiling. That was golden.

"How're we going to do this?" she asked.

"I brought a couple of trash bags and duct tape. We'll get your clothes off and put these in place to keep everything dry."

We finished our lattes, and Connie got ready to shower. I wrapped and taped her arms, and she looked just as ridiculous as I had, but the system worked. I waited in the kitchen while she showered.

"Okay," she shouted from the bathroom when she was done. "Let's get these things off."

Steam fogged the mirror and pink-and-gray tiles, and the aroma of lavender hung in the air. Connie sat on the toilet draped in her robe with a towel around her head. Snip, snip, snip. She watched as I ran the scissors around the plastic bag on her arm. Then I cut through the duct tape and gingerly pulled it away.

"Thank you," she said, inspecting her gauze-wrapped arms. "We'll have to change these out at some point. What a mess this has been."

"I'm so sorry," I said. I felt like I couldn't apologize enough.

Connie grasped my arm, careful to avoid my cuts, and held it firmly.

"Don't," she said. "I want to make something clear." She relaxed her grip. "I did this freely. Of my own free will. And believe it or not, it's been good for me. Made me realize something. Pushed me toward something I've needed for years."

Her expression looked certain. Her stature, even sitting there, more imposing. My friend seemed to have changed before my eyes. Like something long buried had awakened in her.

"You've listened to me dither about who I am and what I do," she declared. "How I've tiptoed around my family for years. Led a double life. Cowered in fear of my father and fearing the judgments of others. Well, this experience changed me—my coming out to you, fighting for my life with Stella, seeing the real harm of Gregory's secrets. It flipped a switch. It's like… I'm done."

Something tectonic was happening. Even the timbre of her voice was different. Clear and more resonant.

"I don't fully understand my abilities," she said, a little less forcefully. "Never have. But I'm finally convinced that they are who I am, how God made me. No apologies. I'm really, really done. No more slinking around like I'm guilty of something. And I think about how this applies to Gregory. If only he'd thrown open those darned compartments, maybe his heart wouldn't have broken. He just didn't understand how it sapped him, the tension of holding all that energy separate. Pushing it down. Dammit, I'm not going to live that way any longer.

"As for this," she said, holding up her arms and looking from one to the other, "I don't hold you responsible. I don't hold anyone responsible. It's just something that happened."

I marveled at this "new" Connie. Her eyes shone, and her smile was open and welcoming.

"Well, even if I'm not responsible, can I at least buy you breakfast?" It came out like a wisecrack.

"Ha. Yeah. You can buy me breakfast anytime."

It was sunny and cold when we walked to the French bakery nearby, the one with a thatched roof façade and cottage decor. I looked at all the people there. I knew something they did not. I knew they had an eternal dimension. Any one of them could go where I went. Now or at the hour of their death. Students in faded jeans or baggy sweats slumped among the rustic tables, buried in books, mainlining coffee. Sweaty cyclists in body-hugging shorts pushing two-tops together to accommodate their merry band. Little kids pestering their parents for more jam. Everything about this earthbound dimension seemed beautiful and less urgent. Less worth judging. Less worthy of angst. My thoughts seemed to ebb and flow with the finger-snapping French pop music pulsing in the background. It used to annoy me. No longer. It was the snow again, swirling around me, cossetting me, protecting me. But this time it was different, as if I would always be protected. A simple thought bubbled up: *I love life.*

Connie and I ordered an omelet—with extra cheese—and some fruit to split and found a corner table.

Once we were settled, I couldn't wait a second longer.

"I don't know any way to say this except to say it," I blurted out. "I've got to find a way to do that again."

Connie just looked at me.

"You mean go out of body?" she said. "Didn't you get enough excitement the first time?"

"Yes. No. No, I didn't. I've got to. I feel like we were this close to the park," I said, holding up my thumb and index finger. "It was like we were just coming to it—we were perched above it—and then everything went crazy."

Connie studied my face.

"You got that close."

"It was amazing," I said. "When we did that hyperjump, warp-speed thing.... I can't even describe it. It felt impossible. And yet we were doing it. Like swinging on a trapeze all the way to Mars."

Connie pushed some of the omelet onto a corner of her toast and took a long time to respond. "It's exciting, isn't it?"

"You've done it, haven't you? All the way out like that?" My fork clattered to the floor, and I quickly grabbed another from a neighboring table.

"Yes, I have done that." She laughed lightly. "With Dr. Koslow and without. That's kind of how I met him."

"Explain?"

"I've kept so much from you—I suppose, as a way of pressing back the childhood trauma and fear of judgment," Connie said. "But that's done."

"So what now?" I said, not expecting what came next.

"Like you, I couldn't resist the pull," Connie said, leaning toward me. "So powerful and seductive. And make no mistake, there are dark forces out there, too. But here's what I've learned: The challenge is to balance the desire to go out with the need to stay in the here and now. Because you are living *this* life." She gestured with her toast. "You're supposed to live it, not spend it trying to go someplace else. Or be something you're not."

Connie voice was strong and assured.

"My family would still disown me if they ever found out all I've done 'out there,'" she said. "But I don't care anymore."

Then her eyes fixed on mine.

"You see who I am," she said. "I'm more grateful for that than you will ever know. But it's taken until now, until this latest episode, to release my fear. Maybe for the first time in my life, I feel free. Really free."

I was in awe of my friend. This was such a contrast to the tentative and conflicted Connie I'd met in college. How gratifying to witness her blossoming from someone closed and fearful into this more open and expansive person.

"Here's something else you need to know," she said almost casually, between bites. "I was subject zero."

"Subject zero? You mean like patient zero?"

I'd heard the term only in connection with epidemiology, what they called the first person to show symptoms of a terrible disease, like HIV.

"When Dr. Koslow first started his studies about twenty years ago, he sent out a notice to counseling and professional psych groups, looking for anyone who thought they might have gone out of body. I was in grad school. Since I'd gone out of body spontaneously as a kid and been looking for answers as to why, I picked up one of those notices. And called him."

My friend was uncovering layers so fast, I was having trouble keeping up.

"I had no idea you were holding back so much."

"Like I said, yesterday Gregory helped me take my final step to freedom."

Yes.

I took another bite of omelet, barely noticing a kid dragging his sticky hand along the edge of our table. Connie wasn't finished.

"Dr. Koslow helped me learn to control my… meanderings. But I can do it—I've helped others do it—away from his lab."

"How is that possible?"

Connie speared a strawberry and popped it in her mouth, chewing, I was sure, on her next words as well as the berry.

"Dr. Koslow is trying to document the experience in a systematic, scientific way. His work is invaluable. But people have been dabbling in this for centuries. Millennia."

"How can that be?"

Connie broke into a knowing smile and arched her eyebrows. "Why do you think monks and nuns spend so much time singing and chanting?"

"So this is like meditation taken to the next level?"

Her eyes crinkled with mischievousness. "Gregorian chants transported those monks. Opened the gateway. The early church was deeply divided over whether that was getting closer to God or… devils' work."

"Same story, first verse."

"And it wasn't just Christians. What do you think those Sufi dervishes were doing?"

The twirling Muslims of the mystic sect who looked like spinning tops flickered in my mind's eye.

"The closest the mainstream Christian church ever came to acknowledging something spiritual was a begrudging miracle or two. That's it. The rest was witch-dunking and the wages of sin."

Connie carefully stretched her arms, respecting their sensitivity.

"We can replicate what you did with Dr. Koslow," she said matter-of-factly. "Albeit with a cruder system."

Was she offering what I thought she was offering? If she was… oh my God.

Be careful what you ask for.

"But here's the thing, Ann…"

I struggled to stay with her as my thoughts flew to the possibility of getting to that space one more time. Finding, touching Gregory for real. No stops. No barriers. My heroin. I was so swept up in the potential that my hands shook. I grasped my coffee cup to quiet them.

Connie touched my hands, almost magically calming me.

"There still are those stories about people becoming so enraptured with the experience that they leave their bodies behind. The idiopathic deaths. They're real. That's part of the reason I trusted Dr. Koslow to guide you. I knew he would be very careful not to let that happen. Doing this without him is much more random. And risky. A home setup like mine is no match for the safety of the lab. And there's no denying the pull to stay. It's very strong."

Her warning sizzled like water droplets on the heat of my desire.

"And just look at you," Connie said. "Your hair is on fire. You're obsessed."

Yes. We came so close.

"I feel like I've got to try," I told my friend steadily, feeling greedy for wanting it so badly and not caring. "I've got to find a way."

"I suspected that would be the case. It was only a matter of time before you'd figure out that it was possible, ever the dogged journalist. So it comes down to this: I'd rather you do it with me than someone you don't know—and that I don't know. We've come this far. I won't abandon you now."

"Thank you," I said, suddenly feeling soft and weepy with a profoundly deep respect for my friend. "I am so indebted to you."

"No. No indebtedness. Eff debts. You feel indebted? Pay it forward someday. Write a book. But you don't owe me."

And so we agreed to meet at her apartment the next week, giving her time to assemble a jerry-rigged setup.

As we rose to leave the cafe, the theme from *The Umbrellas of Cherbourg*, a 1964 French film, played in the background, giving me chills as its haunting strains wrapped around lyrics of forever love and waiting as long as it takes to be "holding you" again.

CHAPTER TWENTY-SEVEN

I picked up the phone to call Elizabeth, then put the receiver back down.

What was I going to say to her?

On the one hand, I was giddy with excitement over the good parts of what had happened. It was an extraordinary adventure, and I was determined to try it again. I wanted so much to tell Elizabeth about it. I had almost connected with Gregory. Our Gregory. I tried to push aside the not-very-pretty underbelly, the earthbound part of the experience that had ended with jagged edges. Nothing complete. Someone almost dying. Gushing over it might come across as insanely insensitive. Elizabeth might not understand at all.

Don't think it to death.

I sighed. All I knew was I wanted to talk to Elizabeth. Needed to talk to her. Urgently. That was how it was.

I picked the phone up and dialed.

"Hello?"

"Elizabeth? This is Ann."

"Hey, how's it going?"

"Okay. You got a minute? I wanna tell you about last night."

"Yeah, I read about it," came her swift reply. "Saw the paper this morning and how Stella destroyed that lab. I was going to call you, but you beat me to it. What the hell happened?"

"A lot that's not in the story," I said.

"Figured as much."

"First, though, you can't tell anyone what I'm about to tell you. I've got to have your word on that."

"Again? Okay. I can do that."

I drew a long breath.

"We—the researcher and I—were experimenting with going out of body. That's what he studies there, and he was letting me try it with him. As a favor to Connie, who's worked with him for a long time."

For once, Elizabeth was speechless.

"What the eff? What the fuck does that mean, 'go out of body?' Whose body? What body? Where?"

"It's called an out-of-body experience. It's where a part of you—your consciousness, what some people call your spirit or soul—detaches from your physical body. I know it sounds like something out of science fiction, but it's what Dr. Koslow studies at the university, and it's what we were doing when Stella—"

"You actually did something like that?"

"Yes, we did *that*."

"Whoa, sister." She said nothing for a moment. "That's a helluva lot to take in right there."

I wiggled my foot and twirled the coiled phone cord absently.

"I know. I know, I know."

"It sounds surreal, Ann. *Un*-real. What the hell were you trying to do? Oh, wait. This is like the reading, isn't it? Trying to do something with Gregory?

"Trying to contact Gregory."

The words spilled out unedited. They were shocking every time I said them.

"Contact *Gregory?*" Elizabeth sounded incredulous. "I gotta sit down for that one. I don't know what to say. You are so far over the edge."

"I felt compelled to tell you.... I thought you'd want to know."

"I do, but Jesus. Talk about something unexpected. I mean, on any level. I don't even know if I believe in what you're describing."

"I'm sorry. You're right." Her doubts tempered my enthusiasm. "I've probably said too much. It's probably too much information. Weird information. I should never have called. Never brought it up. Not yet at least—"

"Did you make contact with him?"

Her question stopped my nattering cold.

"What?" I slowed down. "No. No, we didn't. We got so close. But... no."

Elizabeth was silent again.

"You know this is some crazy shit," she said at last.

"Yeah, but we don't have to talk about it now. I'm sorry I bothered you. I feel like I… I got carried away with my need to talk about it. Didn't consider how it might sound—"

"Stop it," she said. "I just need some time to absorb what you're saying. It's… I've never heard of such a thing. If it was anyone but you telling me this…"

Her tone shifted.

"What the heck was Stella doing at the lab?"

I answered as best I could. I hadn't thought this conversation through. Hadn't thought about what she might ask, or not.

"She found out—I think from her neighbor who works in the same building—that I was meeting Dr. Koslow—he's the researcher—at the lab. I think she figured out the connection. She thought we were agents of the devil, and she was going to protect Gregory's soul."

"Good Lord."

"At least, that's what I've been able to piece together from her rantings and what she did. Something seems to have really snapped. I don't think she knew anything about the specifics of the OBE. Just 'devil work bad.' And 'Gregory mine.'"

"So she attacked all of you."

"Yes."

"I told you she was a nut case."

I yielded the "I told you so" moment to Elizabeth. She had warned me not to try to befriend Stella.

"But back to this out-of-body thing," Elizabeth said. "You really think you did it. That it was real. Not something you imagined, or this Dr. Koslow hypnotized you or something?"

"It was real, I swear."

"Do you have any proof? Anything tangible?"

"I didn't bring anything back, if that's what you mean," I said, suddenly annoyed as my sandpaper sensitivity reasserted itself. I immediately felt small and ineffectual. Like all I had to offer was a weak "Trust me." How could I bring something physical from the nonphysical world? "No secret message, either."

We got so close.

"All I can do is tell you what happened," I said, "and hope you'll believe me. Like there was a point after I separated from my body when I could see our physical bodies in the lab as I sort of floated over them. Then a little higher I tried to touch the brick outside the building, and my hand went right through it."

"Sounds so crazy."

In my mind's eye, I could see Elizabeth shaking her head.

"Yeah," I said.

"Crazy. But maybe real," she conceded.

"I'm not sure why I'm so driven to tell you. Maybe because I feel so bonded with you," I said, words rushing. "It's weird, I know, the way we relate, both loving Gregory. You understand losing him better than anyone. But now I've got this hope I didn't before, and I want to share that. No, it's more than hope. Fire. I'm on fire after what happened. I've got to try this out-of-body thing again. See where it leads. See if it leads to him."

There, I'd said it.

"I can't even comprehend... How're you going to do that?"

"Connie knows a way."

I gave her a synopsis of the spiritual explanation for out-of-body travel and how Connie would use the same chanting technique we'd used in the research lab but with a simpler setup at home.

"I think I'm going to give her a new name," Elizabeth mused. "Cosmic Connie."

I felt protective toward my friend but reminded myself that Elizabeth didn't know everything I knew about Connie's difficult background. "It may sound crazy. But it's real."

"Sorry. You've got to admit it's a lot to swallow. Going out of body. Doing it again. Trying to contact someone who's dead—"

"But if it were real," I persisted. "Consider for just a minute. How would that change your thinking?"

I waited.

"It'd blow my mind. It would... wow... It would change so many things... assumptions we make about life and death..."

"Connie and I are going to try to do it next weekend."

"I'm still having a hard time wrapping my head around this whole deal," she said. "And where do you think I fit in?"

"I-I don't really know," I stammered. "These days I'm so driven by impulses I don't understand. It just seemed right, urgent even, to tell you. Involve you. Like telling you I'm desperate to do it again. I needed to tell you."

"Do you want me there? Is that it?"

"No, I don't think so. I just need you to know what we're doing."

"So let's say you succeed in getting out of your body again. What then?"

"I'll try to find him. Contact him," I whispered, voicing what seemed like a forbidden thought. "I want to try and see him. We came so close. I have to try."

"You sound like someone on drugs," Elizabeth said with no trace of sarcasm. "I'm not trying to diminish your loss—God knows I understand. But the craving I hear in your voice. Are you sure this is a good idea?"

"I… I don't know how to respond to that," I said. Little did she know she was seeing only the barest glimmer of my fevered desire. Ever since I had returned, it seemed like I was burning with love for Gregory. Feeling him nearly in three dimensions. His soul. His energy. It was as if I had touched his outer rings, like Saturn. The aftermath in the lab was so much static noise.

"What if I wanted to contact Megan?"

Another thunderbolt. All this time I've been thinking Gregory. It never occurred to me Elizabeth would want to see Megan. But once she said it, I felt almost ashamed I hadn't thought of it beforehand. My daughter was still available to me—alive—in a way Megan would never be again. I had not been able to fully embrace the pain of that. Elizabeth's pain.

"I don't have an answer," I said. "But maybe I will after we try it again."

"I'm still pretty skeptical, and I don't completely understand," Elizabeth said. "But I get how important it is for you to do this."

"Thank you."

"Will you keep me in the loop?" she said. "I have to go right now, but I want to know what happens. In our weird sisterhood, I'm here for you, Ann. And for Olivia."

"Thank you. That means a lot to me. I'll let you know how it goes."

"Bye now."

"Bye."

After the call, I sat with the cats on the couch and thought of my own daughter.

I looked at Olivia differently in the aftermath of all that had happened. She was more precious to me. I didn't want to miss a minute of her life. I thought back to her expression of triumph when as a young child she tied her first bow, her wonder at chasing a butterfly, her tears over losing her goldfish, and the solemn burial that followed. When I allowed myself to feel the depth of my love for her, it amplified the tug to stay on the earth, pressing me to resist going out of body again.

"What if something happens and I don't get back?" I said out loud to Woody, who was stretched out, all orange and fluffy, on the living room floor. "How awful for her. Could I ever forgive myself?" Woody turned his head and stared at me with green cat eyes, uttering the same chattery sound he made when he saw a bird outside the window.

It's not always your choice.

I tried not to dwell on the risks. Or the consequences. The accountability was all mine should something go wrong. An image took shape in my mind of an astronaut untethered, floating away into space. A suffocating little ball in the middle of nothingness. No, I had to tamp down things like that. Give in, and I'd never make it to the weekend.

Work was crazy all that week, starting Monday morning. There was so much going on—fires, homicides, President Clinton in town, demonstrations—no one in the newsroom had time to ask about the lab incident. But I could tell by the way they looked at me and my arms that they were thinking about it and keen for details. *We know there's more to this story. Can't wait to hear.* Of course they would pry.

As I was arriving at my desk, Raiza was picking up her things to head out.

"Homicide," she announced.

"Whoa." I placed my coat on its hook.

"La dee dah. Gotta go," she said in a bit of a huff. Still unhappy, no doubt, that I'd refused to tell her more about what happened.

"Come on, don't be mad," I pleaded. "I told you what I could. I'll tell you more when I can." I changed the subject. "What do you hear about Stella?"

"I don't know what the *official* line is," she said, pawing through her purse and coming up with her keys, surely a delaying tactic to slow leaving, "but I think she's at Green Hills for a psych eval."

"There's a lot more to this I want to tell you."

"Humph. Can't talk now. On a deadline. But I've done a little research, missy, and I think I know what you were up to."

With that, Raiza hoofed it toward the elevator.

Before I could react, our boss interrupted.

"Ann Stewart! Get over here. We've got a tip, and I need you on it now."

"We'll talk," I called after Raiza, grabbing a notebook and heading for the boss's office.

"Yeah, that."

The whirlwind of pink was gone. Never get between a reporter and her scoop, not even as a friend. I'd have to make good on my pledge to tell her more—and soon.

All week, I walked in two worlds. Work and daily life—the real world—were relentless with their intrusions on my interior world. Or maybe it was the other way around.

Once I was free from the demands of the outer world, my thoughts wandered drunk and unchecked to the out-of-body reckoning to come at Connie's. Caution was a little voice, squeaking from a distant corner. Every so often it would catch me unawares. I'd see Olivia's innocent face. Hear her melodic laughter. Wonder what I was thinking to even consider another OBE.

The desire to return to the park coiled around my feelings for Gregory. Purposefully, even greedily, I allowed it to be fed by my imagination, seeing him in my mind's eye as he had been in life. Something about the OBE had stripped away the muting that had descended after his death. I'd wake up and think I felt his warm flesh next to me or that I heard the back gate close, sure he was standing there in his white sweater, waiting to let himself in the sliding glass door. Maybe I had suppressed my tactile sense of him—too painful to experience in its fullness—or maybe the OBE opened my senses and pores to a more vivid experience of him. I could lie or sit and just drift with the imagery for hours. Drunk. Drugged.

Olivia tethered me to reality just by being herself. She was my heart's safe harbor here on earth. She recentered me, sometimes with something as simple as playing on the floor with Woody and Bernie. Watching them cavort in the evening anchored me in the here and now. She boosted the signal coming from the little cautionary voice within about what I was contemplating.

"You seem weird, Mom," she said one night at dinner.

The coil loosened.

"I do?" Her comment caught me off guard. "In what way?"

"You have a kind of dreamy look all the time and don't much listen to what I'm saying," she said, picking peas out of her chicken pot pie. "Connie seems more interested in me—at least this week."

I was shocked to be so transparent to my daughter. I fancied that I still was pretty good at bracketing those emotions I wanted to protect her from—bad stuff at work, tension between her dad and me. This was the first time she'd ever called me out in this way.

"I *have* been distracted," I said, putting my fork down.

What was I going to tell her? The truth might frighten her or make her ask why she couldn't do it, too. Worst-case scenario: It could land me in custody court. But I couldn't dodge this with a lie if I was going have any integrity whatsoever with her.

She has a right.

"You know the lab accident last week, the one where I got the scratches on my arms…?"

"Yeah, you told me about it. And I saw Connie's bandages. Her cuts looked pretty bad."

"Only a few people know what we were doing in there," I began, unsure how I was going to put this. Olivia put her fork down and cocked her head expectantly.

Dive.

"We were doing an experiment in a research lab," I said. "It was strictly off the books. Do you know what that means?"

"No, not really."

"It means we weren't supposed to be doing it. It was like we were borrowing a car without someone's permission because we were sure we could return it before they knew it was gone."

"Like stealing? Or sneaking out?" Her expression didn't change. She was taking it in.

"No, no. Not quite. But yes, kind of. Borderline. We weren't using the lab for what it was intended."

"That doesn't sound like you," she said, looking doubtful. "Why'd you do that?"

I drew a slow, steady breath, my senses on high alert. I was using every one I had to gauge her reaction. But casually, so as not to create alarm.

"We were trying to see if we could leave our physical bodies and travel outside them." Edited, but not by much.

Olivia's eyes widened before she opened her mouth to speak.

"You were trying to do what? No. That's impossible."

"Actually, it's not. That's what we were doing." Mother's eagle gaze, scanning.

Olivia shook her head, loosening her long curls in soft waves, as if she could shake away what she'd just heard.

"I don't get it," she said, pausing. "Do you mean like the movie *Flatliners*?"

"*Flatliners*. Yes."

"I didn't think that was real."

"I didn't either, until now."

I'd forgotten I'd let her watch the movie with me. Olivia had been super-curious about whether what they were doing in the film was possible.

"But in this case, nobody's heart was stopping. The researcher, Dr. Koslow, uses sound waves—a kind of chanting—to help the 'soul' part of you temporarily release from your physical body. It's weird. You're still tethered—tied to it—but your mind is free to roam."

It was impossible to gauge how much of this was getting through, although she didn't seem fearful or upset. Nothing in her demeanor suggested anything more than intense curiosity.

"That sounds cool."

I smiled. She seemed to be getting… enough of it. Time to introduce the next element.

"We got interrupted when Stella broke into the lab and started hurting people."

"What?" There was that puzzled expression again. "Why'd she do that?"

"Because she had figured out that I was trying to contact Gregory," I said slowly and softly. "She didn't like that."

Olivia just looked at me, inscrutable, for what seemed like a very long time. I couldn't help shifting in my chair.

"Did you?" Her voice filled with longing. An unmistakable urgency hummed below her question. "Did you see him?"

"Almost," I said, tears gathering. "We got close."

"Oh, Mom." Olivia reached across the table for my hand. As our fingers touched, I was flooded with love for my beautiful daughter. Losing Gregory had wounded her terribly, but it also was changing her in ways that made my heart leap. I ached at our mutual pain and her loss of innocence, but I didn't hold back my sobs, as I once might have, mistakenly believing that protected her. My tears triggered her own.

"I miss him, too," she said. "I miss him so much."

Now we were both weeping. Olivia walked around the table to my side to put her arms around me and lean her head on my shoulder.

"I know," I sniffed. "He… was… so much to us. To both of us."

"What you're talking about seems impossible," she said. "But maybe it's not."

I had couched what I had to say in just the right way, I thought. It was something I'd done at other stages of her life, when I'd tried to frame things just a notch higher than her comprehension, to encourage her to stretch and grow.

"But there's one more thing I need to tell you." We both gained control of our sobs, wiping our eyes and she returned to her side of the table.

"Connie is going to help me try again this weekend," I said. "I'm going to try and go out of my body again and find him."

I hoped this wasn't too much.

My daughter stared at me. If she was surprised, she wasn't showing it. Maybe I'd gone beyond surprising her. At least on this topic.

"But how will you do that? You said Stella destroyed the lab."

"She did. But Connie says people have been doing this for thousands of years as a spiritual exercise, going out of body. She thinks we can recreate that."

Olivia seemed to be steadily drinking in my words. Curious. Absorbing.

"So leaving your body is a religious thing?"

"It can be, yeah."

"And if you do this, then what?"

"Maybe I'll get to finish what I started with Dr. Koslow."

"And…?"

Darn it, there would be no wink-wink-nudge-nudge with her.

"And I might make contact with Gregory," I said with quiet resolve.

"You mean see him again? See him alive?"

She leaned toward me pressing her elbows and hands on the table.

"Different," I said. "I'm not really sure how he would look."

"That would be… oh my God… beyond fantastic. I… can I do it, too?"

"No," came the motherly demur. "At least, not now. Maybe after you grow up, if you still want to, you could try. But not now. Not at your age."

"Aw." She slumped back.

"And the thing is, you can't tell anyone about this."

"Why not?"

"Off the books, remember? I know that's a lot to ask. But you can't tell your dad or your friends. Not yet. Wait... I take it back. There is one person you can talk to. Connie. In fact, it'd be good if you talked to her. She can answer questions about this better than me. Do you want me to set something up?"

"Yeah, sure."

With that, she pulled back into her adolescent shell, having reached her limit, and started to clear the table.

We cleaned up in silence, each tuned inward to our own private thoughts. I had managed to conduct a conversation without conveying the danger. But I had also burdened her with a heavy truth. As I watched her glide through the familiar motions of putting the leftovers away, I had second thoughts. She was so young, and still in the grip of a life-changing trauma. Had I made the right decision?

That night after Olivia was asleep, I lay awake second-guessing myself.

Am I doing the right thing? I queried silently as Bernie jumped onto the bed. Woody, I knew, would be snuggled in with Olivia. *I love Olivia so much, I can't imagine life without her,* I thought, absently stroking my black-and-white friend, who insisted on a quick head-butt. *Or more precisely, I can't imagine her young life without me. Am*

I taking too much of a risk, trying to reach you again? I can't imagine anything that would make me risk leaving her—except trying to find you. Connie keeps harping on the dangers of not coming back, leaving my body here to die. I can't do that to Olivia. I know I just can't.

Silence.

I have never loved anyone as much as I love you, I thought, ashamed to even think it, as if I were admitting I loved Gregory more than I loved my daughter. But that wasn't true. The loves were so different. And as Connie so often reminded me, love is not a pie.

Silence.

Perhaps I needed to call the whole thing off. It was the logical, practical answer. My father's answer. A mature person would rise above the out-of-control passion, would see the need here and now on earth to nurture a budding soul. Would push aside the selfishness of desire. Choose the responsibility I'd taken on when I became pregnant with Olivia. There was no escape clause for "don't feel like it," when it came to motherhood. Not for me.

Still, the hunger persisted, even as the rhythmic purring of the small creature wrapped in my arms drew me toward sleep and my questions were answered by silence.

CHAPTER TWENTY-EIGHT

Connie must have seen me hesitate as I surveyed her living room. "You're sure about this?" she said, closing her front door behind me.

My friend had drawn her second set of drapes again, the heavy ones she used to shut out light and sound. The only source of illumination, a gooseneck lamp on a low table, cast a diffused glow across the quilt-covered futon positioned at the center of the room. Except for a miniature electronic console and headphones nestled in the satin-cased pillow, the room looked like it might have been set up for an overnight guest. This was our do-it-yourself, out-of-body lab.

I nodded.

"You're not going to talk me out of it, no matter how hard you try."

"I wouldn't try," Connie said. "I just want to be sure that you're sure."

My attention was drawn to the matrix of knobs and switches on the compact console. It looked like a sound board for a small nightclub act, wires woven neatly into and out of the back. I noticed a second headset next to the gooseneck. And a couple of small, clip-on microphones.

"Who set it up for you?" I asked.

"My friend, Zack," Connie said, "who's an electronic wizard—and into OBEs. He works in a recording studio and does stuff like this on the side."

I sank down onto the futon's firm softness, and Connie sat on one of her big Bohemian floor pillows next to the board.

"We have to approach this a little differently without Dr. Koslow," she said, settling in. "He was my buffer, my protector, for you."

My eyes roamed over the shadowy darkness of the room once more. It was like a warm, hollowed-out, gray womb. A space capsule. Sound was heavily dampened, and light was muted except for a halo around the head of the futon and the console. My stomach fluttered in anticipation. Or was that a shiver?

"I wanted to ask you about that guide thing again," I said. "Like how Dr. Koslow was using them. I'm still not clear what you meant. What exactly are guides, and what do they look like?"

Connie folded her hands in her lap.

"The best I can explain it," she said, "they're like spiritual do-gooders in the beyond. They go around looking to assist others. But that's a really simplistic description."

"But Dr. Koslow wasn't using guides, right? They're not part of his research, right?"

"For a long time, that was true," Connie said. "But when he tried doing his research without them, he made very slow progress—as absurd as it sounds. Those of us who already had some OBE experience tried to tell him about guides. He resisted the whole idea. Finally, he got so frustrated with the pace of the work, he decided to try the guide thing. It was crazy, but it made all the difference. Suddenly things started happening. He decided to simply acknowledge them as a variable and try to explain it in a scientific context later."

"But you don't need an explanation of guides," I said.

"No. My guides are like old friends. And I'm not doing science when I go out of body. Except in Dr. Koslow's lab."

"Are these guides what some people call 'guardian angels'?" I asked.

"Could be." She shrugged. "But that might be looking at it too narrowly."

"And there was that other thing you mentioned that you use, an affirmation?" Connie had already described this to me, but I wanted to hear it again.

"It's vaguely like a prayer," she said, "where you 'affirm'—I don't know—the context for your request. Dr. Koslow eventually adopted these, too, to set the stage for the out-of-body experience in his lab. You just didn't hear him. Another oddity that doesn't fit his 'scientific' box."

"Seems like OBEs are some kind of gateway."

"Probably so," she said. "Which is another reason I'm so cautious. I don't know where it can lead you."

"Fair enough," I said, slipping off my shoes and uncoupling my belt and setting them aside. I picked up fuzzy mittens that lay next to the pillow, giving Connie a dubious look.

She smiled.

"Just put them on. Are you ready to lie down?"

"Ready," I said, sinking back into the reassuring support of the futon. Its firmness made me feel connected to the ground. Wherever my nonphysical body was going, this one was staying put.

Connie pulled a soft flannel blanket over me and tucked it in next to my arms and body.

"Is that warm enough? Or would you like the quilt, too?"

"The quilt," I said. "Please."

She covered me with the faded, hand-stitched patchwork piece, a well-loved family heirloom.

"Good?"

I nodded, sinking into the warmth around me.

Then Connie affixed the headphones over my ears and fastened a microphone to the edge of the quilt closest to my mouth. Immediately, all sound became distant and muffled except her voice.

"Personally," she said into the microphone she'd clipped to her own flannel shirt, "I think an affirmation helps the 'right' guides find you in a cacophony of competing wants and needs out there. Like a beacon."

I could hear her voice clearly through my headphones.

As she continued making adjustments, I started practicing the controlled breathing that helps you tune into the rhythm of your own heartbeat. My racing pulse.

Some people would consider what we were attempting reckless. Our experiment might not go as planned. Even the guide part could go awry. Connie had said whoever or whatever responded to our request for a guide, once I was out of my body, might just as easily be a trickster who wanted to engage in a little cosmic fun at our expense. The nonphysical world sounded quite complicated. None of it mattered. I had to get back to that place, the park.

"We want you to be as comfortable and cozy as possible," she said, continuing to tuck the covers around my neck.

"I think I am," I said, scanning my body for any discomfort.

"Now I want to test the tape."

Connie flipped a switch on the control board that she and Zack had worked all afternoon setting up. The console was next to my pillow so Connie could watch me and reach over to touch me if needed. She would be controlling the board and monitoring me at the same time.

As I lay there, low harmonics resonated in my ears, a Gregorian chant without words, similar to the one I'd heard in the chamber with Dr. Koslow.

"Can you hear that and me, too?" Connie purred.

"Yes." My answer flowed into my microphone and up into her headphones. Unlike mine, Connie had explained, hers allowed in outside noises, so she'd be able to hear anything going on in the larger space. An emergency. A siren. A knock on the door. My headphones dampened all external sound. All I could hear and feel besides her voice was my own pulsing blood.

The chanting stopped.

"Are you ready to start for real?" Connie said, rewinding the tape.

"Yes."

"And just to review, what connects you back to your body?"

"The silver cord."

"And where does it connect?"

"Right here," I said, patting my solar plexus just below my breastbone, under the covers.

"Don't forget. It's your lifeline."

Connie laid a bead-filled, satin eye pillow across my eyelids to complete my cocooning. Body relaxed and swaddled in blankets. Hands and feet enfolded in plush, warm mittens and socks. Ears cosseted in headphones. Eyes given over to blackness.

Connie switched on the tape, and the low thrumming began to fill first my ears, then my head, and ultimately my whole being as I migrated easily to that singular sensation of floating and falling. As the chanting continued, I concentrated on the undulating sounds and my love for Gregory.

Very softly in the background, Connie began the affirmation.

"We are more than our physical bodies. Because this is so, we are able to perceive space and energy that exist beyond the physical world. We deeply desire to be a part of this, to partake of the wisdom therein and to be protected from harm.... We humbly request the assistance of one that..."

I leaned into the words, immersing myself in them. Her affirmation, then request for the assistance of a guide, sounded far away.

This time I embraced the mounting vibrations and bucking sensation, the rhythmic rising and falling and rising before the pop signaling separation. I rolled easily out of my physical body. That was it. I'd done it again. Floating in a gray haze above the physical, I gazed down from the ceiling at the glowing orb of Connie's energy. My body was next to her, and I floated overhead, separate from them. Without Dr. Koslow, I was really on my own.

The next instant, it felt like someone took my hand and swiftly pulled me up and away, deep into a darkened, tunnel-like vortex.

Around and around and around we tumbled—which was disorienting because it was new and unexpected, and I could not "see" where I was. Yet I felt so light. So free. As I bounced from side to side through the maelstrom—a little rougher now—I became aware that I was alone, with no control over what was happening. Whoever or whatever had led me there and set my tumbling in motion was gone. I was alone and untethered. I had visions of satellites careening out of control from their orbits around the earth, gyrating wildly off into space. Suddenly I was gripped by fear. This was happening to me. Except I was bouncing from one side of something to another, across unspeakable distances, galaxy to galaxy. With phantom arms and legs, I scrambled to grab onto whatever I was bumping up against before being tossed head-over-heels back the way I came.

"Help! Help me!" I cried wordlessly, utterly terrified. I threw myself against one wall, then hurtled into another. No, through it. Then I caromed off the sides again for what seemed an eternity before an opening suddenly gave way to nothingness in every direction. I screamed in panic.

"Silver cord," came the strong, urgent words in my head. "Silver cord."

Jerked out of the void, I hurtled headlong through a kaleidoscopic swirl of colors.

"Silver cord." The words became more solid.

Eventually, I lay still, cowering within the safety of the futon and covers.

Connie slid the eye pillow from my eyes as I looked up at her, panic-stricken. She gazed down, placed her hand on my solar plexus, and fixed her eyes on mine.

Slowly, I realized where I was.

"What happened?" I asked weakly.

"You tell me," she said, producing a warm, damp cloth to wipe the sweat from my face and neck. "What happened? Where were you?"

"Somewhere in a round thing. Alone." The words spilled out. "Tumbling. Trapped. Back and forth. Then a void." I shuddered. She discreetly pressed her fingers to my hammering pulse.

"You're okay now," she said firmly. "You're okay."

"Yes. Okay now."

"Safe."

"I got out of my body, and someone took my hand," I said, pushing my headphones back, "and then they just let go of me. Abandoned me."

I started to cry.

"Some obnoxious sprite having a joke." Connie harrumphed in disgust. "There're assholes all over the universe. We can always take this up another time...."

"No," I said, flapping a mittened hand. "I'll be all right. I know you're trying to protect me, but I don't want to wait. We've got to do it again."

Connie regarded me.

"Really?"

"Yeah. I got scared. But I'm not hurt." Freaked out, but not hurt. "You said this might happen."

"Yes," she, said, adding with authority, "and it could happen again. Maybe worse."

"I don't care. One more time," I pleaded, unwilling to give in to my fear. "I want to go all the way. I want to see Gregory. If I freak out again, we'll call it a night."

"God, you're persistent," Connie said. "But you see why this is so dicey. I don't want some other stray entity messing with you."

"I feel like we're so close. We've got to do it again. Now." I was beyond niceties. "You've got to help me."

"I suppose I do. But let's at least take a little break first."

I had to admit, this was a lot more complicated and precarious without Dr. Koslow.

"So these guides you talk about, that you summon," I said, wiping my face and neck with a cotton towel and sipping a little water. "Who would they help? And why?"

"The cosmos is full of energy beings—souls and others, if you will." Connie spoke as easily as if we were chatting about the weather. "Guides are there to help, and I don't know the full 'why.' Some are like freelancers. Like, they'll assist souls that don't know they're dead, souls still hanging around the earth where they used to live. Or maybe clinging to the scene of an accident where they died. A guide might help them move on to whatever's next. But then there also seem to be dedicated guides, like mine, attached to particular people over a lifetime. Maybe beyond."

"What about me? Do I have guides?"

Connie nodded. "I think each of us probably has personal guides. Spiritual mentors. Watchers. It's just impressions I get. From what I've done and seen, and what others have said."

"Where are they now, all these guides?"

"Out there. Here. Around us. Maybe not. It's kind of like a dimensional thing, like trying to describe three dimensions when you only exist in two. And time-space is so distorted. It makes no logical sense next to our linear time. Or maybe I should say our linear time makes no sense in the larger time-space continuum."

"What do guides look like?"

"Sometimes I visualize mine as translucent beings, like humans in long robes. That could totally be something I've made up. Other times, I feel like they're just energy—balls of energy."

"So there are personal guides and then there are drifter guides. Independents in the cosmic soup."

"Ha. Yeah, that's a good way to put it. Plus all those mischief-makers. I'm still not sure where they fit in. Are you ready to go again?"

"Just as soon as I go to the bathroom," I said.

We set up for round two. This time when we went through the chanting and affirmation sequence, I lifted easily out of my physical body and stayed close to Connie. I heard her softly repeating the affirmation and requesting a guide to help me find the park. She begged for an entity that would honor my quest and protect me. Once again I concentrated on my love for Gregory and my desire to find him.

This time something like a hand slipped over mine, only this one seemed to entwine our pulsations like a cosmic harness. Effortlessly, we took one of those jumps, hurtling to what surely was the far side of time-space. All my energy was focused on holding fast to the strange undulating force that gripped me so firmly. I was still alternately terrified and thrilled at these new sensations.

But this time, when fear threatened to undo me, I surrendered to the oscillation of my guide and focused on loving Gregory.

After some period of time, we seemed to decelerate, then stop, at what must surely have been the outer edge of the park. The texture of the energy was different—leaner and more compact—and the greenery under our "feet" squished like moss. Then I noticed the tiny swirling flickers of light rising all around us from the direction we'd just come.

"What are those?" I fluttered.

"Prayers," came the telepathic answer.

Before I could pursue this startling notion, my attention was riveted by our immediate surroundings in a brilliant meadow blanketed by millions of tiny, undulating flowers—points of light brighter than the brightest Christmas display illuminating the soft, mossy carpet that extended in all directions. I wiggled my "toes" among the velvety shoots. It felt like I still had my body, or perhaps an image or imprint of the one I'd left behind in Connie's living room. But no. One glance "down" told me I was nothing but pink light.

"Are we at the park?" I vibrated, jumpy with excitement.

"Yes. But you must continue concentrating on the one you're seeking for me to help you," came the soothing reply. I had the impression of a voice with some kind of force behind it that felt positive, perhaps even familiar, this someone or something that had responded to Connie's request.

The scene before us was so magnificent I could scarcely breathe—figuratively speaking. It was like every exquisite landscape in our world—natural wonders, wild spaces, deep forest, cascading waterfalls, and a few scenes I can't even describe—arrayed as limitless vistas in every direction, all imbued with ineffable love. I noticed other beings here and there sharing the landscape. I could see why people wouldn't want to leave. Who wouldn't yearn to be enfolded forever in this macrocosm of love and peace and tranquility? Despair? Gone. It seemed to have evaporated as my essence coiled and uncoiled in a brilliant pink spiral throwing off starbursts like a summer sparkler.

Then out of nowhere, I was swept up in what I can only describe as an expansive, Cheshire Cat-like smile, wider than all the oceans, enveloping me in a cascade of supernal light.

"Gregory!"

"I think you've found him," flashed the guide's voice before fading away, but I barely noticed. All I could feel were waves of love streaming toward me and into me from a luminescence so brilliant I instinctively tried to shield my eyes.

"Sorry. I'll tone it down a little."

I laughed until I cried at the sound of that familiar sonorous baritone. The release. The knowing. The bottomless moment of recognition. I yearned to reach out and touch him, caress him, whatever he was—this glowing radiance with that signature I'd know anywhere.

"It's true? It's you? You're really here? You didn't die?"

"No. Like I told Olivia in her dream, I didn't die," he emitted. "I just had to leave. I didn't want to go." I felt another blast of love. "But it was my time. My bank account was up."

In that moment, I felt as if I could tumble into him, this light being he had become, and disappear forever.

I... LOVE... YOU.

His words washed over me like a tsunami of unbearable luminescence. And in the next instant I was drawn into the tsunami, swirled around and around inside its waves. Our blending was like an orgasm magnified a thousand times, shooting sparks in every direction, stars colliding and releasing spasms of energy too great to comprehend.

"Oh!" I cried.

The coupling released, leaving me awestruck and tingling.

"We're not supposed to do that," came the vibration, "not full-on like that. But I wanted you to feel the power of love here so that you will hold it in your heart forever."

My own pink shimmers seemed to vibrate.

"We're all energy," he radiated gently.

The moment of coming together was so far beyond anything I'd imagined—it unleashed what felt like a torrent of tears, and my heart simply let go. All sorrow transformed to joy.

As he conveyed these thoughts, blinding white light pulsed and coalesced before my eyes around what looked for all the world like a glowing, iridescent version of the man I loved.

"Pink becomes you."

He nearly knocked me over again with that smile.

As he spoke, I became aware of another presence near his shoulders—what people of some faiths would surely describe as an angel.

"No angel," he vibrated. "That is Andrew." Andrew. Bubba. Gregory's brother.

"Andrew is okay?"

"I'm okay," Andrew flashed. "My brother and I have work to do."

"But the rifle..."

"It doesn't matter now," Andrew flickered, all wisps of electric blue darting in close formations.

I'd given up trying to make sense of what was happening.

"Now turn around and look behind you," Gregory vibrated.

As I turned, I confronted what seemed like a galaxy of individual, bobbing orbs as far as the senses could register. All radiating unspeakable love and kindness.

"Those are yours," Gregory emitted, "your spirit kin. Some of those were also trying to get through when the one you call Sasha reached out for me."

I could discern nothing but a collective, pulsating brilliance. Then slowly names and recognition filtered into my consciousness: Helene, one of my grandmothers. Mother. Boppa, one of my grandfathers. My father. An old schoolmate killed in an accident. A precious teacher who had encouraged me.

"They wanted to say hi before you go back."

Out of the shimmering cluster, several smaller points of light burst to the fore.

"Tiger? Huck? Austin?" I recognized these as some of my beloved cats. Yet the three seemed to dance as one.

"They're telling you they are one spirit, and that they visited you many times in many bodies. They want to thank you for your love."

"Oh, my darlings," I radiated back, wishing I could gather them into my arms for a sweet embrace. In response, they rose as one to nuzzle me.

I turned again to face Gregory and was startled by a brilliant pink corona forming around his head.

"Is that a rainbow?"

"That's Megan."

Megan. She looked like a rose-gold sunburst.

"Yes, and you must tell Elizabeth you see the rose-gold sunburst. Take those words with you."

Then Gregory stretched his hand toward me, and as his finger touched the place where my heart would have been, I felt struck, as if by lightning. All sensibility left me. I could focus on only one thing: This moment. This ecstasy. I could not leave this place. Not now. Not ever. I felt utterly subsumed in Gregory's love and the vibrancy of all these around me. Nothing else mattered. I had to stay. Olivia would be okay, now that I knew what was waiting and how this cosmic community surrounded and lifted her. I knew intuitively that Connie could feel my rapture and understood. This was what all of us were striving toward all our lives. This was the endgame. I wanted to bask in this heightened illumination forever.

"It's not quite as you are conceiving," Gregory vibrated, withdrawing his touch. "Connie will blame herself if you don't go back."

Discomfort raked across my being—Connie.

"But it isn't her fault," I intoned. "This world—the love—why would anyone leave? The absence of pain, the love, utter freedom. I can't bear to go back. She knows. She's been here. She'll understand."

"Olivia will be crushed if you fail to return." I spasmed as he whooshed me into her pain. "Because she cannot feel what you feel or know what you know."

"But I know what's ahead," I flashed. "Her life will be the blink of eye."

Something like the thrumming that had initiated my journey to the park rumbled in the background. Thrumming and a different light.

"She will suffer without you."

Gregory wasn't angry or insistent. He was simply revealing reality without holding back.

"Oh my God, no."

So many unbearable, wrenching feelings diving one into the other. Unspeakable pain. Despair. Anguish. All spiderwebbed against the unfettered ecstasy of this beyond.

How could I leave her alone?

But how could I return? I couldn't lose Gregory. Not again. Wouldn't. Not now. But neither could I abandon Olivia. The feelings, roiling like flames, engulfed me.

Gregory floated closer and reached out again, energetically.

"Go," he vibrated lovingly and decisively, enfolding me one more brief moment in his unbearable brightness. "And take this with you." He lobbed what looked like a small, iridescent ball at me. "You already have its mate." Its mate? "Now it's time. Carry my love with you."

And he flashed like an exploding sun.

Love never dies.

Still tingling, I felt myself soar inward and upward, hurtling across spinning panoramas of stars, across light and darkness, to what seemed like the end of the universe.

"Silver cord."

The barely audible words entered my ears. Connie lifted the eye pillow off my face. I blinked in the soft, shimmering light of her living room. Rivulets of tears streamed from the corners of my eyes and down the sides of my face.

The first thing I focused on was Connie's smile. Tears rimmed her eyes, too. I felt the lightness of her touch on my solar plexus.

"Welcome home."

CHAPTER TWENTY-NINE

"Found him," I said, propping myself on my elbows, sliding the mittens off and blinking away tears. "Felt... touched him.... Touched me—with energy... his energy." My hand went to my chest. "Merged... Love... So much love... Megan... Brother. Oh my God... I..."

My voice trailed off as I struggled to find the words for what had just happened.

"I suspected something was going on," Connie said, her voice like velvet on my newly tuned ears. "I knew you'd found a portal."

"So much more than I expected.... Indescribable."

"I've felt enormous love after returning from the park," Connie said, "but this sounds different. Can you tell me more?"

"Even now, back here, everything's shimmering, vibrating," I said, looking around the room. "Bathed in light. And peace. Wrapped in peace."

I looked into Connie's eyes, and they seemed to glow.

"I didn't want to come back."

A trace of concern darkened her face.

"But I did come back," I added quickly. "He made me. Or something made me."

"I'm glad. Beyond glad."

It was like I was catching my breath after a long run. I was exhilarated. But exhausted. There was so much to process. And yet, that would wait. I felt so light. So clear. Such an enormous burden lifted.

I still ached with missing Gregory, but the pain had changed. Transformed. I knew beyond all doubt that his essence survived. And then it struck me: My essence, too, would transcend this life. Perhaps this was the greater unspoken assurance I also sought.

"What's going on there?" Connie interrupted my musing.

"Just… trying to weigh it all. What it means. I feel so different. About death. Dying. Love."

I fell silent again, my thoughts curling in on themselves.

"Can I make us some tea?" Connie asked. "Then we can continue?"

"Yes, that sounds good," I said, noticing my dry throat.

Connie seemed to understand my need for a little space while I unknotted so many threads, fresh and new. Like I had to realign with earth time-space.

While she was gone, I pushed the quilt aside, stood on wobbly legs and stretched, then plopped down on her Victorian couch. It was as if I were in a trance, or a state of altered perception. I took in the world around me—the air on my skin, the enshrouding darkness—with heightened intensity. Thoughts less swirling than caressing.

Connie tiptoed back into the room with a pot of tea and two ceramic sake cups. She poured us each some of the gray-green brew. I was mesmerized by the way the steam shimmied and curled off the hot liquid's surface.

"Is it always going to be like this?" I asked, noticing Connie's smile.

"No. But the afterglow will probably continue for a long time. Although I hesitate to predict what's going to happen with you because what you did was so much more intense than what I've experienced."

The warm tea felt like liquid silk on my throat.

Absently, I put my hand to my heart again, the way one might finger a locket. The way Stella touched the cross she wore. I was drawn to a warmth there, between my breasts.

"What the…?" I looked down.

Then I remembered. Gregory had thrust something at me, some kind of energy ball—knowledge? information?—to bring back, to share. It sort of stuck to my body, like Velcro. I put my tea down, slipped the orb through my shirt—yes, right through it—and held it out on my fingertips for Connie to see.

"How the heck did you do that?"

The glistening, golf-ball-size sphere rested lightly on my fingers.

Connie's eyes widened, and the sphere cast a liquid reflection of her questioning expression back at her.

"I don't know. And I don't know what it is," I said. "I just have a recollection of it. I think it's like Zuzu's petals in *It's A Wonderful Life.*"

"Zuzu's petals were never like this," Connie said. "I've seen these on the other side, but I've never heard of bringing one back."

Connie reached out tentatively to touch the orb, which made it wiggle and flare. She jerked back.

"Did that hurt?" I asked.

"No." She hesitated. "But there's something inside. A message. A torrent of information. So much I can't even comprehend...." She touched it again. This time her finger slid through the tiny sphere as though it did not occupy physical space.

"Whoa. What just happened?" I said.

"I'm not sure," she said, pulling back slowly.

The orb continued balancing lightly on my outstretched fingers.

Without saying anything, I tried to do what Connie had just done, using the finger of my other hand. As I pressed into the orb, it felt viscous and sticky. It was like trying to push through Silly Putty—simultaneously yielding and resistant.

"What's it doing?"

"I'm at a loss," Connie said, puzzled. "Maybe it's trying to hold on."

I couldn't suppress a chuckle.

Listen to her.

"Because it's clearly intended for you. And Elizabeth."

"How do you know this?"

"I feel it," Connie said. "Some things, I get very strongly. Especially now that I'm not resisting. This is like a trigger. Or needs a trigger. Something to release what's inside."

Still perched in my hand, the orb began vibrating in rapid, liquid ripples. Instead of trying to poke it, I cupped my other hand over it.

"Okay, this is really weird," I said. "Not sure why, but I get a strong sense of the women who've been drawn together by this. It's beyond anything I've ever intuited. I mean, I've never felt so sure, like I need to listen to this intuition. Way beyond a gut check. This is totally different."

"Can you just go with it?" Connie urged.

I closed my eyes. I could "see" the ball in front of me. Feel it buzz insistently in my hands, as if I held a bee there.

Connie cupped her hands loosely around mine.

"I'm feeling something like a yearning," Connie said.

"Yes, there's some sort of amplification needed from a group."

"Are you clear on who this group is?"

"Oh yes," I said, their faces floating up unbidden in my mind. "It must be you and me, and Elizabeth and Olivia. And Raiza. Not sure why she needs to be there, but she does. Maybe this is payback for giving her such lousy quotes for her story about the lab." I laughed. Would Gregory have known about that? Why not, given everything else that had happened.

"And Stella…?" Connie asked.

I closed my eyes to concentrate on the group.

"Not seeing Stella in this gathering." The buzzing in my hands expanded rhythmically into shower-like rays of warmth. "Stella… is… another… thing…."

You said it.

"But these other women—are you thinking there needs to be an actual meeting?" Connie said.

"Yes, and… right away. But that's not all."

My thoughts jumped to the paperweight back in Gregory's chest. The orb and the paperweight were similar in ways—their shape, their mystery—and there was that odd, energetic jolt Olivia reported from the paperweight, which I'd dismissed.

"Do you remember the paperweight in Gregory's chest?" I asked.

"Not really."

"It's weird. It kind of zapped Olivia the other evening when she was handling it. I thought it was just a shock from static. Now I'm not so sure. Maybe we should put them together?"

"There might be something to that," Connie said, touching the orb's energetic pulse again, then withdrawing her hand.

I pressed it close to my heart, where the vibration dissolved into more of a purr.

"Soon" suddenly seemed like a silly concept. Soon in our normal waking sense, or soon in cosmic time?

"Well, the chest is at your place," Connie said. "So maybe meet there?"

"Hmmm. Yes." I thought about the space. Warmth emanated from the orb. "I think that would work. I think that's it."

"Any night—I'm assuming night—work better for you?"

"Wednesday would be good," I said. "Maybe next Wednesday? Gives me time to call folks and let Olivia know."

Oh, geez. What would Olivia's father say about this?

"I'm conflicted about including Olivia," I added.

"Because...?"

"Someone not... in tune with all this... might consider it pretty spooky stuff, not something you expose a child to. Someone... like Olivia's dad."

She is owed.

Connie took a sip of her long-cooled tea and thought for a moment.

"I agree there's some risk," she said. "I'd hate to see you get crossways with her dad. But my intuition, like yours, is to include her. The rest will work itself out."

"I'll set it up then," I said, taking one last sip of tea. "And thank you. Thank you for everything you've done to bring us to this moment. I can't tell you how much it means to me. It's so much more than I ever expected."

"Isn't that the truth?"

My heart felt so buoyant I reached over and hugged her.

Now I knew what was possible. My challenge, I told myself, was to stay to complete whatever work I was here to do. What a strange thought. So unlike how I'd considered anything up to then. This was like my fresh start. I touched the orb between my breasts. As I did so, I realized it was actually nesting on my heart.

I called Elizabeth then Raiza on Monday with my invitation.

With Elizabeth, I was straightforward. I knew she, too, was fixated on Gregory's survival. But more, on her daughter's.

"I did make contact with Gregory," I began. "He's okay. He loves us all."

"I'll be damned." She paused, her voice dropping almost to a whisper. "And what about Megan? Did you see Megan?" Elizabeth's naked anguish made me want to cry.

"Yes," I said. "They are together."

I remembered what Gregory said to tell her.

"She appeared as a rose-gold sunburst."

Elizabeth lapsed into deep, bellowing sobs, as if she were releasing something long submerged. I simply waited, resonating with the flow of sorrow and relief emanating from her. Its depth was heartbreaking.

"You don't know how much that means to me," she said at last. "That aura, that color, was the signal Megan and I had agreed on before she died. She told me she would try to contact me through a rose-gold flare." Her words came in short, raspy bursts. "She's letting me know she's okay."

"Oh, Elizabeth. I had no idea."

Her muffled sobs continued.

"There's one more thing," I said. "He sent back a kind of energy ball for all of us to share."

"An energy ball?"

"I can't explain it. Not now. But can you come to my house on Wednesday night, and we'll all learn what it's about?"

"Yes," she said. "I can do that."

Raiza, as I suspected, was still miffed over my stingy quotes. Yeah, she could hold a grudge.

"Why should I come?" she sniffed. "You gonna do an out-of-body demo, like what you did at the lab?"

Deep breath. She was fishing for confirmation of her suspicions, of course. Guessing.

"Not really. But you are right: I did go out of body."

"And did you see your dead true love?"

Raiza. She never quit being Raiza.

"Yes," I said, drawing the word out slowly, "but not that time. I saw him when I went out of body a different time. On Sunday. Saw him and so much more."

"Pfft."

"I want you to come over Wednesday night," I said, unmoved by her doubt. I no longer felt a need to convince anyone of anything.

"I don't know exactly what's going to happen, but I have a feeling you need to be there. Maybe there's a story? I don't know. But you deserve the scoop if there is."

It seemed appropriate to play to Raiza's scoop-meister nature.

"No 'official' version of things?"

"Unknown. This promises to be an extremely intimate experience, one where people need to feel safe. And Olivia will be there."

"So take it or leave it, not knowing what 'it' might be? That's a pretty limp-dick proposition."

"I'm sorry," I said, without guile. "It's the best I got. It's, like, this is what I'm authorized to offer."

"What? By lover boy himself?"

Sometimes I just wanted to throttle her.

"Yes."

"Well, then. How can I pass up an invitation like that? From a dead guy, yet."

When Olivia got home from school, I was waiting.

"Hey," she said, surprised to see me in the afternoon. "What's up?"

"I wanted to tell you in person about what happened last night at Connie's."

I recounted the experience in simplified terms. Olivia was so overcome it took her several minutes to react.

"That seems so fantastic," she said, with eyes wide and questioning. She was struggling to make sense of it. "Like, out of this world."

"It was. Literally," I said. "And then there is this."

I pulled the energetic orb from its resting place by my heart.

"Holy shit, Mom," she said without censoring herself. The watery ball trembled on my fingers as Olivia swung around to examine it from every angle.

"What is it?"

"Connie thinks it's some kind of message."

"From where?"

"From Gregory. In the afterlife."

"Shit. Shit. Shit."

"Hey, come on. Cool the potty mouth," I admonished weakly.

"That's just freakish, Mom. I mean, what do I tell people?"

"You don't have to tell them anything. Most of them won't believe you, anyway."

"I'm not sure I believe it," she said.

Encourage her.

"Go ahead and touch it," I said, pushing aside my qualms about her father.

She looked at me, then back at the ball, which appeared to be rotating slowly.

Hesitantly, she stuck her finger out. It easily pierced the sphere, just as Connie's had. She jerked it back.

"Mom, this is effing crazy."

"Did that hurt?" I asked.

"No. It… I… I don't know how to describe it," she said, eyes, a mixture of worry and amazement, fixed on mine. "I don't get it. I *know* this is from Gregory. I know it."

She looked at her finger, and tears began slipping down her cheeks.

"I know he's there! He's really out there."

She started sobbing.

"Yes," I said, trying to hold back my own sobs. "Yes, he is."

I pressed the now opaque ball back into its nesting spot and put my arm around Olivia's shoulder.

"This changes everything," she whispered, leaning into me.

"In so many ways," I confirmed.

I watched as she seemed to drink in this information. What a revelation for one so young, to find out that life truly doesn't end with death. Not just for someone to tell you, but to experience by knowing.

"There's more," I said. "Remember the way the paperweight zapped you?"

"Like it shocked me? Um-hm."

"Connie and I both think we need to bring the paperweight and the orb together to unlock what's inside the orb. Nothing scary. Just information. And we think you, Elizabeth and Raiza need to be there with us when we do."

"Can I touch it again?" Olivia said, moving her hand hesitantly toward its resting place between my breasts.

It was like she didn't want to touch me there—I mean, really—but she was drawn to the orb. She barely cupped her hand over it.

"It feels so good."

I could feel it pulse lightly beneath her hand.

"I feel less sad. But also more sad."

"I know. I don't know how to explain that," I said, "but I feel it, too. This is like nothing I've ever experienced. I just know since I got back from the session with Connie yesterday that everything has changed. What I see. What I feel. How I feel. Even how deeply I feel—like how much I really love you."

"And it helps me receive that love, Mom, without feeling embarrassed."

"Well, you are almost a teenager," I said. "Pulling away comes with the territory. It's part of growing up."

"I think I'd like to wait a little longer on that."

"Connie, Elizabeth, and Raiza are coming over Wednesday to see what our presence unlocks. But there's one thing I have to ask of you."

"And that is…?" Wariness crept into her voice.

"I don't know how your dad would feel about this. He might be angry at me for exposing you to it."

"But Gregory was important to me." Unfair! I could hear her unspoken sentiment. "And if there's a message for me, I have a right to it."

"I know. I understand. But your dad might not. Can you agree not to tell him until we have the chance to do it together after Wednesday?"

The week was charged with anticipation for both of us, but we tacitly agreed not to discuss it further. Woody and Bernie alternately jumped up on my lap and nosed the area around my heart, purring loudly and making biscuits on my stomach, looking at me as if I held an explanation. I cherished my simple routines with Olivia: making dinner, cleaning up, shopping the farmers market, hanging out at Half Price Books. Discussing the chest, but not opening it.

The evening of the meeting, we set out some simple snacks—fruit and crackers—and a pitcher of cool water with glasses. No alcohol. Olivia added the finishing touches on the coffee table and scooted the chest to the center of the room.

The doorbell rang and, one by one, the women arrived—Connie, Elizabeth, and Raiza. Even my gregarious pink-haired coworker was subdued.

"I think we're ready to get started," I said after everyone had found a place to sit. Connie and Elizabeth took up opposite ends on the couch. Raiza perched in the overstuffed leather chair from Gregory's apartment, legs draped on either side of the ottoman. Olivia was on the floor near the chest, and I had pulled a chair in from the dining room.

All faces turned toward me. As I reached down the front of my blouse for the energy ball, Elizabeth and Raiza both gasped.

"What the eff is that?" Raiza said. "Did you see that?"

She scanned the room to see if everyone else was seeing the same thing she was.

I brought it over for both to see. Elizabeth just stared—first at it, then at me.

"They've already seen it," I said, nodding toward Connie and Olivia. "As for what it is, we're not quite sure. But when I went out of body at Connie's place—and yes, I did see Gregory, or, more precisely, the billowing energy essence he's become—he sent this back with me."

Raiza was transfixed as I bent over next to her, cradling the orb in my palm for her to examine. I could tell she had questions, like she would burst if she didn't get to ask them. But she remained silent, absorbed in the moment.

"Go ahead and touch it," Connie suggested.

Raiza reached toward the watery mass, and it gave way, seeming to blow apart into droplets. Then, just as quickly, it reconstituted into a whole again.

"What the *eff*? This is unreal."

She looked from the quivering orb to me and back to the orb.

"It's very real," I replied calmly.

The room was still.

"Is this what people mean by *knowing*?" My sassy friend could barely mouth the words.

"It is," said Connie. "Or call it intuition."

"This goes way beyond," Raiza said. "It's just crazy."

"You and I aren't used to dealing with information like this," I said, moving to sit between Connie and Elizabeth on the couch. "It goes way beyond logic."

"So what are we doing here?" Raiza had dropped her notebook and pen on the floor next to the chair.

"We're going to try and unravel the message Gregory sent," Elizabeth said.

"Are you okay with that?" I asked.

"Yeah. Sure." For once, Raiza was speechless.

Olivia piped up. "Mom and Connie think we need to bring out the paperweight that Gregory left in his secret chest." She moved closer to the tooled box, which seemed to have gained additional radiance. "It's where he kept his treasures, like drawings from Elizabeth's daughter, Megan. She died when she was a little older than me."

"I'm so sorry," Raiza said, looking at Elizabeth.

"It's okay," Elizabeth answered. "It's been several years, and Ann has renewed my hope that she is okay." Her voice trembled and her chest heaved, a wave that quickly subsided.

Olivia pushed open the top of the chest. The waxed surfaces slid smoothly apart. She lifted out the top tray, and there in the second tray, the iridescent paperweight gleamed like peacock feathers encased in glass.

"How should I do this?" Olivia said, looking to Connie.

"I think you need to give it to Elizabeth."

As Olivia handed the orb up to Elizabeth, something like sparks danced between their fingers.

"Oh."

Olivia withdrew her hand and sat back down on the floor. She rubbed her palms together lightly, as if they carried a charge.

"It's up to you two," Connie said to me and Elizabeth, "to bring the objects together." Connie more than I seemed to understand how this gathering should flow.

My heart beat wildly as my gaze rose to meet Elizabeth's and I held out the orb. As our eyes met, I was flooded with the full burden of her fear, hope, and anguish. I projected a steady stream of love and joy around and through her. We glowed like embers from the same fire. As our hands drew closer, both the iridescent glass and the orb began to vibrate. When they touched, the orb exploded into a whirlwind of energy that lit the room, enveloping everyone in it. Like a flash of sheet lightning. Ripples of sparkling brilliance. Dancing. Spinning. Electric. Even the cats were transfixed, eyes wide and bodies motionless.

An awareness of what was happening came over me, as if I were graced with expanded consciousness. Hearts, minds, opening. Barriers, defenses, dropping. Love, understanding, flowing. Raiza softening, even teary, at what this broke open for her—something to crack her hard and limiting shell. Connie reassuring her with a titan's strength that she had a message to deliver to the world. She would be a scribe such as she had never imagined. Oliva, with wisdom beyond her years, reaching out to embrace Elizabeth and help her shed the deep, crusted pain of losing her beloved daughter. Shearing away the guilt of perceived failings. Encouraging her to yield to the rose-gold sunburst. And at the heart of it all, Gregory's unifying essence and core message: *You are all loved, and love never dies.*

I don't know how long we all just sat there bathed in the light, basking in the energy, our collective consciousness heightened. Processing, processing. United. Eyes shining. Faces aglow. Slowly, as the luminescence dimmed like a setting sun, the room returned to normal. The paperweight was just… a paperweight once more. And the orb had vanished. I could still feel the hollow where it had resided, next to my sternum. The cats rolled in the floor as if it were blanketed in catnip.

Everyone looked around as if they'd just woken up.

"Do we need to talk about this?" Connie asked no one in particular. Mother hen, checking in.

"No," said Raiza. "Not now. Maybe later, but not now."

By tacit agreement, no one wanted to interrupt their own inner experience. Mumbling only a few words, Connie, Elizabeth, and Raiza picked up their belongings and headed for the door. Wordless embraces were our goodbyes.

Early the next morning, still basking in the afterglow, I asked Olivia if she'd like to walk over to the commons with me. She shook her head. She was sitting on the floor with the paperweight in her hands, both cats vying for her lap, tuxedo on one side, orange tabby on the other. It was as if they couldn't press close enough to her.

"No, Mom. You go. I just want to sit here before I have to go to school." Absently, she stroked the now-inert object.

I was feeling drawn to the place on campus that had meant so much to Gregory and me.

"Okay," I said. "See you in a few."

No explanations were needed.

Pulling my jacket off the hook, I set off for the commons in the frosty air that signaled the coming holiday season. Sitting down on the cool, hard, concrete bench, I was struck anew by how special the vantage point was. Of all the benches around the perimeter of the commons, this was the catbird seat. The morning sunlight cascaded down in shimmering streams, dancing with the emerald-green grass. I'd watched the students and enjoyed their cavorting before, but now it was different. To my eyes, all air and earth were washed in that gossamer brightness that comes right after a rain. Except we'd had no rain. The towering, feathery-plumed cypress and regal oaks encircling the grass glistened, and the students' clothing blurred into harlequin-like patterns of excited color. A speckled gray heeler leapt to grab a stick, then scampered after a rust-colored squirrel darting for the cover of a mighty trunk—a vignette of near-unbearable beauty. The scent of dirt and turf mingled with wet slate, and the dry oak leaves clattered in the wind. It all seemed not just real, but hyperreal, when

I spied a movement in the distance, a blur of curly dark hair and penetrating brown eyes looking my way. There. Then not.

ACKNOWLEDGMENTS

First and foremost I'd like to thank my writers group, Women Who Write, who analyzed, criticized, tore down and built up seemingly every word and line. It was like having three editors, and indeed all of us were or are non-fiction editors as well as writers. Thank you, Sophia Dembling, Eve Hill-Agnus, and Terri Taylor.

I also could not have written this book without the Southern Methodist University Writer's Path program. Director J. Suzanne Frank and instructor Daniel J. Hale helped me understand why I needed to write the last chapter first and provided an incisive, unvarnished overview of fiction writing and publishing.

Jose Ramirez of Pedernales Publishing and designer Eric Labacz transformed my manuscript into a beautiful book, and the wonderful women at Goddess Fish, along with Marissa Neely, helped me get the word out. Theasa Tuohy, thank you for turning me on to Pedernales. The Writers' League of Texas also provided valuable connections. Deanna Roy, you were one of those.

Oliver Tappe and Dr. Scott Taylor, Ed.D, stand out among the special folks at the Monroe Institute, which played a foundational role in the writing of this book as well as my personal grief journey.

I also am indebted to everyone who took the time to read and comment on the manuscript, including Rose Baker, Robin Craver, Joyce Sáenz Harris, Jodi Kaufman, Cheryl Sauve (who also introduced me to Suzanne Giesemann), and Anna-Barbara Tietz.

M.E. Grundman, Shari Reynolds and Gay Lustfield all have crossed over, but their energy suffuses the book's pages. So, too, that of Phillip Bando, who started the whole thing.

Finally, I have to thank my partner of more than twenty years, Alfonso Cevola; my son Ric Martin; and my daughter Anna Pierce for their patience and support. Also, so many cats, including the current trio: Luigi, Coco and Buttercup.

AUTHOR'S NOTE

Everything in this book springs from truth—from my experience with the death of my fiancé in 1998 to the many and varied spiritual/paranormal experiences of those around me. The authors of the books on after-death communications—John Edward, Joel Martin, Patricia Romanowski and Melvin Morse—are real, and the books to which the story's protagonist refers are real. They're part of a substantial body of literature suggesting that some people are legitimately capable of making contact with departed souls. *The Afterlife Experiments* by Gary E. Schwartz, Ph.D. (Atria, 2002) chronicles some of the early scientific studies on this. In the years since Ann's journey, Dr. Schwartz has become an authority in mediumship research and evidentiary mediumship in particular. He has even developed a formal rating system for evaluating readings. One of the foremost evidentiary mediums he has worked with is Suzanne Giesemann, who continues to shape my understanding of the thin veil between those living and those passed. One of the earliest books on out-of-body experiences (or OBEs) is Robert Monroe's *Journeys Out of the Body*, published in 1971. It remains in print, along with two follow-up volumes. Monroe established the Monroe Institute in Charlottesville, Va., to further study OBEs and other consciousness-related phenomena and offer workshops. The institute continues to extend the reach and understanding of Monroe's work today.

— K.P.

DISCUSSION QUESTIONS

1. In the first chapter, shock protects Ann from absorbing the full reality of Gregory's death. What are other ways people might react in such a situation? How do you think you would react?
2. In Chapter Six, Connie suggests that Ann spend some time alone with Gregory's body, perhaps even touching it. What was your first reaction to this suggestion? How did your feelings change—if at all—after reading how it helped Ann process his death?
3. In Chapter Eight, Stella expresses second thoughts at having had Gregory's body cremated. How would you approach the topic of burial vs. cremation with a friend or family member? What do you think is most important to consider in this discussion?
4. In Chapter Nine, Ann dreams about the name Ira, which she takes later to be a reference to an IRA.

Then in Chapter Ten, Olivia dreams that Gregory tells her he isn't dead. What is your best explanation for prescient dreams? How would having one affect you?

5. In Chapter Ten, Connie introduces Ann to the concept of evidentiary mediumship, although she doesn't call it that. Have you ever gotten a reading from a medium? What was your experience like? How did it affect your beliefs? If you haven't had a reading, how does Ann's experience affect your view of them?
6. Throughout the book, Ann struggles to find out whether any part of consciousness survives physical death. How does her need for verifiable facts help or hinder her search?
7. In Chapter Eleven, Ann acknowledges the bond between her and Gregory's ex-wife, both of whom shared Gregory's intimate love. What are other ways this relationship might have played out? How would you handle a similar situation?
8. In Chapter Thirteen, Elizabeth shares the big reveal about her daughter Megan—Gregory's stepdaughter. Does this revelation change how you feel about Gregory?
9. In Chapter Nineteen, Ann shares the contents of the reading with Elizabeth. Ann wants to share the reading with Stella, too, but Elizabeth tells her that's

a bad idea. What would you have said to Ann, either to encourage or discourage her and why?

10. In Chapter Twenty-Four, we learn of Ben's involvement in the cover-up of the hunting accident. How would you describe Ben up to this point? Good guy? Bad guy? In what ways did this revelation change how you felt about him?
11. In Chapter Twenty-Five, Ann goes out of body with Dr. Koslow as her guide. How do you think going out of body changes a person's perspective? How does it change Ann?
12. In Chapter Twenty-Five, Stella all but destroys Dr. Koslow's lab. What is your take on Stella's character? What do you think drives her? Was it ever in the cards for her and Ann to have a friendship? And if so, under what circumstances?
13. How does Connie's experience in the lab in Chapter Twenty-Six change her? What does she release?
14. In Chapter Twenty-Eight, Ann goes out of body with Connie's do-it-yourself set-up. Compare the two out-of-body experiences she has.
15. In Chapter Twenty-Nine, the energy released by the orb touches everyone in the room. How do you think each character—Ann, Olivia, Elizabeth and Raiza—will go forward from this moment?